Adrian Deans

Adrian Deans is a lawyer, journalist and novelist. He is the author of four richly praised previous novels: *Straight Jacket*, *Mr Cleansheets*, *THEM* and *The Fighting Man*, and a sporting biography *Political Football: Lawrie McKinna's Dangerous Truth*. He lives at Avoca Beach with his wife, Karen.

WELCOME TO
ORD CITY

Adrian Deans

FIGHTING MAN PRESS

Published by Fighting Man Press 2020
www.adriandeans.com
Copyright © Adrian Deans

Cover design: Lucy Barker, *www.lucybarker.com.au*

ISBN: 9780648848301

A catalogue record for this title is available
from the National Library of Australia

For all those ratbag politicians who make
me feel so good feeling bad about the world

Welcome to Ord City

It felt wrong.

The two men glanced at each other and the smaller checked the card in his top pocket. There was no need to check the card – he knew by heart the address scribbled there. It was something to delay for a few more seconds what he knew must be done.

The house in front of them was blackened from an old fire but didn't seem to be occupied – which was unusual in Ord City where every available inch was given over to find homes for the flotsam of Asia. An empty house, even burnt out, was a wasteful indulgence.

The larger of the two looked over his shoulder and licked his lips.

'I think we should go.'

'We can't go,' replied the smaller man, irritably. 'He told us to come here … it must be alright.'

But he made no move to venture inside.

They were aware of how still it was – as though they had entered a sound-proof bubble when they entered the laneway behind the large apartment buildings. They could make out traffic din in the distance, but here the lane was quiet and smelled of cooking oil, cabbage and cat piss.

'We should've kept our mouths shut,' hissed the larger man. 'Or spoken to … '

'We tell no one,' insisted the smaller man, as he took a step towards the blackened house, then froze as a sound came from the alley to their right – a plastic bottle had been kicked along the ground.

'A dog or cat?' suggested the larger man, a note of panic in his voice.

Then their heads snapped around as the same noise came from the left, and an empty drink bottle lay in a pool of light under a streetlamp, slowly spinning to a halt.

The smaller man glanced desperately about the alley but there was no escape. He pulled the card from his top pocket and slipped it inside his shoe.

Then, ignoring his whimpering companion, he walked into the burnt out house.

PART ONE

Sunday: Thirteen days before the First Wave

Chapter 1

The Third Click

He knows he's being watched, thought Conan, gazing fascinated at the man's image which filled the screens. His face was mostly obscured by a yellow cap and scarf, and the NO READING on the iris scan suggested highly illegal scan-resistant sunglasses.

The man was in a public library in Ord City and had accessed specifications of the National Broadband Network which could only be found on the Dark Web. Most who wandered into that location got out instantly when they realised what they were looking at.

A second click – and the fellow, using an old-style computer, complete with mouse, had found his way into the engineering maps which highlighted critical linkages. Such access might still only be guilty fascination – the AFP had enough to do without arresting every idle surfer who dallied in the Dark.

It was the third click that mattered. Anyone with half a brain knew they'd be under scrutiny by now. Getting out quickly was enough display of innocence to warrant being left alone, but accessing a third level where specific characteristics of vulnerable linkages might be found meant – to Conan's mind – that the man in the yellow cap with the scan-resistant specs was a person of interest.

The man looked over his shoulder, licked his lips, and made the third click.

At that point Conan could have locked the library remotely, even all the way from Sydney. Instead, he accessed the peripheral vision at that location and immediately had a choice of images. From behind he saw a thin-looking man in a yellow football shirt with FENG in block capitals and the number 9. Abruptly, the man pulled a data stick from the computer, jumped up and strode from the room. Automatically, the peripheral vision network locked in – thousands of optical fibre terminals in light fittings, smoke alarms, any fixed electronic device and even overt surveillance cameras traced FENG 9 as he hurried from the library and out onto the street.

Conan knew he was taking a risk. If he'd closed the library, the man would have been apprehended easily and his data stick confiscated. Letting him outside admitted the chance (albeit small) that the man might get into enough of a crowd or blind spot to defy the cameras and drones. A small thrill of adrenalin tickled Conan's guts as FENG 9 hurried through increasingly crowded streets. The vast amount of visual data coalesced into an all-but-perfect holographic image – occasionally flickering – as Conan hovered invisibly at the fugitive's shoulder.

The man was clearly frightened – constantly looking back for pursuers – and Conan smiled grimly, content to let the man take him either to his refuge or, even better, a meeting with senior confederates. That was why Conan had let him escape – the Big Bosses don't access illegal and sensitive data themselves, they send little fish like FENG 9. But the little fish always swim back to the Big Fish, and then the Big Fish to the WHALES. It was the natural order since the dawn of crime.

FENG 9 turned a corner and Conan realised the people around his subject were increasing rapidly – what's more, many were dressed in similar yellow shirts and caps and Conan suddenly understood the risk. For an instant, he took his eye off the subject to read FENG 9 on another shirt, then when he turned back he realised he was no longer certain that the subject was the same man.

More and more yellow shirts pressed around him as the football stadium loomed overhead, and Conan was already inventing excuses for why he hadn't locked the library.

• • •

'I fucking despair of you, Tooley.'

Conan watched again as Kenny Cook, the chief analyst, replayed the holo of FENG 9's computer search and flight from the library.

'He knew what he was doing,' said Kenny, '… dressed up in Peril gear. He knew he'd be watched, but if he made it as far as the stadium he'd blend in and get away.'

'I was hoping he'd lead us to his contact,' said Conan, rubbing his eyes with his knuckles.

'He's downloaded specs to the Node you arse!' scathed Kenny, threatening Conan with half a donut. 'What were you going to do … wait until he blew it up before maybe letting us know about him?'

Conan kept his mouth shut. He'd gambled and lost so there was little point trying to justify himself.

Kenny Cook was the fattest of the geek overlords who worked in dark rooms high in a Sydney skyscraper to anticipate and thwart crime throughout Australia, or anywhere else if relevant to Australian interests. Their work had changed profoundly since the creation of the quantum supercomputers – still only allowed for G12 governments and approved multinationals, but no one else had a legitimate use for that much processing power.

'In any case,' continued Kenny, 'you were at the briefing about the political status in Ord City leading up to the First Wave.'

'I know,' said Conan, holding his hands up in surrender.

'You know this bloke'll be HT, don't you?'

'I assumed he was,' admitted Conan, '… which is why I wanted to follow him back to base.'

The population of Ord City were overwhelmingly devotees of Habal Tong – a synthesis of the various Asian religions which had grown strongly since the City was established in 2020.

'You were told,' insisted Kenny, '… any chance to clamp down on radical HT sects must be taken and must be publicised.'

'I know. But I seriously didn't think he'd get away and he could have led us to a senior confederate.'

'But he did get away. Meanwhile, the reffo newspapers are accusing us of looking for an excuse to renege on their visas. A public arrest might have cooled 'em down a little.'

Conan was perfectly familiar with the political situation in Ord City, but that didn't stop Kenny teaching him to suck eggs.

'It's Habal Tong, of course, stirring up trouble … saying the government won't honour the seven year visas.'

'Why shouldn't they?'

'They will. They wouldn't dare do otherwise when two and a half million people are watching their every move and ready to explode. Some of their leaders are already complaining we don't provide adequate resources up there … especially policing.'

Something in Kenny's voice warned Conan that the conversation was about to take an irritating turn.

'What policing resources should we be providing?' asked Conan, as Kenny finished his donut and licked his fingers.

'Murder investigation,' said Kenny, and Conan groaned with impending boredom. Murder would normally be the responsibility of the state police but Ord City, within the Temporary Citizenship Zone, was covered by a Commonwealth Act which brought all serious crime under the jurisdiction of the AFP.

'Double murder to be precise,' continued Kenny. 'Gangland execution by the look of it. That used to be your forte, didn't it … gangs?'

'But surely I need to stay on this present case,' objected Conan. 'If he's downloaded specs then clearly there's a potential sabotage situation up there.'

'Which will be monitored by someone else with a bit more responsibility,' said Kenny. 'Virtual investigation is a privilege … an expensive privilege … and when you let arseholes like FENG 9 access critical information and get away you breach the trust the community has placed in you. Maybe next time you'll appreciate your responsibility a tad more keenly.'

'Kenny … you know exactly why I held back,' said Conan, who *really* needed to stay in Sydney. 'If we'd caught this prick … big deal. Whoever's running the operation would simply have passed the baton on to someone else. I wanted the head honcho.'

'How do you know he's not the honcho?' demanded Kenny, reaching for another donut. 'Or a lone wolf? Ever heard of interrogation?'

'He won't talk if he's HT,' said Conan, '… they never do. That's the other reason I held off.'

'There, you see,' said Kenny, grinning, '… you're already an expert on HT culture. Perfect.'

'Are you kidding? I don't know the first thing about HT or Ord City. Surely this is a job for a local.'

'It's been deprioritised … overflow. They're too busy with other stuff, like First Wave security, and I've been asked to send one of my people. You're suddenly the most expendable.'

Conan groaned again sensing politics, and gangland murder was non-political and non-virtual investigation – definitely a demotion.

'If it's any consolation,' said Kenny, 'no one expects you to find the killers. Just get your arse up to Ord City and fly the Sydney flag for a few days. Think of it as a holiday.'

• • •

'Hey Lucia.'

'Hey Conan.'

Conan fell silent – wondering how to breach the subject safely.

'What's up?' she asked, a hint of unprofessional doubt in her voice.

'Wrong number,' he said, then hung up – knowing she'd call him back. Sure enough, about six minutes later, a withheld number flashed up on his phone.

'I can't do tomorrow night Lucia … they're sending me to Ord City. Bloody murder investigation.'

Lucia worked in data and logistics and there was an uncomfortable friendship between the two – not least because of the time they'd 'done it' after getting pissed at a rare work party. Social functions were discouraged in the modern AFP and intimate relations outright forbidden. Lucia had shyly suggested, once or twice since, that if he wanted a relationship she might be willing to resign. But Conan didn't want another relationship.

At least, he didn't think so, and he couldn't have borne the guilt of letting her leave her job and then breaking up with her at any point later.

'Why are they sending you?'

'Because I fucked up a virtual investigation and … where are you calling from?'

'Don't worry, it's safe … as long as …'

11

They both knew all phone conversations were monitored in real time by the Quantum computer – listening for words like 'heroin' or 'gun' or 'crimson' – or any other combination of words that might need closer attention from an AI algorithm or even a human agent. As long as they kept it vague and banal and didn't both use work numbers they were fairly safe to talk.

'Okay … I'm going tomorrow and there's stuff I need to do tonight. Can we catch up when I get back?'

'Sure, Conan,' she said, and he tried not to hear the pain under her carefree manner. It had taken them six weeks to arrange a date. 'But don't you think it odd they're sending you? You don't do murder.'

'Not since I was a state Dee … I guess I've had experience.'

'Plenty of others with more experience,' she said, and he could picture her shrugging.

'Maybe they're busy? In any case, Kenny said no one expects me to solve the case.'

'Then why go?'

'God knows … politics. Something to do with keeping the non-natives happy.'

'Ord City's a weird place, Conan. You look after yourself … I better go.'

'Okay … I'll see you when I get back.'

'Sure, Conan. Maybe.'

• • •

Three people – two men and a woman – sit before a huge picture window looking over a vast city, with an ocean to the north under a pink sky fading to purple. A servant pours tea and departs silently. None of them speak until all have savoured the tea and replaced their cups.

The first to speak is a large man dressed entirely in black.

'It has begun then. There is no turning back.'

A woman in a pink and grey power suit with a necklace of black pearls responds: *'It began some time ago … the preparations have taken years.'*

'The irrevocable step has been taken though,' says the Man in Black, '…

we are now committed ... to see this through to the end.'

'There will be unhappiness,' says the woman, with an eye on the smaller man. It is clear the smaller man is in charge.

'A great deal of it,' agrees the smaller man, speaking for the first time, '... but as long as they are unhappy about the right things, we should have confidence in our mission.'

The last of the pink fades from the sky in the west. It is black to the east.

The woman asks: 'What about the enticement?'

'It went perfectly, as expected,' says the Man in Black.

'But there may be security issues,' she replies.

'We have taken steps to mitigate the security issues,' says the Man in Black. 'It is too late for the mission to be stopped ... I don't see how we can fail at this late stage.'

'I agree,' says the smaller man, '... and I thank you both for your efforts. Future generations will never hear of this, but our secret history will recall your names and deeds for all eternity.'

All three pick up their cups again, and sip contentedly.

The wheels are set in motion.

Chapter 2

The Happy Land
of the Fat Sharks

'Six minutes,' said Ah Cheng, chewing his knuckle and dripping with sweat. He always stank of sweat and, in Asif's opinion, the rose water he splashed over himself to hide the smell just made it worse.

'Plus extra time,' said Asif, then laughed as Ah Cheng winced at the reminder.

'Be serious for once,' growled Razzaq. 'We're not here for the football!'

He'd kept his voice low but he needn't have bothered. Peril matches at Rinehart Stadium were always a sell-out and when 60,000 fans were all screaming their encouragement with the home team a goal down and six to play, Razzaq could have shouted at the top of his lungs.

Asif always sat between the two older men. They were older, but he'd been in Ord City, in the Temporary Citizenship Zone, the longest. Asif was part of the First Wave and in less than two weeks would be eligible to leave the TCZ and go anywhere in Australia, like any normal citizen.

'You have the data?' asked Razzaq, and Asif nodded, as the Melbourne Victory players repelled yet another Ord City attack with their tightly organised defence.

'Asif!'

Razzaq was glaring and Asif, with an effort, turned away from the game and went to pass the data stick to Razzaq.

'Keep it for now. But we need to talk about your mission ... again. Explain the details of the plan ... starting from the moment you are allowed to leave Ord City permanently.'

'The Node is forty kilometres south at the Argyle substation,' said Asif, 'On the day of the mission, drive south along the Argyle Highway until …'

At that moment the Rinehart Stadium erupted with joy as their beloved Horace Hung Feng controlled the ball with his chest at the far post and drilled a shot into the roof of the net from an impossible angle. Ah Cheng leapt to his feet in unison with 60,000 other supporters and started singing the Feng Song.

Razzaq was furious.

'Fuck Feng!' he shouted. 'Fuck the Pilgrims and fuck you Cheng … we have serious business!'

Ah Cheng nodded, chastened, and resumed his seat, while Razzaq fumed and the crowd returned to its standard level of excited buzz. The Melbourne Victory players kicked off again – two minutes left to play.

'Continue,' said Razzaq, and Asif took up from where he'd left off.

'South along the Argyle Highway until the turnoff. There is no sign but it is exactly 14.9 kilometres past the turn off to Halls Creek.'

'You have no authorisation to take that road,' snapped Razzaq.

'No,' agreed Asif. 'If I am questioned, I took the road by error … but the warning signs were in English. How was I to know it was a prohibited road?'

'How far do you drive?'

'Three point seven kilometres from the Highway there is an outcrop of low rocky ridges with several indentations big enough to conceal a car.'

'From this point,' said Razzaq, 'there is no chance of escape if discovered. You must protect yourself.'

'I will have an old Australian army Stehr pistol and four ammo clips.'

'But if capture seems inevitable?'

Asif grinned, watching the game, and held an imaginary pistol against his head.

'What do you have in your satchel?' continued Razzaq, as the crowd started rising again. The Pilgrims were probing about the Victory box, the referee looked at his watch.

Asif tore his eyes away from the game and regarded Razzaq – an angry little man in a yellow tee shirt and white skull cap who worked in a stir-fry restaurant and always smelled of cooking oil. But he was head of the Tong and had to be taken seriously.

'I have six sticks of ... '

The stadium exploded with sound and fury and Asif's head whipped back to the action. The Pilgrims (known to most supporters as the Peril) were clustered in a tight celebratory knot by one of the corner flags and the crowd were on their feet dancing once again. Ah Cheng had raced to the front of their bay where the more active support were clutching at each other and writhing in an orgiastic outburst of adoration.

Razzaq's face was twisted with contempt – eyeing Ah Cheng in disgust.

'I'm glad it is you and not Cheng who carries the burden of our mission,' he said. 'If he was forced to choose between ...'

'Cheng is solid,' insisted Asif, 'and he sees the football as symbolic of our struggle.'

'He does?'

'Cheng says the Ord City Pilgrims have infiltrated the A-League and are successful. Ordinary Australians deeply resent the loss of face when we Asian invaders take points off them but deep down they know of our inherent superiority ... especially in spiritual matters.'

Cheng had indeed said all of that, but he'd said it in the mock-fanatical voice he used for mimicking Razzaq, when Razzaq was not present.

Razzaq looked thoughtful.

'I still say he is dangerously distracted by football. If we changed our objective from the Node to this stadium ... do you seriously believe Ah Cheng could go through with it?'

Asif watched Ah Cheng dancing with the active support as the referee blew full time and felt a wave of affection for his Chinese friend. He knew absolutely that Ah Cheng would violently oppose any plan that jeopardised his beloved Pilgrims, but he said: 'Ah Cheng is a member of the Tong and has fought our fight for many years. We should not doubt him.'

'Maybe not,' said Razzaq, 'but we will watch him. Too much love of Peril is not good for a man.'

· · ·

Asif loved the feel of his neighbourhood.

As he walked home after the game, assailed by the energy, sights and smells of District 11 (also known as K Town after the old Kununurra) he reflected upon his amazing fortune.

Asif had arrived in Australia from Bangladesh in 2022. His family had been forced out of their fishing village by rising sea levels – the floods had become increasingly regular until the water never left. Asif's village was under two metres of water and the movement of vast numbers to higher ground had caused friction and put a lot of strain on the land that was left. Like so many other unmarried sons, Asif was given the task and the duty to get to Australia and commence a new life in a safe and lucky land where he might re-establish the family.

The journey had been hard, and very expensive. It was easy enough to get to Jakarta and there were any number of boats heading for Australia. The prices charged were crippling – the equivalent of two years wages in Bangladesh – but the family had provided the means and were depending on him.

He managed to find a berth on a ramshackle fishing boat which left the port of Surabaya with nearly seventy refugees aboard, including families with young children. The boat should probably have carried no more than twenty so was dangerously overloaded and very low in the water with the bilge pumps straining to keep the vessel afloat. Fortunately the sea was mild but there were dark clouds to the south.

An hour after departure, when it was impossible to leave the ship and swim back to shore, the captain addressed them all. His friendly pre-departure demeanour was entirely gone and, with an evil grin, he held up a hessian sack.

'I have here your passports,' he said, then, without another word, tossed the sack overboard.

Immediately the boat was filled with wails of outrage and despair but the captain just laughed as his two colleagues produced automatic pistols, and the wailing ceased.

'You learn quickly,' he approved. 'That augurs well for your chances of survival.'

He went on to explain that if the Australians knew their true identities and nationalities it made it much easier to send them home. He told them all to choose new names and invent themselves a history. It was simple enough to tell a story of persecution – none of them needed to invent such a story – but the harder it was for the Australians to check their stories the longer they would stay in the country. And with so much international condemnation over Australia's treatment of refugees, there were rumours that the Australians were about to change their laws.

'It might soon be easier … it might soon be harder to get residency … who knows? But unless you're actually in the country you have no chance.'

Asif had brought adequate food and water for the voyage but it was stolen on the first night, so he was obliged to survive on handouts which were grudgingly given and very poor. There was no toilet aboard (except for the crew) so the passengers all pissed and shat over the sides – fathers clutching their children with an eye on the following sharks.

'Sharks in the water, sharks on board … and sharks at home,' said Noor, an Afghan Asif had befriended in Jakarta.

'And sharks in Australia, no doubt,' said Asif.

'Perhaps,' said Noor, 'but from what I hear they are fat and slow … we will make a good life there, my friend.'

'So much effort and danger,' laughed Asif, 'to get to the happy land of the fat sharks.'

The Australian sharks were not fat and slow. On the third day out from Surabaya a patrol boat had appeared out of the storm murk from the south, as the waves freshened and the wind and the children started howling. The patrol boat sliced through the water as the sharks had done, circled the boat once with two large machine guns trained on them, then a voice thundered from a loudhailer like a shout from hell.

At that moment the fishing boat shuddered and seemed to stop.

'The captain has scuttled us,' said a white-faced Noor. 'Let's hope the Australians are merciful.'

The captain, wearing an inflatable jacket, fired a distress flare, laughing as the heavens suddenly opened and panic swept the sinking boat.

'Listen to me,' shouted the captain. 'I am not the captain of this boat. The captain was Bamban Sulo who lost his life trying to save this ship. Is that clear?'

There was confusion among the passengers, so the captain explained again, emphasising his words with a pistol.

'The brave captain, Bamban Sulo, fell overboard while trying to repair the hull. Anyone who tells a different story will receive their punishment in the camps where I already have friends and weapons. Is that understood?'

Waves were beginning to wash over the gunnels and a large fat woman went shrieking over the side, pulling a small child in with her. Without thinking, Asif leapt into the water, swam hard for the panicking woman and tried to calm her as she clutched frantically at his head and shoulders. The child was fine, clinging to her mother's neck, and just as Asif remembered the sharks and his foolishness in entering their domain, a black rubber dinghy appeared next to them and hands reached down to pull them to safety. It took nearly a minute to get the woman into the lifeboat, even with Asif pushing from below, and that was the time he felt most vulnerable – moments from safety but feet kicking madly to attract evil from the depths.

On board the Australian warship they were given blankets and a hot meal and taken to Christmas Island, which he expected to be just a respite, but they were there for many months. Always there were rumours that they would be sent to Nauru, or New Guinea, or even a camp on the Australian mainland. They spoke occasionally with officials and lawyers – always the same questions, as though being tested for consistency to reveal a lie. Asif, despite the warnings of the captain had told the truth about himself. Noor had told the truth about everything, including the captain. This was a serious mistake. Noor may have hoped that his revelation of the captain's behaviour might stay secret, but the captain found out almost immediately and stared at Noor with black-eyed vengeance. Two days later, Noor was found in his cot with his throat cut, but the captain had been in the discipline wing and was clearly innocent. Of course, everyone knew he had ordered the killing, and when he was released from discipline a few days later he was immediately established as king of the camp.

It was in the camp that Asif discovered Habal Tong. HT wasn't really a religion – it welcomed members of any religion. It was more a set of precepts and values that, on one level, encouraged tolerance and unity. But on another level, effectively radicalised and galvanised anyone who felt slighted, insulted or in any way disadvantaged by the Australian mainstream.

The HT group were aloof from the rest of the camp, including the captain's thugs. In fact, they were the only ones the captain's thugs left alone and despite the fact that Asif wanted, desperately, to embrace all things Australian to improve his chances of staying permanently, he found himself inexorably drawn to them. 'All is nothing and nothing is all,' was the most profound and fundamental maxim of Habal Tong and Asif reflected on it constantly – reconciling it with all his previous beliefs and feeling its empowerment.

Somehow the maxim was also interpreted to mean that Australia, as a wealthy first world nation, owed all refugees a living. 'It is the so-called first world,' sneered Tee Tee, the head of the Tong in the camp, 'that caused the sea levels to rise with their industrial exhalations. If they take away your land then by all that is just and right they must provide an alternative. And if they will not do so willingly then we will take what is rightfully ours.'

It was a powerful argument but unpopular with the Australian officials who had made life so difficult for Asif – never believing him but always lying to him about his status and his prospects for staying in Australia.

'I call on you, brothers,' Tee Tee would say. 'I call on Hindus, Sikhs, Jains, Tamils, Muslims, Buddhists, Shinto, Confucianists, Falun Gong and Bahai … even Christians … to embrace the Tong with all your heart. This is no apostasy to replace your birth religion. No. It is a prism to focus the elements of all religions and fuse them into something more … to strengthen your own faith and bring you into a wider brotherhood!'

The turning point came in 2023 when the law changed. After so much international and domestic criticism, the Australian government simply gave up on their various policies to scare refugees away. All in the camps were given seven year temporary visas with a major restriction. They were not allowed to leave the Temporary Citizenship Zone (the TCZ) for the whole of the seven years. If they did, they would immediately be deported. And if they returned the seven year clock would start from scratch.

By the time Asif received his visa, he had been in the camps nearly two years and had been radicalised into hating Australians with their wealth and their privilege and their different rules for different people. He was a hardened member of the Tong and one year later had been easily recruited into a deep cell – biding its time to take revenge on the country that had treated them with such contempt.

'That was a while ago now,' admitted Asif, as he climbed the stairs to the apartment he shared with Tanya – the best part of his good fortune and the source of his growing regret.

'Did they win?' she called as he opened the door.

'Pardon?'

Tanya was tall and blonde – the light to his dark – and, as ever, he found himself dazzled and took a few moments to adjust.

'Oh ... yes. Two, one ... but they left it very late.'

'That must have been exciting.'

She kissed him on the nose and walked back into the room from which she had emerged when he opened the door. Asif poured two cups of chai from the pot she had prepared in anticipation of his return and followed her into the best room of the apartment.

Tanya's studio was supposed to be the living room, but the walls were covered with her strange paintings. The large table was invisible under paints and brushes, but also the clays, wires and bric-a-brac of her various sculptures. And empty water bottles. Like most Australians, Tanya didn't trust the water in Ord City. Even the chai was made with bottled water.

Around the room were easels set up with paintings at various phases of completion. Asif found a place for her cup and sat back in the battered old armchair holding his chai in both hands. Tanya herself was a work of art – beautiful and complex, and utterly beyond his previous experience of women.

'What are you working on?'

Tanya picked up her cup and eyed him over the rim.

'You.'

'Me?'

'Yes ... what do you think?'

She indicated one of the larger canvases which was split in half by an oblique line, dividing two different scenes. One was a flat red desert, and the other was a chaotic ocean of colour and shapes only partly perceived.

'I don't understand it.'

'I think you could if you tried.'

'I am trying. How can such a strange painting be me? It looks nothing like me.'

'It's how I see you.'

Asif looked again at the painting, trying to see what she saw.

'It's half desert and half chaos,' he said.

'Exactly … just like you.'

Asif was shocked, but also intrigued.

'How am I a desert?'

'There are several ways,' she replied, taking a sip of her chai and contemplating her work with fresh eyes. 'For a start you are hot and dangerous.'

'So is lava.'

'But lava is flowing … you are solid, hard, unmoving.'

'Unmoving?'

'And there is mystery about you … an infinite mystery.'

Asif glanced at her, conscious of the data stick in his pocket, but she was still gazing at the painting, as though discovering new insights.

'What about the other part,' he asked, '… the strange shapes and colours like a breaking wave?'

'That is also you,' she said. 'Wild, explosive, overfilled with energy …'

'It looks like the wave will swamp the desert and wash the sand away.'

'The wave can never swamp the desert,' she replied. 'The desert is too great.'

'So the chaos can never wash away the sand to reveal the mystery lying beneath.'

She turned and smiled at him.

'You see?' she said, standing up and taking him by the hand. 'You do understand the painting.'

• • •

Later, as his heart beat slowed, Asif was staring at the ceiling in the semi-darkness, still seeing the painting in his mind's eye – the deep reds of the desert and the striking blues, pinks and greens of the ocean.

'It's more than just me,' said Asif. 'It's us.'

'What is?' she murmured, her eyes closed.

'The painting … it's both of us.'

'You think so?'

'Of course. We are a contrast but also a coming together of different lives and cultures.'

She was silent for a while and he thought she had fallen asleep, but then she said, 'We're not so different. We share the same values.'

Asif was immediately confronted with a vision of Razzaq's angry face. Tanya shared his Habal Tong philosophy but knew nothing of the cell.

'Mostly,' he agreed.

'Not mostly,' she laughed, '… totally. I couldn't love a man who didn't share my values and I know you do.'

'But what about our work?' he said. 'You create and I destroy.'

'You're being deliberately superficial,' she chided. 'You don't destroy. You mine minerals to create the basis for modern life.'

'Through destruction … and I enjoy destruction.'

'You create also … in the most important ways imaginable.'

'I'm not very good.'

Since he'd been with Tanya, Asif had tried his hand at sculpture – carving and polishing the oddly shaped lumps of silvery magnetite he brought home from the mine and releasing their inner lives and beauty.

'You're better than you know,' she said, then changed the subject. 'When you get your citizenship, we should go to Sydney.'

'What?'

It was a bizarre idea. Sydney was a mythical place – the Emerald City in the Land of Oz.

'To live?' he asked.

'No … at least, not yet. I haven't finished my work in OC … and there aren't too many mining jobs in Sydney.'

'Then why go there?'

'Because Sydney is where I come from. My family are there and I'd like you to meet them.'

'I'd like to meet them also,' he agreed, with a sinking heart as he remembered his own family back in Bangladesh. He had sent money over the years but they had never accumulated enough to bring the whole family to Ord City. His mother could have come. His younger siblings could have come. But always they wanted more money so the entire extended family of aunts, uncles and cousins – half the displaced village – could all come out together. And in the meantime, the money was spent on survival.

'Will your family like me?' he asked.

'They already like you,' she said, snuggling her bottom up against him and moments later her breathing was long and deep.

Asif enjoyed several seconds of indescribable bliss as he basked in the glow of his love for her.

Then he remembered Razzaq.

Chapter 3

The Faded Flotsam of Absent Lives

The heat was unbelievable.

Conan had landed in Ord City on the Monday afternoon and gone to the Kimberley Grand Hotel where he had a room on the 11th floor.

The next morning, he opened the door onto his small balcony and was assailed by the crushing heat and humidity. Within seconds the sweat began to bead on his brow and under his arms, but he stayed outside to acclimatise and get a feel for the city, which looked and smelled like Hong Kong or Bangkok. Buildings were clustered together in a riot of town planning and the hot breeze brought him wafts of car fumes, blocked drains and alien cooking. The streets below were choked with traffic and people, and Conan was momentarily shocked that a modern first world country like Australia could allow so much haphazard progress with so little order. Once the doors were open to the teeming desperate hordes the planning and order would always be in catch-up mode.

The city was mostly characterised by apartment blocks and bamboo scaffolding, but there was a CBD of some taller towers, the football stadium further south, and the Army of God cathedral with its huge red and yellow neon cross – that always reminded Conan of hamburgers.

Allowing his eyes to wander, Conan beheld the sun sparkling on Lake Argyle. To the far north there was maybe a glimpse of the Timor

Sea. To the far south, the Ord River disappeared into the dim red distance, but in the middle, Ord City seethed and bubbled – two and a half million getting rich or getting by, as they always had at home.

For many of them – the First Wave as they were known – full citizenship was only days away.

And the city was getting nervous.

• • •

Edward Loong was the Head of Mission at the AFP headquarters in Ord City and was not overjoyed to make Conan's acquaintance.

'You must be Tooley,' he said, ignoring Conan's hand.

'Call me Tools,' said Conan. 'Everyone else does.'

'Call me Loongy,' said Edward, 'Very few call me that.'

'Doesn't really roll off the tongue,' said Conan, unsure of whether Loongy was being friendly, or not.

'You'd think it would by now,' said Edward. 'I'm sixth generation Australian after all … what about you, Buddy?'

'Dunno … third or fourth … not that it matters.'

'Oh, it matters,' insisted Edward, '… more than ever.'

Conan laughed, still uncertain whether 'Loongy' was having a laugh or oddly paranoid about his ethnic heritage.

'What's so funny?' demanded the head of the AFP mission.

'Oh, nothing. Anyway, what've you got for me?'

Edward's eyes narrowed. He suspected Conan was taking the piss somehow.

'I don't know why Sydney thought they had to send someone up here,' he complained. 'This case is already designated overflow … a straightforward gang execution … dime a dozen. You should go back and look after Sydney crime.'

'I will,' said Conan, '… as soon as I can. But in the meantime, I've been sent up to fly the flag.'

'Politics,' spat Edward.

'Politics,' agreed Conan and shrugged. He was already irritated by the distance, the crowds, the weird smells and the heat – now he had Edward's chip to deal with.

Edward muttered something to himself then slid a couple of plastex files across the desk. There was a code on the covers that he could use to access the record bank – the files contained a small number of personal effects found on the bodies. Both men had been Malay Chinese and, apparently, close friends. They had not been known to police as gang members, but everything about their deaths suggested gangland execution. The location, the butchered throats, but most importantly, the DR carved into both of their foreheads. And both had had their left eyes removed.

'Didn't that strike you as odd?' asked Conan, trying to conceal a shudder as he placed the forensic photographs face down on the file.

'What?'

'The DR brandings ... but also the eyes removed? Bit of a mixed message, wouldn't you say?'

Edward laughed.

'Thank God for Sydney,' he sneered, 'sending us their finest officer to shine a torch through the darkness!'

'You don't think it strange that the bodies bear the marks of two different groups?'

'Just part of the usual fun and games up here ... Tools.'

'Left eye missing suggests Habal Tong radicals,' continued Conan, determined to understand the local customs. 'It means the victims saw something they shouldn't have?'

'Their tongues were cut out also,' reminded Edward, with a grim smile.

'But they had DR carved on their foreheads. That's the mark Dedd Reffo leave ... but Dedd Reffo and Habal Tong are mortal enemies.'

'Habal Tong are enemies of no one,' insisted Edward, '... except to those who betray their secrets.'

'The point is,' said Conan, 'presuming these blokes weren't killed by a coalition of two opposing groups ... why would both marks be inflicted on the bodies?'

'As a warning,' said Edward, as though the answer was too obvious for words.

'A warning to whom?'

'To everyone.'

• • •

'Here are the extra files you wanted.'

Conan sat in a spare office grudgingly provided by the AFP who mostly worked in an open plan environment. Hovering in the doorway was Loongy's deputy – Agent Ping – who placed a couple of plastex boxes on the desk.

Agent Ping was tall and slim with dark eyes endlessly amused.

'What's it like having Loongy for a boss?' asked Conan, carelessly allowing his irritation to show.

'Loong's not so bad,' shrugged Agent Ping, '… as long as you know your place.'

'My place seems to be the bottom of his shoe,' said Conan, 'and he's trying to scrape me off.'

'Very funny,' said Agent Ping, and left without laughing.

The plastex files lay open on the desk in front of him – the two murdered men had not carried much on their persons. Both had wallets with plastic and paper cards. One had a number of sticky notes covered in tiny Asian characters and the other (written in English) had a folded list of names, dates and numbers, which was described in the file as a barter record.

He sent the sticky notes to be translated and considered the next item – a business card of one of the murdered men (Michael Wing Ho, importer) with blurred handwriting on the back. The thing that interested him about the card was where it had been found – in his shoe, according to the file. Clearly it was important to the victim if he had taken the trouble to hide it and, as it was his own business card, the importance could only lie in the illegible handwriting.

He placed the card back in its forensics bag and sent it off with the sticky notes to be hyperlit, magnified and translated – to the extent that was possible after the sweat from Wing Ho's feet had caused the ink to run.

The toxicology report listed nothing unusual with the exception of alcohol and traces of Crimson – the latest designer drug – in their blood.

The last thing in the file was a list of phone records for the month. The two men had called each other frequently but it was the last calls that interested Conan. Bruce Fong's last three calls had been to Wing Ho, but Wing Ho's last call had been to an unidentified number.

Just for the shits and giggles, Tools tried the number and was unsurprised when the recorded voice informed the number was no longer in use. He dialled another number and found himself talking to Lucia back in Sydney.

'Hey Conan?'

'Hey Lucia.'

'What can I do for you?'

There was a hint of suggestion in her voice, despite the risk, and Tools grinned, genuinely fond of her.

'I need a trace on a number.'

He read the number out and heard her groan.

'What's wrong?'

'That's a cryp.'

'Is that a problem?'

'No … just a hassle.'

Cryp numbers were unhackable quantum generated numbers – constantly changing. If you dialled the number and were accepted by the owner, then a regular ping would be sent by the owner's phone to your phone to update and thus allow you to go on calling.

'Do you have the phone from which the number was called?' asked Lucia.

'No.'

Another groan.

'Okay,' she sighed, 'I'll do my best, but you owe me.'

'I already owe you.'

'Well, at some point I'll be calling in your tab, Conan Daniel Tooley. And I hope you'll be man enough to honour your debt.'

There was a supercharged silence of several seconds as Conan wondered how to respond in a way that would continue the subtle flirting without putting their jobs in jeopardy. Calls into the Sydney office were routinely monitored for security purposes.

'You know me, Lucia Francesca Baresi,' he eventually replied. 'I'm a man of my word and will stand ready to serve you when I return.'

'Truly?'

Conan winced at her change of tone and said, 'Gotta go. Let me know if you trace the number.'

He hung up and reviewed the meagre contents of the files. Not much to go on without the translations he'd requested. He drummed his fingers against the desktop for a few moments, then jumped up and walked back to Loongy's office.

'Hey, Tools is back! What you want, Sydney investigator?'

'I need to have a look at their flat.'

'Whose flat?'

'Fong and Wing Ho … the dead blokes.'

'What for?'

Conan just stared at Loongy for a few moments, then shook his head to clear it of the *Through the Looking Glass* imagery he was getting.

'It's standard procedure, Loongy … check out the victim's home … try to get some insight. Who knows what we'll find.'

'It's already been checked. There was nothing … just Habal Tong crap.'

'You've been?'

'It's standard procedure … like you said.'

Conan leaned against Loongy's door, trying to imply that he was comfortable – with no intention of going away.

'There was nothing in the files from the flat.'

'So?'

'So … I'd like to see for myself.'

Loongy shrugged, as though indulging a madman, and said: 'Not today, I'm busy. Maybe tomorrow.'

'You don't need to come. I have checked out dead men's flats before.'

'Oh, but I do need to come,' smiled Loongy, unpleasantly.

'Politics?'

'Politics.'

• • •

There being little else he could usefully do, Conan decided to go and have a look at the derelict house where the bodies had been found.

Walking the streets of Ord City was like walking the streets of any oversize Asian city – hot, smelly and teeming with people. Initially a series of camps around Kununurra and Wyndham, Ord City had exploded since 2023 as refugees flooded in from the north and dollars poured in from all over the world – keen to invest in the infrastructure needed to house, feed, clothe and entertain a major new city on the northern edge of Australia.

'Incredible,' muttered Conan to himself as he pushed through the hordes of happy, pissed off, impatient, tolerant, temporary citizens – some of them less than two weeks from full citizenship.

There was graffiti everywhere, like any other city, but it was simply impossible to make out meaning in a multitude of scrawls and styles. Only occasionally did he see English, and that was usually just initials. AINANIA was everywhere – whatever that meant – but it was frequently crossed out or overscored with DEDD REFFO or just DR.

Conan had always taken an interest in graffiti. From his earliest days as a police detective (before transferring to the feds) he had picked up on gang information which the members had happily advertised on walls, assuming no one in authority would understand. Conan understood, which had led to a number of successful arrests and a fast-tracked career.

For a while.

But he was still naturally interested in how the people of the streets communicated and took his time getting to the back-lane address which had been scribbled on Michael Wing Ho's card.

AINANIA he saw again and again, and suddenly twigged its meaning – 'all is nothing and nothing is all' – the most fundamental principle of Habal Tong.

Perhaps the most interesting thing about Ord City was the way so many different races and cultures had blended in such a short time, despite so many ancient conflicts. The reason for the new harmony was mostly attributed to Habal Tong, according to numerous documentaries on religious integration and tolerance, but there was a darker side. Having combined all the best features of its component faiths, HT devotees were confident that they had synthesised the perfect philosophy, free from the trademark doubt that fluttered in the hearts of other believers. This confidence sometimes bred an unpleasantly arrogant fanaticism which was unsettling for the mainstream Australian population, already getting nervous about the imminent First Wave being released into wider society. There were mutterings about embracing Australian values before being let loose and any number of powerful voices were raised in protest. Not least the far right radical group – Dedd Reffo – who were dedicated to keeping refugees out of Australia. They had purchased a submarine from Somalian pirates (renamed the HMAS Eureka) and since 2024 had been sinking refugee boats in international waters, polarising the mainstream community. Most condemned them for cold-blooded mass murder, but others encouraged them and dinner party conversations in Sydney and Melbourne were getting increasingly heated.

The other polarising issue was the number of disaffected Australian youth who were converting to Habal Tong, spouting its tenets like counter-cultural axioms to rock the establishment. The biggest surprise of the 2025 census was the decline in those who regarded themselves as atheist or agnostic.

And clearly, all of those same battles were playing out in graffiti daubed on the walls of Ord City.

'And the murder statistics,' thought Conan as he arrived at the house in Ruddock Lane where the two men had been found, bearing the marks of two violently opposed groups.

It was an evil looking place – burned out and abandoned – and Conan forced himself to ignore the irrational tremors as he walked up the short path, littered with bottles, cigarette butts, syringes, hundreds of little Crimson vials and the faded flotsam of absent lives. The house, of course, was covered in graffiti, with AINANIA and DR the only writing he could make out amid the many alien daubings.

There was blue police tape across the entrance but it was unguarded, meaning the police were no longer interested in the place. That also was odd, reflected Conan, who was beginning to wonder why he'd been sent up when no one seemed to have any interest in the case.

Inside, the house stank of charred wood, damp and urine. There were scores of discarded needles, vials and a carpet of broken glass. Rubbish was piled in every corner and two mildewed mattresses were red-brown with old blood. Conan knew from the file that the bodies had been found face down on the mattresses – which should have been removed. He was also aware that the disfigurement of the victims' faces had occurred while they were still alive – including the removal of eyes and tongues.

Considering the overwhelmingly pacifist philosophy of Habal Tong, its more radical adherents were breathtakingly violent, but the violence was easily integrated within HT philosophy by the aphorisms of Ah Li Wu – the reclusive leader. 'To love is to kill and to kill is to love,' he said, simultaneously defining the relationships of HT couples and empowering his goons.

Mind you, there were mainstream academics who doubted the existence of Ah Li Wu. No photograph had ever been produced but there were paintings of his image everywhere – a Chinese face with a long beard. Indeed, there was a fairly skilled example of his image done with spray cans on the wall in the room in which Conan stood, his nose twitching at the stench.

Conan stared at the picture of Ah Li Wu – appreciating the technique that had produced it and pondering the secret semiotic messages that such street art always carried. It was rumoured that Ah Li Wu would make a first ever public appearance at *Illumination* – a major Habal Tong festival to be held the night before the First Wave, culminating at midnight as the First Wavers became full citizens.

What a night that was likely to be – and possibly it was the reason for Loongy's strange attitude. Obviously he had his work cut out preparing for the big night – such a huge gathering, of such symbolic importance, was a perfect target for Dedd Reffo and after just one morning at AFP headquarters Conan was in no doubt as to their main focus.

Gangland murders were unimportant.

'But not to me,' thought Conan, breathing through his mouth as he hurried from the house and made his way back to the hotel.

Chapter 4

Tim's Time to Shine

'So fuckin' hot,' muttered Robbie Bennett to no one in particular.

His mate, Chris Majkic, was driving but the air conditioning in the old, blue Mazda hadn't worked for years. It had only been Robbie's car for two years but it had been the Old Man's for at least ten before that and had to be nearly twenty years old.

The lack of air conditioning had never been a problem in Melbourne, but it was now. They should've taken the coast road, but no – fuckin' Chris had wanted to take the direct route through the heart of the desert.

One thing that did still work was the thermometer. At Andamooka it reckoned the outside heat (more or less the same as the inside heat) was 54 degrees. Robbie found it hard to believe that planet Earth could sustain such temperatures but, an hour out from Alice Springs, was grateful that the mercury had plunged to a more temperate 45.

'Fuckin' look at that,' sniggered Chris, and Robbie looked up with mild interest at a couple of hitch hikers looming – a chubby young woman in yellow harem pants and her thin, male companion – plainly melting in the sun and pleading with the boys to pull over.

'Whattaya reckon?' asked Robbie, but Chris flashed past as the girl gave them one finger.

'Fuck 'em,' said Chris.

Robbie was a little uncomfortable with the idea of abandoning people to the perilous heat of the desert, but Chris was implacable.

'They would've been trouble.'

'How do you figure that?' asked Robbie.

'We haven't passed any broken down cars,' said Chris, 'so clearly they've been dumped by whoever picked 'em up before. The fat slag was in yellow so she's obviously some fuckin' Habal Tong bitch who wants to convert everyone. That's why they've been left in the middle of nowhere … you wanna put up with HT shit all the way to Ord City?'

'No,' said Robbie, who was relieved to see a roadhouse materialise out of the shimmering heat.

'There you go,' said Chris. 'It won't take 'em long to walk to the roadhouse so they're not in any danger. Someone'll give 'em a lift from there.'

'You wanna stop for a beer?' asked Robbie.

• • •

'Fuckin' cunts!' shouted Lemon at the silvery blue Mazda as it passed.

Tim was all but ready to despair. He sat on their swag, wilting in the heat and wondering where Lemon got the energy to keep railing at the Mazda as it hurtled into the haze up ahead.

Suddenly she turned on him.

'Get off the fuckin' bag!'

Without a word he stood, and Lemon pushed him out of the way. Then she slumped down herself on the bag and pulled out a cigarette.

'Lemon … ' began Tim.

'What?' she snapped.

'How many have we got left?'

'I don't care … *I fuckin' need one*, alright?'

Tim shrugged, helpless. Cigarettes were really expensive now because nearly everyone had given up. Of course, that didn't bother the tobacco companies. Supply and demand meant that it didn't matter how much the price rose for those who still wanted to smoke. They'd pay anything.

Or steal.

It was always Tim's job to do the thieving while Lemon distracted the store people with a disingenuous attempt at evangelism. 'All is nothing, and nothing is all,' she would tell them as Tim hovered in the background, and even the most disinterested shop assistant would eventually be forced to engage with Lemon's irritatingly specious logic. That was Tim's time to shine, and as he stuffed his pockets he would always be thinking, 'Maybe this time?'

But it never was.

'How far to Alice Springs?' demanded Lemon, her nose and shoulders reddening in the mid-morning heat.

'Eighty-five ks.'

There was a silence as they contemplated the impossible distance, then Tim took his courage in his hands.

'Maybe next ride we should lay off the Habal Tong stuff ... '

'Are you fucking mad?' asked Lemon.

'Only as a strategy to stay in the car longer,' placated Tim. 'People get pissed off when we start preaching The Way.'

'It is our duty,' insisted Lemon as she dragged heavily on her cigarette and glared through the smoke. 'Our sacred fucking duty ... to show people The Way ... to share our enlightenment with the world!'

'I understand all that,' sighed Tim, 'but I don't want you to miss *Illumination*. If we keep getting kicked out of cars we're not gonna make Ord City in time.'

'Well maybe if you gave me a bit more support we wouldn't get kicked out!'

'What do you mean?'

'You always leave the talking to me. It's pathetic.'

'Well, what do you want me to say?' he pleaded.

'You could start by agreeing with me occasionally.'

'I always agree with you.'

'It's pathetic agreement,' she sneered, flicking the butt into a thicket of parched dry grass. 'If you want to convince others you have to be more passionate. You have to be convinced yourself.'

Tim knew there was no point in pursuing the argument. He considered retrieving the precious butt to snatch a couple of drags, but stood and stared into the haze to the north-west, which suddenly cleared for a moment.

'Is that a roadhouse up ahead?'

• • •

The beer was cold and tasted like heaven.

There was a bar and bistro attached to the roadhouse and, after filling up on Fifty Fifty, Robbie and Chris found themselves in a cool, dim paradise that smelled like old beer and stale sweat. It was a strangely pleasant smell and Chris breathed deeply as he relaxed into the padded booth seat – cracked and polished by the arses of a million truckies.

'You know what I like most out here?'

'What?'

'The freedom from technology.'

Robbie knew exactly what he meant, but also knew that Chris would need to explain every aspect of his point in case there was some obscure nuance that might have eluded him. Robbie let Chris talk – he was happy in the dim cavern of the bistro and just wanted to relax before braving the heat again. The worst part of the day was yet to come and if he could get Chris into one of his alcohol-fuelled rants then they might spend all afternoon in the bistro and drive on again after the sun set.

'Computers don't rule your life out here,' said Chris, after a long swallow of beer.

Robbie flexed his wrist upon which he wore his OzBrace, which he'd just used to pay for petrol and beer. Chris saw the gesture and shrugged.

'Well … they do, of course, but it's not so in your face like it is everywhere else.'

The boys were both twenty-one and could remember back when Australia still used plastic paper and cards for money, but since the Quantum Revolution in the mid twenties, many things had changed. Cash had disappeared so all transactions were electronic. There had been an immediate short-term recession as the economy adjusted to the end of cash, but it soon bounced back and profound societal changes followed – especially in the field of crime. Robbery was pointless if you couldn't steal cash, or valuables which could be converted to cash. The only point to thieving was if you actually wanted to use what was stolen yourself, or could barter it for something else. As for the legal transactions, every payment for every good or service was auto-analysed in real time and huge dossiers were built up on the actions, movements and criminal potential of every citizen. The end result was that armed robbery and other forms of physical property crime had all but vanished. Electronic transactions and bank accounts were so powerfully encrypted they defied any sort of hacking, and only First World governments and major corporations could afford (or were allowed to have access to) the quantum computers. The only way to steal money was by complex fraud or ID theft, but the penalties for that were so harsh as to make it all but unthinkable.

'You got nothing to hide, you shouldn't be worried about it,' said Robbie, knowing that Chris couldn't resist taking the bait – which would mean at least another hour in the bar.

'It's not about guilty consciences,' insisted Chris. 'It's about the government having too much fuckin' power. They know what we're gonna do before we do.'

'They don't know why we're going to Ord City.'

'No ... but they already know we're headed that way,' said Chris, glancing over his shoulder. 'They know everything about our personalities and particular tastes because they know everything we've ever bought, read, eaten, done or said. Seriously, I would not be surprised if they were secretly analysing our shit.'

Robbie laughed.

'What could that tell them?'

Chris paused, staring into his beer for a moment.

'They'd know you don't eat chilli, rice, tofu or bok fuckin' choi.'

'So?'

'So you're heading to Ord City and you don't eat Asian crap ... that means you're not going up to join Habal Tong. You just got sacked from your job, when jobs are really hard to get ... unless you're a fuckin' reffo. The shit analysers might think it's fuckin' obvious why you're headed to Ord City.'

Robbie laughed, then found himself confronted with a vision of Kate. Instantly he banished that line of thinking, but at that moment the door to the bar opened and Chris swore under his breath. Robbie glanced over to see the fat chick and her skinny boyfriend they'd passed hitching. The fat chick spotted them and marched over bristling.

'You own that fuckin' shitbox Mazda?'

'So what if we do?' replied Chris, flatly.

'Nice pair of cunts youse blokes are! We could've fuckin' died out there.'

'That would've been tragic,' said Chris and Robbie snorted beer though his nose, laughing.

'Fuck off and leave us alone,' said Chris.

The girl turned and stared meaningfully at her skinny boyfriend, as though expecting him to come to her defence, but he just shrugged miserably. The girl glanced about the bar – there were maybe half a dozen other people besides the barman and the waitress.

'Anyone goin' to Ord City?' she yelled.

A couple of blokes looked over without much interest but no one responded.

'Anyone goin' to Alice Springs?' she yelled, and the couple who'd looked over turned away.

'Someone's gotta be goin' to Alice,' she announced. 'We need a fuckin' lift … and we'll pay you back with enlightenment.'

'Order or get out,' said the barman, as a few blokes shook their heads.

The girl was furious but allowed herself to be coaxed into one of the booths by her skinny boyfriend who was whispering urgently.

'What was I saying?' asked Chris, with a last contemptuous glance at the girl.

'You were talking shit,' said Robbie.

• • •

An hour later, Tim finished the last swig of the tepid beer he'd been nursing. Lemon had wolfed down three bourbons and coke but the money needed to be rationed. Tim checked the display on his OzBrace, though he knew the details by heart – $37 to last until the next dole payment, which was four days away – and a schooner was ten bucks.

There was enough there for two bourbons – one of them a double – and Tim weighed the odds of trying to get Lemon tipsy. The only time she ever got amorous these days was when she was a bit pissy. The trouble was, she was just as likely to go the other way and become totally infuriated over nothing – getting her pissed was like tossing a coin, and she already had the shits.

'You want another bourbon?' he asked.

'Of course,' she snapped, and Tim's heart sank, but he rose dutifully and headed for the bar, trying not to notice the scorn on the faces of other blokes as he walked past.

The barman's lips thinned with impatience as Tim ordered a double bourbon and a tap water, leaving him $15 on his OzBrace – enough for one more single bourbon or two packets of Twisties. Food or sex?

Food or a chance of sex, he corrected himself.

'Don't let my mate Chris see you wearing that shirt.'

Tim looked up at the bloke who'd just arrived at the bar, one of the boys from the Mazda who Lemon 'd had a go at. Then he glanced down at his old red and black Wanderers tee shirt.

'Why's that?'

'He hates the fuckin' A-League. He was an AFL prodigy but since all the money's gone out of the game he had to get a job as well as play Reserves.'

'Reserves? Who for?' asked Tim.

'St Kilda … till he told 'em to stick it if they weren't gonna pay him.'

Tim shook his head in admiration, as the other bloke ordered a couple of beers, then turned back.

'Jeez, your girlfriend's got a mouth on her,' he said. 'How do you put up with that every day?'

'She's not always like that,' lied Tim.

'She is a root, I suppose … sort of. I'm Robbie.'

'Tim,' said Tim, shaking hands.

'I'd ask yers over to join us, but … '

Robbie laughed and Tim shrugged.

At that moment, they became aware of some consternation by the door. A few of the truckies had jumped up and gone outside.

'Fire!' someone yelled.

Almost immediately, Tim thought he could smell smoke and remembered Lemon's fag butt in the dry grass.

'It's comin' this way!' shouted someone else, and suddenly there was panic. The music speakers were interrupted by a booming voice from the Road Station HQ.

'All persons evacuate. Repeat … all persons evacuate immediately and head towards Alice Springs. There is a grassfire approaching from the south and only emergency personnel are authorised to remain. All persons evacuate … '

Robbie and Tim walked towards the booth area with the drinks. Robbie handed Chris his beer and they both skulled in unison. Lemon's eyes widened in anger and Tim was amazed to discover he'd accidentally drunk her bourbon. He handed her the water.

'What am I supposed to do with that?' she demanded.

'Throw it on the fire?' suggested Tim, then before she could explode with her usual fury, he collared Robbie.

'I don't suppose you blokes could give us a lift?'

Chris would've refused but it was Robbie's car and what sort of arsehole leaves people to burn in a bushfire?

'For fuck's sake!' swore Chris, as Robbie gave his assent to the couple. Then, grudgingly accepting his humane duty, Chris said: 'Right … let's get out of here.'

Chapter 5

An Evil Child

Conan was falling.

More correctly, he was about to fall from a tall building, having ridden an elevator until it opened onto a long drop in a cityscape he knew only in his dreams. The floor of the elevator seemed to crumble under his feet, then moments later he was awake, with a jolt of adrenalin catching his breath and the dream city fading as he realised his phone was ringing.

He winced with guilt when he saw the number displayed.

'Hi, Ma.'

'Conan?'

He'd promised about a week ago to go over and help her with something or other, but as usual he'd been distracted.

'Where are you?'

'Ord City … it's a work thing.'

'Ord City, WA? I was there yesterday … or last week.'

'It's not a virtual job, Ma … I'm really here.'

'I don't see the point of going anywhere for real these days,' she lectured. 'Virtual travel is just as good … better, because you get to sleep in your own bed.'

Conan's mother lived in a retirement village in one of the many vast estates that had sprung up on the fringes of all major cities in the last twenty years. Conan tended to visit about once a week. Or at least once a fortnight, but it must have been close to a month since he'd seen her – not that she'd notice.

'I lost another boyfriend last night … they can't keep up with me.'

Her boyfriends tended to die in real life because they got overexcited in Virtual Youth – one of the many virtual sex sites but specially catering for the elderly.

'What keeps you goin', Ma?'

'I don't really care about them, so I don't get too excited.'

'That's really profound.'

'It's good advice, Conan … you should try it next time you get married.'

Conan stared at the ceiling fan and refused to take the bait. His mother liked nothing more than to lecture him about his appalling love life while boasting about her many virtual conquests.

'Conan … I need money.'

'You've got plenty of money.'

'Super doesn't pay for Virtual Youth … I have to dip into my capital. That arsehole Keating should have made us pay 20% … or even 30% into super, then maybe I'd have a decent retirement.'

'Well, do without Virtual Youth. If you don't waste capital your super will keep you in pretty good shape for the rest of your life … your real life. '

'You don't understand … I don't like real life any more. Virtual Youth is so much better, but I can only afford it for another six months … unless you help me.'

'Why don't you just start caring?'

'… I beg your pardon?'

'Why don't you start caring about your virtual partners? Then you might get overexcited and … erm … and won't need Virtual Youth anymore.'

'You're evil, Conan. I don't believe I could have raised such an evil child.'

But she was laughing.

'We'll talk about it when I get back, Ma … okay?'

'Okay, Conan. You be careful in Ord City … it's full of weirdos.'

'It is?'

'Trust me. I've been there.'

• • •

Just after nine o'clock, Conan met Loongy outside a ramshackle building in Dutton Close, surrounded by bamboo scaffolding and half the windows blackened from a recent fire. Despite its dilapidated condition, the building was teeming with life – hordes of grimy, happy children mucked about in the street which was also full of dogs, cats, vendors peddling cheap clothing, weird looking fruit and vegetables and makeshift snacks while dozens of motorbikes threaded through semi-abandoned road works and stagnant puddles. The street smelled of exhaust fumes, dead water and frying onions, and somehow reminded Conan of a medieval town he'd explored on Virtual History Channel.

A number of the children suddenly accosted Conan, thrusting battered-looking wares for sale at him, and Loongy snapped at them in Chinese, sending them scampering.

Conan forced himself to remain impassive but Loongy knew what he was thinking.

'Just because I'm sixth generation doesn't mean I can't speak Cantonese.'

'Of course not,' agreed Conan, following him into the building, still uncertain whether Loongy was weirdly paranoid or brilliantly pulling his leg.

The foyer was a shambles of piled up garbage bags, a scatter of small vials and discarded building materials. The elevator shafts were two gaping black holes and obviously not working.

'It's on the fifth floor,' said Loongy, entering a dim stairwell that was lit from several floors up and stank of urine. 'I bet you're wondering: how do people live in this?'

'Not really,' lied Conan, trying not to breathe with all the piss stink.

'This is what they're used to in Asia,' explained Loongy. 'This is what they bring with them … this, and Habal Tong.'

'You're not a fan?'

'You come to Australia, you assimilate!' insisted Loongy, raising his voice. 'You don't like our ways … fuck off back to Asia! Fuck off!'

Conan kept waiting for Loongy to grin, to acknowledge he'd been joking, but Loongy was muttering fiercely to himself, seeming more Chinese every second.

On the fifth floor, they left the stairwell and passed along a corridor with damp carpet that stank of mould. A dog barked from a darkened doorway and faces, old and young, mainly Chinese but at least one family of Indians, or Sri Lankans, peered at them as they strode past until they turned a corner and found two uniformed officers sitting outside a door taped across with blue and white checks.

The two officers leapt to their feet, one of whom was Agent Ping who'd been reading an old paper-style book, which he half hid behind his back.

'Chairs,' remarked Loongy, irritably. 'Where you get chairs?'

'Neighbours,' said Ping. 'They've been very helpful.'

'They better not be from inside,' said Loongy, producing a key as Ping pulled the tape away while giving Conan a look of amused sympathy.

'Well ... here it is,' said Loongy, as they stepped across the threshold into a small and cluttered room, dominated by a large black poster with orange lettering: ALL IS NOTHING AND NOTHING IS ALL.

Conan stood quite still – breathing slowly and feeling his way around the room – trying to imagine what it was like to live there. The walls were crowded with book shelves and football posters, one of which was a picture of a supremely athletic-looking Chinese in the yellow and red of the Ord City Pilgrims, shooting at goal.

'Feng Nine,' said Conan.

'You a football fan?' asked Loongy, a bit less irritable.

'Not really.'

'You should be.'

Conan turned his attention to a huge table under the only window. It was dusty, littered with old-style books and papers, the inevitable Crimson vials and two old lap-top computers at either end.

'Why should I be a football fan?' he asked, noting that one of the laptops was still turned on.

'Football is everything in Ord City. If you want to understand us you have to understand football.'

'Us?'

Conan tapped a key but the screen was frozen.

'Yes ... us! Just because I'm sixth generation doesn't mean I can't be part of Ord City.'

'I guess it might help the newcomers to assimilate.'

Loongy peered suspiciously at Conan.

'Yes … it does help.'

Conan ignored him for a moment to read the frozen screen with a large black and red field covering most of it. In the middle of the field were the words: Access Denied and a pair of keys crossed over each other.

'Locked out,' said Loongy.

Only part of the URL was visible in the address field and seemed to be written in Italian. Conan copied down the part of the address he could see and Loongy laughed, 'Oh look! Sydney investigator finds a clue. What you think it means, Tools?'

Conan ignored him and continued to look among the books and papers covering the desk. Most of it seemed to be scientific or religious. Conan glanced at a book on chaos theory, then picked up a large bible and noted its margins were covered in scribbled notes.

'These guys were pretty churchy.'

'Brilliant deduction, Tools,' laughed Loongy. 'You seen enough yet?'

Several of the pamphlets were glossy plastex Army of God publications. Conan flipped open one with a confused-looking Chinese on the cover, entitled: Can You Be Christian and Habal Tong Too?

'Let's go!' said Loongy, suddenly irritated. 'I've got real work to do.'

'Okay,' said Conan and, as Loongy turned his back, slipped the pamphlet into his pocket.

The door was locked and resealed with tape, and Loongy headed for the stairs without another word to the two uniformed officers. Conan gave Ping an apologetic salute and followed Loongy toward the piss-dank stairs. As he did, one of the neighbouring doors opened and a Chinese woman of quite striking beauty peered out, but immediately lowered her eyes when she saw Conan and closed her door again.

'Now you can write your report,' said Loongy, '… and fuck off back to Sydney.'

'Can I?' asked Conan, still seeing the woman's sad and frightened face in his mind's eye and wondering about the life she had found in Ord City – wondering also whether she knew the murdered men.

'Of course! Two dead Habal Tong … killed by Dedd Reffo. Happens every day. Now fuck off back to Sydney and drink latte by the Opera House!'

Conan laughed and Loongy turned on him fiercely.

'You think I'm funny?'

'Yes, very,' grinned Conan.

Loongy stared again, then stormed down the stairs, somehow leaving Conan with the impression that he was in the presence of a Master Piss-taker.

• • •

The pamphlet didn't say much. It answered its own question in the negative, which is what Conan would have expected. It did, however, give the addresses of a few local Army of God chapters, so Conan decided to visit the one closest to the flat where the two friends had lived.

The streets on the map bore only vague resemblance to the streets and lanes threading the mad jumble of buildings and other temporary dwellings that metastasised throughout the city, but Conan managed to pick his way through teeming hordes of provisional citizens to the Army of God chapter house on the corner of Kerr and Whitlam Streets.

The house was two storey and old brick – one of the places that had obviously been around before Ord City was proclaimed back in 2023. Out the front were numerous placards bearing Christian slogans, and a group of bored-looking children sat on the steps, listening to a young man in a shiny, black uniform reading them a story.

The young man paused to examine Conan as he climbed the stairs.

'Welcome, brother,' he said, in an affected accent that sounded almost British.

'How ya goin'?'

'I'm Lieutenant Michael Rice. Can I offer you guidance?'

'Guidance?' echoed Conan, stifling a laugh. 'Don't know about that mate … I just want to look inside for the moment.'

Conan continued up the stairs and stood in the doorway, aware that the young man had abandoned his story and was hovering at his elbow.

'These are the daily sessions,' he said, referring to a whiteboard in the foyer, and Conan paused to glance at what was available. The board was headed with Children's Bible Story Time, followed by Coffee Shop, various Bible Study sessions, and in the evening was the Daily Service followed by The Great Debate at nine pm.

'Are you in charge here?' asked Conan.

'That depends on what you mean,' said Lieutenant Rice. 'I'm the officer of the day, in charge of the …'

'I'm in charge,' said a voice, and Conan turned to see a woman in a similar black uniform to Lieutenant Rice's, which she filled rather differently. She would have been late twenties or early thirties, with brunette hair pulled back in a severe bun and a tight, humourless smile.

Conan found himself staring for a moment, but pulled himself together.

'Ah … sorry,' he said, recovering, and pulled his ID from his top pocket. 'Agent Tooley … AFP. Can we talk?'

He was still staring at her. It was the eyes that did it. In all other ways she might have been the living quintessence of untouchable female authority, but her eyes gave her away. Her eyes said she was human, and narrowed as she perceived his interest.

'Captain Melodie Roberts,' she said, primly holding out her hand to be shaken. 'Come with me.'

She led him to a stair but stood aside and waved him ahead.

'After you,' said Conan, but she simply raised an eyebrow and he grinned sheepishly, guessing she disliked being followed upstairs by men because of the opportunity it gave to stare at her arse.

He went up the stairs, and she followed, several paces behind.

The upstairs was a long gallery looking down on the hall with several doors leading to offices. Captain Roberts passed him and, yes, her arse was superb. Conan got only one quick peek at its rounded, pert perfection then stared resolutely at the back of her head, in case she suddenly turned.

Her office was the last at the end of the gallery and she gestured him into one of the two chairs opposite her desk.

'So, what can I do for you Agent Tooley?'

'Call me Tools,' said Conan, and immediately felt foolish. She didn't respond, so he pulled his triPod out of his bag and placed it on her desk. Seconds later images of the two murdered men flickered in the air, and her mouth set in a thin line.

'Not again,' she sighed.

'What do you mean?'

'I've already spoken to the police … I've nothing further to add.'

'So you knew them?'

'Yes … as you would know if you people kept proper records.'

Conan, knew there was no record of interview with the Army of God on the file, but made a mental note to check when he returned to the office.

'I've been sent up from Sydney and haven't seen much of the file … but maybe I'll ask some different questions?'

'Like what?'

'Like, what are you doing for dinner tonight?' thought Conan. She got even more attractive as her anger flared.

'Like … were Bruce Fong and Michael Wing Ho members of your organisation?'

'That's the first question they asked me last time,' she snapped. 'We don't have lay members. We have officers and brethren … Bruce and Michael were neither.'

'But you knew them?'

'Like so many in this city, they were searching. They would sometimes attend the Great Debate.'

'Which is on tonight?'

'Yes.'

She was almost aggressive in her answers – eyeing him defiantly – making Conan wonder what he'd done to piss her off so quickly.

'So what were they searching for?'

'For God, Agent Tooley. We get many such people who cannot find what they truly need in their lives, so they turn to us.'

'You must feel very vindicated.'

She stared at him for a moment, then enquired, 'Was that sarcasm, Agent Tooley? Because if it was, this interview is over.'

'Forgive me,' said Conan. 'I didn't mean to sound sarcastic.'

In truth, sarcasm came so naturally when interviewing he wasn't sure whether he'd meant it or not.

'They were Habal Tong?' he asked, trying to sound serious.

'Yes ... but very interested in Christianity.'

'So ... the Great Debate is about converting to Christianity?'

'Sometimes,' she said, still stiff and prickly. 'Mostly it's about comparison. This city is such a melting pot of culture and religion ... it's where we get together with people of other faiths to discuss what we have in common?'

'So you all agree, eh?'

'We do ... on all the important points.'

'Except one.'

Once again she stared at him, as though suspecting him of levity.

'Except one,' she agreed. 'Is there anything else? I really have answered these questions before.'

'Who'd you speak to the first time?'

'I don't remember his name.'

'Was he Chinese?'

'No.'

Captain Roberts rose to usher him out and Conan noted, to his small disappointment, the engagement ring on her finger.

'I'm sorry I can't be of any further assistance ... and I do have work to do.'

Conan switched off the Pod and put it back in his bag as she stood over him, holding the door open.

'One more question, Melodie ... Captain Roberts,' he amended as he saw her anger flare.

'Well?'

'Was there any particular aspect of Christianity that interested these two?'

She opened her mouth to speak, but then paused.

'Yes?'

'It's nothing.'

'What's nothing?'

'There was no proper aspect of Christianity that interested them.'

'Proper? What about improper?'

'Please don't twist my words for meaning, Agent Tooley. I really can't help you with this so I suggest you continue your investigations elsewhere.'

She left the office so Conan had little choice other than to follow her out, but in her haste to be rid of him she forgot to let him go first down the stairs. Conan found himself almost swooning with desire at the sight of her gorgeous bottom in the tight, black, god-fearing skirt.

Halfway down the stairs, she suddenly turned and Conan knew he'd been caught.

'Um … I was just thinking,' he stammered, as she blushed an angry pink.

'Thinking? Is that what you call it?'

'Yes … look, chances are, I'll turn up one night at your Great Debate. Maybe even tonight.'

'Everyone's welcome,' she said, in an ice-hard voice that clearly meant everyone but him.

'Yeah … erm … but if I do turn up, I don't want anyone to know who I am … so don't talk to me.'

'Don't talk to you,' she echoed, reaching the bottom of the stairs and waving him towards the door. 'It would be my pleasure.'

Chapter 6

First Man Eaten

Several hours later, after another frustrating afternoon at the office (where no record of any interview with Captain Roberts could be found), Conan was sitting just across the road from her chapter house, sipping a coffee of surprisingly good quality and enjoying the noise of the street and the evening cooking smells from so many open air kitchens. He'd picked up a tattered print out of the *Ord City Times* and was reading about another refugee boat sunk (allegedly) by the Dedd Reffo sub, the Eureka, and the Giant Array – a huge field of radio telescopes about fifty kilometres south – which was on the brink of some major breakthrough.

Unlike Conan's case, which was going nowhere.

The one small result he'd had was a report back from forensics on the card found in Wing Ho's shoe. The handwriting referred to the address where the bodies had been found, and also seemed to refer to *Epistola Clementis* which was part of the URL he had copied from the locked computer in the dead men's flat. And when Conan did a search on those words he had been intrigued to learn that *Epistola Clementis* was Latin for 'The Letter of Clement'. There was very little on the net about it, but what there was seemed to suggest that the Letter was a controversial document from the early Catholic Church.

Conan had wanted to take the dead men's computers in to go through their search history but Loongy had absolutely refused.

'Case closed, Tools,' he'd said. 'There's too much for forensics to do up here so we can't waste any more time on Sydney politics.'

'Since when is an Ord City double murder Sydney politics?'

'Since you came up to waste our time,' said Loongy. 'I've been talking to your boss … he says you should go.'

'He hasn't told me that,' said Conan, although in truth, there was an email from Kenny Cook which he hadn't opened.

Conan took another sip of his coffee and glanced at his watch.

Something felt wrong. It was clear that Loongy was deliberately preventing him from making progress with the investigation and, in all likelihood, it truly would be a waste of time to pursue it further. Everything pointed to a Dedd Reffo (or Habal Tong) execution and the world would hardly end because of it. But why send him up in the first place if they didn't want the crime investigated?

Conan rubbed at his eyes and felt his frustration seething. First he'd been taken off the remote terror investigation – which was clearly still a massive threat to the NBN node south of Ord City. Then he'd been sent up here on a wild goose chase – a wild goose they didn't want him to catch!

Nothing made sense and Conan suspected he'd soon be back in Sydney and increasingly marginalised – unless he could somehow pull off a huge win from the total fucking shambles of Ord City.

He drained his cup and left the café, ignoring the clamouring street traders and dashing between the hundreds of motorbikes that mostly constituted Ord City traffic.

Just before nine o'clock, he slipped into the Army of God chapter house. The main hall was about a quarter full, some with their heads bowed in prayer and the rest lounging in studied irreverence. At the front of the room, Lieutenant Rice and Captain Roberts – Melodie – sat watching another man in the same black uniform who stood with his palms raised, his eyes closed and finishing some kind of prayer in a sweetly melodious baritone.

'... and please, Lord, open the hearts and minds of all Australians of all faiths, but especially the non-believers. Let your light into their souls and give them the grace ... the peace ... the absolute bliss and joy that we, who already bathe in your light and love, get to know every day. Open the gates to your kingdom of heaven and let your love shine forth to bathe the upturned faces of all humanity!'

'Harr-aruya!' cried a small Chinese man, rather detracting from the enchantment of the baritone.

'... give them freedom from doubt,' continued the Man in Black. 'Give them your faith, your knowledge, your certainty that there is a life eternal … forever by your side in the Garden … Eden restored.'

'Harr-aruya!'

Conan took a chair at the back, slightly away from the others and caught Melodie's eye for a moment. She stared, then turned primly away to watch her colleague finish his prayer. The mellifluous baritone rumbled to a conclusion.

'Harr-aruya! Harr-aruya!'

The little Chinese man, dressed only in blue checked shorts and a white singlet, was in a world of his own, completely oblivious to the impact of his interjections on the devout spell cast by the voice of the Man in Black. Conan found himself thoroughly amused by the theatre – especially when the Chinese man embraced the speaker, chattering excitedly as the taller man suffered the embrace with obviously strained indulgence.

Then Melodie stood and announced, 'We will just take a short break before the Great Debate. Please help yourselves to coffee and tea.'

With that she disappeared through a door at the back, followed by the Man in Black. The congregation all stood and shuffled towards the table at the side of the room where a large urn was plugged in and started helping themselves.

'You were here this morning.'

Conan looked up to see Lieutenant Rice smiling at him.

'I was.'

'Would you like a tea or coffee?'

Conan stood and walked towards the back of the queue, followed by Lieutenant Rice, who struck Conan as the sort of bloke who'd be first man eaten in a horror film.

'Who's that leading the prayers?' asked Conan.

'That would be Major Lammas,' said Lieutenant Rice, his adoration plain.

'Major Lammas,' repeated Conan. 'He has a nice speaking voice.'

'And an even nicer message,' said Rice.

'If you're into that kind of thing.'

Rice cocked an eyebrow as they shuffled towards the urn.

'Not a believer … Mister … erm … '

'Tooley. Conan Tooley … but you can call me Tools.'

Rice smiled and said, 'You spoke with Captain Roberts this morning.'

'That's true … not for long.'

It was clear that Melodie had not reported her conversation with Conan to Rice, whose curiosity blazed.

'Was there anything, perhaps, that I could help you with?'

'What, like … how to hide from a T-Rex?'

Rice's eyes widened, as Conan maintained his serious straight face. 'I'm sorry?'

'Never mind … what's Major Lammas's story?'

'Ah … well, the Major is one of the Ord City War Councillors.'

'Top brass?'

'Exactly. General Jessup … Major Maddox, who runs the hospitals … and Major Lammas. They're the senior officers for the region … although the General's mainly in Perth.'

The queue had shuffled forward as they spoke and Rice reached for a mug.

'I love urn coffee,' he said. 'I actually prefer it to barista.'

'That's fascinating,' said Conan. 'So, why is Lammas here tonight? How does he fit into the local picture?'

Rice gave a tight smile in response to Conan's sarcasm, then said, 'Our chapter house falls within the eastern division of Ord City … which is Major Lammas's division.'

'He's your boss?'

'Well, strictly speaking Captain Roberts is my boss … but what about …'

'Aah yes, Captain Roberts,' interrupted Conan. 'What's her story?'

Conan accepted a mug from Lieutenant Rice and grimaced as he sipped the tepid muck with its nasty tang.

'Captain Roberts?' mused Rice. 'Erm … she's from Melbourne … went to ANU. She studied Asian Languages and joined the Army of God when she was still in first year.'

'She seems full of secrets,' said Conan, watching Rice closely.

'Secrets?' echoed Rice, '… odd thing to say. Still, she is a captain and head of the chapter. She would learn a lot that doesn't make it down to my security clearance level.'

'You have that in the Army of God? Security clearance?'

'I'm sure they have it in all professional organisations,' said Rice.

'But don't you feel left out?' pressed Conan, '... when they're having their secrets?'

Most of the people around the table had drifted pack to the seats but the buzz of the hall suddenly stilled. Conan turned to see that Melodie and Major Lammas had resumed their seats at the front of the congregation.

'Ooh ... time to sit down,' said Rice, grabbing the opportunity to change the suddenly uncomfortable subject. 'Enjoy the Great Debate.'

'What about Roberts and Lammas though?' asked Conan, as Rice tried to scurry away.

'What about them?'

'Are they ... '

'What?'

'Bonking?'

Lieutenant Rice's face went white, and then a deep red. He opened his mouth but then turned and strode back to his seat, leaving Conan grinning in his wake.

The first part of the Great Debate was fairly predictable, and not much of a debate. Major Lammas, who would have been late thirties and looked a bit like a young George Clooney, spoke in that hypnotic voice of his about certain moral themes which united all religions.

'So you say every time,' interjected a smallish, bearded man in a tee shirt and skull cap. 'But despite the commonalities ... you somehow conclude that Christianity is the one true path.'

'Hello Razzaq,' said Lammas, 'nice to see you back again. Well ... Christianity does have one major advantage over other religions. It was started by Jesus.'

'It was not started by Jesus,' said Razzaq. 'Jesus was a Jew ... he simply added his own spin to the Jewish faith, which was much, much older.'

'I think the second covenant with God is a bit more than spin,' smiled Lammas, his fingers indicating inverted commas. 'Our relationship with God was enormously deepened by the words and deeds of Jesus.'

'And further deepened by the words and deeds of the Prophet Mohammed,' said Razzaq. 'Now they are deepened yet again by the tenets of Habal Tong which …'

'Which isn't a religion,' said Lammas, finishing Razzaq's sentence for him.

'No … it is not a religion,' agreed Razzaq. 'Not in the way that 'religion' is normally understood. Habal Tong allows us a better appreciation of our birth religions and at the same time fortifies us with the spirit of unity … of oneness. If Christians could just get over their terrible arrogance regarding Jesus, they might also find something truly profound in Habal Tong.'

'I hardly think Christians are arrogant,' said Melodie, speaking for the first time. 'We are humble … extremely humble.'

'So humble it makes you proud,' sneered Razzaq, getting a laugh from all except the church officers.

'How exactly do you think Christians arrogant?' queried Major Lammas.

'They are arrogant,' said Razzaq, 'because they are the only ones who believe their prophet to be the son of God. No other religion makes such an outlandish claim.'

'Hardly outlandish,' replied Lammas in his smooth baritone. 'But we're not here to argue about which religion is best … we're here to talk about what we have in common.'

'We have nothing in common,' snapped Razzaq. 'While you go on believing your prophet to be a deity you believe yourselves above the rest of us. I find that deeply insulting. We all do.'

Razzaq seemed to be getting angry and the buzz of the room went up a notch. Conan could hardly keep the grin off his face as some of the non-Christians started shouting while Lammas remained implacably calm in the face of their rising hostility.

'Please Razzaq,' said Lammas, 'do try to calm your companions. We are having an intelligent discussion … not a shouting match.'

'What is the point of discussion?' demanded Razzaq. 'Talk, talk, talk is meaningless. The only thing that matters is action.'

'Well, why do you come to the Great Debate, if you think talk is meaningless?' asked Melodie.

'To combat the evil of the Christian message,' shouted Razzaq. 'You are evil! Look at you all … dressed in black like Satan! Doing his work in the name of Jesus!'

'Now you're becoming offensive,' chided Lammas in his magnificent baritone. 'Please moderate or we'll have to ask you leave again.'

'Fuck you!' shouted Razzaq leaping up. 'Fuck you and all Christians!'

With that he swept out of the room followed by most of the other non-Christians, all laughing and shouting at the sad looking figures in black. Conan sat grinning at the back of the room, awaiting developments.

But after the excitement, the evening suddenly ended. The little Chinese man spoke earnestly with the Army of God officials for a few minutes but Conan couldn't quite hear what they were talking about. Then just as he decided to get up and leave also, Major Lammas excused himself from the small man's embrace and glided over to Conan before he could escape.

'How do you do?' he asked, in that bewitching voice, collaring Conan with his Clooney-esque looks.

'I do very well,' said Conan.

'Agent Tooley, isn't it?'

'Call me Tools.'

'Tools,' repeated Lammas. 'I'm Tom Lammas.'

'Captain Roberts' fiancé?'

'That honour is indeed mine … but you've been asking about Bruce and Michael?'

'I have … not that anyone can tell me much.'

'There's not a lot to tell, as far as I know,' said Lammas. 'They were occasional visitors here … but somewhat more polite than Razzaq.'

'Razzaq,' laughed Conan, '… one passionate fellow.'

'He certainly is,' agreed Lammas. 'But what about you, Tools? What's your passion?'

'My passion?' echoed Conan. 'Christ … god knows.'

Lammas' face darkened and Conan felt strangely uncouth for his casual blasphemy.

'Sorry,' he said, lamely. 'I'm not used to these sorts of places.'

'And yet … here you are,' said Lammas, brightening after the apology. 'We can't help you with Bruce and Michael … but maybe we can help with your soul?'

'Oh, I … I doubt that,' said Conan. 'But there is something you can help me with. I'm trying to understand the words: *Epistola Clementis*.'

Lammas' eyes blazed, for a moment, and Conan felt the old instinct – the one he used to get talking to junkies about stolen cigarettes.

But then Lammas smiled and shook his head, 'Ah Tools … just doing your job I suppose … '

'And … '

'And yes … Bruce and Michael were interested in the *Epistola Clementis*, but it had nothing to do with their disappearance?'

'How can you know that when you weren't there when it happened? So I presume.'

'You presume correctly,' said Major Lammas, giving Conan a hard stare. 'But the *Epistola Clementis* is just an obscure document from the earliest days of the church. It has no relevance today.'

'And yet Bruce and Michael were clearly very interested in it. Can you tell me what it was?'

'I'm sure you can find that in any library, Agent Tooley … or google it for the real misinformation. You must excuse me.'

Lammas turned and strode past Melodie and Lieutenant Rice into the kitchen. Melodie gave Conan a last angry look and followed Lammas. Rice followed Melodie, and Conan took a last glance about the room before leaving himself, still grinning at the performance of Razzaq.

• • •

The streets were still full at quarter past ten. Conan found himself enjoying the frenzied activity, the babble of language and exotic cooking smells and suddenly understood Ord City's popularity as a tourist destination. Walking along Whitlam Street, his mouth was watering at the smell of chilli, garlic and frying onions so he bought a box of Singapore noodles with prawns and chicken from a street vendor.

Everyone back in Sydney had warned him not to eat the street food, but he decided to brave it and was rewarded with the nicest stir fry he could ever remember eating. He dumped the box on top of a bin overflowing with similar garbage and continued towards his hotel, enjoying the sights and sounds and the tingle of lime and chilli on his lips and tongue.

So different, he was thinking. So, so different from everywhere else in Australia – all the energy and excitement of Asia with the order and rules of the first world. Some of them, at least.

And that's when Conan realised he was being followed.

At first it was just a sense of being watched – a prickling of the skin that made him feel like bolting. But he quelled the urge to run and feigned interest in another wok chef working like crazy, giving him the opportunity to stand facing back the way he'd come, and saw three Asian men come to a confused stop some fifteen metres away, all of them trying not to look at him.

They're not muggers, Conan knew. No point in mugging these days when cash no longer exists.

The three men all lit cigarettes and Conan took the opportunity to slip behind a truck stopped in traffic and ran, conscious that there weren't many western types on the street at that time of night so his height made him conspicuous.

Doubled over, Conan ran into a side street, then turned immediately into a smaller laneway – much darker than Whitlam Street and which seemed abandoned, if that was possible in Ord City. Heading in what he hoped was the direction of his hotel, he ran into even deeper darkness and was shocked when the lane ended with a high wall. It was too late to get back to the lane's entrance so he ducked behind a skip and stared back the way he'd come.

It was weirdly quiet after the chaos of Whitlam Street and Conan began to wonder who might be chasing him. They looked Chinese, but he'd only had a quick glance in the dim light.

'Didn't take me long to make enemies,' thought Conan. Then, on reflection, he wondered whether he'd simply been mistaken. Why, after all, should anyone be following him?

After another minute or two, Conan stepped out from behind the skip and walked cautiously back the way he'd come. And then he saw three red pinpricks of light – three glowing cigarettes at the entrance to the lane.

He stopped dead still and shrank against the wall to his right. All three cigarettes were thrown to the ground and stamped out in a brief shower of sparks. The darkness was almost complete.

In fact, Conan had a police issued weapon but he'd not bothered with it that evening. Now he had to deal with the consequences, hearing in advance the scathing criticism of Kenny Cook for not following protocol – presuming he'd be lucky enough ever to hear Kenny scathe again.

A motor bike went by the lane and the brief wash of light silhouetted three figures walking towards him, maybe thirty metres away. Not quite panicking, Conan considered the skip as a place to hide, but rejected it as too obvious. He groped along the wall and found a door which was partly open but didn't move when pushed. He sensed the door had swollen with damp and might be forced open, but that would make a noise and alert his pursuers.

He could hear cautious muttering and knew he had only seconds to decide.

A torch flicked on and Conan threw his weight against the door, which flew open with a grating squeal. He had a brief glimpse of stairs in the torchlight and jammed the door shut behind him. Then, in pitch blackness, he groped for the rail and ran up the stairs through cobwebs and what felt like damp hanging laundry.

The door behind him banged open and the torchlight, two flights below, gave him just enough light to increase his pace. His chasers didn't cry out but he could hear their steps and heavy breathing – always about a flight below him. After six flights the stairs ended at a T-junction and Conan went right while tearing his watch from his wrist. Then, just as his chasers reached the top of the stairs, he flung the watch back into the darkness of the left turn. The watch clattered along the floor and the torch light went left as Conan bolted to the right along a corridor with a hint of light through some upper windows. The corridor turned right then left and, his sense of direction completely gone, Conan was amazed to see two uniformed police sitting outside a door sealed with blue and white police tape.

He slowed as they glanced up at him, and Conan knew the immediate chase was over.

'Good evening,' he said, his heart hammering and sweat pouring off his brow.

'Good evening,' responded one of the coppers, neither of whom he recognised from earlier. Both looked Chinese.

'This is Bruce and Michael's place, right? I was here this morning with Loongy.'

'With who?' asked the taller of the two, a senior officer by his stripe.

'Loongy ... Edward Loong,' said Conan, still trying to get his breath back and glancing back the way he'd come. It seemed the pursuit had ended.

The two coppers looked at each other and shrugged.

'You guys know who I am?' asked Conan.

Again they shrugged, and Conan produced his badge. 'Agent Tooley from Sydney. I'm actually investigating these murders ... or supposed to be.'

Their eyes narrowed, and understanding seemed to dawn.

'So ... any chance of opening up for me?'

Yet again the two glanced at each other, then Stripe said, 'I suppose so ... but there's nothing to see.'

'Let me be the judge of that,' said Conan, his breath returning to normal and the sweat cooling under his clothes. 'What are your names?'

Stripe got up from his chair and produced a key ring. 'Senior Officer Greg Lee, and that's Officer Wally Wong.'

'Wally Wong,' repeated Conan, unable to prevent a grin. 'Sounds like you'd have your own postcode.'

Wally Wong stared impassively as Senior Officer Lee pulled away the police tape.

'There really is nothing to see,' he said, opening the door.

Conan followed him into the dead men's flat and, when the light was turned on, just stared.

The room had been emptied.

• • •

'Hey, Conan?'

'Lucia? What time is it?'

Conan hadn't found his watch – an old style watch he wore in addition to his OzBrace. He'd hunted unsuccessfully with a torch borrowed from Senior Officer Lee before he returned to his hotel. After two beers in the bar, he'd gone up to his room about midnight.

And minutes after his head hit the pillow, his phone rang.

Lurching from sleep, he'd answered the phone before he'd properly woken and was struggling to make sense of the conversation.

'I've traced your number.'

'My number?'

Conan still didn't have a clue what she was talking about. He lay with his eyes shut, forcing himself to be civil despite the delicious prospect of sleep.

And then he was wide awake.

'Oh right ... the cryp.'

He sat up and switched on the lamp – eyes burning – and found a notepad.

'Who is it?'

'It's a journalist,' said Lucia. 'Wang Li Kwai ... also known as Ronny Kwai.'

'Ronny Kwai,' repeated Conan, writing it down.

'He's a football journalist known as The Keeper.'

'A football journalist,' mused Conan. 'Why would Michael Wing Ho's last call ... just before he was murdered ... be to a football journalist?'

'Isn't that your job?' said Lucia. '... to find out, using your finely honed forensic brain?'

'Ordinarily yes,' said Conan, 'but there's something very odd going on up here.'

There was a silence as she waited for him to elaborate, and when he didn't she said, 'I hear Kenny's got the shits with you.'

'Kenny's always got the shits with me.'

'This is worse than usual. He's getting heat from somewhere. Someone doesn't want you sniffing around ... someone important.'

Conan felt a sudden wave of affection for Lucia. She was taking a terrible risk in telling him.

'Where are you calling from?'

'Public phone ... better not say where.'

There was another pregnant silence, then Conan said, 'When I get back ... maybe ...'

'Gotta go,' said Lucia, and the phone was dead.

Chapter 7

Bang for Your Buck

Asif packed the last of the Mangalite into the plug and attached the radio-armed detonator, making sure the display showed condition green – safety level. Not that these devices were ever entirely safe.

With infinite care, he lowered the plug onto the others in the pipe, then stood up straight to stretch his back.

'Station four, secure,' he said into his head-mounted mike, and awaited orders.

'All stations secure,' confirmed the leader. 'All retire.'

Asif turned his back on his handiwork and walked into the darkness, lit only by a line of blinking orange lights in the distance. He was aware of the roof suddenly vanishing and felt the lightest of breezes on his skin, which was beaded with the moisture of concentration.

Other lights converged, as his colleagues headed for the blinking lights and Asif recognised the bouncing gait of Ah Cheng despite the fact that all he could see of his friend was the blue-white light from his helmet.

'Hurry up, Asif,' came the leader's voice through his headphones.

'He loves his work so much he wants to feel it,' laughed Ah Cheng.

Asif arrived last at the steel barrier where the lights were blinking and retired behind the baffles with the others. The leader, Kendrick, the only full Australian citizen in the Bang Gang, opened his hand Pod and initiated the fire sequence.

Green turned to yellow.

'Heads down,' called Kendrick.

Yellow turned to orange.

Ah Cheng nudged Asif, 'Why don't you stand closer? I swear you love your work so much, you'd like to be in an explosion yourself.'

'Become a suicide bomber,' suggested Karadzian. 'There's always work for them.'

'Quiet,' snapped Kendrick, as orange turned red and began to flash.

They felt it first beneath their feet – a quivering, then a strong shudder. Then the roar erupted and lit up the mountainside as four explosions tore into its guts. The mountain seemed to crash like a wave, and yet was still standing when the dust settled. Most of it.

Ah Cheng was punching the air and whooping – almost as happy as if his beloved Feng had just scored the winner for the Pilgrims. Asif smiled, liking the Chinese very much and wishing he could express joy as freely.

Joy, of course, was a rare and precious thing in Asif's experience – almost unknown until he met Tanya. Just thinking of her brought a smile to his face, which turned wistful as he lingered behind the baffle when the others went to investigate the results of the blast. Karadzian had left his ordnance esky open and, in a few seconds, Asif had taken a strip of Manga and slipped it inside the false panel in his thermos. They were each accountable for their Mangalite issue, but in all likelihood it would never be missed. Asif took great care to pilfer evenly from his colleagues so that no one person might come under scrutiny. He now had seven strips of Manga – easily enough for the job, but there was no harm in getting more, and it was simple enough to steal.

'Asif,' called Cheng, '… come and see!'

Industrial powered lights clunked on to bathe the site in a white glare. Reddish/brown haematite with shiny veins of magnetite lay in an acre of rubble given up by the mountain. The amount of shiny magnetite among the darker rubble showed this was a particularly pure seam.

In the semi-darkness he kicked a heavy lump and stooped to pick it up. In the light of his head lamp the rock was dark and shiny, and very heavy – magnetite so pure it looked like steel. In his mind's eye, Asif was already reshaping it – paring and polishing to waken the life that lingered within.

Tanya, of course, had taught him. She was a painter and sculptor, one of the many Australians who lived in Ord City by choice. She loved the anarchy, she said, and had inspired Asif's creative side. A side of himself he'd never known existed – not that there'd been any time for it scraping a living in flood-prone Bangladesh.

'What are you going to make of it?' asked Cheng.

'It's a child,' said Asif. 'A small child with its arm protecting its eyes.'

'Sounds like a lot of work,' laughed Cheng. 'Will you have time to finish it?'

• • •

Back in the mess after the shift, Asif sipped an orange juice as the others drank beer.

Habal Tong, of course, had no proscriptions against alcohol, but Asif's birth religion was Islam and he remained devout to all of its rules and precepts. He had only once drunk wine, sharing a glass with Tanya on their first anniversary, and had been racked with guilt for weeks afterward.

Nevertheless, he couldn't help but be a little jealous of the camaraderie of his workmates which he could tell was partly fuelled by alcohol. Ah Cheng, in particular, was an exuberant drinker and gambler and, as ever, Asif found himself speculating as to why he should be a member of his Tong with Razzaq. Cheng didn't fit at all the usual profile, but Razzaq said that was the reason he tolerated the man. 'Cheng is beyond suspicion,' he had said. 'That makes him valuable. We will have an important job one day for Cheng.'

'What are you looking so grumpy about?' demanded Cheng, wrenching Asif from his reverie.

'Nothing,' said Asif, feeling strangely guilty.

'He wants a beer,' said Karadzian. 'Hey, when you get your citizenship, Asif … you should go to Sydney and do a pub crawl.'

'Pub crawl,' snorted Kendrick. 'Knowing Asif, he's part of some deep terror cell … biding his time. He'll only go to Sydney to blow up the bridge.'

The others laughed, led by Ah Cheng, and Asif smirked. Kendrick had made the same joke many times so it didn't bother him, but the mention of Sydney reminded him of Tanya, and he felt a wave of sadness wash over him.

Then Asif felt his phone buzz and pulled it out, knowing it would be a message from her. Uncanny how she would contact him when he most needed her. He peered at the screen of his phone, which simply said: I love you.

Tears sprang from his eyes and the love was so strong it caught his breath, but he glanced up guiltily to see Cheng staring at him. Cheng's stare instantly turned to a grin and Asif put his phone away, more confused than ever.

Chapter 8

Pushing Shit Uphill

Conan could have called Ronny Kwai – The Keeper, as he was known – but decided that simply turning up at his office might yield more interesting results.

Unfortunately, however, Ronny didn't seem to have an office. He was a freelance football journalist who wrote obsessively about the A-League, and about the Ord City Pilgrims in particular. And that's where Conan tracked him down – at training at Rinehart Stadium.

Conan walked into the 60,000 seat arena – weirdly empty despite the frenzy of activity on the pitch – and saw a knot of people sitting in the front of the stand. Ronny was holding court with a bunch of other journalists and officials as the team were put through their paces. Only one of the players had FENG 9 on his back, causing Conan to wince at the memory of a whole crowd of such shirts which had landed him in his present predicament.

Conan knew Ronny Kwai from the pictures on his website and sat within earshot for a while as he talked, sometimes in Cantonese, sometimes in English, about the team and their prospects. Conan had little interest in the conversation – preferring cricket on the rare occasion he took an interest in sport. And even cricket had gone to the pack after the Americans had suddenly become so passionate about Twenty 20. Test cricket was dead.

It was a stinking hot day and, despite his indifference to the game, Conan was impressed with the players' intensity as he sat listening absently to the journos and considering his position. He hadn't bothered telling anyone about being chased, not least as he no longer trusted even his fellow police after finding the flat emptied. Also, he had finally read the email from Kenny Cook which told him, as he'd expected, to wrap up the investigation and get back to Sydney.

And yet all Conan's instincts told him he was on the verge of something important. It was also clear that someone, somewhere, didn't want him looking into the murders, which naturally made him determined that he should.

Still, no point pushing shit uphill if he didn't have a lead. Conan had decided that if nothing came out of the Ronny Kwai interview he'd head back to Sydney and have a long overdue talk with Lucia.

Then training was over and the journos went onto the pitch to talk to a small selection of players who were carefully stage-managed through a boring process of scripted questions and answers, although Ronny seemed to have special status and chatted happily with FENG 9 for a few minutes before Feng went down the tunnel.

Ronny started to follow but Conan grabbed his shoulder. He was quite large, up close, and dressed entirely in black silk.

'G'day,' said Conan. 'Ronny Kwai?'

'Yes.'

'Agent Conan Tooley … AFP. I'm investigating the Fong, Wing Ho murders.'

'Who?'

'Bruce Fong and Michael Wing Ho … about a week ago.'

'I don't know them.'

Once again, Conan felt his antennae tingling as he studied the expressionless face, half hidden by large sunglasses.

'Okay … must've been a wrong number,' he said.

'What are you talking about?'

'The last number called by Michael Wing Ho was your number.'

'Show me the number on his phone account,' said Ronny. It was a comment that would only be made by someone operating an illegal cryp number, and immediately Conan knew Ronny was hiding something.

'I suppose you do know,' said Conan, 'that it is possible to trace a cryp account … just a pain in the arse. But we've already linked Wing Ho's account to yours so the hard work's been done.'

'I don't know anyone called Michael Wing Ho,' insisted Ronny, '…

although many people use an alias in this town. Perhaps I knew this caller by a different name?'

Conan sighed. That also was a statement typically made by cryp users, and journalists in particular were notorious for having cryps to protect their sources.

Ronny smiled, as though perceiving he had the advantage, and said, 'Let's just say, for the point of hypothetical conversation, that I really do have a cryp number – which I don't, because I endorse the state's right to scrutinise metadata for the purpose of security – but if I did, I wouldn't link to an individual by name. I would use a code number.'

'The metadata from your phone and Wing Ho's phone are reciprocal and identical,' said Conan. 'You spoke with him for two hundred and forty-two seconds at 6.39pm on the 9th of January … approximately half an hour before he was killed.'

Ronny shrugged.

'What can I tell you, Agent Tooley? I'm a journalist. I get calls all the time … often from people with urgent messages about breaking news. I suppose it's possible that I did speak with a person at that time … but I don't know any Michael Wing Ho and I don't know anything about a murder.'

At that moment the sound of a roaring crowd came from Ronny's pocket, and he grinned as he pulled out his phone.

'Do you know the Feng Song?' asked Ronny, peering at the screen. 'Ah … excuse me.'

He walked onto the pitch to answer his phone. 'Good morning, Major!'

Conan couldn't hear anything further but strained his ears, wondering how many majors there were in Ord City.

Ronny seemed to stiffen and get slightly more animated, half glancing back in Conan's direction. Then he walked further onto the pitch which was abandoned by all players and coaching staff, and spoke for another couple of minutes as Conan tried not to take too obvious an interest in him. The stadium was very impressive – built to the exact specifications of the Emirates Stadium in London, according to a plaque above the players' tunnel – although mainly decked out in yellow as opposed to the Emirates' red.

'Sorry about that,' said Ronny, his conversation over and suddenly much more friendly.

'Where were we?' asked Conan.

'I was explaining that I couldn't help your investigation,' said Ronny, 'but tell me Agent Tooley ... '

'Tools.'

'Tools,' repeated Ronny with a grin. 'Are you a football fan?'

'Not really.'

'You should be. Why don't you come to the game tomorrow night ... as my guest?'

Conan stared at the grinning Chinese, wondering what had changed in the last few minutes, his antennae sparking like Tesla tubes.

'That's very kind of you,' said Conan. 'I'd be happy to come.'

'Good. I'll be hosting drinks and dinner first, so come to Gate C at 5.30 and ask for Ronny Kwai's private suite. I'll have someone look after you.'

• • •

'Absolutely not.'

Conan had finally bitten the bullet and called Kenny Cook.

'Kenny ... there is something very weird going on up here. I seriously think it needs looking into. We may regret it if we don't.'

'Regret what?'

'I can't say ... but the murders are the tip of the iceberg. I'm certain of it.'

'You're certain ... and yet you've made exactly zero progress on the Fong, Wing Ho case. How can you be certain of anything?'

'I'm certain there are some pretty weird questions to be answered,' said Conan. 'Like, why was the flat emptied without me checking it out properly? Why is an AFP colleague being so obstructive? Who's chasing me? What the fuck is the *Epistola Clementis* and why were Fong and Wing Ho so interested in it? And what is the Army of God and Ronny Kwai hiding?'

'The only question you need to answer,' said Kenny, '... is this one: will you be at your desk in Sydney on Monday morning ... or will I be looking for a new agent?'

It was Friday afternoon and Conan felt a wave of bureaucratic inertia swamping his resolve.

'See you Monday, Kenny.'

• • •

'There's not much about it on the net. I had to go dark.'

'Really?'

Lucia was at her sister's place and had asked him to call her back from a public phone – which he'd located in a bar near his hotel. The call could still be traced and transcribed but it was far less likely than if they spoke on their own phones.

'Did you know there's actually a Vatican Dark Web?'

'Dark Web for everything,' said Conan. 'Pretty spooky was it?'

'Let's just say there are some weird people who want to do seriously perverted shit to each other. That's all you get on Vatican Dark … pervy weirdos … but they knew about *Epistola Clementis* … or said they did.'

'Well?'

'Well, as far as I can tell, the *Epistola Clementis* means the Letter of Clement … one of the early popes.'

'Right.'

'It's all about the pope's authority … where he gets his power from.'

'Fair enough.'

'Conan … you're not taking it seriously!'

'Yes, I am,' he said. 'I'm just waiting for you to get to the important bit.'

'Back in the first century,' she said, her voice singing with sarcasm, 'the pope's authority was pretty important. It still is in some places.'

'But why is it important in Ord City in 2030?'

'I don't know … that's your job. But let me finish will you?'

'Sorry.'

Conan grinned, feeling a surge of affection for Lucia and wishing he was with her.

'Okay,' she continued. 'There was a bit of a scandal about the *Epistola Clementis* many years after Clement's papacy. As the church was becoming the official church of Rome … in place of Jupiter and Thor and all that lot … some bright spark lawyer questioned the source of the pope's authority.'

'Isn't it supposed to come from JC?'

'Exactly. JC gave to Peter – the first pope – the powers of binding and loosing, symbolised by the crossed keys of the Vatican.'

'Crossed keys?'

Conan was remembering the frozen symbol on Wing Ho's lap top – a pair of crossed keys.

'Yes. Jesus apparently said to Peter: whatever you bind on earth will be bound in heaven. Whatever you loose on earth will be loose in heaven. This is the source of the pope's authority.'

'Okay … so what was the scandal?'

'This is the interesting bit,' said Lucia. 'At the critical time – just as Christianity was becoming the pre-eminent religion and blended with the Roman emperor's secular power – there was a big debate about the pope's authority. Some people were saying: we accept that JC passed the powers of binding and loosing to Peter, but JC was the son of God and able to do shit like that. How do we know the same powers were truly passed on to other popes?'

'Aaahh … good question,' said Conan.

'A really important question,' said Lucia, 'because, at the time, the secular authority was stronger than the spiritual authority. If everyone accepted the pope's power came from God himself it was really going to change things.'

'So how'd it turn out?'

'At the peak of the debate,' said Lucia, 'someone turned up what was supposed to be an old letter from Clement … saying among other things: oh, by the way, Peter passed onto me and all future popes his powers of binding and loosing.'

'Very convenient,' laughed Conan.

'It was … not least as Clement wasn't the second pope after Peter. He was third, fourth or fifth … the early records aren't that clear.'

'Wow.'

'Wow indeed. One of the shoddiest stitch-ups of all time. But it worked. Everyone agreed that the letter made the pope the boss and Christianity went on to become the dominant ideology and power source for well over a thousand years. It's still pretty powerful.'

'Wow,' said Conan again, feeling a creepy sort of fear despite his devout atheism. 'I can understand why Lammas doesn't want to talk about it.'

'Who's Lammas?'

'Oh ... one of the blokes up here who interests me. What you're saying is ... without the sudden appearance of this dodgy letter ... Christianity might have lost its momentum and even disappeared around three or four hundred AD.'

'Exactly right,' said Lucia. 'And considering the enormous impact of that one dodgy letter, it's incredible how little information there is on the web ... the legitimate web that is.'

Conan was deeply impressed.

'How did you get all this?'

'I had to play a game with a charming individual called Bishop Satanus,' said Lucia. 'You really don't want to know any more. Let's just say I didn't respect myself in the morning.'

'I owe you big time Lucia. And ... when I get back ... '

There was a heavy silence on the end of the phone.

'Gotta go,' said Lucia, and the phone went dead.

Conan put the phone down and glanced around the bar, feeling weirdly paranoid. There must be some deeply innate superstition in all humans he reflected. Conan had grown up in a Catholic household but had never quite believed in God. He'd tried to believe it, as a kid. Really tried. But the whole thing was so patently absurd and it was pretty clear to Conan, even as a boy, that no one else truly believed. No one lived their life − absolutely − as though they genuinely believed all the ancient hogwash they drivelled on about.

Around the age of fourteen, Conan suddenly understood that he was an atheist − to his mother's dismay − and was constantly amused by the antics of believers. The best part of two thousand years, he laughed to himself. All that history: the crusades, the reformation, the inquisition − the long war with money and science for control of hearts and minds. And none of it might have happened but for some forgotten scribe bodgying up a fake letter to win an argument, back before Adam bowled offies for Eden.

He walked back to his own hotel and sat in the bar, still feeling an odd tingle of paranoid fear. He ordered a beer and glanced about the room, speculating about the lives and motives of those around him. Most were easy to read, wearing their lives on their sleeves, but two men defied his analysis – strangely inscrutable with faces like cardboard.

He pulled out his triPod and got onto the Qantas site, checking out flights home on Sunday. There were three in the afternoon so Conan booked the 12.30, which would have him back in Sydney about eight pm.

If he was on it.

Chapter 9

Head First all the Way

It was Robbie's turn to drive and he was enjoying the opportunity to concentrate on the road instead of the stupid conversation that broke out in the back seat from time to time.

As Chris had guessed, the fat chick – Lemon – was HT and rarely shut up about its bullshit, despite the fact they'd threatened to turf her and Tim out of the car on several occasions. The only other subject that interested her was drop shots.

'I'm fucking brilliant at drop shots,' she said. 'Even that one off the edge of the Grand Canyon that came out last year … my pulse only went from 80 to 84 and that was head first all the way.'

No one responded, which suited Lemon perfectly.

'It's HT of course that makes me so good. When your mind is totally at peace then not even a dive off a clifftop can scare you. That's what makes Habal Tong so good.'

'I'd love to find you a cliff,' said Chris, with a helpless wave at the flat plain ahead, 'but … '

'I wish you would,' she said. 'When you reach a high enough level of HT you can defy gravity. Truly!' she insisted as Chris and Robbie burst into laughter.

'That's why we're going to Ord City,' said Lemon in that really annoying voice that seemed to perfectly blend ignorance with arrogance, 'to climb the HT levels and go to *Illumination* next Friday night. It's gonna be huge.'

'Probably get bombed,' said Chris and Robbie laughed at the look of outrage on Lemon's face in the rear view mirror.

'It will not!'

'Perfect target for Dedd Reffo,' said Chris. 'Thousands of hippies and fuckwits all clustered in one place … I'd light the fuse myself.'

'Existence is nullity and nullity existence,' insisted Lemon, as though that actually meant something. 'I don't care if we do get blown up … I've embraced Habal Tong so my life is already perfect. Dedd Reffo can't hurt me … can it Tim?'

'Erm … no,' he agreed, and Robbie chuckled, wondering whether Tim was totally under the thumb or displaying a subtle form of sarcasm. Tim wasn't a bad bloke.

'Our lives have already reached the pinnacle of human perfection,' boasted Lemon. 'So youse can get fucked.'

Without a word, Robbie pulled over to the side of the road. There was no dramatic screech of tires, no sudden cloud of dust, he simply slowed down and rolled to a halt in the flat red infinity of the Tanami Desert, then switched the engine off.

The car was silent, baking in the blast of heat with no air rushing through the windows.

'Out,' said Robbie.

'What do you mean?' demanded Lemon.

'Get the fuck out of the car,' said Chris, delighted with Robbie's action.

'No way,' said Lemon. 'That'd be murder.'

'What do you care?' said Robbie. 'Haven't you already reached the human pinnacle? Nothing can hurt you.'

'Stop being a smart arse,' sneered Lemon. 'You can't leave us here.'

'Get the fuck out of the car,' said Chris, raising his voice. 'Now!'

Lemon just stared and folded her arms – defiant and immovable.

Robbie turned to Tim, who was staring at the floor in misery.

'Tim … I'm putting you in charge of the back seat. If Lemon opens her stupid, fat mouth once more about Habal fucking Tong, she's out. You can stay, if you want, but she's out on her ear if I hear one more fucking word.'

'Way to go, Robbie,' laughed Chris.

'Have you got that?' demanded Robbie, to Tim, who nodded numbly as Lemon glared at him.

Robbie, turned the key again and was rewarded only with a dying cough from the engine.

He tried again and got just a few clicks. Then nothing.

'Fuck me dead,' said Chris. 'Not again.'

They'd had a bit of trouble with the car in South Australia but had got it fixed in Coober Pedy. Or so they thought.

'Well, well,' said Lemon. 'Looks like we'll all be stranded in the middle of nowhere. How nice.'

'Lemon … ' began Tim.

'What?' she snapped at him.

'Can we just stay calm?' he pleaded as she stared at him with shrivelling contempt.

'But we're all about to die,' she explained, patiently sarcastic, 'which means I can say whatever the fuck I like.'

At that moment the engine roared into life, and Robbie turned back to her.

'You were saying?'

• • •

Two hours later they pulled up at a roadhouse. Robbie drove the car straight into the repair bay and spoke to the bloke in charge while the others stretched their legs.

Then Robbie and Chris headed for the bar/restaurant, with Tim and Lemon straggling in their wake.

'Buy us some food,' said Lemon.

'I beg your pardon?' laughed Chris.

'We're out of money,' she said. 'But we get paid in a couple of days … we can pay you back then.'

'I don't want to spend another two days with you,' said Chris. 'We're only a day or so from Ord City, so after tomorrow I never want to see you again.'

'But … love is money and money is love,' quoted Lemon triumphantly, as though revealing some logical flaw in his argument. 'So just buy us some food anyway. And a drink.'

'No fucking way,' said Chris, with a glare at Robbie in case he was feeling generous.

Robbie and Chris went to the bar and ordered beers and steak sandwiches, while Tim and Lemon poured water from a jug and sat staring at them. Robbie felt a little guilty, at least as far as Tim was concerned, but Lemon was so fucking irritating – and it wasn't as though she'd starve, from the look of her.

'I say we leave 'em here,' said Chris.

'What?' demanded Lemon.

'We've done 'em enough of a favour,' said Chris. 'Let some other poor bastard take 'em the rest of the way.'

'But we've got no money,' wailed Lemon. 'We can't support ourselves here.'

'You can't support yourselves with us either,' said Chris. 'So it simply comes down to whether we'd prefer you in the car or out of it.'

He raised his hand.

'I say out.'

The others looked to Robbie, all being aware it was his car and that he therefore had the casting vote.

'I'll give youse a head job,' said Lemon.

'What?' cried Tim, as Chris snorted beer through his nose.

'I'll give youse both a head job if you take us all the way to Ord City … and buy us some food and drink.'

'I don't want a head job,' said Robbie, but Chris was laughing.

'A Habal Tong head job,' he laughed, 'from a chick who's reached the human pinnacle. I could really get into that.'

'Lemon,' objected Tim, but she glared him into silence.

The steak sandwiches arrived at the table and Chris launched into his with gusto, with Lemon and Tim watching every bite like dogs waiting for scraps. Robbie picked up his own feeling momentarily awkward, but the toast was hot and crisp and the steak so perfectly tender that he managed to forget about their passengers, until the haggling.

'Okay,' said Chris, 'we'll take you to Ord City for a head job … but that's all.'

'I don't want a head job,' repeated Robbie.

'Food also,' said Lemon.

'What are her headies like?' asked Chris, of Tim, who continued to stare at the table.

'How would he know?' laughed Lemon. 'My HJs are the best.'

'Alright,' laughed Chris, 'I'll get you a packet of Twisties.'

'I want a steak sandwich,' said Lemon. 'And a bourbs … '

'A ride and a packet of Twisties,' insisted Chris. 'Take it or leave it.'

'Two packs.'

The deal was struck, with the further details that Chris was not allowed to touch her and it had to happen in the dark so he couldn't watch her.

'I do have my fucking dignity,' insisted Lemon, one paw stuffed in a Twisties bag.

Robbie was more than a little embarrassed, mostly on Tim's behalf, and when he arrived back at the table with three beers, Chris was too amused by the prospect of his HTHJ to notice or comment. Tim gratefully sipped his beer and muttered a voiceless thank you as Chris and Lemon started giggling, negotiating further small details of their transaction and clearly on much friendlier terms than they'd been just minutes before.

Chapter 10

Thirteen is Lucky

At 5.35 on Saturday afternoon, Conan walked up to Gate C of Rinehart Stadium. There were only a handful of people around, this far from kick-off, but in an hour or so the place would be a sea of yellow – with hundreds of FENG 9 shirts among the many thousands of fans.

Conan laughed at himself and shook his head. Life would have been so different if he'd just closed the library that day. Of course he'd replayed the incident asynchronously and had been able to follow the bloke a lot better when he'd not taken his eyes off him. But even then there was margin for error when the bloke had turned into a tunnel and joined with hundreds of other fans. The camera coverage hadn't been perfect as he swung from a stairwell into the tunnel and the bloke's appearance was so middle-Asian neutral. He did have a fairly distinctive triangular mole pattern on the part of his face that was visible, but after the tunnel there'd been no shot he could use for a close up. FENG 9 was long gone, with his download of the NBN Node specs.

Conan managed to dismiss that old problem to focus on the present. He'd had another fruitless day. His mother had called again to hassle him for money he didn't have, and he'd tried to confront Loongy about the cleared out flat, but Loongy had just shrugged and said the case was declared closed. When Conan pressed the matter, Loongy had simply said, 'Why do you care, Tools? Fuck off back to Sydney and go for a ferry ride. Fuck off back to Sydney and buy real estate!'

'Why the fuck was I sent up here if no one wants me to look into the case?' he wondered, for the hundredth time. 'And why did Ronny Kwai invite me to the football?'

At Gate C he was just behind a deeply sun-tanned couple, both in khaki shorts and Hawaiian shirts. They also asked to see Ronny Kwai and were asked for their names.

'Jen Khataten and Richie Farr,' said the young woman, who looked like she'd just stepped out of the pages of Vogue, despite her bogan chic attire.

'Conan Tooley also,' added Conan, to the beautifully lacquered Chinese girl with a clipboard, checking off names.

'Come this way,' she bowed to the three of them and they were ushered into a lift.

'Jen and Richie?' asked Conan, and they smiled at him.

'Conan Tooley, but call me Tools.'

The lift moved so smoothly they were barely aware of it. Conan found himself staring at the woman and being a little jealous of the man. Conan would never get within coo-ee of such a stunner and, despite being inside a lift, left on his sunglasses to preclude an accusation of perving.

'I hope you're not perving, Tools,' said Jen. Conan knew he'd blushed, but thankfully the lift had reached its destination, so further embarrassment was suspended.

They were received by yet another beautiful Chinese-looking girl in a similar outfit to her colleague downstairs and taken down a short corridor to a set of double doors which were open wide. Above the door was a golden plaque inscribed with "Private Suite A2 – Mr Ronald Kwai".

Ronny Kwai himself could be heard laughing within and Conan felt his mood lifting. He had decided not to worry too much about the case, seeing as no one else was worried about it. He was just going to enjoy himself, and maybe flirt a little with Jen Khataten if he could get drunk enough to lose his inhibitions.

Conan was just behind the other two as they entered the large room and felt a different kind of jealousy as he made out the magnificence of the place. The room (or suite of rooms) was like a large city apartment, with a seated balcony overlooking the stadium, right on the halfway line. It was on the top level and like something Caesar might have owned if still swanning about in the twenty-first century.

'How does a journalist afford this?' wondered Conan as he stared about at the hors d'oeuvres, the sushi and cold seafood in trays of ice, the well-stocked bar and the army of white-jacketed wait-staff. In the centre of the room was a large, round dining table set for thirteen with white table cloths and gleaming silver. Even the light was expensive. There was some quality of the light that seemed to sparkle and glow with money and Conan knew he would never again rub so closely against the lives of the rich. Another reason to get stuck in and make a total cunt of himself.

Ronny, wearing a Peril shirt with KWAI 13 on the back, shook his hand and smiled but didn't say much, his eyes raking the room for more important people to talk to. Conan happily allowed himself to be passed over and attacked the bar.

He downed a double shot of single malt to get the ball rolling, then headed for the balcony with a cold Coopers Red. Jen and Richie were admiring the view and also drinking Coopers so, suitably reinforced, Conan joined them.

'Do you come here often?' he asked, and grinned at his own clumsy question.

'We don't go anywhere often,' said Jen. 'We spend so much time in the middle of nowhere it's a relief to meet other humans.'

'Not least as she spends most of her time trying to talk to aliens,' added Richie.

'Aliens?'

'Have you heard of the Giant Array?' she asked.

'No. Oh ... yes. The telescopes down south?'

'Correct.'

'Right ... you guys are astronomers?'

Yet a third kind of jealousy seeped into Conan's soul as he regarded the two beautiful people who, not only looked somehow superhuman with their glowing good health and spectacular looks, they were also engaged in fabulous careers! It was just ridiculously unfair that some people got the looks *and* the brains. And the money no doubt.

'I am,' said Jen. 'Richie's the local director of the NBN. We're only twenty ks apart which out here makes us close neighbours.'

Conan gave Richie another look and this time recognised him from certain files he'd been researching around the time of his fuck up back in Sydney. He'd been wearing a suit and tie in the official photographs.

'But the Giant Array,' mused Conan, trying to rise above his jealousy, '… didn't I read that you guys have made some big discovery?'

Before she could answer Conan swore with surprise at the vast holographic display that flashed into life above the pitch – a slow motion replay of the last game's highlights.

'You've never been to a football match before?' asked Richie.

'I've never seen the holos so huge and live,' admitted Conan. 'I don't often go to sporting events … well, never really. Obviously I've seen holos a million times, but not like that.'

'What do you for a living,' asked Jen, and Conan hesitated. In social situations, he usually gave the old vague public servant answer, but Ronny Kwai knew he was an AFP investigator so, in case it came up later, he admitted the truth.

'AFP?' queried Richie. 'I've always wondered exactly how the police jurisdiction works up here.'

'Well … it's a bit confused,' admitted Conan. 'This is Western Australia, which is normally policed by both state and feds, depending on the nature of the offence, but because Ord City has special status under the Immigration Act … and the Ord River Zonal Citizenship Act of 2023 … us feds have additional powers. Just about everyone here is a migrant so, the way it works … most crime is covered by federal law, with a few exceptions like traffic and the like. Oh fuck!'

Conan had briefly turned and saw Ronny Kwai greeting Major Lammas, with whom was Captain Melodie Roberts, staring coldly at Conan.

'Friends of yours?' asked Richie.

'They're no friends of mine,' muttered Jen.

Conan turned back to the stadium to collect his thoughts. The gates opened at six o'clock and very shortly the yellow tide would start to rise. Already from outside he could hear the buzz and announcements from external tannoys advising that the evening's game against Sydney FC was a sell-out.

'It's always a sell-out,' boomed Ronny, arriving in their midst, with yet another Chinese girl.

'This is Dr Ming,' said Ronny, introducing her. 'She's a scientist like you lot … well, except for you, Agent Tooley.'

'Call me Tools,' said Conan. 'But what makes you think I'm not a scientist?'

'Surely criminal investigation is an art more than a science,' said Ronny. 'But please excuse me.'

He hurried back inside, haranguing his wait staff in loud Cantonese and pointing at the table.

'Hello! How are we all?' asked Ming, all breathless, sparky enthusiasm like a C-list celebrity.

'Have you been on TV?' asked Conan.

'TV?' echoed Ming, with a dazzling smile. 'I hope not.'

She looked oddly familiar but Conan dismissed the notion and shrugged.

'You must have one of those faces,' he said.

'Yes, I suppose all we Chinese girls look the same to you,' said Ming, but she laughed at his embarrassment and the conversation moved on safely.

'What sort of doctor?' asked Richie.

'Oh … medical,' said Ming. 'Paediatrics.'

'You must be busy,' said Jen.

'You'd think so,' said Ming, 'But you're Jen Khataten … from the Giant Array?'

'I am,' smiled Jen, as Ming started gushing her excitement about Jen's work.

'Anyone after a drink?' asked Conan, but his was the only empty glass so he went in search of a top up.

Inside, Ronny Kwai was speaking with Major Lammas and Captain Roberts, plus another large woman in the Army of God uniform, and yet another woman whom Conan recognised as Joan Chard, Chief Administrator of the Temporary Citizenship Zone.

As he approached, Melodie peeled away to examine the bar, and so Conan found himself shoulder to shoulder with her.

'Long time no see, Captain Roberts.'

Her head snapped around and she gave him a look that would have frozen the nuts off Errol Flynn.

'Hello, Agent Tooley.'

She accepted the mineral water that had been poured for her.

'And goodbye,' she added, leaving him in her wake.

'Lovely to chat,' he called after her, and once again found himself face to face with a grinning Ronny Kwai, this time with Joan Chard at his elbow.

'Have you met our esteemed Chief Administrator?' asked Ronny. 'Colonel Chard ... allow me to introduce Agent Tooley of the AFP.'

'Call me Tools,' said Conan, shaking her hand.

'You're the fellow sent up from Sydney,' she said. 'Any luck with that?'

Conan stared at her, sensing more unfriendly fire, and said, 'No. In fact I've been told to wrap it up and come home.'

'Bit of a waste of time,' she shrugged. 'Still ... plenty of ice addicts back in Sydney.'

'That's a state matter,' sniffed Conan. 'But they're all into Crimson now.'

Crimson was the latest designer drug to terrify the middle class. Users would believe themselves absolutely indestructible and jump off buildings or cliffs in a bid for immortality. As often as not they wore a helmet-mounted camera to film their defiance of gravity, and the films – called drop shots – were played in holomax theatres to hordes of teenagers wearing bio-suits that displayed their pulses on the chest. Everyone in the theatre would be linked and the person with the lowest change in pulse at the end of each shot would win money transmitted directly to their OzBrace accounts. So much money was involved there were even professional drop shot gamers, but anyone caught taking Crimson to artificially lower their pulse was more scorned than Lance Armstrong (who'd been elected president for one term in 2024).

'Why is it called Crimson?' asked Chard.

'Dunno ... maybe the big crimson mark they make when they hit bottom?'

Ronny laughed, but Colonel Chard looked as though she had just encountered a revolting odour.

'Well ... I hope you make the most of your visit,' she said and walked outside with Ronny to admire the view.

'I sure am popular,' laughed Conan, and once again found himself looking forward to seeing Lucia. Why had he taken so long to realise how perfect she was?

Needing to reconnect with friendly folk, Conan grabbed another Coopers and headed back outside to where Richie and Jen were talking with an animated Dr Ming.

'It's just so exciting,' she enthused. 'When can we see the pictures?'

'They're still being back-filled from the data and analysed,' said Jen, 'but it's pretty special. I could show you some rushes but it's mostly guesswork until we get our turn on the Quantum.'

She suddenly grinned and whispered in Richie's ear, but he shook his head.

'Richie has access,' said Jen, 'but won't let me jump the queue. Not even if I … '

She whispered again in Richie's ear and he laughed.

'You're making it awfully hard,' he said.

'That's exactly what I was trying to do.'

They all laughed, and at that moment a roar came from outside the stadium and yellow shirts appeared among the concourses below.

'Six o'clock,' shouted Ronny, clapping his hands, and wait staff scurried to make the dining table ready. 'We shall be seated in five minutes,' he announced to the guests, then shouted again in Cantonese at the wait staff.

For the first time the internal tannoys started welcoming the crowd and giving details of the evening's entertainment. People (mainly in yellow shirts) were pouring into the lower concourse and vast holographic advertisements hovered about the stadium. Conan could still see the sun lowering to the west-north-west, but it was already dim on the pitch far below and the huge banks of floodlights were warming up.

Then someone banged a gong inside and Ronny called the guests to the table.

'There are place cards where I have seated you,' he called out. Conan, to his delight, discovered his card next to Captain Melodie Roberts, with Dr Ming to his right.

'Result,' laughed Conan and was not at all perturbed by the white-faced look of fury on Captain Roberts' face as she sat, thereafter keeping most of her back to him.

Ming at least was friendly and, as the waiters fussed about the table pouring white wine, beer, mineral water and jasmine tea, she explained to him about Jen Khataten's work.

'It's really exciting … they've managed to get pictures of the actual creation of the universe … the Big Bang itself.'

Conan was aware of a muffled exclamation of annoyance to his left, but Ming continued, 'The Giant Array telescopes can see all the way back to the very beginning of time … in this continuum.'

'How can you see time?' asked Conan.

'You can't,' said Dr Ming, 'but you can see what was happening when it started.'

Waiters surged again distributing san choy bow and Conan was unsurprised to find it excellent − perhaps a little spicier than usual, but he liked it that way.

'Welcome everyone,' said Ronny Kwai raising his glass. 'I hope you enjoy the food and, of course, the football. Go Pilgrims!'

Everyone raised their glasses in acknowledgment and Ronny said, 'You'll note there are thirteen of us. I always have twelve guests to my soirees because thirteen is lucky. Some say one and three adds up to four … which means death … but I say that's taking superstition too far. At some point you have to be scientific!'

He laughed loudly at his little joke but only Conan joined him. In particular, the Army of God people were frowning, no doubt wondering whether they'd been invited to make up the numbers.

'Does everyone know everyone?' asked Ronny.

There were a number of non-committal shrugs so Ronny went around the table naming each individual and giving a one sentence description, usually just a job title. The third Army of God member − the large woman with multiple chins − was Major Marjory Maddox, director of St Thomas Aquinas, the private hospital run by the AOG.

'I work there,' whispered Ming, as the introductions continued, mainly other local officials and businessmen, as well as those Conan already knew.

'So … Dr Khataten,' said Ronny. 'When do we get to see your pictures?'

'Oh,' Jen put her hand over her mouth to finish chewing and said, 'I was just saying to Ming … we've got all the data in but there's too much to be properly processed by the computers we have on site. We're just waiting for our turn on the Quantum. There's a bit of a queue.'

'Why do you need a computer to show pictures? asked Greg Ferrier, director of one of the water purification facilities on the Ord River.

'Because radio telescopes don't take pictures in the visual spectrum,' said Jen. 'They take in a vast amount of data from radio waves and convert that data to an image we can see. But the Giant Array has more than ten thousand dipoles ... special receiving stations like giant white spiders, also linked with the ALMA in Chile and another in South Africa ... and produces an unbelievable amount of data. Only the Quantum computer can deal with that ... and of course there's only one in Australia, which is mostly taken up by the military, money transactions and law enforcement. Science has to wait.'

'Such a shame,' said Major Lammas, getting a tight smile from his AOG colleagues.

'The data sets are unbelievable,' continued Jen, with a glance at Lammas. 'If you could picture all the atoms of the world's oceans as individual bits of data ... that's about a ten billionth of what we're dealing with.'

There was a bit of a silence as the diners attempted to wrap their heads around the numbers involved, then everyone reached for their glasses in unison.

'Definitely need the Quantum to make sense of something like that,' said Conan. 'My boss, Kenny, explains quantum computing like this: imagine if back in 2020 the computing power and scrutiny of the entire planet was focussed on just one person ... Well, that focus and scrutiny is nothing compared to what we have in 2030, but it's focussed on everyone ... all the time. The computer never stops thinking about you and your standard patterns. It makes predictions and learns from its mistakes. Eventually, the computer knows what you're going to do long before you know yourself ... which is pretty handy for law enforcement.'

'And would be very handy for science,' added Jen. 'Pity ... '

'Oh well,' said Lammas. 'Just gives you more time to cook up a story.'

'I beg your pardon?'

There was a sudden silence. Even the noise from outside seemed miles away as Jen stared a challenge at Major Lammas.

'Convert the data,' he laughed. 'Scientific code for cook up a story.'

'You don't accept science, Major Lammas?' asked Ronny, grinning from ear to ear, and in that moment Conan understood the guest list. Ronny Kwai was a journalist whose stock in trade was conflict.

'It depends what you mean by science,' said Lammas in his compelling baritone. 'Demonstrable advances in medicine or engineering with obvious, tangible benefits are fair enough. Even advances in computer gaming like those appalling drop shots are demonstrable science … although the church deplores the idea of young people seeking fulfilment through fantasy.'

'Just one fantasy at a time, you reckon?' asked Conan, getting a withering look from Lammas and Captain Roberts.

'But so-called cosmology,' Lammas continued, '… relying on arcane mathematics and vast oceans of data … requires a massive leap of faith.'

'The maths and data are not arcane,' said Jen. 'Not for those who've done the groundwork.'

'Done the groundwork,' quoted Lammas. 'Scientific code for been indoctrinated.'

There was a bit of a buzz about the table as opinions polarised.

'The fact that you don't understand it doesn't turn it into fantasy,' said Conan. 'Don't drag science down to your own level.'

A number of people laughed. Ming gave Conan a delighted smile, but Captain Roberts glared at him and moved her chair further away, as waiters placed steaming dishes of fried rice about the table, accompanied by a Szechuan stir fry that smelled sweetly of onions, garlic and chilli.

'You're not a believer, Agent Tooley?' enquired Lammas.

'No … and neither are you.'

'I beg your pardon?'

The ice in Lammas' voice had frozen all other conversation and the entire table was now focussed on Conan.

'Okay,' he said, feeling a little drunkenly immortal. 'This is what I reckon about god. Not only do I not believe … I don't believe you believe. I don't believe anyone has ever believed, one hundred percent, because the whole thing's absurd. It's about power … that's all. Money and power. The Army of God is your power base … Major … and don't tell anyone different because it's a lie.'

There was a stunned flash of outrage around the table but Conan grinned, despite the uneasy suspicion that The Army of God might be able to pull strings to damage his career, such as it was. Lammas was silent until the anger on his behalf subsided.

'I'm surprised you're not working for the diplomatic corps,' he said. 'But you're right … belief in God is a kind of power, but it's only personal. How can I, or the church, have power over others when we share the same belief and are all equal under God?'

'But you're not equal … are you, Major?'

'My rank is purely administrative. We are a large organisation … for which I daily thank God … and need to delegate authority for the purposes of governance and logistics. It is not power to be wielded like a pharaoh … or even a federal police agent.'

It was a well made point and Conan laughed with the others. 'I suppose it's true that I do wield some authority on behalf of the state … but at least the need for that authority is based on something real.'

'You're claiming the church is not real, Agent Tooley?'

'It probably wouldn't be,' said Conan, '… if not for the *Epistola Clementis*.'

And there it was, the black look on Lammas' face that once again sent Conan's antennae into tingling overdrive.

'The what?' enquired Ming.

'Shall I explain?' Conan asked Lammas. 'Or will you?'

Lammas composed himself, took an elegant sip of wine, and said, 'Agent Tooley is referring to an old document from the early church. It has no modern relevance and is probably apocryphal … but some anti-church crusaders will try to tell you it debunks the whole of Christianity.'

'Ridiculous,' sneered Major Maddox, her chins wobbling with indignation.

'I thought so too, when I heard about it,' laughed Conan.

'Why haven't we heard about this before?' asked Ronny. 'If it's so important?'

'That's the interesting point,' said Conan. 'There's hardly anything anywhere about the *Epistola Clementis*. It's like there's been a massive cover up.'

'Covering what, exactly?' asked Major Lammas.

'The way the church cooked up a story,' said Conan, getting a delighted laugh from Ming, but mostly silence and confusion from the others.

Ronny, playing host, deftly changed the subject at that point so Conan took the opportunity to tuck into the chicken and prawn stir fries and was blown away by the explosion of flavours which went perfectly with the Margaret River Semillon that one of the waiters kept topped up by his right hand.

Others gave their attention to the food also and the buzz of conversation returned.

'You have some interesting ideas,' said Ming, smiling at Conan. 'I'll bet you're a Scorpio.'

'I'm a strange case,' said Conan, 'I was born in October but I'm actually Pisces.'

'How interesting.'

Conan laughed, as a fresh dish of cubed beef in a tangy pink sauce was placed within gorging distance.

'I think you might have got me into trouble,' said Ming.

'How'd I do that?'

'Major Maddox runs the hospital where I work, and the look she gave me when I laughed at your joke ... I think my days are numbered.'

'Oh ... sorry about that.'

'Doesn't matter,' she said. 'My department has so little work these days.'

'Really? In paediatrics?'

'They've opened a new specialty hospital for newborns ... near the stadium ... but only AOG staff are transferred there, which means I'll have to look for something else.'

Ming excused herself to find the bathroom, leaving Conan in a bubble of semi-pissed silence. He'd reached that point of early intoxication where he felt fantastically light-hearted and full of goodwill towards his fellow man. And woman, irrespective of how she might feel about him.

'Just kidding, Mel,' said Conan, nudging Captain Roberts.

'Did you say something?' she asked.

'Didn't mean to upset your boyfriend. I suppose he does believe … in something.'

'Do you have any idea how offensive you are?' she asked, and then got even angrier as Conan laughed.

'I'm just giving Ronny the drama he craves. That's why he sat us together.'

Captain Roberts slammed her fork down on the table (only Conan, Ming and Ronny were using chop sticks).

'Take this any way you like,' said Captain Roberts, reaching for her glass, 'but I don't wish to talk with you any further. I will ignore anything you say from this moment onward.'

'You are the most beautiful woman I've ever seen,' said Conan, getting a wide-eyed, open-mouthed response.

'Heh … didn't ignore that,' he smiled, as she turned away in fury.

'Still making friends, Tools?' called Ronny across the table. He had clearly followed the exchange and was grinning delightedly.

'See what I mean?' said Conan to Captain Roberts' obstinate back.

· · ·

Captain Roberts was true to her word and did not respond to any further comments. Ming however was full of interesting information – not least that the two AOG Majors were locked in a death struggle for a vacant colonelcy.

'It'll probably be Lammas … the AOG is as sexist as any other organisation. That's part of the reason I don't care if I'm sacked.'

The dinner finished and Conan felt both over-full and delightfully pissed as he sat in the balcony seats with Ming, Jen and Richie watching the game. The football didn't much interest him but the stadium, the crowd and the huge holograms that flickered in and out were utterly spectacular. The crowd, in particular, was like some vast yellow organism pulsing with anger and ecstasy as the game unfolded below. And deafening. Whenever they weren't loudly cheering or complaining they were endlessly choreographed in songs and dances led by bare-chested young men on platforms with megaphones. When number 9, Horace Feng, scored a goal just before the end to break the deadlock there was pandemonium. It was like a mediaeval painting of purgatory the way the Ord City fans leapt and writhed in terrifying unison, careless even of hellfire if only Feng could score. The goal was replayed in a massive slow-motion hologram in the air above the pitch and Conan was open-mouthed at the spectacle.

'I love the chaos of crowds,' said Ming, '… the way they move … the patterns they make.'

'It's certainly an education,' said Conan. 'The members at the SCG don't carry on like this.'

There were only minutes to go and Conan realised the crowd were singing the song from Ronny Kwai's ringtone.

'What are you doing afterwards?' asked Ming.

The question so surprised Conan he took some moments to answer.

'Erm … nothing,' he said. 'Getting ready to go home I guess.'

'You're going home to Sydney?'

She actually looked disappointed and Conan felt rather odd. It was a while since any woman had taken an interest in him – except Lucia – and even she seemed to run away whenever he tried to talk about it.

'They're wrapping up the case, so I have to be back in the office by Monday morning.'

'Well … that still leaves tonight,' she said. 'Shall we do something?'

Conan felt himself burning with a weird, sheepish embarrassment that somehow turned into excitement.

'Sure … what would you like to do?'

'Go dancing? Go to one of the rooftop bars in K-town?'

There was a sudden wave of anxiety that surged through the stadium and Conan looked back to the game where a player in sky blue was racing by himself towards the Ord City goal, rounded the keeper with a piece of athletic trickery, then tapped the ball into an empty net.

There was a full second of silence, and then a thunderous lamentation as the crowd perceived that victory had been snatched away.

'Scorer for Sydney FC … Matthias Palmquist,' announced the voice from the tannoys as the hologram showed again the intricate step movements the player had used to get around the goalkeeper and then score with such nonchalant ease.

'I'm in your hands,' said Conan, and she gave him a smile sweet enough for a toothpaste commercial.

• • •

It was a beautiful night, reflected Robbie. Cool after the heat of the day, with no moon just yet and the stars blazing above like icing sugar splashed over dark chocolate.

They were somewhere between Rabbit Flat and Halls Creek, in the middle of nowhere. They'd pulled over for the night and Tim and Lemon had put up their tent about ten metres from the car. Robbie and Chris always slept in the car with the seats laid down.

They'd brought a few take-aways and Chris didn't bat an eyelid when Robbie offered Tim and Lemon a beer to share. Chris was in an excellent mood and kept asking Lemon whether it was dark enough yet to trigger the terms of their agreement.

'It'll be dark enough in the tent soon,' she decided, snatching the beer from Tim. 'But no touching.'

Robbie was mortified, on Tim's behalf, not least as Lemon seemed so keen to go through with the HTHJ (as even she was calling it by this point). After a while Tim walked away so Robbie got another two beers and went after him.

Catching up with Tim he said, 'I reckon you could do with one of these.'

Tim thanked him and sipped gratefully. 'She's not so bad.'

'Really? I don't know how you put up with it, mate.'

'You just have to remember the basic tenets,' said Tim. 'All is nothing and nothing is all … sex doesn't matter and we have no problem with it being used as a lever to get what we need.'

Robbie just stared at Tim in the moonlight.

'Well, you did get a pack of Twisties I suppose.'

'Half a pack,' muttered Tim, and then despite himself managed to laugh. 'I know how it looks,' he said, 'but I've always been crazy about her.'

'Crazy?' echoed Robbie. 'More like insane, I would have said … but whatever floats your boat.'

There was a bit of a silence, broken only by Chris and Lemon laughing in the background. Then Tim said, 'You and Chris seem like pretty different blokes.'

'We're not so different.'

'So, why exactly are you headed for Ord City?' asked Tim.

'Oh … just for the hell of it,' said Robbie, vaguely. He and Chris had agreed that no one should be told why they were going to Ord City, although Robbie had his own private reason. Kate had told him that she …

His mind immediately sheered away from that line of thinking.

'Ord City seems like an interesting place,' he said.

'It is for Habal Tongers,' said Tim, 'but there's not a lot there for other people.'

'Don't know about that,' said Robbie. 'There's been a few docos about it … the melting pot of Asia and all that … and probably the easiest place in Oz to get work these days.'

That much was true. Parts of Australia had been in recession for the last five years – since the Quantum Revolution had rendered so many jobs redundant. But there was always work in Ord City – especially in construction.

'What sort of work you looking for?'

'Anything really. Preferably something in the mines … that pays the best.'

'What did you do in Melbourne?'

'Motor repairs, but the conditions have been getting so much tougher because there's fewer and fewer jobs and they can get away with whatever they like … until Chris told 'em to stick it.'

'He seems to be good at that.'

'Yeah,' Robbie laughed. 'He always speaks his mind, regardless of the consequences. You have to admire that.'

'Unless you're the one who has to deal with the consequences,' said Tim, walking away into darkness.

Robbie shrugged and headed back to the camp site where Lemon, partly fuelled by further beers from Chris, had finally agreed it was time. She disappeared into the pup tent and said she'd call when she was ready. Robbie sat on an old truck tire where Chris was grinning with anticipation.

'Are you sure you want this?' asked Robbie.

'Are you kidding?' laughed Chris.

'No. Just strikes me as a tad grubby … and you don't know where she's been.'

'Aah … you're just feeling sorry for her boyfriend,' said Chris, taking a slug of beer. 'Besides … I see my HTHJ as a political act.'

'A what?'

Chris laughed, and took another reflective slug.

'Habal Tong are just a bunch of reffos and reffo lovers … the natural enemies of Dedd Reffo. If we're truly committed to fighting the good fight we have to be ready to take on the enemy in any context.'

'Sounds like a long bow to me,' said Robbie, grabbing the last beer.

'In the moment I come in her mouth,' sniggered Chris, 'I'm gonna tell her I'm a member of Dedd Reffo … choke on *that* bitch!'

Robbie shook his head sadly and in that moment, Lemon called out from the pup tent. 'Okay, ready … but no touching.'

'I feel like an Anzac warrior going into battle,' said Chris, as he finished his beer and headed for the tent.

• • •

It was pitch black in the tent and smelled of unwashed clothes, plus that dry plasticky smell that tents always seem to get.

'Lie down and get it out,' said Lemon, and Chris did as he was told, still giggling as he shifted uncomfortably in the confined space.

'Okay,' he said. 'Ready to rip.'

He could hear Lemon also giggling and he had to admit, despite everything, he couldn't help but like her a little. He felt a hand on his thigh and then breath against his cock, and then a glorious sensation as warm lips closed around him and started sliding slowly up and down, sometimes harder, sometimes softer – an excruciating pleasure.

'Oh, you're good at this,' murmured Chris, barely able to speak as her mouth continued to draw him towards oblivion. He wanted to hold her head but she'd said she'd stop if he touched her so he resisted the urge, but started thrusting upwards to get a bit more friction to relieve the glorious pain.

Harder and harder he thrusted, feeling her choking slightly and grinning at that, even though he could hear her laughing. Chris felt his brain twitching, almost clenching with imminent climax. A roaring seemed to fill his head as the burn in his cock was like a fuse about to reach a packed charge of dynamite. She laughed again and it vaguely occurred to Chris that she was amazingly skilled – to be able to maintain such incredible HJ momentum while also able to laugh.

In that instant, Chris perceived what was happening. And yet he was too close to climax to stop himself. He grabbed Tim by the head and pounded furiously into his mouth until his brain exploded in kaleidoscopic shards. Then he was pounding his fist into Tim's face – holding him by the hair in the dark and smashing with his fist, not stopping until he realised Lemon was still laughing.

Chapter 11

A Meaningless Distraction

Conan lay in the wolf light before dawn, trying to get back to sleep.

Ming lay next to him, her body curled into his and almost unconsciously he began stroking her silken skin. Again.

It had been an unbelievable night. Ming had taken him to her favourite rooftop bar in old Kununurra (or K-town as it was called by the locals). It was much darker than the surrounding metropolis so stars blazed above them and the air was laced with jasmine and frangipani. Conan had felt a little under-dressed in such a place – crammed with beautiful creatures (like Ming) – but the alcohol, and her presence, soon put him at his ease.

'I love the way you put them in their place,' she said. 'I've always been so scared of them ... those black uniforms. They run the hospital like a concentration camp and jobs are hard to get so most accept their rules and arrogance like slaves.'

Medicine didn't pay anywhere near as well as it had done in the past – partly because of the oversupply of doctors in the last ten years, but mainly because health science had made such massive advances in the Quantum Era.

'But there are still many problems,' said Ming, 'especially up here with all the overcrowding, poor sanitation and endless issues with the drinking water.'

The conversation had mostly been about each other and Conan quickly established that they had never moved in similar circles despite his vague sense of having met her before. Then at some point, Conan had realised they were holding hands across the table.

'Why are you so nervous?' she asked him.

'I'm not nervous … just had a strange thought.'

'Yes?'

'Every woman I've ever … been with.'

'Yes?' she laughed.

'Erm … they've … Well, they've all been bog-standard Aussie chicks.'

'I'm an Aussie chick,' protested Ming, smiling.

'Of course you are,' he back-pedalled, '… but, the others were all Anglo-Saxon … if you catch my drift.'

There'd also been Lucia, obviously, but despite having Italian parents, she was the most bog-standard of the lot.

'How old are you?' she asked.

'Thirty-six.'

'Wow. Thirty-six years on planet earth and never done it with a Chinese girl. That's an epic fail.'

'It is,' he'd agreed, 'but maybe you could … you know … get me sorted with that.'

'I'd love to help,' she said, taking a provocative sip at her cocktail, 'but I'm an Aussie chick. Maybe I could find you an immigrant?'

By this point Conan had to fight the urge to just grab her and kiss her, but she pulled her chair round to his side of the table and the next thing he knew he *was* kissing her – stars and alcohol whirling in his brain with the taste of tequila, lime and cherry lipstick.

Almost without further conversation they'd left the bar and walked hand in hand to her apartment, about half a kilometre away, and from there Conan's problems began. With the exception of one drunken fumble with Lucia, he hadn't had sex since his ex-wife (Lisa) walked out two years prior. And he couldn't really remember how to do it. Not with any finesse.

Fortunately, Ming sensed his coyness and took the lead, slowly building his confidence, and by the time they collapsed onto clammy sheets, Conan was more or less back into stride – and ready to go again when he woke, enjoying the way her natural scent mingled with the piney disinfectant that pervaded her apartment.

'Was it different?' she murmured.

'Was what different?'

'Doing it with a Chinese girl.'

'Ah … but you're not a Chinese girl,' he said, cupping his hand over her breast. 'You're an Aussie chick.'

'To tell the truth, I'm only half Chinese,' said Ming, then started talking in Cantonese.

'What does that mean?'

She snuggled harder against him and said: 'Ngou oui lei … it means: stop poking me in the bottom with a broomstick.'

But she rolled over smiling, and before he knew it Conan was once more devouring her with all his seven senses.

A short while later as he lay waiting for his heart to slow …

'Breakfast?'

'Mmmm.'

Ming jumped out of bed and started pulling clothes on, to Conan's disappointment.

'I'm just going down to the bakery … back in five.'

'You want me to come?'

'No. You lie there … or have a shower. Won't be long.'

She jumped back onto the bed, looking like a teenager in a pink *Hello Kitty* sports top, kissed him on the nose, then snatched up her OzBrace and a hot pink phone and skipped out the door. Within seconds he was aching for her return.

In the shower, Conan considered his position.

He was supposed to be on a plane at 12.30, which meant being at the airport by 11.30, which meant he'd have to be back at his hotel by 9.30 to pack, check out and get a cab.

It was 6.55, so he had about two more hours with Ming before he'd have to go back to real life.

At that point a wave of depression struck him. The prospect of slinking back to Sydney and confronting Kenny Cook filled him with inertia. In all likelihood he'd be busted back to tax evasion, or even airport duty. And what really pissed him off was that he didn't properly understand what had gone wrong in the first place. It was like someone was pulling strings in the shadows to deliberately fuck up his life. The only thing going well was meeting Ming.

That thought had two immediate corollaries. One was that he suddenly felt guilty about Lucia – despite owing her nothing as far as sexual fidelity was concerned. The other was a reckless desire to abandon his job in Sydney and make a new life in Ord City. It was a tad irresponsible, having known Ming substantially less than 24 hours. Maybe he could get a transfer – although the idea of working with Loongy was even worse than going back to Kenny.

Conan finished dressing and walked out into the open plan apartment to find the coffee maker, which was soon filling the apartment with the fresh smell of Sunday morning. He opened the French windows onto the balcony and walked outside to admire the day and the cute old neighbourhood – like a forgotten part of the main city glowering to the south, west and north. He could see the small arcade of shops about a hundred metres away and glanced at his watch: well after seven.

He sipped his coffee and, to his surprise, realised he'd made a fairly momentous decision. When Ming returned, he was going to ask her to be his girlfriend. And if she said yes, he would move to Ord City – irrespective of whether he could arrange a transfer.

With the realisation of his decision he felt excited and started to get impatient for her return. He looked again down the street towards the shops – hoping to spot her gorgeous figure flitting along the footpath that was just beginning to fill up with joggers and early shoppers.

He checked his watch again: quarter past. She'd been gone over twenty minutes – probably closer to half an hour, yet she'd said she'd only be five minutes.

He thrust down a frisson of anxiety for the over-protective paranoia it surely was. In any case, he couldn't leave her apartment to go looking for her as he didn't have a key. He'd just have to wait.

He glanced at his phone but realised he didn't have her number – didn't even know her surname. He went back to the kitchen, where the pine disinfectant smell was reasserting its dominance over the coffee, and examined the fridge where, sure enough, a couple of print outs were stuck with magnets in the name of Dr Ming Li Chen.

He walked back onto the balcony and swept the street again for a sight of her, and five minutes later rang Lucia at work.

'Hey, Conan.'

'Hi, Lucia … I need an urgent favour.'

'How's the investigation going?'

'Really badly ... but something's come up. Can you get me the phone number of Dr Ming Li Chen in Kununurra?'

'It's not in the White Pages?'

'No ... silent. This is urgent.'

'Okay ... Dr Ming who?'

'Li Chen.'

'You sound worried.'

'I am worried. Have you got it?'

'Almost.'

'Can you text her number to me? I'll run it through my sim locator.'

'Ming's a she?'

Lucia's voice had gone flat and Conan felt a terrible guilt, but he didn't have time to deal with that.

'Have you got the number?'

'Yes.'

Conan's phone pinged.

'Thanks Lucia ... gotta go.'

'Bye Conan,' she said, tearing his heart with the desolation in her voice.

'See you soon,' he said, aware that there was every chance he'd never see her again.

Two minutes later, having left a note on the kitchen bench in case she returned before he did, and having found the spare key in a kitchen drawer, Conan ran down the street towards the shops. He had a fix on Ming's sim card, which was not far away.

As he approached the shops he could see a bakery sign and prepared himself for embarrassment – expecting to find her inside joking with the owner. But just before he got to the bakery the phone finder app told him he was right on top of her sim card. Glancing about in confusion, he noticed an overflowing garbage bin.

On top of the garbage was a hot pink phone.

• • •

Captain Melodie Roberts lay blinking in the early morning dazzle, trying to decide how she felt.

The unaccustomed weight in the bed next to her remained somehow a mystery. When she and Tom had been engaged, she had allowed herself to be convinced that sexual relations prior to marriage were permissible with one's fiancé, but that first time had felt strangely wrong, and last night – the second time – had been even more disappointing.

Tom had seemed ardent and amorous at first, but the physical transaction was over too quickly – just as she was getting interested – and Tom had retreated within a cold, moody shell, making her feel guilty and somehow a failure. Somehow she had not satisfied him and she had to wonder whether it was just the fact that they weren't married yet? Maybe he felt as guilty about that as she did and that's what was turning the sex into a hasty, sordid embarrassment instead of the wondrous transformation she'd read about.

She put her hand out to stroke his shoulder, but at that moment he farted long and loudly and her hand recoiled as though burned. Even worse was the realisation that she probably did that herself in her sleep and was mortified at the idea he might hear her. It's quite horrible being reminded we are animals, she reflected, determined not to judge her fiancé despite the awful smell that continued to waft from under the sheets.

Maybe she should have a shower?

The idea of making herself clean was suddenly all-consuming but as she rolled over to get up she felt his hand and turned back to see him smiling at her.

'How do you feel?' he asked her.

'Wonderful,' she lied, hoping that was the right thing to say.

He reached out for her and she returned his embrace, until she felt his hard penis against her leg and tried to move away without being too obvious about it. But he pulled her closer and forced himself between her legs so she had no choice but to accept him. Remembering the few seconds the previous night when it had started to feel alright, she shifted herself around him until the beginnings of a pleasurable sensation could be discerned and she tried to kiss him, but his eyes were screwed up and his teeth gritted angrily and, before she properly understood what was happening, something hot and wet was running down her leg and the Major swore with frustration.

'What have I done?' asked Melodie, horrified to hear him swear but even more upset to think she'd let him down again.

'It's nothing,' he muttered. 'Nothing.'

She held him tightly, feeling his penis go soft against her leg and wondering what the big deal was about sex. As far as she could tell it was uncomfortable, embarrassing – even painful. Maybe she was doing it wrongly?

'Tom?'

'Yes?'

'I … I don't think I'm doing it properly.'

'Of course you are,' he snapped. 'There's no problem.'

'Are you sure?'

'Of course I'm sure. How could you possibly get it wrong? It's only the man who can get it wrong … although nothing *is* wrong.'

Melodie lay reflecting on his words for a few moments, then said, 'Well … if you're sure there's nothing wrong … fine. But if for argument's sake there was something wrong, what would it most likely be?'

'What do you mean?' he asked, sounding angry again.

'Well, you said only the man can get it wrong … what is it he can get wrong, and why can't the woman get something wrong?'

'The woman is just the receptacle,' he said. 'The man does all the work to fill the receptacle … it's the work that matters.'

'That doesn't seem fair.'

'Just part of the burden of being male,' he said, his voice redeeming some of the baritone magic it had lost in the last minute or so.

He rolled onto his back and Melodie lay there, wondering how long she should stay before it would be polite to get out of bed and have the shower she craved.

'I was unhappy with the seating arrangements last night,' he said.

'So was I. That Tooley is a creep.'

Yet, even as she said it, Melodie was aware that she was just a little intrigued by Agent Tooley, and that thought angered her.

'He's harmless enough,' said Tom. 'Just another atheist intellectual … boring. But I didn't like the effect he had on Dr Chen. Did you see they left together?'

'No. I was trying not to notice him at all.'

There was a bit more of a silence as Melodie wiped her thigh with the sheet and prepared to get out of bed.

'She already asks too many questions,' said Lammas, almost to himself. 'I don't even know why she was invited.'

'What questions does she ask? I didn't know you knew her.'

'She's one of Marjory's creatures,' he replied, frowning. 'I do believe you're jealous.'

Melodie felt herself blush.

'I am not jealous … although she is very attractive.'

'Is she? I hadn't noticed.'

Melodie so desperately wanted that shower but for some reason felt oddly coy about getting out of bed. She'd just had sex with her fiancé but she didn't want him looking at her naked body – especially in its dishevelled, post-coital state – which meant she had to stay, for the moment.

'So what sort of questions does she ask? Doesn't she work at the hospital?'

'Yes. Obviously that's Marjory's jurisdiction but, being on the Board of Governors, I must take an interest.'

'Alright … but you still haven't answered my question.'

'Which question?'

'What questions does Dr Chen ask?'

He gave her a tight-lipped smile and reached across to stroke the hair away from her face.

'It's nothing. I shouldn't have mentioned it.'

'But now you have mentioned it … '

The smile faded and he rolled onto his back.

'You know there are aspects of my work I simply can't talk about. Suffice it to say that she asks questions beyond the ambit of her remit. That's what happens when you employ non-AOG doctors.'

She was silent for a moment, mulling over the tidbit of information and trying to decide whether her curiosity was satisfied.

'Of course, there aren't that many AOG doctors … ' she said, trying to get him talking again.

'No. We really must do better in the recruiting department. Marjory's failure there is one of the many reasons the colonelcy will be mine … and when I am her direct superior I shall insist we employ only committed Christian doctors.'

Melodie disliked Thomas obsessing about the vacant colonelcy, but he was at least less circumspect than usual and she couldn't help her curiosity.

'So Dr Chen asks questions of management which are none of her business and will not accept correction?'

Lammas laughed.

'Unlike you my dear. You do accept correction when you ask the wrong questions ... as you are doing now.'

'I'm just curious,' she defended. 'The more I know, the more I can help you.'

'Perhaps ... but knowledge is dangerous.'

'Knowledge about the hospital?'

'That's enough.'

Lammas was suddenly stern, but still smiling. 'Once again you have wheedled information out of me to which you shouldn't have access at your security level.'

She smiled back, determined to take the moment as far as she could.

'So you disapprove of Dr Chen talking to Agent Tooley because of his interest in the *Epistola Clementis*?'

'I couldn't care less about the *Epistola Clementis*,' he said, and Melodie felt a chill at the menace in his voice. 'The *Epistola* is a meaningless distraction, but the things he said about me and my belief were outrageous ... unforgivable. And she laughed ... *laughed* at her superiors being mocked. I don't see how we can keep her on after that. She will never respect us.'

'Is she good at her work?'

'It doesn't matter how good she is,' said Lammas, cold and final.

He rolled onto his stomach and closed his eyes, so Melodie took her opportunity and dashed for the shower.

Chapter 12

Random Abos

Conan sat in an interview room at the K-town state police station.

His interrogator, Sergeant Marsh, was a middle-aged Aboriginal man who managed to convey a rumpled Sam Spade air, rubbing constantly at his face and scalp while sipping tepid coffee and occasionally jotting down parts of Conan's story on a Missing Person form.

It wasn't much of a story. Ming had gone to the shops and not come back. Then he'd found her phone and her OzBrace in a bin but didn't know the code to unlock it to check for calls.

'Any enemies?' asked Sergeant Marsh.

'None that I know of,' said Conan. 'But I only met her yesterday.'

Sergeant Marsh rubbed again at a red, inflamed part of his scalp, then scribbled a bit more on the form.

'Well … that's probably as far as we can take it for now,' he said, in a winding up voice honed on hundreds of previous dickheads wanting him to do something.

'There's something else,' said Conan.

Sergeant Marsh didn't answer, just stared tiredly at Conan, pen poised and waiting for him to get it over with.

'Whoever has done this …'

'Presuming anyone has done anything,' interrupted Marsh.

'I suppose … but whoever. It might have been because she was with me.'

'Why?' asked Sergeant Marsh, as though indulging an imbecile.

Conan pulled out his plastex ID.

'Because I'm an AFP investigator from Sydney … and someone up here doesn't like me.'

Conan had not wanted to mention his own status due to the inevitable political slant that would be added to the conversation, but at last Sergeant Marsh took an interest.

'From Sydney? I reckon there'd be plenty who don't like you … including me.'

'I was sent to look into the Fong, Wing Ho murders,' said Conan, 'but I'm due back in Sydney this afternoon.'

Sergeant Marsh groaned, and rubbed again at his eyes and scalp.

'What's more,' continued Conan, 'there have been some pretty weird aspects of my investigation … which has already been closed … and some arseholes chased me the other night.'

Sergeant Marsh groaned again and Conan might have laughed if he hadn't been so worried about Ming.

'So now I'm worried that Ming's disappearance has something to do with me and my investigation.'

Sergeant Marsh was silent for some time, his face buried in his hands. Then he banged the pen down on top of the Missing Person pad and said, 'Let's go for a walk … I need a fag. And some decent coffee.'

Conan glanced at his watch, nearly ten, and Marsh said, 'What time's your plane?'

'Twelve thirty … but I reckon I'll have to miss it.'

Marsh nodded and led the way outside, a cigarette already in his mouth. They crossed the road which was comparatively empty (by Ord City standards) and headed for a coffee cart.

'Your shout,' said Marsh. 'Long black with three sugars.'

'Three sugars?' queried Conan.

'You got a problem with that Tooley?'

'No. Call me Tools.'

'No worries, Tools. I'm Dave.'

They collected their coffees from the ancient Vietnamese barista and strolled back towards the station to where an inviting red brick wall offered a seat in the sun. Dave lit another cigarette and said, 'Okay Tools … get it off your chest.'

Conan explained some of his experiences of the last few days, emphasising his frustration with the apparent wild goose chase, the politics and the strange behaviour of Loongy.

'I know Loongy' grinned Dave. 'Weird sort of bloke, but not dodgy.'

'Well … maybe he's been leaned on,' said Conan. 'But nothing makes sense.'

'So who chased you?'

'Three Asian blokes. No idea who they were and haven't had a problem since … until now.'

'I suppose I could order up the CCTV footage for the street,' said Dave, stubbing out his cigarette on the wall. 'Come on.'

They went back inside and Conan couldn't help but notice how dingy it all was in comparison with the AFP offices. Dave even had to get by with an old style computer.

'You want to use this?' asked Conan, pulling his Pod out of his satchel.

'Wouldn't know how,' said Dave, tapping away at his keyboard. 'Right … here we go. Argyle Street this morning between twenty to seven and quarter past … between numbers sixty and a hundred.'

He sat staring at his screen for a moment.

'That's odd.'

Conan got out of his chair and went round to Dave's side of the desk. Dave clicked on his mouse and Conan saw the screen showing the street outside Ming's house and the time 6.42 at the bottom of the screen counting by thousandths of a second.

There were few cars and almost no people.

Then the screen went black.

'Fuckin' wiped,' said Dave.

Conan felt a cool freeze tingle up his spine.

'Wiped? Fuck.'

Neither of them spoke, both aware that only very high authority could have arranged for the video to be wiped.

'It could be just a glitch,' said Dave. 'They do happen … especially up here.'

He fast forwarded the screen and the pictures cut back in at seven o'clock, with the street looking perfectly normal. Fast forwarding again to 7.35 they watched Conan run down the street then pause and reach into an overflowing garbage bin.

'It's no glitch,' said Conan.

Dave groaned and started rubbing at his face and scalp again.

• • •

It was quiet in the car.

Mostly.

Chris had hardly spoken – just sat fuming in the passenger seat – and there was barely a peep from the back where Lemon sat grinning and Tim nursed a broken face. Robbie had insisted on taking him as far as the first hospital they came to and Chris had agreed with very poor grace. After that, he'd said nothing for several hours and they were less than a hundred ks from Ord City, winding along the river flats as the sun was setting in the west.

Tim was in a very bad way: two black eyes, a broken nose, one tooth missing and another broken, possibly a broken jaw, and a bleeding scalp from where a handful of hair had been torn out in Chris's fury.

Robbie was aware of the basic facts but curious about the details, not that he could really ask at that moment. Maybe not ever.

'You realise you can't mention us,' said Robbie, to the back seat. 'When you get to the hospital they'll want to know how you got hurt. Nothing to do with us, right?'

'Tell 'em you were hitching and got picked up by random Abos,' said Chris, breaking his long silence. 'You mention our names … you cop another fuckin' hiding. Both of youse.'

Robbie's eyes flicked to the rear view mirror and he saw Lemon grinning from ear to ear.

'Dunno what you're so pissed off about,' she said. 'You wanted an HTHJ and that's what you got. Tim's Habal Tong, isn't he? Not our fault if you discriminate against men.'

Robbie expected Chris to explode with anger at her deliberate goading, but to his surprise, Chris said: 'You still owe me a heady, bitch. A deal's a deal.'

'No way,' laughed Lemon. 'You already came so that's it … mission accomplished.'

'Not by you,' insisted Chris. 'The deal was you.'

Lemon just laughed and Robbie found himself grinning.

'What's so fuckin' funny?' demanded Chris, and Robbie shook his head, barely holding back laughter.

The next thing he knew Chris was laughing as well, and then Lemon was squealing like she was about to piss her pants. The three of them howled with laughter until Robbie caught a glimpse of Tim's broken face and remembered it wasn't funny.

A green sign loomed up on the left – 55ks to Ord City.

'Should be able to see it soon,' he said, as the laughter ebbed.

'*Illumination* is gonna be brilliant,' said Lemon. 'You guys should join Habal Tong so you can come with us.'

'What'd I tell you about HT crap?' demanded Chris, but he was still laughing and there was little threat in his voice.

'You wouldn't be so fuckin' uptight if you made it past the first level,' said Lemon. 'Take Cocksucker here … he's so far up the levels it doesn't matter what anyone says or does to him. He's found peace and perfection … haven't you, Cockie.'

'Yeth,' mumbled Tim through his mangled mouth.

'You guys'll never appreciate what a profound achievement that is,' said Lemon, all HT arrogant again.

'Thank fuck for that,' said Robbie, and Chris laughed.

'So why are youse goin' to OC?' demanded Lemon. 'You keep avoiding the question.'

'No we don't,' said Chris. 'We're lookin' for work.'

'And having a holiday,' added Robbie. 'But what the hell is that?'

He was staring into the distance and the others followed his eye to where a dirty brown haze hovered above the darkening horizon.

'Welcome to Ord City,' said Chris, but Robbie started pulling over. There was a gorgeous picnic area on the banks of the river, with a decent looking toilet block and sheltered tables.

'We'll never find a room tonight,' said Robbie. 'Hit the Big Smoke in the morning?'

They pulled up in a gravel car park and sat for a while just staring at the beautiful scene, the wide river golden in the fading light and Ord City brooding in the distance like a pile of embers shrouded in smoke.

Chapter 13

The Powers That Be

Asif felt weird, meeting Razzaq without Ah Cheng being present. It was against the rules of the Tong.

What's more, the meeting was unscheduled and a complete surprise, also against the rules. Razzaq had accosted him in the street and told him to meet at a particular time and place. Asif had complied with the irregular instructions and had been doubly uneasy when he realised Ah Cheng would not be present.

'Ah Cheng doesn't need to know,' said Razzaq, in a coffee shop across the road from the restaurant where he worked. 'If he doesn't know, he can't divulge information under interrogation.'

'What information?'

Razzaq eyed Asif, as though judging his resolve.

'Your mission has been brought forward a day … to Friday. And the target has changed.'

Asif felt a tremor of trepidation. He had been at peace with the original target (in which human casualties would likely be nil, or at least negligible) and could tell from Razzaq's excited demeanour that the new target was somehow an escalation.

'Why?'

'Does it matter?'

Asif was silent as Razzaq lit another of his pungent clove cigarettes. He was grateful as the smoke helped to mask the strong smell of unwashed bodies and cooking oil that Razzaq carried with him.

'Well?' demanded Razzaq.

'I will always do as the Tong requires,' said Asif, holding Razzaq's eye despite the angry glare of scrutiny.

'Good. In fact the target has not changed … the true target. The true target has always been, but it was necessary for you to believe in the NBN in case of infiltration or interrogation. It is now too late for infiltration, and little time left for interrogation … if you were apprehended. Still, we must prepare for the true target.'

'Which is?'

Razzaq looked over his shoulder into the noisy street. Then he wrote on a scrap of newspaper and held it up for Asif to read, before setting fire to the scrap of paper.

Asif watched the scrap curl up and blacken, then be crushed into powder by Razzaq's thumb.

• • •

'What's wrong?'

Tanya's beautiful face was more curious than concerned, and once again Asif was amazed at how well she could read him.

'Nothing … it's just that I have to work.'

He was about to join Ah Cheng for a three day stint – fourteen hours on, ten hours off – hard work but the money was good. Not that that mattered.

'Oh well … you'll be back on Wednesday. I might have a surprise for you.'

'Another painting?' he asked, glancing around the studio for something new. 'Or a sculpture?'

'You'll see.'

Asif picked up his backpack, kissed her, and left the house. Ah Cheng was waiting with his motorbike and Asif smiled as he clambered on behind.

Without a word, Ah Cheng roared off into the early evening traffic, absolutely in his element as he slipped through the chaos of bikes and cars, none of them observing the road rules but all of them getting quickly where they needed to be.

• • •

Three people – two men and a woman – sit before a huge picture window looking over a vast city, with an ocean to the north under a pink sky fading to purple. A servant pours tea and departs silently. None of them speak until all have savoured the tea and replaced their cups.

'Only days to go,' says the woman.

'Yes ... but there is still much to do,' reminds the smaller man. 'And nothing must go wrong,'

'Nothing will go wrong,' says the Man in Black. 'We have everything in hand.'

'Something already has gone wrong,' says the woman.

'It has been dealt with,' says the Man in Black.

The last of the pink fades from the sky in the west. It is black to the east.

'And yet he is still here,' says the woman. 'He was supposed to be on a plane this afternoon.'

The Man in Black shrugs as he sips his tea.

'His case has been closed and he will be back in Sydney shortly.'

'The risk was worth it?' asks the smaller man, '... exposing him to our friends?'

'There can always be unintended consequences,' says the Man in Black, '... but the risk was contained.'

'Unintended consequences are always the greatest risk,' says the smaller man. 'That is why our actions must be kept to a minimum. I do not like this ... unnecessary complication.'

'It has no impact on our main strategy,' says the Man in Black. 'That is entirely under control, you have my word.'

All three pick up their cups again, and sip reflectively.

They are changing history.

• • •

'What do you mean ... missed your plane?'

Kenny Cook was pissed off.

'I got caught up in a local investigation ... I've been in the K-town cop shop all day.'

'So you can get on the red eye flight and still be back tomorrow morning.'

There was an angry silence as Conan pondered his best move.

'Kenny … something very strange is going on up here. I seriously think it needs to be investigated.'

'There's nothing strange, Tools. Your investigation was suspended because the locals reckon the murders were obviously DR … or HT … with no prospect of a quick resolution. They need to keep their focus on Friday night so they've pulled all resources for it. You're a distraction they don't need. Simple as that.'

'I don't buy it. What about the …'

'It doesn't *matter* what you buy,' interrupted Kenny. 'The powers that be have shut up shop, so you've no further authority up there.'

'What about the other case?' asked Conan. 'The bloke in the library downloading NBN specs … has that been followed up?'

'Not yet, although they've been advised to ramp up security out at the node.'

'Well, you could extend my authority to look into that for a few more days.'

'Why on earth would I do that?'

'Because it's important, Kenny. I've never known anything like this. The AFP are hiding evidence from me, the Army of God are hiding something else, Ronny Kwai knows something, I've been chased by goons and now a friend has been abducted … probably for associating with me. The evidence of her abduction was wiped by someone with enough authority to do so. And, on top of all that, the city feels like a powder keg waiting to blow.'

'And in all of that,' said Kenny, 'I don't see a single clear cut offence that falls within AFP jurisdiction. It's all either state police or airy fairy bullshit.'

'Two days,' said Conan. 'Give me two days to try and work out exactly what it is we're dealing with. You can make it my birthday present.'

Kenny laughed and in that moment Conan sensed he was weakening.

'Okay … two days,' said Kenny, 'but stay away from AFP headquarters. Loong doesn't want you around.'

'No probs.'

'There won't be any further extension,' snapped Kenny, as though pissed off at himself for relenting. 'You give me an offence plus a name plus evidence within two days or you're on your way home. You got that?'

'Yep. Absolutely,' said Conan.

He hung up, lay back on his bed and stared at the fan revolving just fast enough to touch his sweat-beaded skin.

Then he lurched up off the bed and walked to the balcony, letting the heat into his room despite it being nearly ten o'clock at night. The city lay pulsing and gleaming below, like a live thing brooding on its secrets.

'Now what the fuck do I do?' he wondered aloud.

PART TWO

Chapter 14

Good Behaviour

The papers were full of *Illumination* the following morning, the Habal Tong ceremony on Friday night preceding the First Wave that kicked in at midnight. Huge celebrations were planned although there were still community spokespeople who called on the government to state unequivocally that the First Wavers would be confirmed in their citizenship. The government kept seeming to avoid the question and Colonel Chard, as the Chief Administrator of the TCZ was refusing to comment despite the rising tide of anger that leavened the general air of excitement.

'The seven years is contingent on good behaviour,' the *Ord City Times* quoted lawyer Alison Wong, leader of the TCZ Action Group, '... which potentially means the good behaviour of the entire community. The legislation is capable of that interpretation, which means citizenship could be refused to the many for the crimes of an activist few. Why won't the government confirm one way or another whether good behaviour is an individual or community responsibility?'

Conan sat in the café across the road from the local Army of God chapter, making a list of notes and questions to help guide his next movements.

Ronny Kwai was a possible source of information but Conan didn't really have any sort of hook to hang him on, and clearly he was determined to protect his sources, like any journalist.

Likewise, the Army of God. Conan was certain there was something going on there but he didn't have a clue what, so there was no pretext to justify further questioning, or even surveillance, he admitted to himself as he watched the building.

He'd spoken to Dave Marsh but there was no further word on Ming or the missing footage so effectively there was only one further line of investigation.

He paid for the coffee and left the café, wandering the streets around the AOG chapter house, taking in the sights and smells, and trying to make himself conspicuous. He hung around the street vendors where he'd been followed a couple of nights back, enjoying the frenzied activity and exotic aromas. A man in a sweat-drenched singlet with a cigarette in his mouth was working a huge wok over a butane lamp, expertly sweeping prawns, vegetables, chilli, garlic and noodles about with another mouth-watering meal made every minute.

Conan was so fascinated by the chef's performance he almost failed to notice the two men staring at him from a laneway. Tearing his eyes away from the stir fry star he met the eyes of one of them, grinned, and ran.

A glance back over his shoulder told him they were haring after him so he deliberately ran for the same side alley as a few nights before. The difference was that, this time, Conan had brought his weapon with him which he pulled as he ran into the lane and turned to face his pursuers.

The two men raced into the lane and skittered to a halt, shouting in Cantonese and staring round-eyed at his gun.

'On the ground!' shouted Conan. 'Now!'

But neither of them moved a muscle.

'I said down!' barked Conan, as they simultaneously grinned. Instinctively he turned, just in time to see a baseball bat being swung at his head.

• • •

Robbie stared out the window at the buildings, traffic and people – total chaos – and somehow felt his spirits lifting.

After an easy night by the river they'd driven into town and encountered the first real traffic since they'd left Melbourne. It was fucking anarchy but, somehow, Chris had found a place to park in the old part of town – Kununurra – which wasn't quite as overwhelming as the rest of it. Chris could see the problem though …

'Look at this,' he said. 'This part of town with the old buildings represents the old Australia … our Australia … and it's totally swamped by all these huge fuckin' towers full of Asians.'

'Not swamped,' said Lemon, from the back seat, '… improved. Those towers represent the wisdom of Habal Tong coming to fill Australia with light.'

'So why is it so fucking dark?' asked Chris. 'It's nearly nine thirty in mid January and I can't see the sun yet.'

'You don't know how to see it,' replied Lemon in that infuriating sing-song style of hers, but to Robbie's surprise Chris laughed.

Robbie got out of the car to stretch his legs and was immediately assailed by the sound and the smells of Ord City – the heat he was used to.

Tim got out of the car, blinking in the dim light. His face was bruised black and purple, but he seemed to have largely recovered from the beating and was not interested in going to hospital.

'Hey Cockie,' said Lemon, 'it's Monday … should get paid today.'

Welfare payments had moved from Thursdays to Mondays back in the early 20s as it was believed that Mondays were less socially active, so people were less likely to spend the lot partying in the first couple of days.

Lemon and Tim checked their OzBraces but both were still on zero. They'd buzz when a deposit was made, but you'd miss it in your sleep.

'Well, I guess this is where we say goodbye,' said Chris. 'I won't say it's been a pleasure meeting you.'

Robbie opened the boot and Tim pulled the big swag out and dutifully hauled it onto his shoulders.

'Good luck, mate,' said Robbie as Tim held out his hand. 'What are you going to do?'

Tim shrugged.

'Find a temple and sort out some digs, I guess. But accommodation won't be easy with *Illumination* on this week.'

'We'll be right,' said Chris. 'If we can't get a room we'll just stay in the car.'

Robbie nodded but his heart was sinking at the prospect of

nowhere decent to stay. He'd kill for a shower.

Lemon had wandered over to a telegraph pole to read a poster and shouted, 'Bingo!'

She turned in excitement and said, 'Habal Tong temple at 121 Whitlam Street. Let's go Cockie.'

She shook Robbie's hand and then, to his surprise, gave Chris a passionate kiss which he seemed to return.

'You still owe me a heady,' he said.

Lemon grinned as she nudged Tim. 'The man's insatiable ... don't cut him with your teeth next time.'

Chris roared with laughter as Robbie winced with embarrassment. Then Lemon waved and led Tim away to consult a local street map.

'Well ... that was interesting,' said Chris. 'Where now?'

'Accommodation?' suggested Robbie. 'Or a pub?'

'Might be a pub with a room or two,' reckoned Chris and the two of them started towards the water at the end of the street, where there'd have to be pubs.

There were several, but all were closed at that time.

'Quite like the look of that place,' said Robbie, as they paused out the front of the Courthouse Hotel. It was across the road from the river, widening as it joined the broad bay just north of Argyle, and lined with tall buildings to the north-east, south and west.

There was a café open next door so they went in for breakfast and to kill an hour until the pub opened. The coffee was good enough but the papers were full of crap about Habal Tong and their bullshit fuckin' festival on Friday night.

'What about that Lemon?' laughed Chris, dropping a printed copy of the *Ord City Times* onto the table.

'I've already forgotten her,' said Robbie.

'Yeah, fair enough ... imagine putting up with her all your life.'

'Why would you bother?'

'I dunno,' mused Chris. 'It's weird.'

'What is?'

Chris didn't answer, but picked up the newspaper again and started scouring the ads towards the back.

'I've heard,' he said, lowering his voice, 'that they always advertise their whereabouts in the local paper.'

'Who do?'

'Who do you reckon?' said Chris, raising an eyebrow.

'Aah,' replied Robbie, as light dawned.

Chris's brow creased in concentration as his eyes swept the ads pages.

'That'll be it,' he said, turning the paper around and pointing at a small boxed advertisement. 'Institute of Demography ... that's one of the standard aliases. And there's an address in Whitlam Street, which is where we parked.'

'Cool,' said Robbie.

'I reckon we get a room ... sink a couple of quick ones, then go introduce ourselves.'

'Cool.'

• • •

'Boy are you guys lucky,' said the Old Duck at the pub. 'There's not a room to spare in Ord City right now, but someone just cancelled two minutes ago.'

The room had a double bed but the Old Duck reckoned she'd get it changed to twin singles over the course of the day. And it was pretty good. Stinking hot, but clean and Robbie exulted under the shower, washing away days of dust and sweat and then changing into a clean shirt and shorts.

When Chris was dressed they trooped back down to the bar which was already half full at eleven o'clock on a Monday morning.

'Yeah, gets a little noisy,' said the Old Duck, pulling a couple of Emu Exports, which were surprisingly cheap.

It was a beautiful pub – old Queenslander in style, with rooms upstairs and a rooftop bar that opened at night. The front balconies were a riot of bougainvillea but the interior was dim with that sweetish smell of sweat and old beer that all the best pubs seem to get. Robbie and Chris found a high table by a window and settled back to enjoy themselves.

'Now ... we can't hang around here all day,' said Chris, licking froth off his lip. 'If we get too comfortable we'll never make it down the road ... which is why we're here after all.'

Robbie nodded, already scheming to spend as long as possible in what he reckoned was just about the nicest public bar in Australia.

'Feel like a game of stick?'

'Why not.'

• • •

'A fucking queue?' shrieked Lemon in outrage. 'I'm not standing in a fucking queue!'

The queue stretched from the doors of the temple, out onto the street and around the corner.

'There's no option,' said Tim. 'If we want to be registered for *Illumination* we have to get accredited.'

'Accredited? What is this … Nazi Germany?'

Tim winced, as Lemon shouted, and did his best to settle her down.

'It's fair enough, Lemon … there's gonna be thousands … millions maybe at *Illumination* and they have to be organised.'

'They don't have to be fucking organised!' she shouted, getting even louder. 'They just have to believe in The Way! Am I right?'

A couple of people in the queue nodded and Lemon grinned.

'All is nothing and nothing is all. That's all you need! You don't need some fucking piece of plastic round your neck. Am I right?'

A few more nodded and a couple even muttered their agreement.

Lemon started striding up and down the line, haranguing the absent organisers and stirring up the crowd as Tim wilted with tiredness. His battered head was still giving him a lot of grief.

'Standing in queues goes against everything Habal Tong teaches us,' shouted Lemon. 'If you truly believe that all is nothing and nothing is all … *truly* believe it … then you ought to know that whatever is due to you will come regardless of your actions. Your rights are a given … born simply from who you are and what you believe. To stand waiting in a queue is to obey an artificial rule imposed by an irrelevant force. It's wrong!'

'She's right!' shouted a filthy looking bloke with long, brown dreads.

Lemon gave him a delighted high five and he also left the queue, marching up and down with her as she continued to goad their colleagues.

'Habal Tongers don't wait in line,' she shouted. 'You're like lambs in a fucking abattoir.'

'Baaa-aaaa,' shouted her dreadlocked companion. 'Baaa-aaaa!'

'Baaa-aaaa!' echoed a few more, laughing. Then a few more joined in.

'Baaa-aaaa!'

More of them left the line and started milling about Lemon, laughing and baaing in a mad self-parody which perfectly underscored the most profound axiom – all is nothing and nothing is all.

'Let's go!' shouted Lemon.

'Where?' they asked her.

'Anywhere but here!' she replied. 'The only way to scour the queue from your soul is to leave it and go wherever your heart guides you. So let's go! Now!'

She pointed towards the river and first a trickle, then a whole host of the Habal Tongers broke away from the line to race for the water. Tim hefted the backpack and prepared to follow.

'Where do you think you're going?' demanded Lemon.

'Erm … I thought we were leaving.'

'You're not. You're staying in this magically shortened queue to arrange my accreditation. I'll meet you at the temple in half an hour.'

With that she ran after the crowd, still shouting and laughing as they baa-aaed and mooed and neighed themselves hoarse.

• • •

Four beers later, Robbie and Chris had reached the point – go to the Institute of Demography to make enquiries, or stay in the bar.

'It's not like we have to join up today,' said Robbie. 'I reckon we deserve a little R'n'R after that trip through the desert.'

'Maybe,' agreed Chris, lining up a shot on the yellow, then pausing to chalk his cue for the requisite backspin to bring him back for the green.

'And this is a pretty nice bar … '

'True,' agreed Chris, smacking the yellow into the top pocket and grinning at Robbie as the white rolled back neatly to line up the green. If he sank that he'd have a perfect shot on the black.

'And … it's just about lunchtime,' said Robbie, as the green disappeared in the side pocket. He wanted Chris to win as that would put him in a positive mood and more susceptible to the temptation of a lazy afternoon.

The black was a straight poke, but still a longish shot. Chris lined it up and cracked the ball cleanly into the far pocket.

He grinned for a second then dropped his cue onto the table.

'Time to stop fucking about,' he said. 'Let's go.'

Chapter 15

A Decent Feed

Conan was shivering.

He was dimly aware of himself emerging from a dream consciousness to a level below full consciousness. He wanted to return to the dream. It was the only way to escape the cold.

Dream figures slipped around him like ghosts in a long corridor. His mother was talking to him, wanting money.

'They want to move me out of the home,' she was saying. 'I can't afford it anymore because of Virtual Youth.'

'Okay,' said Conan, but then she was gone and Lucia had taken her place.

'You owe me, Conan,' said Lucia.

'I know,' said Conan. 'I know.'

'But you won't pay up, will you?'

'I will.'

'No you won't. No one ever pays ... no one knows me. No one wants me.'

Conan was overcome with a devastating sadness. Almost enough to impel him into waking, but he managed to cling to the dream – still shivering.

'Why are you so cold?' asked Ming.

He was lying in bed with her, covered by just a sheet and it wasn't enough.

'I can make you warm,' she whispered and held him. She smelled wonderful and he felt himself drifting off again, suffused in the smell of Ming.

'He doesn't look too bad.'

Conan opened his eyes.

Two men with oddly bland faces – like cardboard – were watching him.

He closed his eyes again, trying to return to his dream of Ming but he was too cold. The shivering forced him back to the surface of conscious thought and his eyes seemed to open of their own accord.

He was staring at a strange ceiling and was vaguely uncomfortable, and cold under just a sheet. The two men, if they had truly existed, were gone.

Besides the cold he felt stiff and oddly numb. He tried to touch his face and was aware of a tube attached to his hand and a thick gauze bandage around his head. There were machines around him and the pine smell of disinfectant.

There was also a weird pain in his groin and, to Conan's considerable surprise, realised he had a raging erection.

And at that moment a young woman with a clipboard walked into his room.

She was Chinese and for an instant he thought it was Ming, but her eyes widened at the tee-pee in Conan's bed, and she blushed.

Conan also was embarrassed but there was nothing he could do about it. She averted her eyes to read something on her clipboard as Conan imagined himself in a cool mountain stream ... a cool mountain stream ... a cool mountain stream ...

'How are you feeling?' she asked him.

'Where am I?'

'Thomas Aquinas Hospital. Do you remember getting hurt?'

'Not really.'

And he didn't. He had a vague recollection of being chased and then being hit, but it was all very blurry.

'You were found in an alleyway ... unconscious and bleeding. Are you a tourist?'

'No.'

'You live here?'

Despite his woozy state, Conan's protective instincts kicked in to avoid answering questions.

'Thomas Aquinas ... that's the Army of God hospital?'

'Yes.'

'How many other hospitals between here and where I was found?'

'I don't know,' she said returning her attention to the clipboard.

Conan closed his eyes and tried to clear his head. He knew there were three hospitals close together in the middle of Ord City, plus another couple further out. He also knew that the other general hospitals in the centre of town were public, whereas Thomas Aquinas was private.

'Strange they'd bring me here instead of a public.'

'You go wherever there's a bed,' she said, without looking up from the clipboard. Then she examined the drip leading into his hand.

'Is this hurting you?'

'No ... just uncomfortable. How bad am I?'

'Loss of blood ... severe bruising ... but no broken bones. You'll live.'

Finally she met his eye.

'Please tell me your name.'

'My name? You don't know?'

'No. There was no ID ... no wallet or OzBrace ... when you were brought in. Of course, your picture was entered into the admissions computer but there was no match. That happens sometimes when a patient is injured and no longer resembles their own stored image.'

Conan groaned, bored in advance by the need to get his various cards and OzBrace replaced. The nurse was waiting for Conan to give his name and in that moment he made a decision. He didn't want the Army of God to know he was in their hospital so he wouldn't use his real name. AFP investigators were supposed to give a code name in difficult circumstances which would alert their superiors and let them smooth the path, but Conan didn't want Kenny to know he was in trouble.

'Erm ... Craig Bowen.'

'Middle name?'

'Anthony.'

'Date of birth?'

She continued to write down his invented details and Conan knew he had only a short time to get out of the hospital before his subterfuge was revealed. There were serious penalties for identity crime, and even more serious consequences for a man in his position.

'I'll be back soon,' she said. 'Would you like something to eat?'

'No thanks.'

She left the room and immediately Conan sat up, ripped the bandage from his head and pulled the tube from the back of his hand. He held the rumpled sheet hard against his skin to stop the trickle of blood then swung his feet out of bed – wincing with every move. Every muscle activated awoke memories of trauma, although he knew he'd been sedated and the pain would be worse later.

Standing up he was woozy and unbalanced but staggered across the floor to the cupboard in the corner, which contained his clothes. He flung off the flimsy gown and struggled into his torn and soiled suit. There was blood on his shirt and the elbow was ripped out of his left sleeve, but escape was more important than sartorial splendour.

Patting his pockets he realised that all his personal effects were gone except his phone and the key to Ming's apartment.

'Where's the patient?'

Conan stiffened as he recognised Major Lammas's voice outside his room and without a second thought stepped into the cupboard which had contained his clothes. It was barely big enough to hold him and he didn't have time to close the door properly, but he heard footsteps, and then:

'Isn't this the room?'

There was a knock close by, and then a door opened.

'He's not in the en suite,' said a woman, an older woman by the sound of her.

'That's odd,' said Lammas. 'Surely he hasn't discharged himself.'

'Well he's not here now and we're late.'

'Yes … sorry about that. I just thought it would be amusing to see the smug Agent Tooley reliant on our goodwill and mercy … but never mind.'

'We don't even know it was him, Thomas,' said the woman. 'He was so beaten up, it could have been anyone.'

'It was him, I'm certain.'

Conan heard their footsteps depart, and immediately left the cupboard and sidled to the doorway. Glancing down the corridor he could see Lammas and another black uniformed woman – probably Major Maddox – striding towards the elevators. He waited until they entered, then shuffled as fast as he could manage (which was not very) towards the lifts, just in time to see the doors roll shut and arrows indicating the lift was descending.

There was a stairwell next to the lifts so Conan went down as fast as he could, pausing at each landing to listen for voices. By the time he reached the lower ground floor he was covered in sweat, tired and sore, but the old hunting instinct was strong. He glanced around the corner and saw Lammas and Maddox disappearing down a long, yellow-lit corridor that looked like it had been built decades before the rest of the hospital. Conan followed, keeping close to the right wall where a number of linen trolleys were parked, the only cover in case they stopped or turned.

The long corridor twisted around a couple of dog-legs – each of which required cautious navigation – then suddenly they were outside and walking through a car park. Conan's heart sank, as he could hardly follow if they got into a car, but they proceeded through the car park, past a boom gate, and into a laneway.

The city had entered the violet hour as dusk settled and the noise, smells and heat slowly registered on Conan's part-sedated brain. He felt more alert but also sick and tired as he merged with the bodies going about their evening business. Fortunately, Lammas was tall, which was why Conan saw him turn right into a narrower lane with fewer people. They were heading slightly downhill and soon entered a warren of laneways thick with people shouting in Urdu, Farsi, Thai and Cantonese and clustering around the stalls and outdoor kitchens of a night market.

Conan felt a sense of urgency and pushed through the crowds – unnoticed as most were doing the same. The air was filled with glorious cooking smells and Conan's mouth was watering. It was a long time since he'd eaten and, with the drugs leaching from his system, his hunger returned like a form of torture. He'd lost sight of Lammas and Maddox but pushed ahead anyway until he found himself by the waterside. There were people streaming along the promenade and Conan found himself dawdling, hunting instincts waning, but still casting about for his lost quarry.

There was a floating Chinese restaurant – an old ferry boat – moored alongside a pier which was lit up like a New Year's festival. It was a frenzy of activity and the sound and smells were a torment, so attractive did it look to Conan who was just about ready to surrender. Sitting down at that restaurant for a couple of cold beers and some spicy Szechuan was suddenly his concept of heaven.

That's when he saw Captain Melodie Roberts.

His initial thought was that she must be going to meet the other two and his hunting instinct surged back into place.

What's more, she wasn't wearing her uniform. Instead of the severe black skirt and jacket she wore tan culottes and a light floral top, typical tourist wear.

She also, despite the hour, had dark sunnies that obscured most of her face and seemed to be watching the floating restaurant. Conan stepped behind an old power pole from where he could watch her.

In different gear she seemed softer somehow, more like the girl next door than the dark dominatrix of the church. She was staring intently at her phone and had an ear plug in place, and that's when Conan finally twigged.

There was a shop in front of him selling mainly touristy rubbish, including racks of cheap plastic sunglasses. Conan took a pair of pink-lensed sunnies and slipped them into his pocket while pretending to look at another pair, then strolled casually towards Captain Roberts.

But at that moment she thrust her phone into a satchel and strode towards the floating restaurant. There were two Chinese bouncers at the bottom of the gangplank but they smiled at Captain Roberts. With his new sunnies in place (and everything looking strangely brighter) Conan followed her, nodding at the bouncers as he went. Their grins faded to polite frowns, noting his dishevelled appearance, but they didn't stop him.

The restaurant was like a controlled, fragrant riot with waiters swooping and shouting amid the din of conversation. It was obviously popular because it was three quarters full even though it was early for dinner. Captain Roberts was escorted by a waiter as Conan hung back, sweeping the room for Lammas and Maddox.

And there they were, sitting at a large table in the stern corner on the waterside. Captain Roberts was shown to a table in the middle of the restaurant, obscured from the corner table by a potted palm.

'Table for one?'

Conan realised a waiter was talking to him.

'No thanks, I'm with her.'

He took off in Captain Roberts' wake and slipped into the seat opposite her, barely repressing laughter at the look of surprise on her face, followed by her usual hostility.

'What do you think you're doing?' she asked between gritted teeth.

'They let anyone into ASIO these days,' he replied as she glared.

'I'm not in ASIO.'

'ASIS then, or ASD … or ONA. You're using a unidirectional listening device and those don't get handed out to just anyone.'

'Shut up!' she snapped and thrust the phone again into her bag with the evident intention of leaving.

'Hang on,' said Conan, grabbing her hand.

'What?'

He nodded towards Lammas and Maddox, both of whom had their backs to the rest of the restaurant.

'Don't you want to see who they're meeting … listen to their conversation? I'll bet you can get a decent feed on them in here.'

'I'm not staying here with you,' she hissed. 'And you look ridiculous in those glasses.'

'That's better.'

She blinked at him, then said, 'What are you talking about?'

'Criticising my appearance makes us sound more like a couple.'

'A couple?'

Her face went pink and white with fury and Conan raised a finger to his lips.

'Couples are invisible,' he said, '… but single women dining alone attract attention … especially a woman as beautiful as you.'

'Please don't do that,' she said, but Conan could sense her anger fading, the part of it above the surface at least.

She glanced over at Lammas and Maddox, still by themselves at a round table set for several people.

'Of course,' said Conan, '… if they look this way we'll have to convince them we're a real couple and kiss … like in the movies.'

'In your dreams,' she sneered. 'Besides, you look like you haven't washed in weeks.'

'It's days, not weeks … and I've been in hospital after getting bashed.'

'You were *bashed*?'

For the first time she looked something less than furious and peered at the bruising on his face that was partly hidden in the dim light.

'By whom?'

'A gang of Chinese blokes … I'm asking the Ord City police to be on the lookout for three men with black hair.'

'You want drinks?'

A man with black hair appeared at their table with a Pod and stylus.

'I'll have a Tsing Tao if you've got it,' said Conan.

Captain Roberts mouth was set in tight line of disapproval, but eventually asked for a glass of white wine.

'What about food?' asked the waiter.

'I'm not hungry,' said Captain Roberts.

'Yes you are darling,' said Conan and her eyes blazed for a moment, but then she glanced again at the menu and asked for the prawn and crab omelette.

'I'll have the special fried rice and the hot Szechuan chicken,' said Conan. 'As hot as the chef can make.'

'That's pretty hot,' said the waiter. 'I better call fire brigade now.'

'Just bring beer,' said Conan, and the waiter laughed as he walked away.

'You're paying by the way,' said Conan. 'My wallet and OzBrace were stolen.'

'Real gentleman, aren't you.'

Conan glanced over his shoulder at Lammas and Maddox.

'Well come on, Mel, spill the beans. Why are you following them and who do you work for?'

'My name is Captain Roberts.'

'Too much of a mouthful,' said Conan, shaking his head.

'Well, don't call me anything. I'd much prefer it if you left.'

'But we both know that won't be happening, so why not tell me who you work for.'

'You know for whom I work … the Army of God.'

'Who you really work for … the ones supplying you with the field gear.'

'I don't know what you're talking about. The listening app is available to anyone.'

'It is?' asked Conan, realising as he spoke that it made more sense than his original suspicion. 'But why are you spying on your fiancé?'

Mel cast her eyes down to the table.

'It's none of your business.'

'If it's anything to do with my investigation it's very much my business.'

'I've already told you ... I know nothing about Bruce and Michael.'

'But there's something you're not telling me. There's *definitely* something Lammas isn't telling me.'

Their drinks arrived and Conan sighed with pleasure as the cold beer fizzed in his throat. He glanced through the palm leaves at Lammas and Maddox again, still sitting by themselves, and made a decision. It was an unorthodox and unauthorised decision that could get him disciplined (more so), but Conan was certain that Melodie Roberts had a part of the jigsaw that was eluding him.

'Okay Mel,' he said, ignoring the flash of anger on her face, 'I have a proposition. I'll tell you a bit more about my investigation and then maybe, in return, you'll tell me a bit about yours.'

She sipped her wine but made no other sound or gesture.

'Right ... the Fong and Wing Ho murders are not the only reason I'm here in Ord City.'

She continued to ignore him.

'I'm also investigating a potential Habal Tong terror cell which has downloaded specifications for the main NBN node south of the city.'

'And what on earth does that have to do with me?' she demanded.

'Nothing ... probably.'

'So why tell me about it?'

'I'm giving you a broader perspective. This city is a powder keg, in case you hadn't noticed.'

'It's always a powder keg.'

'And now it's sitting in a ring of naked flames. And for some reason no one will talk to me about it, not even my colleagues.'

'Well, maybe it's something to do with your personal style ... you should reflect on that.'

'Also, I've been chased twice, beaten up, and my friend Ming has been abducted.'

Melodie's eyes widened.

'Dr Chen?'

'She went for a walk to the shops yesterday morning and never returned. And what's more, the CCTV footage for that part of the street, at the relevant time, has been wiped. It can't be hacked, so … do you have any idea what level security clearance would be needed to pull a stunt like that?'

Mel turned to glance at Lammas then swallowed the rest of her wine in a single gulp.

'What?' said Conan, sensing she might be about to add to the conversation.

'Nothing,' stammered Mel, then ducked as a waiter led another small entourage past them.

Conan recognised Colonel Chard, the Chief Administrator of Ord City, flanked by a couple of heavies. She made directly for Lammas and Maddox and sat at their round table, while the heavies sat at a table for two, partly obscuring Conan's view.

'Interesting,' said Conan.

'They meet all the time,' said Mel. 'It's not the conspiracy you're looking for.'

Conan suddenly grabbed the arm of a passing waiter.

'Another Tsing Tao thanks mate … and what was the wine?'

'Brookland Valley from Margaret River,' said the waiter. '… good Western Australia wine.'

'Bring us a bottle … and another glass.'

Mel didn't object, and when the waiter had gone she said, 'What time did Dr Chen disappear?'

'Just before seven yesterday morning.'

Mel nodded, thinking, and Conan could sense her thawing a little further.

'He didn't like her laughing at your rudeness,' said Mel.

'What rudeness?'

'Telling Thomas he didn't believe. That's profoundly offensive, as I'm sure you know … but she laughed and it upset him.'

'Why should it upset him? What connection does she have with him?'

'She works for an AOG hospital and Thomas is one of the two most senior officers in Ord City … most senior when he is made a colonel shortly.'

'So? She's not a member of the AOG and he's not yet in charge of the hospital.'

'It's a matter of respect … anyway, don't start speculating about his involvement.'

'Why not?'

'Because I can guarantee he had nothing to do with it.'

Their drinks arrived and both sat back in their chairs to allow the waiter to pour Conan's beer and top up Melodie's glass.

'How can you guarantee something like that? You don't know all his movements … which is obvious or you wouldn't be here following him.'

Mel snatched up her glass and looked away angrily, as Conan cursed himself for going in too hard just as she was opening up.

'Sorry,' he said. 'I …'

'No, I don't know all his movements,' said Mel, interrupting him. 'But I know where he was all Saturday night and Sunday morning.'

'You do?'

Conan saw her face darken in the half light and realised she was blushing.

'Okay,' he said, twigging to her embarrassment. 'So you know where he was but you don't know he didn't arrange something.'

'It would have been difficult … I was with him every moment between the time we left the stadium to halfway through yesterday morning. He spoke to no one else.'

'Every moment?'

'Yes,' she said, defiantly, but colouring even darker.

'So every time he went to the bathroom … and you never slept.'

'No, of course not, but …'

'So he may have sent a message to someone while you or he were in the bathroom … or while you were sleeping?'

At that moment their food arrived. The smell of the sizzling Szechuan chicken was like paradise and Conan felt his mouth fill with saliva like Pavlov's dog.

'Unlikely,' said Mel.

Conan gave himself up to the glorious food for a moment,

savouring the exotic smells and flavours that went so perfectly with the cold beer. Melodie picked up her knife and fork and dabbed at the omelette.

After several restorative mouthfuls, Conan remembered his investigation.

'I've learned all about the *Epistola Clementis* in the last couple of days.'

'Good for you.'

'Fascinating story … if it's true.'

'It's an apocryphal story,' insisted Mel. 'And it happened too long ago for anyone to know anything for certain.'

'Unlike the resurrection,' grinned Conan, unable to resist the cheap shot, which she simply ignored.

'Whether or not it's true doesn't really matter,' said Conan. 'What matters is that Bruce and Michael were interested in it … *so* interested that it was written on a card found in Wing Ho's shoe and was the last thing researched on his laptop. We know they spoke with the AOG about it … at the Great Debate perhaps … but no one from AOG will talk about it. Can't you see why that interests me?'

Melodie glanced over at the other table and said, 'They never *stopped* talking about it. It was an obsession with them, and every conversation would eventually be drawn around to it … questioning the entire basis of the church. How can we do our good works when our fundamental reason for being is cast into doubt?'

She took a thoughtful sip of wine. 'The only thing that puzzles me is they learned about the *Epistola* from Tom.'

'Really?'

'Yes … he certainly regretted telling them. That's probably why he hates to talk about it now.'

'I wonder if they wanted to get the press interested in the story,' said Conan. 'The last person Wing Ho rang was Ronny Kwai.'

'He writes about sport.'

'He's a journalist … and a lot richer than journalists tend to be. I've no doubt he's a significant player in this town.'

'But writing about the *Epistola* … it's hardly news, or a motive for murder,' said Mel. 'The church has suffered much stronger attacks than that over the centuries.'

'And look how many millions have been killed because of it,' laughed Conan, and once again cursed himself for going in hard when she was being responsive.

'But I agree with you,' he said, trying to mollify. 'It's not a motive for murder in secular Australia in 2030.'

He finished his second beer and picked up the wine.

'What's this like?'

'Very nice.'

Conan poured himself a glass and topped up hers, wondering whether it was the glass and a half of wine which had relaxed her slightly.

'Aren't you going to try and hear their conversation?'

'I don't think there'll be anything much to hear just yet ... they're clearly waiting for others.'

Conan shrugged, just as Ronny Kwai was shown to the round table by two fawning waiters.

Neither spoke for a few moments and Conan felt both his antennae and the hair on the back of his neck rising.

'Sure you don't want to turn on that listening app?'

Mel pulled the phone back out of her bag, inserted one of the ear plugs, and positioned the phone on the table.

'Does it record?' he asked.

Mel nodded, and listened for a few moments.

'It's hard to get a clear feed in all this noise, but they're still waiting for someone else.'

'Did they say who?'

Mel ignored him so Conan tucked into the last of his chicken. It was bloody fantastic.

It was also fantastic that he seemed to be making progress – on two fronts. One front was the investigation. The fact that the four were all meeting was not, of itself, significant. They had all been present at Ronny's party a couple of night's previously, so they were hardly a secret cabal. But Conan's instinct told him differently. Something was up.

The other front, of course, was Mel. He sensed that she was increasingly relaxed with him and found himself speculating on the future of her relationship with Lammas. It couldn't be healthy to feel as though she needed to follow him about. And she was so beautiful ...

'What are you staring at?'

Her eyes seared and Conan felt like he'd been jabbed with a cattle prod.

'Sorry ... I didn't realise I was staring.'

'You're too familiar, Agent Tooley. Don't presume on my good will because I tolerate you at this table. I don't wish to make a scene ... that is the only reason I haven't left.'

'You also want to find out who he's meeting,' said Conan. 'But sorry if I offend you.'

'If I believed you truly *were* sorry I might feel more kindly disposed ... but I suppose that's what comes of dealing with criminals all the time. You pick up their manners.'

Conan didn't know whether to feel angry or amused. He was also disturbed by how attracted he was to her despite the fact that he had committed in his own mind to Ming just the previous morning – Ming who in all likelihood needed him desperately at that moment. And, of course, the Lucia question would always complicate his relationship status.

'I truly am an arsehole,' thought Conan in a moment of startling insight. 'I don't deserve a partner if I can't stay constant for more than five minutes. Isn't that what my mother keeps telling me?'

Mel was fiddling with her phone, moving it and realigning it to get the best feed.

'No, my mother tells me the opposite,' thought Conan with a smile. 'She tells me the only way to succeed with a partner is not to care about them.'

Mel stiffened in response to something she'd heard, and he wanted to snatch the other ear plug. He opened his mouth to ask a question but she held a hand up.

Then the waiters were clearing their plates and Conan felt they were being hurried along. He knew they needed to stay longer so poured the last of the wine into their glasses (rather overfilling them) and said, 'Can you bring another bottle? And the dessert menu?'

The waiter stared for a moment, but nodded and hurried away with the empty bottle.

'What on earth are you doing?' demanded Mel.

'I'm presuming that you don't want to leave just yet and getting us a reason to stay longer.'

Mel glanced down at the cleared table and understood.

'I see ... but I can't drink any more wine. Why didn't you just order dessert?'

'You can't linger over dessert. A bottle of wine buys us the best part of another hour.'

'Well, you'll have to drink it,' she said, taking a sip from her own glass. 'Actually, it's rather good, isn't it.'

'Very,' said Conan. 'Now what was so interesting on the listening app a minute ago?'

'It was nothing,' lied Melodie in a faltering voice that made Conan laugh out loud.

'Will you shut up?' she hissed. 'Stop drawing attention to us.'

Conan blew her a kiss as the wine arrived and a couple of menus were dropped on the table with very poor grace.

'I do think they want us to leave,' he said. 'Who are they expecting, do you think?'

'I've no idea.'

A couple of other tables were cleared proximate to the round table, and both were populated by more heavies.

'I advise you to start being very friendly,' said Conan. 'If they keep swapping customers for security guards we'll start to look conspicuous unless we behave like a proper couple.'

Mel glanced around unhappily. Then she shrugged and said, 'You're right. I'll endeavour to be friendly ... but it's not easy, Agent Tooley.'

Conan grinned, and took her hand. She stiffened, for a moment, but didn't pull away.

'It might help if you start calling me Conan. That's what a girlfriend would call me.'

'Isn't Dr Chen your girlfriend?'

If Conan was surprised by the question, he was more surprised by the fact that he didn't really know the answer.

'Well, no ... not really. We're friends but ... '

He shrugged and looked again at the round table where everyone seemed a bit tense.

'What about you and the Major?' asked Conan.

'What about us?'

He had to hang onto her hand which she'd nervously pulled away in response to his question, but then she settled again.

'This isn't normal couple behaviour,' said Conan, '… fiancée stalking fiancé through a crowded city.'

'Surely it's one of the clichés of your detective fiction,' sneered Mel, and then laughed despite herself. The first time Conan had seen her show any sense of humour.

'At first I thought you must be working for ASIO,' said Conan, feeling her hand relax, although the prim frown was quickly back in place. 'But that's clearly not the case. So … just curious about his movements, huh?'

'In fact that's the truth,' she admitted. 'And I'm more than a little ashamed of myself … not least as these are people he talks about all the time, so it's not as though he's hiding anything … '

'And yet?'

She was silent and glanced surreptitiously at the round table while sipping wine.

'And yet … I can't tell you Agent … Conan … what exactly it is that gnaws at me. But I feel unused … a wasted resource.'

'You feel you should be sitting at that table right now and party to all the secrets.'

She stared at him and blushed, then took another sip of wine and didn't object when Conan topped up her glass from the new bottle.

'It sounds childish, doesn't it.'

'It's not at all childish,' said Conan, examining her hand with the engagement ring. 'Why shouldn't you be part of the inner cabinet? You're clearly very talented.'

'Please don't patronise me.'

'I'm not patronising Mel, I'm admiring.'

'And don't call me Mel.'

'That's what I'd call you if you were my girlfriend … and for the next hour or so you are my girlfriend so just relax will you. Mel.'

Again she smiled, almost despite herself.

'You're not so bad yourself … I suppose,' she said, sipping wine again.

'My mother thinks I'm too nice to women, which is why they walk all over me.'

'They do?'

'I was married,' he said. 'Another of your detective story clichés I'm afraid ... it's a hard life for a partner.'

'Do you really *want* a partner?'

'Of course I do. Doesn't everyone?'

'I used to think so,' said Mel, sipping wine again. 'But I'm not so sure now. I can see the upside to being single.'

'Really? Odd statement for an engaged woman.'

He felt her hand tense and wondered if he'd gone too far again, but she relaxed and said, 'I'm in an unusual relationship. Tom is active in politics and has a high public profile. On top of that there are all sorts of security aspects to his work and all of this ... inevitably ... comes between us. We talk about it all the time, but ... '

'But talking about it doesn't help you feeling ignored and wasted.'

'I suppose that's true. I ought to be stronger ... Tom would be furious if he caught me. I don't know what's come over me.'

'You're rebelling against an unequal relationship,' said Conan.

'I am not! And we're not unequal.'

'Maybe not true inequality,' back-pedalled Conan, '... like a woman having to walk five paces behind her husband ... but even artificially imposed inequality like yours is going to be hard on a couple who in all other ways should be equal.'

Mel sipped wine – partly mollified – and glanced again over at the round table. You could twang the tension like an overwound string the way they all sat without speaking, drumming their fingers and looking at watches.

'Whoever they're waiting for is late,' said Conan, topping up her glass again, and his own.

'You're an unusual man,' said Mel. 'Few men would even know an equal relationship was a thing ... let alone talk about it so articulately.'

'That sounds suspiciously like a compliment.'

'Don't get carried away.'

'Can I ask a personal question?'

She stared at him for a moment, then said, 'It depends on the question.'

'Personal about me ... not about you. I'm curious as to why you were so immediately unfriendly when we met. What had I done to upset you?'

'Two things,' she said. 'First of all, I was busy and you were wasting my time with a lot of questions which had already been asked.'

'Fair enough. And the other thing?'

'You are lecherous.'

Wine exploded from Conan's nose and mouth as he reacted mid-sip to her statement.

'Lecherous?' he exclaimed, wiping his face and dabbing at his shirt.

'Yes … I saw that look in your eye the moment we met … and caught you staring at my bottom.'

Conan couldn't help but laugh.

'Sorry,' he said. 'I really don't mean to be like that, it … it just happens,' he finished lamely.

'And that's just not a good enough excuse,' she said. 'You are a civilised, sentient being … you ought to be way beyond all that.'

'I'm still an animal,' said Conan, '… fundamentally. We all are … even you.'

'I am not!'

'Of course you are. We have a body as well as a soul you know … and your body is extremely attractive.'

This time she really did snatch her hand away, but the movement caught the eye of the waiter so she hastily took his hand again, after another sip of wine.

'I don't mean to be offensive, Mel … these are just the facts of life. The race would die out if men and women stopped finding each other attractive. And just because I find you attractive doesn't mean I'm about to chase you into the cot.'

'About to *what*?'

'Nothing.'

'No dessert.'

They looked up at a stony faced waiter who placed the bill on the table.

'No time for dessert … drink up quickly please.'

He splashed the second bottle into both their glasses without quite emptying it and took it away before they could object.

'Great service here,' said Conan. 'It's pretty obvious they want us to go.'

A glance around the restaurant showed it was now less than half full with a quarter of the tables filled by heavies.

'What on earth is going on here tonight?' wondered Conan.

Mel picked up the bill and held it against her OzBrace until it buzzed green.

'You were talking about equality,' she said primly, but there was a smile beneath the stern facade again and Conan was encouraged.

'Being equally attracted to each other is just as important as all the other parts of an equal relationship,' he said. 'Probably the most important part as none of the other stuff matters if there's no chemistry to bring you together in the first place.'

They were holding hands again.

'Isn't that how you got together with Tom? Chemistry?'

Mel took another big sip of wine.

'I admired him. He ... well, you've heard his voice ... and he's so passionate about our work.'

'But what about the chemistry ... the overwhelming physical attraction?'

'It's none of your business.'

'So ... no chemistry?'

Her eyes blazed, again, and he knew he'd gone too far, but she reached for her glass and finished nearly all of it.

'Can I ask *you* a personal question?' she demanded, with the careful enunciation inspired by too much alcohol.

'That depends on the question,' he smiled, realising she was a little tipsy.

Suddenly she blushed.

'What?'

'It's too personal,' she said, now slurring a little. 'I shouldn't be asking.'

'That's okay, Mel,' he soothed. 'You're my temporary girlfriend in an equal relationship with no secrets. Ask away.'

'Well, how old are you?'

'Thirty-six.'

'Thirty-six ... been married before. Many other girlfriends?'

'A handful over the years ... I'm not exactly Don Juan.'

'But ... you're fairly experienced.'

Conan frowned for a moment, scarcely believing the turn of

conversation.

'Are you asking how many times I've had sex?'

Again she blushed, but she didn't look away.

'Well,' said Conan, both surprised and amused by how effective alcohol could be at removing inhibitions, 'I couldn't tell you exactly how many times ... but a few hundred I suppose. Why?'

'I've done it twice.'

Once again the wine exploded from Conan's nose and mouth.

'Sorry,' he gasped. 'Why are you telling me this?'

'Because there's something I want to understand ... I don't think I'm doing it right.'

'Good God!'

'Don't blaspheme, Conan.'

'Sorry ... but ... how old are you?'

'Thirty-one.'

'And only done it twice ... despite being so amazingly beautiful.'

'What's superficial beauty got to do with morality.'

'Nothing, but it has a lot to do with opportunity. Blokes would've been hunting you since you were twelve.'

'For the truly moral that doesn't matter. I only lowered my resolve to stay celibate after engagement ... and now I regret it.'

'Why?'

'Because we weren't married ... so the sex didn't work.'

'Didn't work? There's no such thing as sex not working. It always works.'

'Not for me, and I'm certain Tom didn't enjoy it.'

'Well ... he's an idiot.'

The waiter snatched the paid bill tag away and tried to take their glasses but Conan hung onto his own and demanded Mel's be placed back on the table.

'Closing shortly,' said the waiter. 'Drink up ... time to go.'

'Yeah, won't be long, pal,' said Conan.

'He's *not* an idiot,' said Mel, as though nothing had happened.

'Of course he's an idiot,' said Conan. 'And if you really were my girlfriend ... '

He paused.

'Yes?'

'Yes what?'

'If I really was your girlfriend?'

Conan licked his lips, feeling a little drunk and wondering what were the perfect words to take the surprisingly intimate conversation to the next level, but there was a sudden silence throughout the restaurant and Conan could see all eyes looking over his head.

He turned and saw a small Chinese man walking toward the round table and then some applause broke out. The little man, looking a bit like Ho Chi Minh with the round spectacles, walked up to the table and bowed, as the others all stood and bowed in return.

'Time to go,' hissed the waiter accompanied by one of the heavies.

'Okay,' said Conan, turning away from the round table and pulling Melodie to her feet.

'Come on darling,' he said as she openly stared, to the obvious anger of the waiter and his burly companion.

Eventually she allowed herself to be dragged away, as Conan tried to leave inconspicuously, with the waiter and bouncer dogging their footsteps.

• • •

'That's Ah Li Wu.'

'I know.'

They were standing out on the street, looking back at the floating restaurant.

'I didn't know he was real,' said Mel. 'I thought he was a sort of … composite Chinese bogey man … invented to scare children.'

'Nope. That's the reclusive … semi-divine … founder of Habal Tong, meeting with your lot, Chard and Ronny Kwai just a few days before *Illumination* and the First Wave.'

Mel was still shaking her head in astonishment.

'I think it's time you told me everything you managed to hear up there.'

'I can play it back for you,' she said, 'but there wasn't much. They were trying to make small talk while occasionally referring to *him* and the fact that *he* was late. They never said his name or why they're meeting.'

'I saw you react at one point,' said Conan. 'What was that?'

'Tom made a joke about you being in hospital,' said Mel. 'I thought it in poor taste but … shouldn't we be trying to hear their conversation now?'

'We should … but there's no way we're getting back in that restaurant, and the river, while not *entirely* full of crocodiles, is full enough.'

'We could steal a boat,' said Mel, 'and park about thirty metres away. We'd …'

'Steal a boat?' he echoed, amazed at how much she'd changed in an hour. 'Why not just hire a boat?'

'From where?' she demanded, and Conan saw her point. There were a handful of tourist boat hire places, but none were nearby and none were open after dark.

'Borrow a boat is what I really mean. Come on.'

She started striding along the riverfront which was mainly boardwalks and concrete piers. There were any number of boats but most were overlarge, and there were plenty of people around.

'We need to find a rowboat,' she said.

'Do you know how to row?'

'No … but how hard can it be?'

Conan was aware that Mel was more than a trifle tipsy and felt guilty that he'd encouraged her to drink and now she was inviting danger. Still, he couldn't deny that he was enjoying himself and the sudden change in her demeanour was exciting.

Searching away from the brighter lights they soon found an old style row boat tied up to some rusty metal steps. After a quick glance around Mel clambered down and stepped aboard, almost falling as the boat moved under her weight.

Conan ignored her giggling as he pulled the boat closer by its rope, and then worked at the knots until it was free. He pushed the boat away from the steps and went to take the oars, but Mel said, 'What do you think you're doing? This is an equal relationship, right?'

She crammed next to him on the thwart and they both took an oar. And immediately started going in circles as they rowed in opposite directions.

'Sorry … for the purposes of rowing,' said Conan, 'one of us has to be captain. You or me?'

'You can do it,' said Mel. 'But only because you asked nicely.'

She smelled wonderful and Conan could feel himself becoming aroused as she moved against him, struggling with her oar.

'Stop,' he commanded, as she started giggling again. 'Like this ... okay.'

He reached back with his oar, and she matched him and slowly they made progress.

'Let's go first out into the darkness of the bay ... and then approach the restaurant and ... see what we can hear.'

They pulled together for a few strokes, moving reasonably silently, and slowly got the hang of it.

'What's that?' she said.

'What?'

'Red lights in the water, like eyes.'

'Probably a croc.'

'Really?'

'Either that or reflection from the city lights. Dive in and find out.'

'They can't come in the boat can they?'

'Probably not. They'd just smash the boat though, if they wanted us. Like cracking a walnut'

'Shit!'

Conan was so surprised he stopped rowing.

'Melodie Roberts!'

There was a bit of a silence, then, 'Oh dear. I never swear ... and I'm mortified. I've obviously drunk too much.'

'It's okay to swear when you're in mortal danger,' soothed Conan. 'There are crocs everywhere.'

And there were. The river – widening into Lake Argyle at this point – was full of red glowing eyes, all of them staring at Mel and Conan.

'They might be freshies,' said Conan, '... because there're a lot of them and salties tend to be solitary. But don't panic ... just keep rowing evenly and they'll leave us alone.'

He could feel her shivering despite the warm night and looking over his shoulder started rowing a little harder to bring the boat to starboard and start heading towards the floating restaurant.

It was about two hundred metres away and, as they glided slowly closer, Conan was pleased to note their boat was a dark green colour which didn't seem to reflect any of the city lights blazing around them.

'Sound travels a long way over water,' warned Conan, 'so talk in whispers from now. And maybe we should set up the listening app?'

They paused while Mel fumbled in her bag for her phone, then gave him one of the ear plugs.

'I won't turn it on yet,' she said. 'No point until we're a bit closer.'

They recommenced rowing – fairly adeptly now – and were soon gliding about fifty metres from the restaurant's stern.

'I reckon we can get about ten or fifteen metres closer before we're in danger of being spotted,' said Conan.

Mel switched on the app and immediately there was noise, indecipherable, like hundreds of people shouting on the other side of a thick wall.

They took another couple of pulls and again glided to a stop. There were snippets of coherent conversation now and Conan dropped the anchor overboard. There was little discernible current but the boat soon aligned itself with the flow – drifting at anchor some thirty-odd metres from the round table – which they couldn't see as that was on the upper deck.

Conan could make no sense of the babble but Mel kept training the phone on a particular point and occasionally there were a few scraps of words that may have come from the round table.

'That was Tom,' whispered Mel, '… asking about the hospital.'

'I didn't hear,' replied Conan.

'And that was Maddox,' said Mel, 'talking about Ferrier.'

'Who?'

'You met him at Kwai's on Saturday … runs one of the purification plants.'

'Oh right … why would they be …'

'Water's always been a big deal up here,' said Mel. 'The infrastructure has always been a couple of steps behind the population which has risen so quickly since 2023. There are four plants now along the river with another two planned.'

'Has Ah Li Wu said anything?'

'I don't think so … but I don't know his voice.'

At that moment Conan could clearly hear Lammas asking about payment and a woman's voice – possibly Colonel Chard's – dismissing him. 'Payment will be made as originally agreed and not otherwise.'

'I have run risks. I am more exposed than you others.'

'That is why you are being paid. Now … '

Conan was suddenly dazzled by a spot light and the loud roar of a motor boat drowned out all other noise.

'Crap!' said Conan.

The boat was coming quickly but would have been a hundred metres away.

'Over the side!'

'What?'

Without another word, Conan picked up Mel and threw her into the water. Then he dived in after her and struck out for the bank about thirty metres away. His head was mainly under water but whenever he broke surface he seemed to hear shouting and the motor boat getting louder. The steps of a pier were only ten metres away. Then five. He was aware of Mel swimming strongly just ahead of him and was relieved that he hadn't had to help her – they would have been caught for sure otherwise, and were still more than likely to be. There were also the crocodiles he remembered at that moment and could just about feel jaws closing on his feet as Mel reached the stairs, which were suddenly blazing with light and there was shouting behind them.

'Quickly,' said Conan, as Mel dragged herself out of the water, somehow still clutching her handbag. She fled up the stairs as Conan followed dripping. There were people shouting from the water and a couple shouting from the top deck of the restaurant, but Conan simply ran. Grabbing Mel's hand he flew across the well-lit road into a slightly darker alley, which was still crammed with people and food stalls.

The shouts behind them faded and after taking a couple of turns designed to keep them more-or-less in a straight line away from the river they slowed to a walk and realised they were both laughing.

'Oh damn … I've lost my phone in the river,' said Mel, but she was still grinning. 'What do we do now?'

They were in Whitlam Street and Conan realised they were just one block from Argyle where Ming's place was. He felt his pocket and was relieved that the key had survived its dunking.

'Come with me.'

• • •

Ming's place was exactly as he'd left it.

They closed the door and were suddenly self-conscious about the fact that they were still holding hands. Conan opened his fingers and she gave his hand a squeeze before blushing and letting go.

They were all but dry again after walking through the balmy night, but they smelled of diesel and mud and a shower was uppermost in Conan's thoughts.

'Let me show you the bathroom.'

She followed him through the apartment.

'This is Dr Chen's place?'

'Ming's place, yes.'

'But she's not your girlfriend … '

'No. My only girlfriend right now is you … unless our temporary fling is over.'

'Not quite,' said Mel, then smiled. 'It's been a very strange night, Conan. I know I've drunk too much but I feel … different … liberated somehow.'

'That's a dangerous thought,' laughed Conan. 'You never know where liberation might take you.'

He led her through the bedroom to the en suite and switched on the light.

'You can have first shower,' he said, as she leaned against him in the doorway.

'Back in the restaurant,' she said, putting her arms around him, '… you were about to tell me what you would do if I really was your girlfriend … in a truly equal relationship.'

Conan had been aware of her thawing towards him but the sudden increase in momentum was almost frightening.

'Well … as equal partners,' he said, 'I suppose we ought to shower together.'

She just smiled.

'… which takes our pretend temporary relationship up a pretty big notch ... and you're engaged.'

Mel examined her hand, then slipped the ring off her finger and dropped it into her handbag, which was still soaking wet.

'Okay,' said Conan, and immediately started removing his clothing.

Mel watched for a couple of seconds, then started unbuttoning her nice floral top which was streaked with something evil from the river. Soon they were down to just their underwear and Conan turned on the shower – which like all Ord City showers had a water saving head that permitted only a moderate stream.

'Get in as you are so you can wash your undies while we shower,' he said.

'Aren't we going to take them off?' she asked, sounding oddly disappointed.

'And reveal our animal selves?' laughed Conan.

He threw their soiled clothes into the washing machine, dimmed the lights as low as they could go, then joined her under the water, reaching for the soap and washing every inch of her body, relieving her of bra and then panties as he went.

Then she took the soap and returned the favour while he stepped out of his undies that were already leaving nothing to the imagination given his arousal. When they were both naked they finally kissed and he just held her for a while, leaning against the shower wall, almost delirious with pleasure under warm water in the dim light.

'I can't believe this is happening,' he whispered. 'Two hours ago I would have said you hated me more than any other man on the planet.'

'I did,' she said, '... or thought I did. But I'm suddenly very conscious that I'm an animal. It feels natural with you, somehow.'

He turned the shower off and they stepped out, examining each other in the dim light. Conan took a fluffy pink towel from a rack and draped it around her shoulders, kissing her again as he dragged it down her body. Then he pulled another towel for himself off the rack, banishing any weird or guilty thoughts about it being Ming's place, and rubbed himself briskly.

Mel hung her towel back on the rack then walked into the bedroom and pulled back the sheets. Then she lay on the bed, waiting. Conan was so overcome by the beautiful sight he almost felt the need to kneel on the floor in worship, but he sat on the edge of the bed and just consumed her with his eyes.

'The strangest thing of all,' said Mel, 'is that even during sex … with Tom, I couldn't bear him seeing me naked. But I love you looking at me now.'

'Staring lecherously?'

'Yes … stare all you want.'

But Conan couldn't look anywhere but her eyes, grey and smouldering, and he kissed her again, nestling against her flesh, feeling himself hard against her thigh and then her hands running over his chest and sides.

She was moaning, deep in her throat, then she was laughing and all but shouted, 'We're animals Conan! Let's do it like animals!'

• • •

Sometime later, as they lay in darkness, she seemed to be talking from out of a dream. 'So *that's* what it's supposed to be like.'

Conan said nothing, afraid of spoiling the moment. Then Mel said: 'As I said, I've only done it twice before … but it only lasted seconds and then he would pray and scourge himself.'

'Scourge?'

'He has a small whip … made of leather but lined with tiny crystals.'

'Good God.'

'He wanted to whip me as well, but I wouldn't have it.'

Conan started to laugh and she pushed him.

'Don't laugh at me, Conan.'

'I'm not laughing at you, but it strikes me that sex with Lammas is like doing it with Thomas Hobbes … '

'Nasty, brutish and short?' she mused. 'Very funny.'

A sudden change came over her mood, but Conan had been expecting it.

'You're wondering what to do now?'

'Yes.'

He rolled over and reached for his watch.

'It's only eleven o'clock. Feels later.'

'I should probably go home.'

'Do you live with him?'

'No … but he sometimes drops in.'

'So you were out … and you lost your phone.'

'I suppose.'

'You don't have any dry clothes either.'

'There must be something of Ming's I can borrow.'

Mel would have been marginally bigger than Ming but very fit and shapely.

'Your own will be dry in the morning.'

'You want me to stay?'

'Of course.'

She went quiet again and Conan knew she was exploring further parts of her conscience now that the excitement and alcohol had partly worn off.

'I can't believe this evening. This is *not* how I expected it to turn out … in bed with Agent Tooley.'

'You could have got odds of a billion to one a few hours ago. Shame there were no bookies about.'

Again she smiled absently and went silent.

'You're worried about the future?'

'Yes.'

'What parts of it exactly?'

He reached out for her and found her lying on her back, with her arms behind her head.

'All of it. My certainties have crumbled.'

'What will you do about Lammas?'

'What *can* I do? I have an insight now into what an equal relationship means. It's the only relationship worth having and I don't think he's capable.'

'Do you have any idea what he's up to?'

'No. I was disturbed by his mention of payment and running risks … but maybe it's nothing? With *Illumination* happening in just a few nights I suppose it makes sense for the main groups to get together to discuss it.'

He slipped his arm under her neck and pulled her towards him.

'Do you mind me holding you?'

'No. I like it.'

They lay in silence for a while with just a sheet over them. The temperature was perfect and the bed like a womb for a pair of twins.

'Has he ever mentioned Ah Li Wu before?'

'I've been trying to remember exactly that,' she said. 'Habal Tong are the enemy. The people he most rails against in his sermons and speeches. Well … Habal Tong and atheists.'

'I'm an atheist.'

'Yes, I know.'

'Does that bother you?'

She was silent for a while and he understood that she was undergoing another of her self-torments.

'It depends,' she said at last.

'On how much we see each other in the future?'

There was another silence. 'Conan … it is truly frightening how well you know me already. I'm not used to being understood, and I'm not entirely sure I could cope with it over a long period. It's almost violating.'

Conan felt suddenly cold, as though the inevitable receding had commenced.

'So you like being an animal … you like being held … but you don't like being understood?'

'That's not what I meant,' she said. 'Talking to you is so different from any other person I've met. It would take some getting used to.'

'My ex-wife said I was too intense.'

'Is that why she left?'

'How do you know I didn't leave her?'

'I just know.'

Now it was Conan's turn to collect his thoughts before answering. 'She said I was too hard … I've never really tried to interpret that.'

'What about all the other women in your life?'

'There haven't been that many … long term I mean.'

'Maybe they worked out quickly you were too hard?'

With that she reached down and held him.

'Yes … definitely too hard.'

'That's your fault for being such a beautiful animal.'

Chapter 16

The Indigenous Game

Chris was in his element.

Robbie was having an okay time, but had been glancing at his watch for an hour and was more than ready to go.

He had also reached that point where he'd just about drunk himself sober. He was tired, toxic and too beyond caring whether they'd fit in with the others.

As for that, it had been a successful day. The local office of the Institute of Demography had made them very welcome after a routine screening.

'Why do youse want to join up?' asked the bloke in charge – a tall, raw-boned redhead with tatts up to his chin.

'Too many wogs and no fuckin' jobs,' said Chris, and Robbie shrugged in agreement.

The bloke, whose name was Jimbo, pursed his lips and considered.

'What do youse do for work?'

'Both mechanics,' said Chris. 'Or used to be.'

Jimbo nodded in understanding.

'Yeah … cars are all self-diagnosing and repairing … anything built in the last five years, anyhow.'

He led them from the front office through to a large back room which was well populated, although nearly all males. A bit of a party was under way.

'We're supposed to give you a proper screening to make sure youse aren't cops or spooks,' said Jimbo, 'but I reckon I'm a fair judge of character.'

'Oy!' he shouted and the room was almost silent.

'This is Chris and Robbie from Melbourne … best city in the

world,' said Jimbo. 'I reckon they're alright but get to know 'em and anyone reckons they're not fair dinks … come and let me know.'

With that, Chris and Robbie were provisional members of Dedd Reffo. Beers were on sale from a huge communal esky – just marginally above cost price – so heaps cheaper than any pub, and there was a pool table around which most of the blokes were clustered. It was standard pub rules – no need to play your own ball and you could only lose in-off when on the black. It was an old coin operated table but they had a big supply of goldies which were used to start games and emptied out at the end of every night. Chris and Robbie sat a coin at the end of the queue and waited their turn.

They got chatting with a few other blokes and Chris was quickly popular when it was learned he'd played for St Kilda.

'Fuckin' makes me sick what's happened to the game,' spluttered a big, fat bloke – Pauly. 'That's what you get letting in so many fuckin' foreigners. They take all the jobs and they all play fuckin' wogball. There's no way Oz would've made the World Cup Final without so many fuckin wogs, and that's what's fucked AFL.'

'Don't get me started,' snarled Chris, who started railing against the injustice of soccer-loving foreigners flooding in and killing the indigenous game.

'It's just like what happened to the Aborigines,' said Robbie, trying to get involved in the conversation.

'What is?'

'Foreign invasion … and now Aussie Rules fans are second class citizens.'

'It's not like that at all,' said Chris, a bit pissed off.

'You saying AFL fans are all pisshead petrol sniffers?' demanded Pauly, his eyes blazing with anger and alcohol.

'No,' back-pedalled Robbie, staring at Pauly's old Ford Racing Team tee-shirt. 'It's just that …'

'Fuck the Abos!' snarled Pauly, stepping forward belligerently.

'Aah, don't worry about Robbie.' said Chris, throwing a protective arm around him. 'He's just a bit too smart for his own good sometimes, aren't you Rob.'

Pauly backed down with a bit of a warning stare for Robbie, but clinked long-necks with Chris.

That had been hours ago and everything had been fine afterwards. Mostly. Chris and Robbie had held the table for some time until Robbie deliberately went in-off after becoming uncomfortable with their success when playing Pauly and his partner for about the third time. If it was an attempt at trying to make up to Pauly, it didn't work.

'Suck shit, smart cunt!' Pauly had gloated when Robbie offered his hand.

An hour or so later, Robbie was just about over it and ready to go.

'There hasn't been anything formal,' he said to Chris.

'What do you mean?'

'Well, no speeches or any sort of briefing on the status of the world and what they have planned … '

'That's tomorrow night.'

'Yeah?'

Chris tipped up his bottle and drained the last of it.

'Jimbo told me. They don't invite everyone to the planning meeting but … he's a St Kilda fan.'

'Cool. You wanna head off back to the pub?'

'Yeah, alright … holy *fuck*!'

Robbie followed Chris's eye and was utterly gobsmacked at what he saw.

Standing in the doorway, grinning like a loon, was Lemon.

• • •

Tim was amazed at how quickly Lemon had managed to turn herself into a minor HT celebrity.

But less amazed at how quickly she had alienated the entire local hierarchy. Her ability to use HT aphorisms to pursue her own interests or justify her actions may have impressed the Indians – even after they learned that she had been accredited for *Illumination* while leading a revolt against the queue – but the Chiefs were having none of it. Lemon had a way of making a reward seem like the inevitable end to a reasoned HT proposition, but the Chiefs were all the same, realised Tim. They knew she wanted the reward in the first place so no amount of aphoristic posturing would see her getting her way with them.

Which meant Lemon was not given immediately the place in the local hierarchy (including a free room at the temple) she thought her due. A normal person would have accepted that and started working their way up the ladder – learning the rules and laying out a long term plan to negotiate every rung.

Not Lemon. When she wasn't appointed a Leader at once, she started screaming.

'Pack of useless cunts youse are! Can't even see a born Leader right under your noses. Well get fucked! I'm taking my leadership abilities where they'll be appreciated!'

With that she dragged Tim out of the temple and down to the waterfront where they found a pub and treated themselves to a feast, their OzBraces having buzzed during the day with their fortnightly dole payment.

Tim spent most of the time soothing and reassuring Lemon as she vented her fury at the small-minded idiots that passed for Leaders in the local Tong, but secretly he was delighted. This was his favourite time, when it was just him and Lemon. This was the time when she was most likely to remember who loved her best and, just maybe, return that love, for a while.

He got her several double bourbs while drinking his favourite Coopers Red, and they had steak and chips with garlic prawns on top. It was the nicest meal they'd had in yonks and, despite the dent it was making in Tim's OzBrace, worth every cent while her mood continued.

'You're the only one who really gets me,' she told him.

'I adore you, Lemon.'

Her smile repaid everything and he felt himself melting all over again.

'What are you crying for?' she demanded.

'Nothing … I'm just happy.'

'Well cut it out. Now … we need to find out where Chris and Robbie have gone.'

The warmth and happiness of the last two hours vanished.

'Why?'

'So we can sleep in their car … what else?'

Tim nodded at the reasoning, but was still uncomfortable with the idea of Lemon meeting up with Chris again.

'It's getting on … won't be easy to find them tonight.'

But it was surprisingly easy, as it turned out. Everyone knew the Institute of Demography was a Dedd Reffo front and there were posters everywhere advertising the whereabouts of the local offices. The very first address they tried on Whitlam Street, there was no one manning the door so Lemon and Tim walked through a corridor into a loud piss-up with Chris and Robbie in the thick of it.

'Lemon!' said Chris, 'What are you doing here?'

Lemon didn't answer at first, just grinned at Chris who was grinning back like a cat with a bird, as Tim's and Robbie's hearts sank.

'What happened to your Habal fuckin' Tong?' demanded Robbie, loud enough to engage the interest of those closest, and there was an electric silence awaiting her response.

'Fuck Habal Tong!' shouted Lemon, engaging the rest of them. 'We've seen the light, haven't we Timmy … all is nothing and everything's shit. And too many fuckin' wogs, eh!'

There was some laughter and cheering. Lemon, being the only woman present, was immediately popular and even Jimbo was soon laughing at her unique way of viewing the world through the expression of grievances and perceived slights.

Pauly made a fast play for her affections but it was obvious she only had eyes for Chris. Tim found himself excluded from the main conversation and was actually contemplating leaving when Robbie pushed a beer into his hand.

'Thought you'd seen the end of us, huh?'

Tim accepted the beer but was uncertain how to respond, and before he could help it was crying.

'Chin up, mate,' advised Robbie. 'You don't want this lot to see your weakness.'

Tim wiped his eyes with his sleeve.

'I don't know what to think any more. Everything was pretty fucked up before, but at least I had Lemon … or thought I did. I just feel like walking down to the bay and sticking my head under the water until … '

'Come on, mate … snap out of it! She's not fuckin' worth it!'

To Robbie's surprise and amusement, Tim threw a punch at him which he deflected easily, despite the many beers he had on board. Fortunately, no one else seemed to have seen the attempted punch but Tim started crying again and took off.

Robbie watched him go and might have forgotten about him, except that it was obvious that Chris wouldn't be ready to leave for a while, so he grabbed a couple more beers from the esky and followed.

It was still warm outside, despite being nearly midnight, and Robbie was happy to get out and clear his head. Tim was striding down the centre of the road but there was little traffic by Ord City standards – mainly motorbikes. Robbie followed on the footpath where some of the food hawkers were still open. He'd never been into Asian food but found himself intrigued by the exotic smells, and he hadn't eaten since lunchtime.

Still, no time for that. His was a mission of mercy and he quickened his pace to catch up with Tim who had taken a left and was heading for the water.

At the end of the street, not far from the pub at which Robbie and Chris were staying, Tim paused on the boardwalk looking out over the bay which was bathed in silver light from the almost full moon.

'Crocs'll get you before you've had time to drown.'

Tim turned to see Robbie holding out a beer, and after a few seconds sighed and accepted it.

'Thanks.'

Robbie sat on the edge of the boardwalk, his feet dangling about six feet above the mud flat that was glistening silver. After a few moments Tim sat a couple of paces away.

'I don't know much about women,' said Robbie, 'but one thing I've learned is this … you can't make them love you.'

'Have you tried?'

Robbie was silent for a few moments, his head filled with unwelcome memories.

'You can make yourself worthy of being loved,' said Tim.

'You reckon Chris is worthy?' asked Robbie, and there was another long silence.

'She doesn't love him,' said Tim. 'It's just a thing that will play itself out. It's happened before.'

'And you go on putting up with that?'

'All is nothing and …'

'Everything's shit,' interrupted Robbie. 'I heard that from Lemon herself. What happened with your HT mob?'

'We didn't fit in,' said Tim, taking a long swig of beer.

'So now she wants to join Dedd Reffo? Bit of a turnaround … '

'She reckons her leadership abilities might be better appreciated there.'

'Yeah? Well if she becomes a leader, I'm out.'

Of course, the thing most preying on Robbie's mind was the sleeping arrangements – not least that there had been a double bed in their room that morning and he wouldn't be surprised if they'd forgotten to change to twin singles. It'd be bad enough getting through the night in a double bed but if Chris brought Lemon back, Robbie would have little choice other than to sleep in the car. Maybe his best move was just to head to the room now and be asleep before Chris arrived to negotiate.

'Why don't you fuck off back to Sydney?' asked Robbie. 'That's what I'd do in your shoes.'

'We've come this far,' said Tim, shaking his head. 'Might as well see *Illumination*. They say Ah Li Wu himself is speaking.'

'He doesn't exist, does he?'

'Illusion is reality and reality illusion,' said Tim. 'Of course he exists.'

If Tim had any evidence for his proposition he kept it to himself and Robbie felt himself succumbing to a tidal wave of sleepiness.'

'Look, I'm heading off to bed so … so don't do anything stupid. You wanna sleep in the car?'

Tim turned and stared at Robbie, then said: 'Thanks Robbie … right now you'd have to be my best friend in the world.'

'Well, don't count on me for anything. I'd say we were temporary co-travellers rather than friends.'

But he grinned, 'Come on, dickhead … the car's this way.'

Chapter 17

The Light of His Obvious Desire

Emerging slowly from sleep, Captain Melodie Roberts had never felt so wonderful.

Somehow, everything in her dream world was in perfect balance, but the very acknowledgment of that perfection changed it – like measurement changes the state of a photon.

Gradually her analytical brain entered the dream to make sense of it. There was imperfection somewhere, threatening the rosy warm blur in which she could happily spend the rest of her days.

With Conan.

And there it was. As soon as she remembered Conan she remembered Thomas, and that was the problem.

She moaned aloud and felt Conan's arms tighten about her, realised he was moulded perfectly to her back and poking hard through the tops of her thighs. She stirred, momentarily shocked, but then relaxed and found herself pushing against him, adjusting subtly so that every tiny movement was a teasing arousal.

'If you keep that up you'll be molested,' he murmured. Melodie laughed and rolled over to slip her arms round his neck again. Then his mouth was on hers, tasting sweetly of his natural, warm flavour.

Half an hour later they were in the shower and she found herself coy. Not embarrassed – certainly not that. She loved the way he looked at her and felt proud, if anything, in the light of his obvious desire, but there were decisions to be made.

'What are you going to do?' he asked, while kissing the back of her neck.

'What do you want me to do?'

'I want you to be happy.'

She searched his face and saw nothing to make her wary or uncomfortable, but it wasn't exactly the answer she wanted from him.

'I need to get home and sort myself out,' she said. 'Sort my life out.'

'Do you want me to come with you?'

'I'll be okay.'

'Am I going to see more of you?'

'There's not much you haven't seen,' she said. 'But yes … if you want.'

She refused breakfast, feeling an urgent need to get home and reappraise. She knew she was falling for Conan – falling very hard – but she had to deal first with the imperfection in her life before seeing him again.

'What will you do today?' she asked, as she prepared to leave.

'Well … the chase is back on, I reckon. Maybe I'll go see Loongy … or maybe I'll just look into a couple of things on my own.'

'Will I see you later?'

'I'd say call me,' he said, 'but … '

'Oh damn … I'll have to get a new phone.'

Conan wrote his number down on a green sticky note.

'Give me a call when you get a phone. I'll take you to dinner … or cook for you if you prefer.'

'You can cook? Let's do that.'

She kissed him goodbye and was surprised by the depth of regret as she left him. It was all she could do not to turn round and declare her undying love, but that was ridiculous after only one night, so she forced herself to keep walking, enjoying the sights and smells of the waking city before the heat made it all unbearable again.

It was a half hour walk to her apartment and she needed all of that time to explore her feelings, marvelling at the extent of her transformation over the course of one evening. And yet, somehow, she was not surprised. It seemed that, as she played back her inner tape, her strong dislike upon meeting Conan was a protective response to how naturally attracted she was to him. As an engaged woman it was inappropriate attraction, and yet here she was – walking home with her engagement ring off her hand and knowing it would not be going back on.

She arrived at her apartment hot and sweaty and ready for another shower, but when she opened her door, Tom was sitting at her dining table and she screamed.

'Thank you, darling,' he said in that deep, rich baritone she'd always admired. 'Lovely to see you also.'

'Tom! Sorry … you gave me a fright.'

He was going through her brief case, she noticed, but thrust down her indignation.

'Are you looking for something?' she asked, unable to keep the asperity out of her voice.

'I was,' he replied smoothly, 'until I found Jesus. Now I need never search again.'

Tom was using his glib public voice and Melodie shivered with a premonition of trouble.

'I found your phone,' he said.

'Really? How did you know it was lost?'

'Because I have you on phone tracker app … have done forever. It means I can monitor your location and even listen to your conversations, if I wish.'

She stared at him, fear replacing her initial anger.

'Those conversations have never been particularly interesting,' he continued, 'which is exactly what I wanted for my fiancée and future wife … conversations unlikely to embarrass me.'

'Where is my phone?' she demanded.

'I've left it with the technicians to see what can be recovered after its dunking in the river. I suspect last night's conversation would be substantially more interesting than usual … especially as you are not wearing your ring.'

'What are you talking about, Tom?' she asked, nervously hiding her hand behind her back.

'And after you lost the phone,' he continued, ignoring her question, '… where did you go and with whom?'

'How dare you come in here and interrogate me!' she replied, determined to take back the initiative.

'I have, of course, examined CCTV footage from last night, so I have some of the answers … but I'd prefer you volunteered the rest rather than have to dig it out of you.'

'I would like you to leave, Tom,' she said. 'Now.'

'I asked you a question,' he repeated, the flatness of his voice terrifying.

It was clear that their relationship was over. The imperfection would soon be deleted.

• • •

The media reports were all about *Illumination*. Conan read numerous stories from numerous angles, mostly about the fear of a Dedd Reffo terror incident but also about the locals' ongoing concerns that the government would find a reason to renege on the seven year visa deal. Colonel Chard was reported as saying the government had no reason to renege and every reason to comply: 'The population is growing at such a rate that we urgently need to start spreading Ord City residents around the rest of the country.'

Conan closed his Pod and stared into the Ord City chaos for a while, then decided to go to work.

Loongy refused to see him so Conan walked into the state police station and was amused at the disorderly scene. It was like some old clichéd cop shop from the seventies and a million miles from the glass techno-towers inhabited by the AFP and the other Homeland Security offices.

Dave Marsh groaned as he walked in but introduced him to a couple of bored colleagues before suggesting they go for coffee.

It was another stinking hot day in Ord City and the clamour of the street was already deafening at nine o'clock. The Vietnamese barista took their order and worked his cart efficiently as Dave hoovered his way through a couple of cigarettes.

'No news on Ming,' shrugged Dave as they received their coffees.

Conan felt a tinge of guilt that he hadn't been more focussed on her disappearance, although he had little doubt that if he worked out what really was going on then resolving her disappearance would be part of it.

'That's not why I'm here.'

So what's up?' asked Dave.

'I was wondering whether you can lend me a boat.'

Dave sprayed hot coffee and swore with irritation.

'Jeez! You don't want much, do you.'

'I want to go upriver and have a look at a couple of things,' said Conan, amused as ever by Dave's manner.

'Look at what exactly?'

'So you do have a boat?'

'Maybe … but its use has to be authorised. I can't just go for a fuckin' picnic.'

'How do you get it authorised?'

'I'd have to suspect a breach of state law and, as you know … most of the laws around here are Commonwealth.'

'What about failure to observe the boat safety rules … is that state?'

'I suppose so.'

'Well, you have reason to believe that certain irregularities under the Maritime Act of Western Australia have been perpetrated by persons unknown somewhere south of Ord City.'

'Jee-zuss … what's this really about?'

'I'm not sure, but another piece of the puzzle was dropped onto the table last night so I want to check it out.'

'Why not use the AFP facilities? They've got heaps of boats.'

'Loongy won't see me. Reckons I should be back in Sydney.'

'Jee-zuss.'

But an hour later they were chugging out of the small police marina in an old half cabin cruiser, Conan covered in sunscreen and sipping on a sparkling water. Dave had insisted Conan provide the picnic.

From the water, the city looked like a poor man's Bangkok. The blend of high tech and street market – high rise and humpy – was a riotous mass of contradictions, with people everywhere. Thousands and thousands milling about, clamouring for attention, buying and selling, and somehow getting by. At the same time they were good for Australia – inspiring an economic boom hard on the heels of the quantum recession – and Conan was suddenly really pleased he had come to experience it first hand rather than just some cheap virtual tour.

At that moment his phone rang and he answered automatically, hoping it was Mel.

'Conan?'

'Oh … hi, Ma.'

'No need to sound so excited.'

'Sorry, I'm … in the middle of something.'

'Catching crooks are you?'

'Trying to … '

There was an awkward pause and before he knew it, Conan was filling the silence with news he wasn't quite ready to divulge.

'I think I've met someone.'

'You *think* you've met someone? When will you know for sure?'

He laughed, with one wary eye on Dave, who was cautiously navigating through a flotilla of canoes and tinnies filled with produce and goods for sale.

'That's nice, Conan … I hope she'll be able to look after you in your old age. It's terrible being old and alone.'

'Let's not get too far ahead of ourselves,' he said, ignoring her plea for sympathy.

'So what's her name?'

'Melodie … Mel.'

'Melodie? She sounds like a bogan. Got a sleeve tattoo I suppose?'

'No, she doesn't … and it's not nice calling people bogans.'

'You'd better bring her around, I suppose,' said his longsuffering mother.

'Well she works up here in Ord City,' said Conan, 'but I'll see what I can do. Gotta go, Ma.'

'Bye Conan … but you haven't forgotten I hope. I really do need help with money.'

Conan put his phone away as Dave lit another cigarette and said, 'Fast worker, aren't you?'

'What do you mean?'

'First Ming, and now Mel Roberts … all in a couple of days. Didn't have you pegged as a trouser man.'

'Well, I'm not,' laughed Conan. 'Not normally … and I wasn't really trying for either of them. They just seemed to fall in my lap.'

'That's the secret,' said Dave, opening up the throttle as they emerged from the thicker water traffic and headed upstream. There were still hundreds of buildings lining the shore but Conan knew they'd start to thin out in a kilometre or so as the river narrowed to the south out of Lake Argyle.

'What secret?' asked Conan, his heart strangely light despite the circumstances.

'Women hate it when you try too hard. A confident bloke doesn't have to try, and they love confidence.'

Conan nodded as they chugged southward under the largest of the bridges connecting Ord City across the Ord River.

'Can't believe how quickly this place has grown,' he said, wanting to change the subject.

Dave said nothing for a while, but then he lit yet another cigarette. 'So, how's Tom Lammas responded to the new situation.'

'He doesn't know.'

'Wouldn't want to be on his wrong side,' said Dave. 'The AOG can make things pretty hot for them they don't like.'

Conan considered Dave for a moment, then decided to take a risk.

'Have you ever seen, or heard of anyone seeing ... Ah Li Wu?'

'Habal Tong Ah Li Wu?'

'Yes.'

'No, but he doesn't really exist, does he? He's a corporate symbol ... like the Marlboro Man.'

'He does exist. He was at a meeting last night with Lammas, Chard, and Ronny Kwai ... and another of Lammas's people ... the one who runs the hospital.'

Dave stared at Conan. 'How do you know it was Ah Li Wu?'

'I've seen his picture on walls ... and Mel said it was him.'

'I've seen Colonel Sanders' picture on walls,' laughed Dave. 'But just supposing it *was* him ... what are those lot doing at a meeting together?'

'It has to be something to do with *Illumination* ... Friday night.'

Conan recounted most of what he'd seen and heard the previous night and Dave's eyes grew wider as he listened.

'And what are we looking for today?'

'I don't know exactly, but there are a few places of interest upriver and … as I have no other leads.'

'And what about the people who bashed you?'

Conan's fingers automatically went to the parts of his head that were still sore and bruised.

'Still no idea who that was … who ordered it, I mean. Or why.'

The buildings were getting sparser but the light industry was getting heavier as they proceeded south, and in the distance they could already see escarpment, desert and mulga. They passed under the last of the bridges and picked up a little more speed.

'Any idea what we're looking for?' asked Dave.

'Where are the water treatment facilities?'

'Water treatment?' echoed Dave. 'There's a few along the river. We'll get to the first of them shortly.'

'Do you know which one is run by Greg Ferrier?'

'Who?'

'Greg Ferrier. I met him at Ronny Kwai's football dinner and heard his name mentioned last night.'

'Wouldn't have a clue, sorry,' said Dave. 'I don't move in your exalted circles. What does it say on the net about him?'

Conan pulled out his phone and started googling: *Greg Ferrier, water plant.*

'I'm getting nothing … the signal's crap out here.'

They chugged along another kilometre and Dave said, 'There's the first of the treatment plants.'

Conan examined the nondescript facility with buildings, metal stairs, gantries and a large reservoir tower. There was no observable activity – no moving parts – and they chugged past it heading south.

There were two more fairly identical plants on the west bank, again with no discernible activity, but when they approached a newer looking facility on the east bank there were numerous cars and transit vans and any number of technicians and suits standing about. A large sign on the bank said *Ord City Water Treatment Facility DELTA*.

'It's gonna be that one, isn't it?' suggested Dave. 'Delta.'

Conan pulled out his mini-binox and peered at the site, not really understanding anything that was happening, but perceiving a fair bit of energy about the place. There were a few technicians racing around but most of the people looked like spooks with their dark suits and sunnies. As he panned the binox across the scene he saw one of the suits was also using binox and staring straight back at him.

'Well, well,' said Conan, 'they seem as interested in us as we are in them.'

Conan ignored the bloke with the binox and continued sweeping the facility, trying to understand what was happening, but it was just some impenetrable industrial complex and he could have stared for a hundred years without gaining the slightest insight.

'What do you wanna do?' asked Dave. 'Stop for a closer look?'

Conan was looking at the bloke with the binox again and saw him speaking into a headset microphone.

'No … keep going,' said Conan. 'Let's try and look like we're not snooping.'

Dave opened the throttle again and Conan felt strangely relieved to be putting distance between them and the treatment plant.

A minute or two later they passed the last of the human constructions and, as they rounded a bend of the river saw a huge crocodile slide off a mud bank and into the water.

'Fucking hell!' exclaimed Conan. 'Did you see that?'

'Had to be five metres,' said Dave. 'They can be as long as seven and weigh over a tonne, but anything over two metres can kill you.'

'Far out!' continued Conan, still a little unnerved at the reminder of how dangerous the river could be. 'I actually jumped into the harbour last night … despite the fact there were crocs everywhere. I just forgot about them.'

'Never do that,' laughed Dave. 'We'd have to average five deaths a year up here … mostly reffos swimming in the harbour. They never learn, although I suppose there's no shortage of the buggers.'

Conan felt a shiver across his shoulders as he glanced at the thin fibreglass hull.

'Do they ever put holes in boats?'

'Crocs? I guess they could … if we hit one.'

Conan forced himself to think about something else.

'Beautiful country out here,' he said, and it was true. Just a couple of ks south of habitation it seemed pristine, remote and wild. Birds flocked and shrieked, bickering over every scrap of food and space.

And every hundred metres or so there'd be another crocodile half in half out of the water.

'Never used to see 'em south of Argyle,' said Dave, 'but they've really multiplied in the last few years. And for every one you see there are plenty more you don't.'

The river was about a hundred metres wide at this point with the occasional small island. They continued south as Conan collected his thoughts.

'How far's the NBN node from here?'

'Fair way,' said Dave. 'As the crow flies ... at least ten ks but you wouldn't go by boat. It's a couple of ks east of the river.'

'What else is out here?'

'Nothing ... apart from a few mines and the flying saucer place.'

'The what?'

'You know ... the place with all the weird metal shapes where they're looking for ET.'

'Oh right ... the Giant Array. How far is that?'

'From here? Thirty odd ks by road but a lot less by river ... maybe twenty.'

'Have we got enough fuel to get there?'

At that moment a helicopter seemed to come from nowhere, passing only a hundred metres or so overhead before continuing south, following the river.

'Croc spotters,' said Dave. 'Tourists.'

'Loongy reckons I'm a tourist,' said Conan. 'For the head of an AFP section, it is beyond weird the way he carries on.'

'Don't underestimate him,' said Dave. 'You don't get his job without being a bloody smart operator.'

'That's what I'd have thought,' protested Conan. 'So why is he deliberately cutting me off? Isn't he on my side?'

'He's on the side of the AFP,' said Dave. 'So ... to the extent he thinks your operation is in the best interests of the Ord City branch of the AFP ... then yes, he's on your side.'

Conan stared at the disappearing helicopter, contemplating Dave's words and the quicksand they implied.

'I'm way out of my fucking depth up here.'

'You only just worked that out?' laughed Dave.

They continued south, with Conan still totally in the dark as to what they were looking for. He needed to report to Kenny Cook on the latest developments, inconclusive though they were, but increasingly his mind was turning to Mel. She probably had a new phone by now and was maybe trying to call him. And he hadn't told her he'd be out of range – she might think he was avoiding her!

Suddenly Conan's quixotic crusade seemed a ridiculous waste of time despite the numerous nagging questions. A beautiful young woman wanted to have dinner with him and, amid all the crocodiles, heat and frustration, Conan decided his priorities were completely wrong.

'Yeah, fuck it,' he said, gesturing at a small island, midstream, with a thick cluster of trees and a sandy beach. 'May as well have lunch and get back to civilisation.'

'You're the boss,' said Dave, easing back the engine as another helicopter zoomed overhead.

• • •

Asif sat with Ah Cheng and the rest of the Bang Gang in a demountable room which managed to be hot and breathless despite the air conditioning on full.

A woman was explaining an odd looking rubber shirt with a special cap.

'This is the ultimate in safety gear to prevent an accident,' she said. 'The cap has sensors which pick up on brain waves … and this display on the chest, back and wrists shows the decision status.'

Apparently the suit could be worn by a person with sufficiently disciplined thoughts to finalise a blast sequence. It was an extra check to prevent premature explosions after all other checks had been made.

'Once you are absolutely certain that no one is in an unsafe place,' said the woman, 'the crew member in the blast suit can send a subvocal command to the detonator. But the command must be sent three times, and the decision status can be seen by other crew members to indicate imminence of explosion … green, yellow, orange, red.'

There was a bit of a confused silence, then Kendrick, the foreman, said, 'Am I missing something here?'

'What do you mean?' snapped the woman, immediately irritated that she was being queried.

'Well, you're calling this an additional safety check,' said Kendrick, 'but if you ask me, these suits are fuckin' dangerous. Half the blokes who work out here are bloody maniacs. What if someone's wearing one of the suits and decides to top himself, and take everyone else with him?'

There was a murmur of agreement, but the woman waved their worries aside with a flick of her hand.

'They are not dangerous,' she insisted. 'There is a mandatory minute between every change in decision status and the status can clearly be seen. You would have at least three minutes to disarm the detonator manually in the unlikely situation that an operator went feral.'

'But where's the need?' objected Karadzian. 'It's not as though blast accidents are happening all the time.'

'Exactly,' agreed Kendrick. 'I can't remember us ever having an accident. Our safety processes are already perfect so, if it aint broke … '

But the government was offering tax incentives to use the safety suits and the company executive had decreed their use, so that was that. The next step was for each of them to be tested for compatibility. Only those with the most disciplined minds could send a sufficiently coherent command. It was quickly established that Kendrick, Karadzian and Ah Cheng were utterly hopeless and unable to shift the monitor from green to yellow to indicate the first step in the blast chain.

'It's up to you, Asif,' said the woman. 'If you can't do it I'm afraid this crew will have to be broken up to allow for someone who can operate the suit.'

Asif felt the pressure from his colleagues. They had been a tight, happy crew for nearly two years and the idea of being broken up sent the room temperature soaring. The rubbery cap was placed over his head and the rest of the thin suit taped tight across his back and shoulders.'

'What do I do?' he asked.

'Just imagine an explosion and think: bang,' the woman suggested.

Asif complied and the indicators immediately turned yellow.

Ah Cheng was whooping and punching the air, as Kendrick and

Karadzian smiled with relief.

'That is excellent.' said the woman. 'Although you others should continue training to use the suits in case Asif goes on leave or is sick. Now … let us turn to the matter of security. The suits are valuable, and under no circumstances are they to be removed from the work site. Is that understood?'

All four of them shrugged.

What possible reason could anyone have for taking a blast suit?

• • •

Robbie felt like five kinds of shit.

Obviously he had a hangover, but that was the least of his problems. Chris and Lemon were now openly a couple. Not only that, Lemon was so popular amongst the Dedd Reffo boys she'd overnight become one of the informal hierarchy and was already throwing her considerable weight around. Tim had been sent to get coffee for the Leaders and Robbie was mortified on his behalf. Did the prick have no pride?

Despite his contempt, Robbie couldn't help feeling sorry for Tim. Love, Robbie understood, blinds you and makes you do stupid things. He'd been there himself, after all. Stupid love was the main reason he'd left Melbourne – to put as much distance between himself and Kate as was possible. And there were few places further from Melbourne than Ord City.

Robbie had, at least, had the double bed to himself. He'd been pissed off when he got in last night that the twin singles hadn't been put in, but then relieved when he'd woken and found himself alone. That relief had been tempered by the realisation that, if Chris hadn't come back, he must be with Lemon.

And that meant trouble.

Trouble was now ordering everyone about – even Jimbo and Pauly leapt to do her bidding. And it was just plain weird how Lemon was now going on about all the fuckin' reffos takin' over and how it was important to make a powerful statement. The same Lemon who'd been pissing them off with her HT crap for the last few days and how Asians were the most highly evolved of all the races.

And before he could help himself, Robbie had gone on the attack.

'How come you hate Asians so much?' he demanded, 'Only yesterday you reckoned they were the example we should all be following.'

'I never said that,' said Lemon.

'Yes, you fucking did,' said Robbie, ignoring the warning signs from Jimbo and Pauly and appealing to Chris to take his side, or at least acknowledge her change of tune.

'My only interest in Habal Tong was to learn about my enemy,' said Lemon. 'Someone has to find out what the cunts are up to.'

'Best way to do something about 'em,' agreed Jimbo. 'Have someone they trust on the inside.'

'They trust me,' said Lemon with that annoying smugness that Robbie found more irritating every minute. 'I reckon I could walk in and out no problem … plus Timmy and I are accredited for *Illumination*. We could get up to all kinds of hi-jinks. But after that I want to get on the Eureka and sink a few fuckin' reffo boats!'

The others laughed but Robbie had another premonition that everything was turning to shit.

Tim walked in with a tray of coffees but Robbie got up and left. He really needed some headspace but knew Chris would not be coming with him, unless Lemon tagged along and that was the last thing Robbie wanted.

Somehow Robbie found himself back in the bar where he and Chris had been playing stick the day before, and halfway through his first beer was unsurprised when Tim plonked a schooner down on the table.

'The world has changed,' said Robbie.

'It'll play itself out,' shrugged Tim. 'It always does.'

Robbie shook his head with bewilderment and disgust.

'Seriously,' he said, '… what on earth do you see in her?'

'It's hard to explain if you don't see it already,' said Tim, with a thoughtful sip of his beer. 'She's like a force of nature … intoxicating. You saw how Jimbo and Pauly are falling over themselves to win her approval.'

'That's because they're a couple of white trash misogynists who've spent half their life in gaol and the other half in the public bar. They're not used to mixing with women … as I suppose she must be called.'

'What about Chris?' said Tim. 'He's been smitten from the moment they met … just took him a while to realise.'

'That's what I don't get,' said Robbie. 'She's fat … she smokes … she's got an epic sense of entitlement. She's everything Chris hates.'

'That's why he likes her,' explained Tim. 'Love is hate and hate is love.'

'Shut the fuck up with that crap,' threatened Robbie, but after a moment he went to the bar and got another two beers.

It was going to be a long afternoon.

Chapter 18

Losing Yourself in Something Bigger

Conan sat on a comfortable log and, after hesitating, accepted a third beer from Dave.

They'd landed on the island and were sitting in a sandy clearing, facing south west, having munched through a barbequed chicken with bread and salad – plus beers. Dave's price for getting the boat out.

Every now and then a helicopter buzzed overhead, but apart from that they could have been a million miles from anywhere. The river flowed slow and brown and on the western bank they could see another huge croc half out of the water with its back to them.

'Can he see us?' asked Conan.

'Yeah … he knows we're here,' said Dave. 'But this time of year … this time of day … it's too hot for 'em to get out of the water.'

'You sure?'

'Yeah … safe as houses, mate.'

Conan was only partly reassured, but the boat was only a short sprint away and he reckoned he'd be faster than some dozy crocodile.

But when he wasn't worrying about crocs his thoughts turned constantly to Mel. He was starting to get impatient about getting back within phone range, but Dave was in no rush and it would have been ungracious to hurry him along after talking him into coming out.

'So … where are your thoughts as far as this whole shemozzle is concerned?' asked Dave.

'I'm just about ready to give up,' admitted Conan. 'You don't have any jobs going in the state coppers do you?'

'Hah!' laughed Dave. 'Mr City Slicker Fed workin' for me? I'd fuckin' love that … but I'm not puttin' on a bloke who gives up at the first hurdle.'

'It's hardly the first hurdle,' objected Conan. 'There's been nothing *but* hurdles, and no one wants me up here anyway.'

'Well, what do you know for sure?'

Conan collected his thoughts and started counting on his fingers.

'Okay … there's Feng 9 who downloaded specs to the NBN node. There's two murdered blokes both bearing the warning marks of Habal Tong and Dedd Reffo. There's this business with the *Epistola Clementis* and a connection with the Army of God. There's a further connection with Ronny Kwai and the murdered men, and Ronny Kwai has twice been at social functions with Lammas and Maddox … and Chard.'

'And now with Colonel Sanders … I mean Ah Li Wu,' said Dave.

'There's something going on at that water treatment facility … And on top of all that, my colleague at the AFP office couldn't be less helpful and my boss in Sydney wants me to come home. Oh … and I've been chased twice and bashed once by mystery assailants, and Ming disappeared less than twelve hours after getting involved with me. Plus the CCTV footage of the incident was wiped by someone at the very top.'

'Dangerous bugger to know, aren't you,' said Dave, draining the last of his beer. 'But if you ask me, there's quite a few bits of the jigsaw there.'

'Maybe,' said Conan, 'but I can't even tell whether the pieces I've got are all from the same puzzle.'

'Kwai seems to be the link … if it is just one puzzle.'

'I ought to haul him in for questioning,' agreed Conan. 'And I would if there was any sort of co-operation from Loongy. What the fuck is going on there?'

They sat in silence for a few moments, both staring at the crocodile on the western bank. Two or three small birds were jumping on and off the croc's back and pecking at it – cleaning no doubt, but risky business.

'May as well head back,' said Dave. 'You wanna have another look at that treatment plant?'

'I don't think so.'

Both of their heads whipped round in unison, to see four blokes dressed in dark camouflage gear with green painted faces and holding hi-tech-looking rifles.

'Get up,' said the leader. 'Hands behind your backs.'

'What the fuck ...'

'Shut up!' snapped the leader, threatening Conan with his rifle.

Dave and Conan stood and their hands were bound roughly with plastex wire. Then black hoods were pushed over their heads and pulled tight. A helicopter could again be heard, much closer now and strong hands took Conan by the shoulders and pushed him forward.

• • •

Over the course of the afternoon, Robbie asked Tim for his life story, which was more interesting than he would have expected. He'd grown up in a fairly well-to-do sort of family on the North Shore of Sydney – private school – but had always been a bit of an outsider.

'I didn't like the way everything seemed to always come back to money,' said Tim. 'Everything was always ... when you looked deeper ... somehow about money. Even religion. It drove me mad trying to find something that wasn't infected by a deep-down, hideous lust for cash.'

'I can understand that,' sympathised Robbie.

'That's what fascinates me about HT. It's not at all about money. It's more about the abnegation of the self.'

'The what?'

'Losing yourself in something bigger,' said Tim, warming to his theme. 'Modern western life has too much focus on the individual. We should all be putting the community first ... and the planet first ... instead of tearing it all apart with selfish, short term gain that turns communities against each other and fucks up the earth for future generations.'

'So explain to me,' said Robbie, 'how any of Lemon's actions have ever been to benefit anyone besides herself.'

'Lemon has all the same underlying values as me,' insisted Tim. 'But her best contribution has always been through leadership. She just needs to land a leadership role and then she'll start pushing the main program.'

'Really? She's gonna promote HT after landing a leadership role within Dedd Reffo … the sworn enemies of Habal Tong?'

'All is nothing and nothing is all,' shrugged Tim. 'She'll make them see that in the end.'

Their glasses were empty and Tim was red-faced as he checked his OzBrace.

'Your shout, isn't it?' asked Robbie, with a grin.

Tim muttered something but Robbie just laughed and headed to the bar.

'Explain again how Habal Tong has nothing to do with money,' he said.

• • •

It was hard to estimate time with his head in a sack, but Conan reckoned they'd been in a strangely silent motor boat for at least half an hour. He knew they were headed south because he could perceive the sun through the black material – high to his right at approximately two o'clock.

He had stopped protesting or questioning their assailants as to identity or purpose. Their questions were ignored and the men spoke no words to each other. Conan recognised the calm professionalism with which they went about their business and guessed they were ex-military types working for god-knows-who.

The softly purring motor throttled back and Conan sensed they were slowing down. Some brief orders were given and the boat juddered to a stop – clearly beached, so it must have been a zodiac, or similar inflatable vessel.

'Get up.'

It was not easy to get up with their hands manacled behind their backs, so Conan and Dave were dragged to their feet and helped over the wide gunwale. Then rifles were poked in their backs and they walked, splashing through ankle deep water and then hard mud.

'Down.'

'What?' asked Conan, beginning to be frightened. He hadn't really feared for his life until that point. He'd expected to be taken somewhere for questioning but the circumstances suddenly seemed to have only one possible purpose.

'Down,' was the implacable response, from the only man to speak so far.

A hand on his shoulder forced him to his knees and then the manacles were cut. A flare of hope flashed through Conan's heart as the hood was removed and he blinked in the bright light, trying to make sense of his surroundings.

They were on another island in the middle of the river, but not so heavily wooded as the one where they'd stopped for lunch. He and Dave were kneeling on hard wet mud and close by were a couple of large concrete blocks with steel rings implanted.

Directly in front of Conan, lying in the mud, was a pink, Hello Kitty top – torn to shreds and edged with red.

'Oh fuck,' said Conan, recognising Ming's top.

'Hands,' said the leader, as Conan and Dave were pulled around and forced to lie in the mud. Their hands were re-manacled to the iron rings set in the concrete.

'Back in the boat,' ordered the leader and the other men with guns obeyed immediately.

'What the fuck are you …'

Conan's words were choked off as the leader's rifle was immediately in his face.

'No doubt you have questions,' said the leader. 'Suffice it to say … someone doesn't like you. So I suggest you make your peace with God before the crocs get here.'

'I'm an atheist,' said Conan.

'Really?' laughed the leader, walking away. 'You won't be in five minutes or so.'

As the men returned to the boat, another zodiac zoomed silently onto the beach with another two camouflaged men on board. They bent to lift something and struggled ashore carrying an inert body with a similar black hood.

Conan didn't need the hood to be removed, immediately recognising the floral top and tan culottes.

'You fuckin' sick cunts!' he shouted, no longer caring about the gun.

'She's not dead,' said the leader. 'Just a little sleepy. Wouldn't want to cheat the crocs of their sport.'

'Like I said,' muttered Dave. '… you're a dangerous bugger to know.'

One of Mel's hands was manacled to the iron rings and the last of the men returned to the boats.

Conan was already craning his neck as high as it would go, looking for any encroaching reptiles, but had an idea they would steer clear while the boats remained. He gave an experimental tug at the manacles but the plastic cut into his wrists, so he stopped.

The boats pushed off and the leader gave them a wave, before turning north and disappearing quickly around a bend in the river. There was almost silence.

'Well … a few more pieces for the jigsaw,' said Dave. Conan ignored him, trying to check out Mel. She didn't look injured and seemed to be breathing normally.

'Any chance of slipping the manacles?' asked Conan.

'Don't pull on them,' warned Dave. 'You'll only make 'em tighter and … well, it's not pleasant.'

'Oh fuck,' said Conan, as something like a giant log appeared at the water's edge.

The log blinked, and then began its slow, sinuous way towards them.

'Fuck off!' shouted Dave and Conan in unison, and Melodie stirred.

'Get away! Fuck off!' continued Dave. Mel said drowsily, 'Is that you Conan?'

'Yes! Fuck off!'

'I beg your pardon?'

'Not you, Mel! The fucking crocodile! Fuck off!'

Conan felt like his brain could snap with horror as the monstrous croc – mud-grey and glistening – paused part way up the bank and considered them with gleaming yellow eyes. Then another huge head appeared at the water's edge.

'What crocodile?' asked Mel. 'Where are we?'

'There are two crocodiles' shouted Conan, hoping the noise had made them pause. 'And we're tied down on the banks of the river. Shout and yell for fuck's sake.'

Melodie added her muffled shrieking to Dave and Conan's raucous din but the crocs took another few paces forward as Conan pulled his legs as far up the bank as he could get. The larger of the two crocs paused again, just a few metres from Mel, eyes blinking in the bright sun and muttering a deep throaty growl like an idling lawnmower.

'What's that noise?' screamed Mel and Conan found himself yelping for help – his mind seizing with white noise terror. The croc took another two paces forward, then a rock struck it between the eyes.

Conan gaped, as hands grappled at his left hand, which was suddenly free.

Then his right hand was free and he leapt up.

Ming, stark naked but covered with mud, was already cutting at Mel's hands so Conan looked desperately for a weapon. There were a few more rocks and he snatched them up and started flinging them at the crocodiles only three metres away.

He hit the closest one square on the snout and it turned its head. Then he hit it again on the side of the head and it took a few paces back towards the water.

Mel was up and Ming was cutting Dave free as Mel whipped her hood off and started screaming at how close the crocs had come. She ran, as Dave got up and also bolted away from the bank. Conan threw one last rock the size of a half brick and the larger croc took a few more paces back to the water as the other stared balefully at its escaping lunch.

Conan followed the others into the mulga and forest in the centre of the island.

Chapter 19

Awkward Stiffness

Ming led them to a small clearing in the central copse, which was pleasantly shady. Already Conan had adjusted to his salvation from the crocs and was embarrassed in advance by what Ming would think of his new relationship with Mel – who was clinging tightly to him and sobbing with relief.

Ming stared at them, and light dawned in her challenging eyes.

'Would you like a shirt or something?' asked Conan.

'Why?' she responded. 'Does my nakedness offend you?'

'It's fine with me,' said Dave, but Conan was cringing with embarrassment as Ming glared at him, looking like a swamp demon in her mudskin. He knew also that he ought to be giving Ming a hug – given both his salvation from the crocs and their own recent intimacy – but it was simply impossible with Mel still hanging onto his arm and crying into his shoulder.

'I'm really glad to see you, Ming,' said Conan, further embarrassed by his own awkward stiffness.

'Are you?' she enquired, staring at Mel. 'Didn't take you long to get over your Asian fetish I see.'

Conan winced, but there was no comeback to something like that.

'What happened to you?' he asked, trying to steer the conversation to safer ground.

'What happened to me?' she echoed. 'After leaving you naked in my bed? Well … I was snatched off the street on my way to get your breakfast. That's what happened. And what exactly did you do to try and find me?'

'Hang on,' said Dave, interrupting. 'You can have your recriminations later. First off … where are we and how do we get away?'

The island was about half the size of a football field, shaped roughly like a diamond and mostly covered with low mulga with a central knot of trees. In the sandy clearing, Ming had dragged three logs into a triangle as a feeble defence against crocodiles. Both banks of the river were about sixty metres from the island in midstream. Without even trying they could see several large crocs either side of the island and in all likelihood there were plenty more.

'Don't even think about it,' said Dave.

'Think about what?'

'Swimming. You wouldn't get ten metres.'

'Well, what about you?' said Conan. 'Haven't you got some black fella bush skills to get us off the island?'

'I can certainly track a crocodile,' said Dave, '… but I can't outswim one.'

As if by silent agreement, they all sat on the logs – Conan and Mel together on one, with Dave and Ming singly on the other two. Ming continued to refuse the offer of clothing from Conan but eventually accepted Dave's khaki police shirt.

'It's not from modesty that I've covered myself in mud,' she explained. 'It protects from the sun and mosquitoes … and maybe hides my scent from the crocs. I advise you all to mud up as well.'

Mel grimaced but Conan instinctively knew it was a good idea, especially with his Celtic skin that was already damaged from growing up in Sydney. He pulled out his phone and saw the blank space where a signal ought to be.

'They keep the spectrum free of human radio traffic out here,' said Ming. 'The radio telescopes couldn't work effectively otherwise. But we can't call for help.'

'So we wait for a helicopter,' said Conan, 'and jump about waving.'

'Not your best idea,' said Ming. 'The croc spotter choppers don't come this far south. Any chopper is likely to belong to whoever it is that put us here … and I'd rather they continued to think I was dead.'

Conan remembered the torn pink top back at the water's edge and understood that Ming had left the top there herself to convince her assailants that the crocs had done their work.

'Well how do we get away?' demanded Mel, in a small voice.

'I've been wondering that for the last three days,' said Ming.

'And what have we got to eat?' asked Mel.

'I'll be right,' grinned Dave, '… plenty of bush tucker out here. Don't know about you gubbas but.'

No one laughed at his joke and there was silence.

Then Conan said, 'Okay … so who are we dealing with? Why did someone try to kill us? Who are they … and why are you here?'

They all looked at Mel, who blushed and said, 'I was also snatched off the street. I had an argument with Tom … my ex-fiancé.'

She glanced sidelong at Conan. 'And I ran out of the apartment, and the next thing I knew a car pulled up next to me and men took me.'

'So … it's got to be the AOG, doesn't it?' said Conan.

Mel shook her head. 'I can't possibly believe Tom would want me killed.'

'But AOG is the only link between you and Ming … both snatched off the street and brought here. What was the argument about?'

Mel blushed and moved away from him.

'Sorry,' said Conan, pulling her back, 'None of my business … okay.'

Mel allowed herself to be drawn back to his side, then said, 'No, it is your business … it's all of our business if we've been brought here. The argument was about you, Conan. Tom discovered we'd spent the night together at Ming's and he …'

'You spent the night together at my place?' interrupted Ming.

Conan winced with further embarrassment. 'Well … I'd just been chased and bashed,' he said pointing at the damage to his head. 'I couldn't go back to my hotel.'

'And where did you think I was?' demanded Ming.

'I knew you'd been abducted … or worse … I had nowhere else to go.'

'Or worse,' she repeated, her eyes flashing dangerously. 'So you thought I was dead … and instead of grieving your dead lover you've been fucking someone else in her bed. How romantic.'

'Can we please try and stay on topic?' soothed Dave and there was a tense silence for a few moments. Then Conan, despite his intense humiliation, found his forensic brain kicking back into gear.

'You were manacled to the concrete blocks like we were?' he asked Ming.

'Of course.'

'So how did you escape, if there was no one else to cut you free? And where did you get a knife?'

Ming stared at him for a moment, once again triggering that nagging sense of having met her before.

'I was lucky,' she said. 'They only tied one hand to the block, and I was able to find a shell with a sharp edge.'

'What kind of shell?' asked Dave.

'I don't know,' snapped Ming. 'Does it matter?'

'But you used a knife to cut us free,' persisted Conan.

'I found it afterwards,' said Ming. 'And lucky for you I did.'

She lowered her eyes and, in that moment, Conan remembered a beautiful face glimpsed in a doorway.

'You were in the apartment,' he accused, all breathless epiphany. 'The apartment near Bruce and Michael's place. You knew them.'

Ming looked up, her expression changing from wounded innocence to defiance. Then without another word she bolted. Conan and Dave jumped up and followed as she ran through the mulga, shrugging off Dave's shirt as she went, and then splashed into the river and struck out for the eastern bank.

'Ming! Don't be an idiot!' shouted Conan as a couple of swirls in the brown water demonstrated interest in the commotion. Ming was swimming strongly and was only twenty metres from the far side when the swirls in the water caught up with her.

There was an explosion of splashing as two monstrous crocodiles emerged from the water, locked in each other's jaws and tails thrashing. But beyond that Conan saw Ming emerge from the water, her skin shining copper in the setting sun.

She blew him a kiss, then strode east through the mulga and was gone.

• • •

Robbie had lost count of how many shouts he'd bought. The light was getting soft and golden outside and the bottles behind the bar were all the same glowing red as the sun hovered low in the west.

It was also soft and golden inside his brain.

Tim was a pretty good bloke and quite funny once he opened up. In fact, he seemed pretty smart with the exception of his obvious blind spot. He was fuckin' mad when it came to her, but Robbie couldn't help but admire Tim's dedication to a lost cause. Maybe if he'd hung on a bit longer with Kate she'd have …

'I suppose we ought to head back to the Reffs,' muttered Tim.

'Fuck 'em.'

'What do you mean?'

Robbie stared into the dregs of another schooner and shrugged.

'I know we came all the way from Melbourne to join up … but they're just a bunch of fuckwits in there, and I hate the effect they've had on Chris.'

'Well … he always struck me as the more zealous of you two,' said Tim.

'I do agree with him,' clarified Robbie. 'Mostly … but I'd prefer our leaders to have a bit more style and nous than arseholes like Jimbo and Pauly. Not to mention your mate.'

'Dedd Reffo's ideology is ugly,' said Tim. 'Stands to reason they'll have ugly leaders.'

'Including Lemon.'

'She'll change them,' said Tim with his usual deluded confidence.

'Yeah, right,' laughed Robbie.

He was suddenly feeling very pissed and not at all in the mood for dealing with arseholes.

'I gotta eat something,' he said. 'You wanna steak?'

Tim blushed and started to stammer something but Robbie waved him to silence.

'It's okay, dickhead … I got it.'

• • •

'Where the fuck's Robbie?' wondered Chris aloud.

'We can't wait for him,' said Jimbo. 'Under the circumstances … it's probably best he's not here.'

Chris gave Jimbo a hard stare, but he understood – Robbie had not wholeheartedly embraced the Dedd Reffo boys, for some reason. And clearly they sensed that and were not entirely ready to embrace him.

'He's only new,' said Jimbo, sensitive to Chris's conflict, 'and we can't have too many new blokes at once in the planning group. The honchos'd have a fuckin' fit!'

One of the honchos was present that evening – Mungo, a heavily tatted skinhead in an old, leather biker vest with faded unreadable colours. He was surly and inscrutable at first but Lemon soon had him laughing at her comical impressions of Asian stereotypes.

'Me rikee,' she kept saying to just about every suggestion the others made, but eventually they got down to the main business.

'Right,' said Mungo, 'Check the fuckin' door.'

Pauly got up and reefed the door open to make sure there was no one eavesdropping, then closed it and returned to the table.

'Habal Tong have got their big fuckin' festival Friday night,' said Mungo. 'Our orders are to fuck it up.'

The others all grinned and waited for him to explain.

'The best way to fuck something up is to make people scared,' said Mungo. 'So what is HT most scared of?'

'Being sent home,' said Jimbo, '… not getting their full citizenship.'

'Bingo,' said Mungo.

'No, it's not,' said Lemon.

Mungo turned to her incredulous. 'I beg your fuckin' pardon?'

'They fear the same thing everyone fears … deep down.'

'Which is what?'

'Pretty fuckin' obvious,' chuckled Lemon. 'They fear death. We best fuck up their festival by issuing threats and making them too scared to go.'

The others sneered.

'We've been sinking their fuckin' boats for yonks,' said Jimbo. '… the ones that don't sink all by themselves. Fear of death doesn't stop 'em coming.'

'Only makes it more attractive,' said Pauly. 'Australia or martyrdom … it's win, win.'

'They've also got statistics on their side,' said Mungo. 'Less than one in fifty boats get sunk. The risk is pretty low.'

'Yeah … they're not scared of death,' said Jimbo. 'Especially their leadership. For them the big issue is conversion of temporary citizenship to full citizenship. So how do we stop that?'

'Well ... that's why we're here,' said Mungo. 'We fuck up their full citizenship by scaring mainstream Australia ... who are already split on the issue. How are all these new fuckin' citizens gonna behave once they can live anywhere?'

'And how many deep cell terrorists will be among them,' demanded Jimbo, '... waiting to blow up the Opera House or the MC-fuckin'-G?'

'Exactly,' said Mungo. 'We have to scare the fuck out of middle Australia ... and once the government puts a moratorium on new citizens from Ord City, this place 'll go off. Couple of decent riots ... a few well timed explosions ... the public demands a permanent ban on new citizens.'

'So how do we scare middle Australia?' asked Lemon.

'Easy,' said Mungo, '... we start the riots ourselves.'

'And set the explosions,' grinned Jimbo.

'But I'll tell youse fuckin' what,' said Mungo, tossing a weird looking rubber garment, attached to a skull cap onto the table. 'If you're scared of death yourself, you're in the wrong fuckin' game.'

• • •

Robbie was pretty smashed, but Tim was worse.

They were walking the streets, looking for Robbie's car but Tim kept falling over and Robbie had to hold him up. What's more, Tim had started crying and Robbie was awkwardly consoling him.

'It's okay, Timbo. Things aren't that bad ... you just need to go back to Sydney, I reckon.'

Even as he said it, Robbie realised he wanted to go back to Melbourne and would rather be just about anywhere than Ord City with its heat, its humidity, its weird smells and weirder people.

'You're my best mate,' sobbed Tim.

Well, Robbie didn't know about that, but he felt pretty sorry for Tim who deserved a shitload better than what life had dished out so far.

He plonked Tim's almost comatose figure down on a bus stop bench and tried to get his bearings. The car was parked only two blocks from the pub where Robbie and Chris had a room, so it should've been easy to find. Somehow they'd taken a wrong turn and Robbie was getting increasingly irritated by the throngs of people pushing past with their shouting and laughing and general bullshit.

He tried to check out some street signs to work out where they were, then recognised a 24-hour mini-mart that was only a block from the pub.

Fuck it.

Robbie dragged Tim up off the bench where, of course, he'd fallen asleep, and half carried him across the road and down towards the pub. Chris hadn't come home the previous night and Robbie guessed he wouldn't tonight either. He and Lemon had scored a room in the Reff club house – one piece of news Robbie had spared Tim.

Fuckin' women. Robbie found himself thinking about Kate again. She'd told him she wasn't interested and deeply regretted the one time she'd been in his bed. Somehow (he couldn't quite remember the details after a really big night) she'd stayed over and nature had played its inexorable course. The next morning he woke up on top of the world, but she was cold, monosyllabic and swiftly on her way.

She avoided him for days but when he finally cornered her she told him it had been a mistake and she didn't want to get involved with him. Despite all the great times they'd had together, he was too much like a brother, she'd said.

She liked him too much to fall in love with him, she'd said.

She wasn't capable of being the woman he needed her to be, she'd said.

And now, hauling Tim through the houseguests' door and up the stairs to his room at the pub, Robbie was suddenly struck with just how much he still loved Kate and how he needed to get back to Melbourne and try one more time to convince her that they were perfect for each other and their lives would be totally fucked up if they didn't get married.

Married?

'Jeez, I am pissed,' giggled Robbie. A great warm glow seemed to spread through him as the old fantasy kicked in – standing in the Botanic Gardens as she approached him barefoot, in a white dress with flowers in her hair. All their friends and family around as she stared into his eyes, smiling, and said, 'I do … with all my heart.'

Robbie dumped Tim on the bed which only had a sheet on it given the heat and absence of air conditioning. There was, at least, a fan which Robbie turned on. He turned off the light, removed his clothing and got under the sheet, leaving Tim dressed and outside the sheet to insulate their bodies from each other in sleep.

But sleep wouldn't come.

Robbie was so excited by the fantasy he found himself contemplating calling Kate to tell her how he felt. He looked at his phone and was surprised to see it was only nine o'clock, which meant it was midnight back in Melbourne. On a Tuesday night.

Was that too late?

In normal circumstances, certainly yes, but the circumstances were hardly normal. The circumstances were momentous – or potentially so. And if she truly did feel the way about him as he believed, deep down, that she did, then she wouldn't mind the hour.

Fuck it.

He scrolled down his list of contacts, found her number and hit call, his heart pounding with adrenalin as he heard the phone ringing. But after a few seconds her voice mail kicked in, 'Hello, you've called Kate. I can't answer just now but leave a message and I'll get back ASAP.'

A few seconds ticked away as Robbie racked his brain for something profound and meaningful to say. He kicked Tim to stop him snoring, then the long beeeep sounded.

'I love you,' said Robbie, his voice heavy with alcohol and emotion.

Then he hung up.

. . .

It was a beautiful wedding. So perfect he couldn't recall the details, but he seemed to sink into her soul, consumed by her eyes. They were walking through the garden, lost in each other, and then suddenly they were naked.

He wanted to take it slowly, to draw out their love over hours, days, years. But she was insistent, pulled him onto the soft grass of a secluded glade and began kissing his face, his neck and chest. She straddled his hips and, as he reached for her breasts, lowered herself onto him, guiding him in, squeezing with impossible pleasure.

His brain seemed to fill with the white noise of inexpressible love as she increased her rhythm, covering his face with kisses as he grabbed her by the hips and thrust upwards as the burn began in his groin.

'Oh Kate,' he breathed. 'Kate my darling … I … '

'What the fuck?'

Brilliant rainbow shards seemed to shatter in his brain as Robbie thrust upwards on the sweat sodden sheets. Tim was gagging, then furiously wanking Robbie's bursting cock and kissing his stomach.

'What the *fuck*?' repeated Robbie in a haze of tears and fury.

He stopped coming, shuddered with revulsion, then swung a fist in the dark, connecting with Tim's ear. Then he lurched up off the bed, grabbed Tim by the hair and smacked him again and again until Tim, unresisting, was just curled up and crying on the bed.

'What the fuck did you do that for?' demanded Robbie, absolutely furious but already regretting his violence.

'You said you loved me,' cried Tim.

'What? Why the fuck would I say that? I'm not a fuckin' poof!'

He felt Tim get off the bed in the darkness, then moments later the door opened and he saw Tim's silhouette just before he closed the door and vanished.

For a moment, racked with guilt, Robbie thought about going after him to apologise, but …

He needed some space after all that – a fucking shitload of space. He could just about have cried himself over the way his beautiful dream had turned into such hideous reality but …

Maybe he'd apologise in the morning.

Chapter 20

Don't Wake the Reptiles

In the hour before dark, they'd smeared their arms and legs with mud to protect from sun and insects, and Dave had shown them how to dig for pencil yams and collect edible seeds (most were poisonous, apparently). They then debated whether a fire was a good idea, but in the end, the yams needed to be cooked so they built a ring of stones in the centre of the clearing and set up a little blaze – which might also prove handy for keeping crocs at bay.

Dave wrapped the yams in some kind of leaves then thrust them into the coals and added more kindling. Then they reverted for the twentieth time to their previous conversation.

'ASIO?' wondered Dave.

'No way,' said Conan. 'I've met plenty of ASIO people in the line of duty and there's no way they'd carry on like that.'

Ming's behaviour was certainly a mystery and they discussed its implications (and her likely alignment) long into the evening.

The one benefit of her departure was that Conan no longer felt conflicted or embarrassed regarding his feelings for Mel, and Mel was clearly very into Conan. She leaned against his shoulder and contributed little to the conversation, except to insist passionately that Ming was a plant.

'You met her at Ronny Kwai's football party, right?'

'Yes.'

'You never wondered why she was invited … when everyone else was a mover and shaker?'

'Except me,' said Conan. 'I did wonder why I was invited. He was quite unfriendly when I first spoke with him, then he spoke on the phone with someone he called Major … I presumed it was Lammas

'... and after that he was weirdly friendly.'

Dave tossed some more dried wood onto the fire.

'So ... Ronny invites you for some obscure reason, and you meet a girl who wants to jump your bones within an hour of meeting you. How often has that happened in your life?'

'Only twice,' laughed Conan, giving Mel a squeeze, but even she laughed.

'No seriously,' amended Conan. 'We seemed to be a little team against the rest of the room and gravitated naturally together. Looking back, it seems obvious now that she was manoeuvred into place ... But why? What's the point?'

'Find out what you know? Who you're investigating?'

'Ronny knew I was interested in him and a possible connection with the murdered pair. And she didn't ask me anything about the case before she disappeared ... and clearly that was a set up also.'

'And now you reckon she was in a flat just a couple of doors down from the dead blokes,' said Dave.

'Yeah ... and I wouldn't mind having a look in that flat right now,' mused Conan.

'Not easy from here,' said Dave. They fell silent as he dug at the wrapped leaves, from which an aromatic steam poured forth.

'Pretty much done,' said Dave, which was just as well as they were all ravenous. The seeds had done nothing to quell hunger despite (according to Dave) their high nutritional value.

They all edged forward as Dave unwrapped a blackened leaf to reveal a couple of long thin yams. They were very hot but sweet and far more filling than the seeds.

With the moon rising the night was suddenly loud with the singing of insects and some ominous grunting from the river. Despite their predicament, Conan found himself enjoying the feel of Mel's body against his and wishing they were alone, but it was time to get serious.

'We have to get out of here,' he said. 'If the paramilitary blokes come back we're screwed right? And if Ming's really on their side ... as I reckon she must be ... then she's gonna tell them we've escaped the crocs.'

'That doesn't make sense,' said Mel. 'If she's on their side they must have known she was here and was going to cut us free ... which means they don't really want us dead. They just want us out of the way.'

The others considered, then Conan said, 'Maybe … but I don't want to meet those blokes again without a special assault group at my back. I reckon we need to get back to civilisation quickly.'

'So how do we get off the island?'

'One of us will have to swim for it,' said Dave, as a loud splashing and grunting sounded from not far off.

Dave was joking, but Conan said, 'You're right. Ming made it across, so one of us can do it also.'

'Are you mad?' asked Mel.

'Probably,' said Conan. 'But I can't see any other way unless we wait for a boat or a chopper which may take days and may not be friendly.'

'You're not to do it!' insisted Mel, clinging to his arm.

'I didn't say it had to be me,' said Conan, with a glance at Dave, who grinned and shook his head.

'If you *are* gonna do it,' said Dave, 'the best time is dawn. The crocs are all pretty dozy then, after a long cool night.'

'Don't encourage him,' said Mel, but Dave laughed.

'Conan saw those two huge crocs fighting this afternoon,' he said. 'There's no way he'll set even a toe in that water.'

• • •

Just before dawn, Conan stood at the water's edge staring across the river to the far bank. In the pre-dawn glow there was only one croc visible, unmoving about forty metres downstream, but it's the ones you can't see you have to worry about.

Sixty metres.

Probably closer to fifty, but it looked a very long way for a swimmer – more than the length of an Olympic pool. Conan had stripped just to undies, with his long-sleeved shirt tied around his neck, and for the first time Dave and Mel realised he was serious.

'Conan,' pleaded Mel.

'Sshhh,' he told her in a loud whisper. 'Don't wake the reptiles.'

He took a deep breath and marvelled at how cool it was before the heat of the day. But that was good. The cold-blooded crocs would be a tad listless at this time. That was the theory.

'I'm gonna breast stroke,' said Conan, 'but if you see any crocs coming … feel free to shout.'

'Conan, please!' said Mel, but he ignored her. They had to get off the island and he felt a sense of responsibility, that it was his fault they were trapped there.

He also had the sense of an opportunity slipping away – that the game was going on without him and the only way to pull something out of the fire was to take the bold and necessary action.

He took another breath. It was perceptibly lighter, and he could now make out another massive croc about fifty metres upstream. Could it be those were the only two close by? He just about fancied his chances if they were.

There was a hot pink glow to the east and Conan knew the sun was about to peek over the horizon, which would quickly take the cool out of the air.

'If you're gonna go, you'd better go,' whispered Dave.

Conan took another deep breath, winked at Mel, then walked down the mud bank into the water. He could hear a whispered argument going on behind him but managed to block it out. He needed to concentrate totally on not disturbing the water and alerting the monsters.

He glanced left and right, but both crocodiles were unmoving and apparently disinterested.

He waded to his knees but then the water got quickly deeper and he balanced on the balls of his feet, crouching in water up to his neck, took a last quick glance at the two crocs then pushed out like a giant frog, breast-stroking as smoothly and silently as he could.

The water was cooler than he expected and smelled of rain and mildew. It was muddy brown, full of insects and leaves, and felt somehow slimy, as though the passage of giant slugs had left a trace that coated his skin and somehow slowed him down.

But the far bank was definitely getting closer.

'Croc coming!' shouted Dave. 'Forty metres!'

Conan didn't need any further advice. He heard Mel scream as he pounded at the water, thrashing towards the bank. He took a great gulp of water trying to breathe and kicked furiously, always imagining jaws about to close on his legs.

He couldn't see the eastern bank. He couldn't see anything and had the idea he might be swimming in circles. He wanted to stop and rub the water out of his eyes to get his bearings and almost laughed at how stupid that would be. He then lifted again, thrashing arms and legs as wildly as possible, but then his hand scraped against the river bed and he knew he was almost safe. One more stroke and he reached down with his feet. But he slipped on the steep slope being scoured by the current and had to take a couple more frenzied strokes, clawing at the mud to haul himself into the shallows. Then he was up and running until he reached the top of the bank. Only then did he turn, chest heaving with exertion, to see the giant crocodile staring up at him from immediately below, before it slid backwards into the deeper water.

'Hey, Conan!' shouted Dave, 'You forgot your shoes! Better come back, eh?'

Conan laughed, full of adrenalin but shitting himself with delayed terror. He untied the shirt and squeezed it out, then considered the land to the east. It was flat, grassy savannah with stunted gums, she-oaks and hundreds of termite mounds. Knowing he had to hit the highway eventually, he gave the others a wave, then took off east as the sun finally lifted over the horizon.

The difference in temperature was immediate and he was glad he'd brought the shirt after worrying it might slow him down during the swim. His main problem was the ground. It was soft enough for bare feet but, with all sorts of nasty thorns, ants, scorpions and snakes about, he picked his way carefully. In fact, after an hour of walking, his focus was so fully on the ground that he was only twenty metres from the first of the structures when he came across them.

Conan's eyes widened as he lifted his gaze to see them – rank upon rank, thousands of giant white spiders, stretching as far as the eye could see.

• • •

Asif always had a feeling of pure freedom at the end of a three day shift, riding on the back of Ah Cheng's bike with the cool wind streaming past. He enjoyed the speed and Ah Cheng's expressive exhilaration as he flew around corners, but most of all he enjoyed the thought of days at home with Tanya.

Probably his last days at home with Tanya.

Asif thrust that thought away and concentrated on the distance – not moving, in contrast with the green-red blur closer by, a green-red blur that reminded him of Tanya's painting. His life was a blur and he was losing sight of the horizon.

The horizon should have been his citizenship, now only a couple of days away, unless there was any truth to the rumours in the papers that suggested the government would find an excuse at the last minute to delay, or refuse the First Wave.

'They cannot!' Ah Cheng had insisted in the mess. 'There will be mass riots if the First Wave is delayed. They wouldn't dare!'

Ah Cheng had grinned at Asif, knowing that the two of them shared a secret and, for the thousandth time, Asif found himself speculating as to what had driven his friend into the Tong. Ah Cheng was such a simple lover of life, so apolitical. Why had he joined?

It was always so sudden, the transition from desert highway to high rise around Lake Argyle, and Ah Cheng had to slow appreciably. But he still moved far quicker than most of the Wednesday morning traffic – slaloming his way through slower vehicles and the myriad obstacles such as food carts, road work and pedestrians that so characterised Ord City.

The smells also – blocked drains, sesame oil and fried garlic – so different from the dry, fragrant fume of the desert. Asif breathed deeply and felt a strange sense of joy, coupled with a feeling of loss.

He patted Cheng on the shoulder.

'Can we stop?'

Ah Cheng immediately pulled up onto a footpath, getting a few shouts for his trouble and shouting back until everyone adjusted to the new arrangement.

'What's up Asif?'

'Can we get a coffee? I want to talk about something.'

Ah Cheng shrugged but switched off the bike and removed his helmet. Then he followed Asif into a street café where they sat on broken plastic chairs under a faded umbrella with an ice cream logo painted white on red.

They ordered coffee and the two friends sat watching people and traffic for a couple of minutes until a pot of Turkish coffee was brought with two small cups.

'I love the coffee here,' said Asif.

'It's good,' agreed Cheng, 'but I'd rather have a beer. You should also.'

Ah Cheng never stopped tempting Asif to drink alcohol, but it wasn't going to happen. Not now.

'I'll have a beer with you next week,' said Asif.

Ah Cheng frowned.

'That's if there is a next week,' continued Asif.

Ah Cheng looked up at him tight lipped.

In that moment, Asif could no longer hold back and despite the direction from Razzaq not to mention the change of target, he couldn't help himself, knowing he would get support from his friend.

'I think it's very sad,' said Ah Cheng quietly.

'You agree with me?' asked Asif. 'It is a bad target?'

'I think it's very sad that you should betray the tong after nine years of faithful secrecy.'

Asif was deeply shocked. This was not the response he'd anticipated from Cheng.

'But … I haven't betrayed the tong.'

'You were told not to tell me. You disobeyed.'

'Only because I wanted your opinion,' said Asif. 'You are part of the tong and should be aware also of the changed target.'

'Of course I'm aware,' said Ah Cheng. 'Who do you think gave the order for change to Razzaq?'

Asif was stricken – dumbstruck with adjustment to the new reality.

'You mean … you? You are senior to Razzaq?'

Ah Cheng did not answer for a moment, but sipped his coffee and stared thoughtfully at the traffic.

'You put me in a difficult position, Asif. I no longer know whether you can be trusted … but there are only two days before the mission must be fulfilled. I cannot find a replacement in that time unless I undertake the mission myself.'

Asif started to speak but Ah Cheng held up a stern hand to silence him.

'Do you still believe in the purity of our purpose?' demanded Ah Cheng.

'Of course.'

Asif had a vision of Tanya – and the text she had sent him – but he banished it from his mind.

'Are you prepared to go ahead with your mission … the new target?'

Asif swallowed, but nodded as Ah Cheng stared hard at him.

'I will consider the matter,' said Ah Cheng. 'I ought to have you shot for your betrayal, but there is no time. And under the circumstances …'

Asif stared white faced at the man he thought he had known, fear replacing the comradely affection he had always had for Cheng.

'You will be watched, Asif. The moment we suspect any unwillingness to go ahead with your mission, you will be shot. And so will your woman. So play the part you were born to play.'

Asif nodded.

'Understood?'

Asif nodded again.

Ah Cheng stared piercingly then reached into his bag and pulled out a rubbery-looking garment which he placed on the table. It had a skull cap attached and Asif recognised the blast suit in which he had recently trained.

'I was going to give this to Razzaq to pass on to you,' said Cheng. 'But you may as well have it now.'

• • •

'Hello darling! How was work?'

Tanya glanced up as he entered but was deeply absorbed in a moment of creation, standing back from a canvas, holding two brushes in her right hand.

'It was okay,' said Asif, dropping his bag in the old armchair. 'The usual.'

He kissed the back of her neck and examined the painting – a wild woman with blonde dreadlocks, raging naked through a dark forest.

'What do you think?'

'She looks like you.'

'You think so? There's a fresh pot of chai in the kitchen.'

Asif disengaged and walked into the kitchen where he quickly transferred two new manga strips into the plastex box he kept at the back of the fridge inside a packet of haloumi. Tanya hated haloumi.

He then poured himself a chai, and went back out to Tanya's studio. She was once again in the world of the painting, humming to herself as she added umber shading to the woman's inner thighs and belly.

'It's you and it's not you,' said Asif.

'Why's that?'

'Because she's scared ... and you're the bravest person I know.'

Tanya laughed delightedly, 'I'll have to redo the eyes because she's not scared ... she's elated ... utterly joyous.'

'Also ... she's too fat,' said Asif. 'You have a much nicer figure than that.'

Again Tanya laughed.

'She's not fat, darling ... she's pregnant.'

For the second time in half an hour, Asif was stricken, as Tanya grinned at him with love and inexpressible joy.

'It's a self-portrait, my darling.'

PART THREE

Chapter 21

Chaos Theory

Conan walked through long avenues of the white, metallic spiders, all about two metres high by three metres wide. He'd seen a picture of them in the paper so knew immediately they were the receiving dipoles for the Giant Array telescopes and stretched over several square kilometres. Somewhere in the centre would be the node where all the data was collected, and no doubt an office from which he could call for help.

The node was proving difficult to find and he began to feel uncomfortable in the hot sun despite it being barely nine o'clock. It would be sweltering soon so he really needed to find the shade. There were footprints in the dirt path he was following, which was reassuring. At least two people had come this way barefoot and Conan wondered whether he might catch up with Ming, even though she was half a day ahead of him.

There was a slight rise in the ground ahead so Conan hastened forward, hoping to see the node beyond. But as he reached the crest a woman appeared to his right, head down and focussed on some instrument. She was tanned very brown and completely naked.

'Oh shit!' she said, glancing up at him.

'Doctor Khataten, I presume,' said Conan. 'You're looking well.'

Jen Khataten glanced about nervously, then shrugged.

'There's little point running for my clothes, I suppose … you've already seen the goodies.'

Conan laughed, impressed at her coolness under pressure.

'You're half naked yourself, Agent Tooley. What are you doing here?'

'Call me Tools.'

• • •

Ten minutes later they were inside Jen's office and she was once again dressed, in a white dust coat she pulled off the back of a chair.

'I usually work by myself and I like having an all over tan,' she explained as she placed her instrument on a desk and guided Conan to an old landline telephone.

'None of my business,' said Conan, '… so no need to explain. But … erm … Richie's a lucky man.'

Jen grinned back at him and left him to his call. He rang the AFP headquarters, gave the emergency code and was quickly put through to Loongy.

'Tools? What the fuck you want?'

'G'day Loongy … I've got an emergency on my hands. I need a chopper real quick to pick me up from the Giant Array.'

Loongy was incredulous.

'You want a chopper? I thought you'd gone home to Sydney to grow hipster beard and see abstract art.'

'Seriously, Loongy … we've got an emergency. Can you send the chopper?'

'You don't have good explanation, you fucking well pay for it,' said Loongy, but he agreed to send the chopper.

'You could do with some clothes also,' said Jen, returning to the small kitchen cum office. 'There's a pair of Richie's shorts that will probably fit you … somewhere.'

She handed him a cup of black tea (no sugar) and disappeared through another door as Conan examined her work space.

Considering what was going on at the Giant Array, with all its impressive hardware, the office was unspectacular and unpopulated. There were a couple of large triPods and an old tridee diorama screen, but apart from that it was all higgledy piggledy files, banks of old style CDs and books scattered everywhere.

'So this is where the magic happens?' asked Conan, picking up a text on chaos theory as Jen returned, having changed into a kaftan. She tossed a pair of khaki shorts at him.

'This is it,' said Jen. 'Still waiting for our turn on the Quantum to make sense of all the data, but I know what we're gonna see.'

'The Big Bang, yeah?' asked Conan, vainly trying to make sense of the weird looking equations in the chaos text.

'The Big Bang itself ... the very dawn of time.'

It sounded impressive but Conan shrugged.

'Won't it be just ... a big flash of light?'

'Yes ... but we can run it a billionth of a second at a time and follow it mathematically. The implications are ...'

'Mathematically?'

'Of course. You don't think we just want to gawk at the pictures, do you? There's a PhD in every micro-second after the beginning.'

'Well, I hadn't really thought about it,' admitted Conan, tossing the book back onto the table. 'You seem to be all by yourself out here.'

She glanced at him sharply, then shrugged.

'Most of the work is done by the dishes, dipoles and computers. It just needs someone to run a few tests occasionally and respond to any hardware problems. There's not a lot to do most of the time.'

'It must get lonely ... all the way out here.'

'I'm not always by myself ... and I do get relieved, every now and then.'

'Is chaos theory relevant to your work ... or just an interest?'

Dr Khataten glanced at her watch and regarded him with a hint of impatience. 'Chaos is central to my work. It is the only construct capable of explaining turbulence ... what happens in an explosion, like the Big Bang. Chaos predicts very precisely the way rapidly expanding gases and plasmas behave.'

'You can explain an explosion with mathematics?'

'Yes. Well ... *I* can't. The equations would fill a whole library ... but the Quantum computer could do it in seconds and I could understand the answers.'

'The answers to what?'

'The questions asked by the researcher. Are you going to put those shorts on?'

'Oh ... right.'

Conan stepped into the shorts as Jen blew on her tea and surveyed him thoughtfully.

'I've been getting some grief in the paper from your mate.'

'I don't have any mates,' said Conan, '... in case you hadn't noticed.'

'Major Lammas,' continued Jen. 'He's pressuring the government to stop funding my research ... reckons it's the ultimate blasphemy to look upon the work of God in the moment of His creation.'

'Well, maybe it would be,' said Conan, '... if there were any such thing as God.'

'It's such a boring argument,' said Jen. 'If there really is a God then what does it matter if we understand the way she does stuff? Wouldn't she want us to understand?'

'The church feels threatened when science comes up with explanations which aren't in the Bible,' said Conan, aware that he was trying to impress her. 'I've always been amused by perfectly rational people in the twenty-first century giving credence to a genesis myth based on the science available to the ancient Hebrews. They didn't understand geology ... or biology ... so God did it. End of.'

'As I said,' said Jen, glancing at her watch again, '... it's a boring argument. When does your chopper get here?'

Conan was taken slightly aback by her change in tone, and a little disappointed.

'I'm not sure. But I gave the emergency code so fairly quickly I'd hope.'

He suddenly felt a tad guilty, sitting around chatting over tea while Mel and Dave were still trapped on an island surrounded by crocodiles.

'Well, I need to get on with it,' said Jen getting up and putting on a wide-brimmed sun hat. 'You can wait here for the chopper.'

She filled a flask with water, tossed it in a shoulder pack and went to depart.

'Don't you need this?' said Conan, holding up the instrument she'd been poring over when he met her.'

'Oh thanks ... wouldn't get far without that.'

The instrument also went into her bag and she was gone.

'How very odd,' said Conan, as the thud of a chopper became audible in the distance.

• • •

Twenty minutes later, Conan was back in his own clothes in an unmarked black chopper with Mel and Dave. Little was said on the journey back to Ord City, not least as the two pilots were blankly uncommunicative behind mirror shades. Dave stared thoughtfully out the window while Mel clung to Conan, her face buried against his shoulder.

Conan had a lot to think about. More pieces had been added to the jigsaw, but once again he had the impression that there were too many pieces – that there was more than one puzzle mixed up in the box.

One thing did not puzzle him though – Mel's obvious attraction, which was exciting and full of promise for the future (notwithstanding his guilt regarding Lucia). As the chopper settled on top of the AFP building, she said, 'Don't get separated from me Conan … I don't trust these people.'

Conan nodded, but knew they would shortly be separated as a matter of protocol.

'They'll want a statement from you … by yourself … but it shouldn't take long. Just tell 'em the truth.'

'Of course I'll tell the truth,' said Mel, with a touch of her old prickliness back. 'I always tell the truth Conan … and you and I have a lot to talk about.'

As anticipated, Agent Ping and a couple of other blue uniformed functionaries met them at the helipad and escorted them to a lift that descended deep into the building. Eventually the lift opened on a long, white corridor that glinted purple in light that had a weirdly antiseptic look. They were ushered past numerous closed doors until Dave was shown into the first of three rooms with their doors ajar.

Mel was untangled from Conan, who smiled encouragement before being shown himself into the last of the rooms where Loongy was waiting for him.

'Hey Loongy,' said Conan, ignoring the flash of irritation that inspired.

'I have orders to put you straight on a plane,' said Loongy. 'Do not pass go … do not collect one hundred dollars.'

'Why?'

'It doesn't matter why! Orders are orders.'

Conan sat in the chair opposite Loongy while Ping remained

standing inside the door.

'Don't you want to hear what happened to me?'

Conan was still bruised from his Sunday night beating as well as the scrapes and sunburn from his subsequent ordeals.

'Write a report when you get back to Sydney … send me a copy for the file.'

Conan shook his head in frustration.

'Loongy … don't you get it? There is something massively weird going on in Ord City and I'm all round the edges of it. There were blokes with guns, mate! Guns! We were tied down on the river bank and left for the crocs! It's bloody amazing I'm alive!'

'Well … thank God you are,' said Loongy, 'but now it's time to go home. Your boss said come home now. You don't come today you suspended. Investigate while suspended, you under arrest.'

'But … this is ridiculous. Why isn't anyone taking my investigation seriously?'

'Investigation closed,' said Loongy. 'And where is your OzBrace? It's against AFP regulations not to wear it. How can we track you … when you're in danger?'

'It was stolen when I was bashed,' said Conan, once again wrong-footed by the weird Through-the-Looking-Glass feeling he got when talking to Loongy. 'Not that the AFP seems to give a rat's about one of its officers being assaulted.'

'You report it?'

'Not yet.'

'So how can we give a rat's? How can we give anything if you don't report? You don't make any sense, Tools.'

'Okay, so I've reported. Do you give a rat's now?'

'No. So will you go home today or do I have to put you on a plane myself?'

Conan took a deep breath and tried to ignore the knot of angry frustration building in his chest. Surely that wasn't good for him.

'You need to bring in a Dr Ming Li Chen for questioning,' he said. 'Ronny Kwai also.'

'What charge?'

'Erm … '

To his embarrassment, Conan couldn't think of a single offence that their behaviour suggested, nor link either of them to the offences which had certainly happened.

'Look, I ...'

'What have they done ... allegedly?' demanded Loongy.

'Aah, fuck it ... don't worry about it.'

Chapter 22

The Shadow Group

Robbie woke with another blazing hangover.

The sun seared through his tightly shut eyelids and battered his brain like a stick stirring up a hornets' nest. Every movement of his head increased the pain as exploding rainbows shattered his perception, and toxic waves of nausea rippled his guts.

The memories were worse.

They seeped back into his consciousness like so much oily scum and he felt fury at Tim and his disgusting antics. Then he felt an even bigger fury at himself for his violent response. Finally, he felt a devastating sadness for the dream he'd had of Kate, and how the whole journey to Ord City was wasted. He still loved her and no amount of distance had made it better.

He reached for his phone and was unsurprised to see that she hadn't responded to his message. It was after ten in Ord City, which meant it was afternoon in Melbourne. She would've heard his drunken protestation of love hours ago, and ignored it.

A profoundly deeper sadness hit him as he realised that now he didn't even have the fantasy of her loving him to cling to. Putting his feelings into words (and her silent response) meant he had nothing left but the reality of her absence in his life.

At least that was better than Tim's lot. Imagine going about desperately in love with a woman who had nothing but contempt for you and exploited your love to get her way all the time?

Robbie shuddered on the sweaty sheets, feeling sorry again for Tim, but then revolted as his hand brushed the dried semen on his thigh. For fuck's sake!

Robbie didn't want to think about it anymore but he couldn't help feeling sorry for Tim and a dreadful remorse for bashing him. Okay, he hadn't wanted Tim to do what he'd done, but that didn't make violence okay. Tim had been really upset when he'd left and Robbie felt a chill premonition. What if Tim did something rash?

'Jee-zuss,' moaned Robbie as he rolled off the bed and headed for the shower.

The hot water against his skull was nowhere near as hard as he would have liked but he did at least start to feel vaguely human again after several minutes of scrubbing. He got out of the shower and examined himself in the fogged up mirror, all crazed and rusting around the edges.

'I'm getting old,' thought Robbie, for the first time in his life, which was both depressing and somehow empowering.

He swallowed some aspirin, put on the last of his clean tee-shirts and contemplated a trip to the laundrette. That would have to wait. He had to know Tim was okay and maybe apologise before he had time for domestic chores.

With no better ideas, he headed for the Dedd Reffo house. It was conceivable Tim would have gone looking for Lemon, despite the likelihood she was with Chris.

'Why are people so weird?' Robbie asked aloud, getting some odd looks from the people streaming past him on the footpath. It was already stinking hot and the alien stink of Ord City was more oppressive than ever. The cooking smells were bad enough but there was an all-pervading dead water stench coming from hundreds of puddles and broken pipes – as though none of the plumbing actually went anywhere.

Late morning at the Reffo house was pretty quiet with the exception of Pauly snoring on a beaten up lounge. There was no one else around and Robbie shocked himself with the depth of the loathing he felt for Pauly. What the hell was Chris doing with a bunch of ratbag losers like Jimbo, Pauly and their dropkick cronies?

He turned to leave but was stopped by a shout.

'Hey, Robbie!'

Robbie turned to see Chris wearing only his St Kilda shorts and grinning like the old Chris.

'Hey Chris,' said Robbie. 'Have you seen Tim about?'

Chris laughed.

'I saw what was left of him. Someone's given him a proper fuckin' smacking, which is no less than the cunt deserves. You want a coffee?'

Chris didn't wait for an answer but started clearing away some of the crap around the kitchen sink and filled the jug, from which a giant cockroach emerged when he switched it on. Chris must have seen it, but to Robbie's disgust he ignored it and left the jug to boil.

'Any idea where Tim went?'

Robbie was aware that a lot had changed since he and Chris had last been alone together and felt slightly weird talking to him.

'Off with Lemon somewhere.'

Chris was grinning as he wiped a couple of mugs clean-ish and scooped instant coffee out of a large open tin.

'So ... you and Lemon, eh?' asked Robbie.

'Naaah. She's a bit of fun, but could you imagine taking that home to meet your folks? I gave her the arse.'

Robbie raised his eyebrows, feeling a glimmer of hope that things could go back to normal.

'How'd she take that?'

'How does she take anything? Bit of a screaming fit, but Tim 'll look after her.'

Robbie watched Chris sniff the milk, shrug and pour some into the mugs. He handed one to Robbie with HMAS Eureka on it. There was an insect wing revolving in the centre and Robbie placed the mug on the table with no intention of ever touching it again.

'And how are you getting on with Jimbo and Pauly and all the rest?'

'Pretty good.'

'Did you go to the planning meeting?'

'Yeah ... sort of,' said Chris with a glance at Pauly still snoring on the couch.

'Sort of? What does that mean?'

Chris just raised his eyebrows and gave an imperceptible nod towards Pauly, which Robbie interpreted to mean either that he couldn't or wouldn't talk about it.

'Let's go outside,' said Chris.

Robbie, for the sake of politeness, picked up his mug and followed

Chris through the back of the house into a small, cluttered yard with some badly weathered outdoor furniture and an obviously stolen beach umbrella advertising soft drink.

They sat in the shade and said nothing for a few minutes. They'd always been capable of long companionable silences, but Robbie was tormented by any number of conversations he needed to have with Chris, but didn't know where to start.

'What's the room at the pub like?' asked Chris.

'Okay … but the air conditioning's fighting a losing battle, and they never gave us the twin singles.'

'Still just a double? Fuck that.'

'Are you okay to stay here a bit longer?'

'Yeah … ' Chris glanced back towards the house, '… but if you play your cards right, there might be a room here for you.'

And there it was. The bone of contention rude and raw on the table.

'How would I have to play my cards?' asked Robbie, unable to keep the derision out of his voice.

'You know what I mean,' said Chris. 'You haven't really joined in. The boys sense it. They won't fully trust you until they know you're one of us.'

'Us,' repeated Robbie, trying to keep the revulsion off his face as he glanced at his coffee.

'Yes … us. That's why we came Rob … to join the Reffs and take back fuckin' Australia. Remember?'

'Yeah. I guess I was expecting something a bit more than … '

Robbie trailed off and gestured all round at the ramshackle building with its yard full of debris and dog shit.

'Have to make the best of what we've got,' said Chris, both defensive and accusing.

There was a bit more of a silence, then Robbie said it.

'I'm thinking of heading back to Melbourne.'

'Yeah, I've been waiting for you to say that,' said Chris, disgustedly. 'What happened to our big resolution … to join the Reffs and do our patriotic duty?'

'Sorry, man. I'm just not as into it as I thought I was … and there's also the Kate thing.'

'What about the bitch?' snapped Chris, 'I thought you didn't want to talk about her.'

'I don't,' said Robbie. 'And yet … I can't get her out of my fuckin' head and part of the reason for coming up here was to try and do that. I'm completely screwed.'

'Fuck her!' said Chris. 'If she can't see what a top fellah you are she's not worth a pinch of shit.'

Robbie grinned, despite himself, enjoying the old Chris passion.

'I reckon we'd better go for a beer,' said Chris.

'I reckon you're right.'

• • •

Conan, wearing a replacement OzBrace and accompanied by Mel, knocked at the door of Ming's apartment and was relieved when she didn't answer. He opened the door and was unsurprised that the place was exactly as he'd left it. Clearly she hadn't returned so he collected his gear and had a quick look around. He hadn't really noticed before how starkly furnished it was – no book shelves, very few clothes and almost nothing in the way of documentation. It was as though the apartment had been set up as a shell – as though she didn't really live there.

'Can we please go?' asked Mel and Conan understood her discomfort.

'Okay … let's go.'

They went back down the stairs, Conan still feeling utterly bewildered by the whole experience and a total failure as an investigator. They walked to the cab rank in a moody silence, Conan staring balefully at the traffic and wondering how long it would take to get to the airport.

Not that he really wanted to get to the airport.

'You know, Mel … if you and I are to have any sort of future, I'm gonna need you to be a little more forthcoming about your feelings.'

'Isn't it obvious how I feel?'

'Well, yes … but don't you want to talk about it?'

'Alright. I feel betrayed by the Army of God … I've been abducted by strangers and had my life threatened by crocodiles and mosquitos

... I'm too scared to go home to my own apartment and you're heading back to Sydney.'

'I don't *want* to go,' he said, knowing she was being deliberately unfair. 'What choice do I have?'

She didn't answer and they climbed into the first cab.

'Airport,' said Conan, and the Indian cabbie laughed.

'You are hopefully not in a hurry,' he said. 'There is much traffic today.'

'Do your best,' said Conan and took Mel's hand, which was stiffly withheld until she sighed and leaned into his shoulder.

'So what are you going to do?' she asked.

'Dunno. If you want me to I'll quit the AFP and we can go travelling together. Have you been to Europe?'

'Only the UK,' said Mel, '... very briefly ... and Paris for a weekend. I'd love to go back to London but ... erm ... '

'It's okay, I've got some money,' said Conan, '... if I can keep my mother's claws off it.'

They crawled along in the stifling heat with all the windows down and the car filled with exhaust fumes.

'Could've walked to the airport quicker than this,' said Conan. 'So what about the AOG?'

'What about them?'

'Are you going back?'

'I can't decide. I don't trust them ... at least I don't trust Thomas, although I refuse to believe he had anything to do with my abduction.'

'Who was it then?'

'It had to be something to do with my connection with you ... the people Ming works for perhaps?'

Conan nodded. The same thing had occurred to him.

'Okay, the people Ming works for ... let's call them the Shadow Group. Who are they and what do they want?'

'They want you to stop investigating the murders and the infiltration of the NBN node.'

'Why?'

'I don't know, Conan ... that's your job. But surely if they don't want you to investigate it means they have something to hide themselves regarding either the murders or the node.'

'Or both.'

'Or both,' agreed Mel. 'So who are their members … besides Ming?'

'I don't know, but they have some serious influence if they can get my investigation closed down. Are they the people we saw meeting at the Chinese restaurant?'

Mel considered, wrinkling her nose against the car fumes and the cigarette the cabbie had lit up.

'I sincerely doubt Thomas is involved, although I suppose it's not impossible … or at least that he has some link with them. But maybe Chard, Kwai and Ah Li Wu are in it.'

'Chard would have the authority to get the CCTV erased,' mused Conan, watching a group of wok chefs all working frantically as the car filled with a glorious smell of garlic, onions and chilli, briefly overcoming the cigarette smoke. 'Okay, let's assume Lammas and Maddox are not part of Shadow Group … but they've met them twice and Thomas wanted to be paid, so they're maybe negotiating some sort of deal or arrangement? What would the AOG want if that was the case?'

'I've no idea,' said Mel. 'My head is still spinning from the idea of Thomas sitting down to dinner with Ah Li Wu. Habal Tong are our greatest challenge … that and atheism.'

'And the *Epistola Clementis* … which so interested Bruce and Michael. That was a kick in the teeth for Christianity, yeah?'

'I rather doubt that,' said Mel, 'but I suppose you might interpret it that way … from a small-minded atheist perspective.'

'But Bruce and Michael weren't atheist,' said Conan, ignoring the jibe. 'They were both Buddhist … interested in Christianity and devoutly Habal Tong.'

'That's right.'

'And Ming was in an apartment just a couple of doors down from them … '

The cab was stuck in a gridlock of honking cars and Conan glanced at his watch.

'I'll never make the flight at this rate.'

'I am thinking the traffic will clear when we get around the next corner,' said the cabbie, sensing Conan's anxiety.

'But when will we get round the corner?' asked Conan.

'That is indeed the question, sir, that I have been pondering for some time now. The traffic monitors are not working today.'

Conan drummed his fingers against the brief case on his lap, and made a decision.

'Just let us off here mate. I can't afford to sit in traffic.'

'Oh, but sir, I am very much thinking that ...'

'This'll be fine, thanks pal.'

The cabbie sighed but scanned Conan's proffered OzBrace and unlocked the doors. Conan, with only his briefcase and a small cabin bag, slid out of the taxi and waited for Mel while many cars started honking anew at the stationary vehicle – the traffic was moving again.

Conan glared at the fickle traffic, then pointed down a side street. 'Bruce and Michael's apartment is just down there.'

'But, didn't they say not to investigate or you'll be arrested?'

'They said a lot of things. Come on.'

Conan led Mel down the crowded side street, turned into another much narrower street and soon found themselves outside the building in Dutton Close where the murdered men had lived.

Remembering the squalid lobby with its old graffiti and urine bouquet, Conan was a little embarrassed to take Mel into such a place.

'Breathe through your mouth,' he advised as they entered the hot, dark stairwell and began climbing, occasionally pushing past people coming the other way. Mel was making small noises of disgust but she followed him closely up the five flights of stairs, and both were sweating when they reached the top.

There were still remnant bits of blue police tape around Bruce and Michael's door, but that was no longer the address which interested Conan.

'This is the one,' he said, pausing outside the second last door before the stairwell. 'I think.'

'What are you doing?'

Conan pulled something like a pen from his top pocket and unscrewed it.

'This is a handy gadget,' he said. 'It reverses the lenses on a peep hole and lets me see inside a flat.'

He held the device up to the peep hole and peered in.

'Except when the peep hole has been taped over. Bugger.'

He put the device away and pressed his ear against the door, but there was so much background noise in the building, it was hopeless trying to hear inside one apartment.

'I've usually got a stinger ... an electronic device for opening locks ... but I didn't bring it with me.'

'Conan, you're not thinking of breaking in are you?'

'I am a bit.'

'But you'll be arrested!'

'Not if I can somehow turn this whole shemozzle around with a result.'

'And how likely is that to happen?'

'God knows ... but I sure as hell won't get a result if I just head back to Sydney with my tail between my legs.'

Conan leaned against the door, testing its resistance.

'Shouldn't you at least get a warrant or something?' she hissed urgently.

'I should do, yes,' said Conan, putting his heel next to the lock, picking his spot, and then driving it hard into the wood. There was a loud crack, but the door held. He kicked it again, harder, and felt something give. Then he threw his shoulder at the door, hitting just above the lock and fell through as it burst open.

'Quick.' Mel was staring white faced and motionless at his handiwork and had to be dragged through the doorway.

No one had protested his entry so the likelihood was that no one was present. Nevertheless, Conan left Mel by the entrance and flitted through the apartment using standard field technique, clearing each room before returning to the main living area and beckoning her.

'Look at this.'

Mel paced warily down the hall and paused in the open doorway, arms folded, staring at the furniture stacked in the middle of the room surrounded by boxes.

'What is it?'

'It's Bruce and Michael's stuff ... moved from their flat down the hall to here.'

'Who on earth would do that ... and why?'

'Why indeed, young Melodie. As for who ... I think that's pretty clear. Only the AFP could have done this.'

'The people you work for?'

'The very same.'

Conan started opening boxes.

'What are you looking for?'

'I'd love to find their laptops. Come on … help me look.'

Reluctantly, Mel started opening boxes and glancing inside.

'It's just a whole lot of junk,' she said.

'It is,' agreed Conan, holding up an Army of God pamphlet.

'Very funny … oh shit … I mean, golly!'

Conan looked over as she pulled a familiar-looking book out of a box.

'Isn't Ming a paediatrician?'

'She said she was.'

'Well … look at this.'

The book was a text on chaos theory: *Asymptotically Approaching Certainty: Chaos As The New Normal.*

It was written by Dr Ming Li Chen.

'Bloody hell,' said Conan. 'That same book was on Jen's desk back at the Giant Array … but I didn't notice the author.'

Conan pored over the contents, reading aloud the names of chapters: 'Quantum Analysis of Plasmatic Behaviour … Cosmic Morphology and Hive Consciousness … Plasmas and Peoples: Predicting Populations and the Chaos of Crowds … '

'What on earth does it mean?' asked Mel.

'It means we have another link,' said Conan, turning a page and staring at a phone number written in the top margin.

'Maybe two links.'

• • •

'Hey Lucia?'

There was silence on the other end of the phone.

'Conan?' she whispered, after a while.

'I don't have long, and I need another favour.'

'Please don't tell me you're still in Ord City. They said you were on your way home.'

'I am on my way home … sort of … but I need you to identify

227

another number for me.'

Lucia groaned.

'You're in so much trouble, Conan … and so will I be if I help you.'

'Lucia … this is really important.'

'I can't help you, Agent Tooley.'

She hung up but, as he knew she would, she called back seven minutes later.

'Where are you?' he asked. 'Public phone?'

'Of course.'

'Okay … now I'm still not entirely on top of all this but I know that something massive is brewing in Ord City … so massive that even our bosses are being leaned on to stop my investigation. Someone very high up is dodgy as fuck.'

'Conan!'

Mel had registered shock despite his request she keep silent.

'Who's with you?' demanded Lucia.

Conan frowned at Mel and shook his head.

'I can't say … just someone helping me.'

There was another silence.

'She scolded you for language, like a mother would … or a girlfriend.'

'Please Lucia … can we just sort out this number?'

He opened the book and read the number scribbled at the beginning of a chapter called: Non-Linear Dynamics in Purposive Pharmacology.

'That's another cryp,' she said.

'I guessed it would be.'

Yet another silence, then, 'You know, Conan, there is a reason I've always been prepared to help you … '

'… I know.'

'We've kinda talked about it over the years … but never properly.'

'I know.'

Conan winced with embarrassment, profoundly aware of what an arse he was.

'I think we should talk about it now. Then maybe I'll look up your number for you.'

'You know we can't talk about it now … and we've only a little time.'

Conan and Lucia both knew the Quantum computer constantly scanned all phone conversations and could possibly identify them from their voice signatures and then locate them via their OzBraces.

'Can't talk about what?' hissed Mel.

'I think we should both leave the AFP,' said Lucia, 'and go travelling, like you always said we should.'

'Lucia, I have to get off the phone. Call me when you've traced the number, okay.'

'Yeah, okay, Conan … maybe.'

Chapter 23

A State of Pure Ecstasy

'Are you happy?'

'I cannot begin to tell you how happy,' lied Asif, forcing a smile.

He and Tanya were sitting in their favourite café, where they always went when Asif returned from a shift in the mines. It was very popular with Habal Tong devotees and, with *Illumination* only two days away, there was a bit of a party atmos happening.

'I feel so wonderful,' said Tanya, and indeed, she was glowing with good health and budding maternity. 'I mean ... I feel dreadful in the mornings but, apart from that, I've never felt so alive.'

Asif's thoughts kept returning to the painting she had done of herself – a naked, wild woman running through a forest in a state of pure ecstasy, so full of life she couldn't get the happiness out.

'It is wonderful,' said Asif, sticking to short sentences because of the lump in his throat, and the deep sense of loss that was already consuming him.

Tanya sipped her lemon and ginger tea, her eyes sparkling with love and the future.

'Maybe we should move to Sydney?' she said.

'Sydney?'

'Yes ... I think the climate would be much healthier for the child ... not to mention the medical services, and my family is there. I'll need them.'

'Of course,' said Asif.

'And you know what else?' said Tanya. 'I'm going to hold an exhibition, and the sales can go to bringing your family out to Australia ... all of them.'

Asif felt the last of his resistance crumble and tears ran freely down his face.

'What's wrong?' she asked, her own eyes brimming.

'I am sorry, Tanya darling … I am just so overcome with love and happiness. It is more than I can bear.'

'Oh Asif … '

They clasped hands across the table, both of them crying and thinking of what the future would surely bring.

• • •

'How about this place?' asked Mel.

'It looks a bit HT,' said Conan, dubiously.

'It is, but they do great coffee and the food is very good.'

Conan allowed himself to be dragged into a hippyish café, full of alternative looking types with all sorts of exotic food and drink for sale. They ordered coffee and a couple of wraps, and sat in the only vacant chairs at a share table – one end of which was occupied by a couple holding hands with tears in their eyes.

'Are we disturbing you?' asked Mel.

The woman with long blonde dreadlocks looked up, smiled, and shook her head.

'Lucia was upset?' asked Mel.

'Yes,' sighed Conan. 'It's … erm … complicated.'

'It always is with you.'

'She's not my girlfriend,' said Conan. 'I owe her nothing … '

'But?'

'But … I know she's always had a bit of a thing for me, and she's maybe feeling a tad exploited. She shouldn't be helping me when I'm persona non grata.'

Mel nodded and reached for Conan's hand.

'So … she's not part of your baggage?'

'No … I don't really have any baggage.'

'Except Ming … and your ex-wife.'

'Ming doesn't count, and my ex is long gone. She hates me.'

'Because you were too hard?'

The coffees and food arrived and Mel smiled her thanks at the Indian girl who had brought it.

'God knows. The point is … she's out of my life. If you're up for it, I'd love us to be a couple … a normal couple.'

Mel almost snorted cappuccino through her nose.

'A normal couple? Us?'

Conan felt mildly insulted.

'We could at least try,' he said.

Mel gave him a stern look, which slowly morphed into a smile.

'I've been thinking about your offer,' she said. '… to go travelling.'

'Great.'

'Where shall we go and when shall we leave?'

'Well … as soon as this case is wrapped up … '

'Now!' said Mel, suddenly full of enthusiasm. 'Let's have an adventure. Let's just walk away and go.'

'I'd like to,' said Conan. 'I really would … '

'But you won't.'

'I just feel so maddeningly close to a breakthrough … despite everything … '

'They don't *want* you to investigate, Conan. The Shadow Group seem to give orders even to the AFP, so you're never going to break through. But we could break away.'

Conan was playing with his phone, willing Lucia to call with the cryp identified.

'Even if you did break through … who can you trust with it? You're clearly in very dangerous territory here.'

Conan shrugged.

'I just can't stand giving up when I'm …'

Conan paused mid-sentence, staring over Mel's shoulder.

'Yes … when you're what?'

He put a hand up to stop her speaking.

'What's up?' she insisted.

'I just found a major piece of the jigsaw.'

• • •

'Are you finished?'

'Yes.'

Asif drained the last of his tea, held the thin plastex bill slip against his OzBrace until it buzzed, then got up.

'What do you want to do?' he asked her. 'Go home, or go for a walk?'

'Let's just go home.'

Tanya took his hand and they left the café, blissfully unaware that they were being followed.

Chapter 24

The Land Where
Everything is True

'Does it hurt?'

'It's okay,' said Tim, despite the pain.

'It looks like it must hurt,' said Lemon. 'Why did he do that? I thought you were friends.'

'I thought so too.'

They were in a bar together and Tim was happy because Lemon was sad. She'd been dreadfully upset when he'd found her that morning, crying and carrying on about what a ratbag Chris was. But a while later she'd noticed the damage to Tim's face and for the first time in a long time was solicitous about his feelings and even bought him a couple of drinks as his dole money had been blown already.

'What makes you happy, Timmy?'

'Being with you … when it's just us and no one else to confuse things.'

'What things?'

'You know what I mean.'

She gave him one of those dazzling smiles she reserved for special occasions and he felt his heart lurch with love as she took his hand.

'Why do you love me so much? I know I'm not the best girlfriend … some of the time.'

Tim's eyes filled with tears and he kissed her hand.

'All is nothing and nothing is all,' he said.

'Do you really believe that … with all your heart?'

'Of course I do. It's the most important rule of my life.'

She drained one of the bourbons in front of her and sipped on the next.

'What would it feel like …,' she wondered, '… to be nothing?'

'Peaceful,' he mused, delicately touching his broken nose.

'Peaceful,' she agreed. 'But if nothing is all, does that mean we should aspire to being nothing?'

'I suppose it does.'

Lemon nodded and ordered him yet another drink. He couldn't remember the last time she'd been so generous and found himself feeling optimistic about the future once again.

'What do you want to do about *Illumination*?' he asked.

'Oh … we should definitely go.'

'But what about Dedd Reffo?'

'What about them?' she snapped.

Tim held up his hands in apology. 'Sorry Lemon … I get a bit confused with your various strategies and infiltrations.'

Once again she smiled.

'That's okay, Timmy. You've been very hurt and it must all seem a bit strange. You deserve to find peace.'

The sun was setting outside and Tim, after the humiliation and bashing from Robbie, wondered whether he'd ever felt so happy.

• • •

Chris and Robbie had been drinking all afternoon.

Their conversation had ranged across all their usual topics but had continually come back to two main issues: Dedd Reffo and Kate.

It had been a very honest session – more than once they'd nearly come to blows. But as the sun disappeared over the western horizon and the sky turned velvety pink and purple, they reached what Robbie called The Land Where Everything is True: a state where they understood each other so perfectly it was impossible to disagree.

'Kate's gonna come to her senses,' insisted Chris. 'How can she not when you'd be so perfect for each other?'

'God, if only it were that simple,' said Robbie. 'Love isn't logical. It never does the obvious thing.'

'Love isn't logical,' repeated Chris. 'That's really profound man … you should write it down.'

'Who's gonna read it?' laughed Robbie.

'You never know,' said Chris. 'You might be famous one day.'

'For what?'

'I dunno … first man on Mars? Serial axe murderer?'

Robbie sprayed beer in laughter as he often did when Chris was in form.

'That's how to get famous,' enthused Chris, '… just kill a bunch of cunts and everyone'll know your name forever.'

'I don't want to be famous that badly,' said Robbie.

'Really? I do.'

Chris's face had changed and Robbie was no longer sure whether he was joking.

'You'd kill to be famous?'

'For the right cause I would. Fuckin' oath.'

A different mood descended and Robbie would have preferred to change the subject but Chris was off on one of his rants that had always seemed so funny back in Melbourne.

'There're too many people already in this fuckin' country and with the seven year visas about to start letting 'em out of Ord City we're gonna be fuckin' swamped.'

'Can't kill 'em all,' said Robbie.

'Don't have to kill 'em all,' said Chris.

'What do you mean?'

Chris took a swig of beer and glanced over his shoulder.

'Couple of well placed bombs at *Illumination* … the government puts a moratorium on the visas while it gets sorted out. No one wants terrorists loose in the community.'

'But you'd be the terrorist,' objected Robbie. 'Hypothetically, of course.'

'No one'd know that,' shrugged Chris. 'I'd even wear a bomb suit myself if that was the only way to get close to Ah Li fuckin' Wu.'

Robbie was shocked that Chris could even be joking about such a thing. They had of course come all the way from Melbourne to join a far right extremist group with a track record of mass murder, but that reality had always seemed like a game – a bit of a joke even – to Robbie lamenting Kate's rejection and not particularly caring where Chris led him.

'You are joking, aren't you?'

Chris stared at Robbie for a long moment, as though coming to a decision.

'Maybe ... maybe not. I'd see it as a patriotic duty.'

'The mass murder of innocent people is patriotic?'

'Keeping the cunts out by any means possible is a patriotic duty,' insisted Chris. 'I would lay down my own life so other Australians could live in a country unswamped by Asians and Habal fuckin' Tong.'

'It's not worth dying for,' insisted Robbie, feeling pissed again.

'You reckon? I don't want to live in a country fucked up by feng shui, bok choi and Habal fuckin' Tong, so it's win win. The thing is ... why don't we do it together?'

Robbie felt a cold horror creeping over him as he realised Chris was serious – or almost serious.

'No way, man. No fucking way.'

'What else have we got to live for?' demanded Chris. 'There's no jobs except for reffos ... we don't have women in our lives.'

Robbie winced as an image of Tim flashed into his mind.

'We'd be like a couple of those Anzac heroes who jumped out of trenches when the whistle blew,' said Chris. 'They knew they were gonna die in front of the machine gun nests but they did it anyway, for their mates. I'd fuckin' well do it for you, man.'

'But we're not Anzacs in a war, Chris. We're two ordinary blokes in 2030. It's a different world.'

'You saying the Anzacs weren't ordinary blokes?'

'No.'

'Of course they were ordinary blokes ... until they got out of the trench and became heroes. That's what I'm gonna do and if you were truly my mate you wouldn't let me go alone.'

Robbie opened his mouth to speak but didn't know where to start, he was that confused and worried.

'And it's not like it'd hurt or anything,' slurred Chris. 'Over in half a second, mate ... you wouldn't feel a thing.'

At that moment Robbie's phone rang. He glanced at the caller ID and his eyes widened.

'Holy shit!'

'Who is it?' asked Chris.

'It's Kate.'

‘I'm feeling a little adventurous Timmy.’

Lemon had been getting amorous over the last hour or so and Tim's face was no longer hurting. That might have been the alcohol but it might also have been something to do with the blood draining from his brain and concentrating elsewhere. He was that hard it hurt and was dying to get Lemon somewhere private – not that they really had anywhere private unless it was back at the Dedd Reffo house.

She'd slid round to Tim's side of the booth and was kissing his neck and his ear, her breath smelling sweetly of bourbon and Twisties.

‘I'd like you to do something for me … something special.’

‘Anything.’

‘This is something I've never tried before … the person who did it for me would have to love me more than anyone else in the world.’

‘Lemon, you know that's me,’ he protested, feeling a little hurt.

‘It could be you,’ she teased, kissing his cheek and running her finger up his thigh, ‘but how can I really be sure?’

‘I'd do anything for you Lemon. I'd die for you.’

‘Would you?’

• • •

Chris watched the spectrum of expression pass across Robbie's face as he sat with the phone against his ear.

He said very little after the initial excited greeting, just sat listening, his face going from delight to desolation over the course of a couple of minutes. Then he hung up and stared at the table.

‘Bad news, huh?’

Robbie didn't answer for a while, but took another slug of beer and rubbed his face in his hands.

‘She said she'd been worried about me,’ he said, eventually.

‘That's promising.’

‘Worried I was still carrying a torch for her when she'd already made it clear she wasn't interested.’

‘That's less promising. But fuck her man … if she's not interested, her loss.’

Robbie felt a surge of emotion and a lump in his throat. It was difficult to talk without crying but he forced himself to be strong.

'She did say one thing,' he said. 'It was sorta nice … I guess.'

'Yeah?'

'She said she loved me too much to get involved with me.'

'What a bitch!'

'What do you mean?'

'Don't you see what she's doing there? Telling you no, but at the same time giving you some sort of hope for the future.'

'Maybe,' agreed Robbie.

'She's keeping you interested in case she decides there's no one else by the time she's fuckin' thirty.'

'So what do I do?'

'I know what I'd do,' said Chris angrily. 'Give her some fuckin' guilt to choke on. Let the stupid bitch realise what she's lost and how fucked up her life will be without you.'

Robbie looked up slowly, the emotion suddenly gone and replaced by a cold, hard resolve.

'Over in half a second you reckon?'

Chris nodded, and Robbie stared into the dregs of his beer.

'Okay fuck it,' he said. 'I'm in.'

• • •

Four people – two men and two women – sit before a huge picture window looking over a vast city, with an ocean to the north under a pink sky fading to purple. A servant pours tea and departs silently. None of them speak until all have savoured the tea and replaced their cups.

'So,' says the elder woman, '… two more nights.'

'Everything is in place?' asks the small man.

'Everything,' confirms the larger man. 'Although it is a pity the federal agent made his way off the island.'

'He must be very brave,' mused the smaller man. 'But no braver than our young heroine.'

The younger woman inclines her head.

'Thank you,' she says. 'I can at least confirm that his investigation has led nowhere.'

'And yet he found his way to me,' says the larger man, dressed entirely in black.

'He had the phone records of the dead men,' shrugs the older woman. 'It was not possible to have those erased before they were accessed by the AFP.'

'So what about the AFP?' asks the small man. 'Are they compliant?'

'They have ordered Tooley home,' says the younger woman. 'But it is not clear whether he has gone.'

'What keeps him here?' asks the smaller man.

They all look to the younger woman.

'He has become involved with Captain Roberts … romantically involved.'

There are tight smiles, then the older woman says, 'That will not please our friend.'

'He is humiliated,' agrees the younger woman, '… but is not the kind of man to become unpredictable. As we have seen.'

The others all sip tea and consider.

Then the smaller man says, 'He did ask for the amended target, did he not?'

'He did. Exactly as we contrived.'

The others smile.

'Even still,' continues the smaller man, 'I am disappointed he is so easily manipulated. Perhaps we should talk again with his rival?'

'I think that is wise,' agrees the older woman. 'I will arrange it.'

All four sip their tea contentedly.

There are only two more nights.

Thursday: Two Days Before the First Wave

Chapter 25

Grinning Like Punch in a Nightmare Side Show

On Thursday morning the media was full of *Illumination* and the arrangements for Friday evening.

The main event was at Rinehart Stadium which would be set up like a rock concert with seating for over a hundred thousand accredited Habal Tongers, but many times that number were expected to fill the surrounding squares. It was going to be an epic celebration with people from all over Australia and Asia attending (even though Habal Tong was a uniquely Ord City phenomenon).

But beneath all the excitement was the security fear. It was known that various anti-HT groups would be staging demonstrations and Dedd Reffo in particular were expected to be active. The police would be everywhere but that wouldn't deter anyone bent on trouble. A further complication was the hordes of drop shot and death game thrill seekers expected to turn up in pulse-display bio-suits to cluster around any likely danger spot to prove they weren't scared of the terror threat.

Conan tossed the paper aside and finished the last of his toast. They were sitting in the café across the road from the place to which they had followed the couple the previous night.

They had followed the couple because the man had a very distinctive triangle of moles on his cheek. The same triangle of moles that Conan had seen a dozen times re-watching the man download specs for the node and then walk through the streets of Ord City towards Rinehart Stadium.

They had seen the couple enter the small apartment building, then lights had appeared on the first floor. Conan had climbed up to peer in the windows for a while but had seen nothing interesting. The woman seemed to be some sort of artist and the man did little more than sit in an old armchair and drink tea.

Conan had contemplated breaking in – or even trying to get a warrant – to make an arrest, but he knew that would only lead to trouble so decided to wait until the man did something more outwardly interesting.

They had retired to Mel's place for the evening, despite her fear it was under surveillance, and had some pretty torrid post-crocodile sex, before sleeping the sleep of the dead.

And Lucia had not called.

The next morning they'd been back very early to the stake-out and were just in time to follow the couple – to whom they referred as Moleface and Blondie – back to the same café where they had first encountered them.

But they had continued to do nothing out of the ordinary, although Moleface did seem a little jumpy and Conan was increasingly tempted just to go over with his badge and gun and confront the bloke.

'I knew you'd be here.'

Conan looked up and was amazed to see Dave Marsh grinning at him.

'Here? I've never been here in my life. Why would I be here?'

'Kenny Cook told me. He's monitoring your new OzBrace.'

'Kenny? How do you know Kenny?'

Dave laughed and sat in a spare chair next to Mel, who smiled and chastely accepted his peck on her cheek.

'He knew we'd been on the island together,' said Dave. 'He figured you'd trust me … so he got in contact.'

Conan shook his head, having trouble adjusting to yet another weird development.

'Dave Marsh and Kenny Cook,' he mused. 'I wouldn't trust anyone in cahoots with Kenny Cook.'

'Well he trusts you … that's what he wanted me to tell you.'

'He trusts me?'

'He does now. There's been a development.'

'What sort of development?'

'Kenny said to tell you that Lucia is gone.'

A cold freeze crept over Conan's heart.

'Gone? What do you mean gone?'

'Apparently she tried to look up some phone number and all hell broke loose. A bunch of blokes from fuck knows which agency descended on the building and spoke with the head of the AFP in Sydney. Then they all swarmed into her ops room and she was gone in seconds. No one knows where.'

Conan was devastated, and wracked with guilt. But he glanced back to Moleface and Blondie and swore furiously.

They were gone.

'Jeez Dave … you bloody well distracted me from the best lead I've had the whole time.'

'We know where they live, Conan,' said Mel, and Conan nodded.

'Right,' said Dave. 'Kenny says you're back on the case, but unofficially.'

Conan felt his eyebrows rise, as he sipped coffee.

'Unofficially? That sounds dodgy and Kenny hates dodgy.'

'The whole thing's dodgy,' said Dave. 'But wait'll you hear the next bit.'

'Well?'

Dave grinned and pulled off his OzBrace.

'He suggests we swap OzBraces.'

'Oh fuck, no.'

'Conan!'

'Sorry Mel, but fuck! This is highly irregular … not to mention illegal and totally against our regulations.'

'Kenny wants me to go to Sydney with your OzBrace,' said Dave, 'so anyone else who happens to be monitoring you will think you've gone home.'

'But Kenny will be able to monitor me through your OzBrace,' mused Conan. 'This is a world of trouble if we get busted.'

'I think OzBrace fraud is the least of our worries,' said Dave. Conan nodded, pulling his OzBrace off under the table and handing it to Dave.

'Cool,' said Dave. 'I'm off Sydney. Don't fuckin' ring me till it's all over.'

With that he jumped up, gave them a grin and was gone.

'What now?' asked Mel.

'Back to Moleface's house I suppose ... but you shouldn't be getting involved anymore.'

'Are you about to become a boring chauvinist?'

'No ... it's just that there are rules. Operational rules which ...'

'Like the ones you're following with your OzBrace?'

• • •

'What is wrong with you today?

Tanya was irritated. She was trying to explain her trip to the ultra-sonographer as they shopped for groceries, but Asif was a million miles away and she'd had to retell the story three times.

'Nothing.'

'You're jumping at shadows. Is there something you need to tell me?'

Asif's heart sank as he contemplated the devastating impact his actions the following morning could have on Tanya, and on his unborn child. How had it come to this?

'The only thing I need to tell you is how much I love you.'

Tanya smiled and her eyes filled with tears.

'You're crying, Asif. Why?'

'Because I love you so much it hurts.'

Tanya threw her arms around his neck, not caring about the public display.

'I knew I made the right choice with you,' she said. 'You won't be surprised to know that old friends and family warned me off getting involved with a refugee ... you might be a boogie man terrorist and all that crap ... but they hadn't met you. They don't understand the depth of your emotion and most importantly, your ability to express it. That's so rare in a man.'

Asif's frame shook with sobs as she continued to make things much, much worse. Was there any way out of his mission? Could he go and see Cheng and make some sort of deal?

Immediately, he knew such an approach was impossible. Ah Cheng had said the instant he suspected Asif had lost his resolve he would be shot. And so would his woman.

'I think it's a good idea that we go to Sydney,' said Asif.

'Fantastic,' said Tanya, disengaging and continuing her hunt for groceries as Asif returned to his wary surveillance of all in sight.

'Or rather, you should go, but maybe I should stay here for a while,' he said. 'This is the only place I can get work.'

'Are you mad?' asked Tanya. 'Do you think I'd leave the father of my child?'

Asif was having trouble concentrating on the conversation, he was so attuned to the presence of every other body around them, any of whom could be Ah Cheng's Watchers.

'It's just ... what you said about the climate being bad for the child. I worry about that ... and maybe you should go soon.'

'I almost think you're trying to get rid of me,' teased Tanya, lifting a slab of bottled water into the trolley.

'No, no ... let me do that,' insisted Asif.

'My pregnancy isn't turning you into a chauvinist, is it?' she laughed, and Asif felt himself burning with embarrassment and confusion. A Chinese woman seemed to be following them, idly checking out the same groceries and close enough to hear their conversation.

'Are we finished?' he asked.

'Finished what?'

'The shopping. Is there anything else we need?'

Tanya stared at him, perplexed by the sudden change of subject and his weirdly swinging moods.

'A few things ... but we can go home if you want.'

Asif forced himself to smile as the Chinese woman strolled serenely past.

'No. Let's finish.'

They gathered the last few items, pushed past the pay scanner and were on their way, Asif resisting the urge to constantly turn and check whether they were followed.

As they reached the front of their small block, his eyes swept the street. And there they were, sitting in the café across the road – a man and woman that he picked out as anomalous.

Playing back his mental tape he realised they were the same non-Asian couple who had sat at his and Tanya's table the previous afternoon. It probably meant nothing. But here they were again …

Asif's instincts screamed at him to run, but how could he possibly leave Tanya?

• • •

'There they are.'

'Don't stare at them,' advised Conan. 'The art of surveillance is to watch without watching.'

'You've done this before?'

'Heaps of times.'

Mel had a big grin on her face and Conan understood exactly how she was feeling, having seen the same thing in dozens of rookies.

'You're not supposed to be enjoying it.'

'I can't help it,' she said. 'It's quite exciting this cops and robbers lifestyle.'

'It's not exciting, Mel,' he said, pointing at the bruises that still darkened his face. 'It's serious. Remember the crocodiles? Remember Bruce and Michael?'

'Sorry.'

But she was still grinning and Conan sighed, sneaking another peek at Moleface standing at the door across the street with shopping bags while his partner fumbled for a key. Then, as he followed her in through the door, Moleface turned and looked directly at them.

'Shit!'

'What's up?'

'He's made us.'

'He's what?'

Conan shook his head in exasperation.

'He knows we're watching. I just made eye contact and saw it in his face.'

'So what do we do?'

• • •

'What's wrong Asif?' demanded Tanya. 'You're like a cat on a hot tin roof … and you're sweating. Are you alright?'

'I'm fine … fine,' muttered Asif, dumping the bags in the kitchen and walking over to the window that looked onto the street.

'You don't seem fine.'

'I am … but I need to go out for a while.'

Tanya stared at him.

'You need to go out?'

'Yes … just for a little while.'

'Why?'

'Erm … I can't say. It's a surprise.'

'Well you're acting very strangely and it's scaring me.'

Once again his eyes welled with emotion.

'Please, my darling … trust me. I won't be long.'

With that he picked up his keys, ignored her protest and slipped out the door to their apartment. But instead of heading down the stairs to the street entrance, he strode along the landing and down the back stairs to the communal laundry and the small yard which led onto a lane.

He glanced up and down the lane, then took off to his left intending to circle all the way round and in through the back entrance to the café to check out the Watchers. But no sooner had he started down the lane a woman stepped out from behind a derelict car.

It was the woman from the café.

He spun around to see the man – thirty metres away – and then he bolted, straight at the woman. She jumped out of his way but there was a shout from behind and Asif knew he was being chased. He fled through the alley – supercharged by adrenalin – swung left then right onto the main street in an effort to lose his pursuer in the crowds.

People shouted or got out of his way as he dodged around food carts and then charged across the road heedless of traffic. Two motorcyclists slid onto the road in an effort to miss him and horns blared. People ran towards the incident and Asif knew they would help screen him from the Watchers.

He snatched a glance over his shoulder and couldn't see them so dodged into an alcove doorway, lungs heaving with exertion in the stifling heat and humidity.

'Now, what do I do?' he wondered. He couldn't go home, that was clear. He knew no one but his work crew and some friends of Tanya's, and none of them could be jeopardised.

Razzaq perhaps? Could he somehow be an intermediary between Asif and Cheng?

Too risky. Razzaq was a fanatic and probably Cheng's assassin.

The Army of God?

Asif had accompanied Razzaq a couple of times when he had gone to the Great Debate to shout at the Christians. They pursued an alien agenda but they seemed safe. Maybe he could pretend to be a convert and they might hide him, and send a message safely to Tanya to tell her to go to Sydney.

He readjusted his headscarf to hide his face as best he could. Then, with a glance in both directions, he left the alcove and walked quickly the several blocks to the Army of God chapter house on the corner of Kerr and Whitlam.

He paused across the road, aware that if he was still being watched, entering the AOG building would be a fatal error. He decided to sit down in the café across the road and take stock, and that's when everything changed. Razzaq slipped into the café and, in that moment, Asif despaired. He assumed Razzaq was following him, but to his amazement Razzaq sat at another table and showed no sign of having seen him.

Even more amazing was the large man with the deep voice who entered the café a minute later and sat with Razzaq. Coffees were brought to them, without being ordered, which suggested they were regular customers.

Asif could not hear their conversation but he could hear the deep baritone buzz punctuated by Razzaq's more nasal tone. He could also tell that, whatever they were discussing, they were in agreement.

• • •

'He's in the café,' said Mel. 'Shouldn't you go in and arrest him?'

'Maybe,' said Conan.

'Maybe? Why maybe?'

'Because there are another interesting pair in there, sitting at a different table.'

Melodie peered into the café from behind a garbage skip across the street near the chapter house where she'd worked the last three years.

'My goodness,' she said, the blood draining from her face. 'Tom and Razzaq?'

'They didn't part on the best of terms when I saw them last,' said Conan, '... but look friendly enough now.'

'I ... I don't understand,' said Melodie. 'Thomas meeting with Chard and Kwai ... and even Ah Li Wu ... I kinda get. They're all major players and he's comfortable dealing with such people ... but Razzaq? Who's Razzaq?'

'Don't lose sight of Moleface,' said Conan. 'He's just gone into the rear ... he might be trying to get out the back way. He's got form for that.'

Conan quickly weighed up his options and decided he only had one.

'Stay here while I check out the back lane.'

'But ... what if they leave?'

'Moleface is more important. Let's stick to the main game.'

With that he kissed her on the forehead and slipped through the slow moving bikes into a side-street, and then into a narrow lane behind the café filled with overflowing garbage receptacles. Sure enough, Moleface was walking quickly in the opposite direction. He was wearing a headscarf but also the yellow FENG 9 shirt, which brought a grim smile to Conan's face.

Another agony of indecision. Should he run back to get Mel or should he continue following?

'I'll lose him if I lose sight of him,' thought Conan, and that made up his mind.

• • •

'Oh no,' thought Mel as Tom and Razzaq got up from their table and went their separate ways.

Conan had been gone for ten minutes so she supposed he was following Moleface. She still hadn't bought a new phone so couldn't contact him. And now Tom was walking across the road, and Razzaq was walking away down Whitlam Street.

Thomas she knew. Conan would be more impressed if she discovered some information on Razzaq.

She sidled around the skip, keeping it between her and Lammas as he trotted up the stairs into the chapter house, then dodged the traffic and went quickly after Razzaq.

• • •

Asif glanced quickly over his shoulder a couple of times as he walked through the maze of lanes parallel with Whitlam Street. He seemed to have eluded the Watchers.

It was time to think straight. Who were they? Surely Ah Cheng's people, but they didn't look like the sort of people he'd associate with – although the woman's face was vaguely familiar.

Of course, there were any number of ordinary Australians into Habal Tong. Asif had met a few but they mostly disgusted him with their twisting of axioms to suit their own immediate purposes. Is that what he was dealing with?

If yes then he doubted their resolve, and relaxed a little more.

What if they weren't Cheng's people?

Impossible. Who else could be following him? But why chase him? He had done nothing to demonstrate loss of resolve, except possibly running from the Watchers.

Asif cursed his stupidity.

He had panicked when he should simply have acknowledged their presence and gotten on with apparent normality.

'Fuck!' he said aloud. Asif never swore.

'Fuck! Fuck! Fuck!'

He stopped.

There was only one thing to do.

• • •

Conan, with just nose and fingers sidling the wall at the corner of the alley, saw Moleface stop.

He stood motionless for several moments, then turned and walked back the way he had come.

Conan waited until his quarry was just a couple of metres away then stepped out in front of him.

He saw a fit looking man of about thirty or so, wiry and tallish with a milk coffee complexion and black eyes, glowering with fear and rage.

Asif saw a tired, sweaty man who looked out of place in Ord City – like a tourist perhaps. The man said nothing but stared pointedly.

'I shouldn't have run,' said Asif. 'I panicked … but I have not lost my resolve … I swear it.'

'Your resolve?' asked Conan.

'For my mission.'

'I see,' said Conan, remembering the scene in the library as Moleface downloaded specs to the NBN node.

The sensible thing to do was pull out his gun and badge and arrest him, but then he'd have to take Moleface back to Loongy at the AFP HQ where he would almost certainly lose control amid people he didn't trust, despite Dave Marsh's message.

'I think you and I should have a little chat,' said Conan.

• • •

Mel pushed through the teeming hordes of excited people. So many were wearing the yellow of Habal Tong and dancing about in celebration for *Illumination* the following day.

The smell of incense was everywhere, dry sandalwood and fruity bergamot – celebratory smells for the Habal Tong festival. And also, of course, for the first large tranche of temporary citizens who would reach the end of their seven years and be free to go anywhere in Australia – forever.

Mel realised she was tired of Ord City as she forced her way through the joyous crowds, sometimes losing sight of Razzaq, but always finding him again. He was about twenty metres ahead and in no apparent hurry. He stopped to watch a couple of stir-fry cooks and bantered with one who dripped with sweat as he worked frantically.

Mel was also getting hassled by street vendors and pawed by children, wanting her to stop. That sort of thing never happened when she wore her AOG uniform – no doubt they thought her a tourist.

What fun it would be to do this sort of thing for a living, she thought, as Razzaq took off again, turning into a labyrinth of lanes that twisted and turned in ways that made no earthly sense.

There were fewer people off the main drag so it was easier to keep Razzaq in sight. He was no longer dawdling but marching purposefully through the paths and alleyways, never once glancing back. Her confidence grew. Conan would be impressed when she came back with information on how to locate Razzaq. Mind you, few of the lanes had names and fewer houses had street numbers and she'd have to find some other way of identifying his address to lead Conan back.

In that moment she realised her focus on Razzaq had wavered and he was out of sight.

'Damn,' she cursed under her breath and paused at an intersection of five alleyways.

'Oh well,' she thought. I can at least bring Conan to here and tell him Razzaq's house must be close by.

She turned to retrace her steps and found a number of men standing in her way. She didn't try to push past them but turned again to go another way. And there was Razzaq, grinning like Punch in a nightmare sideshow.

Chapter 26

Changing the Rules

Conan and Asif sat in a booth in the back of yet another café. It was dark and dusty, with the ever-present smell of mildew under a sweet incense pong, but both were at least confident they could not be seen or heard.

Asif was amazed to learn that Conan was not one of Ah Cheng's Watchers.

'Then why were you following me?' he wondered.

'Because of that,' said Conan, pointing at Asif's cheek.

'Because of what?'

'You tried to disguise yourself when you downloaded specs to the NBN node in a library ... but you left your cheek exposed and that's a fairly conspicuous pattern of moles you've got there. I've been looking for you ever since.'

To his surprise, Asif was relieved that Conan was a member of the police rather than one of Ah Cheng's people.

'So you have found me,' shrugged Asif. 'What now?'

'That depends.'

'On what?'

They both leaned back as a waitress brought a tray to the table – coffee for Conan and a pot of chai for Asif. The waitress left them and they both sipped their drinks, appraising each other.

'Why don't you start by telling me about yourself and why you were downloading classified information from the Dark Web?'

'How do I know you aren't really part of ... erm ... a certain group, trying to lure me into a fatal disclosure?'

'I can't answer that beyond re-confirming my identity,' said Conan. 'But here's your choice ... you talk to me right here in a nice café, or you talk to me in a hyperlit basement in the bowels of the AFP building. Up to you pal.'

The fact was, Asif desperately wanted to trust the tired looking man. Even if it meant going to prison for a while he seemed to offer the only way out of the nightmare in which Asif had somehow found himself. The only barrier in his mind was Ah Cheng. If he was capable of such extraordinary acting to maintain his cover, why shouldn't other people in his network be similarly capable to win his confidence?

'That I downloaded specs from the library computer is something the people I fear would know,' said Asif. 'Tell me more details of that scene and what happened afterwards ... if you truly were watching remotely.'

'You were wearing that shirt,' said Conan. '... and scan resistant sunglasses. You copied the NBN specs onto a data stick then left the library and headed towards the football stadium. I can describe the exact route you took ... I can even show it to you.'

Conan lifted his triPod out of his bag and set it up on the table and Asif was amazed to see himself sitting in the library, nearly two weeks prior, pull a stick from the computer then get up and stride through the streets. It was terrifying but at the same time reassuring.

'I doubt whether anyone beyond the AFP would have the gear to pull this off,' said Conan.

Asif nodded slowly. 'Very well. I believe you are who you say you are.'

'And you are still resolved to undertake your mission, you were saying?'

Asif swallowed drily. This was the key moment that would dictate the rest of his life.

'No,' he said. 'I have completely lost my resolve and want nothing to do with the Tong. I joined a long time ago when I was young and embittered by my treatment in the old camps.'

'The Tong?'

Asif glanced nervously about the room but they were in a small booth in a backroom separated by a heavy curtain. No one else was within sight.

'It is a sleeper cell ... a small group of three but linked to a network of other cells through the leadership.'

Asif explained about Ah Cheng and Razzaq, at first reluctantly, but once he had said enough to surely get himself killed if the tired man was not who he said he was, Asif found himself relaxing and speaking with greater confidence.

'They expect me to undertake a mission on behalf of the Tong, which could see me killed ... but if not killed then certainly gaoled for the rest of my life. If I refuse they will kill me ... and my family.'

'That is a pickle,' agreed Conan. 'So what's the mission ... blowing up the node?'

'It was,' said Asif, 'but just a few days ago they changed it.'

• • •

Mel was sitting on a chair with her hands tied and her head in a bag.

Again.

There were several men in the room with her, most chattering excitedly in Cantonese or Arabic. But Razzaq questioned her in English.

'You are the woman from the Christian place?' he demanded.

'I am an officer of the Army of God,' she confirmed.

'So why are you following me? Is Major Lammas so worried about our agreement he has to send a spy?'

The room stank of unwashed clothes and old cooking fat, and the chatter of the other men was disgusting. She knew Arabic from her university days and had picked up Cantonese from her work in the mission. They thought she didn't understand so spoke openly of what they would like to do to her and it was all she could do not to scream with fear and anger.

'Major Lammas didn't send me,' she said, mastering her terror and revulsion. 'I was just taking a walk through the area in which we have our congregation.

'Your congregation,' sneered Razzaq. 'You presume to evangelise your Christian filth in these streets where all other faiths are united?'

'We presume nothing,' said Mel. 'We do God's work. That is all.'

'Well, I don't believe you came here to do God's work,' said Razzaq. 'Although only God knows why you thought you could come to these streets and pass unnoticed.'

'I have always passed unnoticed in these streets,' insisted Mel. 'And I wasn't spying.'

Razzaq snapped at the other men in Arabic and told them to keep their goat tongues to themselves. But if Mel was relieved by that she was horrified at his next comment.

'I think I will call Major Lammas and let him know I have his chicken in a bag.'

It took Mel a couple of moments to realise he was referring to her and the thought of being collected by Thomas froze her blood.

'No please! I don't want him to know where I am.'

'You don't want him to know your mission has failed?' laughed Razzaq.

'No ... I ... don't want anything to do with him.'

'Are you not his woman?' sneered Razzaq. 'Living unmarried like animals rutting in their own dung?'

'How dare you!' flared Mel, but Razzaq laughed and the ribald comments of the other men resumed.

'Maybe I should let these men have their way?' mused Razzaq. 'You are no better than a whore after all ... but all spies are whores.'

Mel wanted to scream but knew it would only amuse her captors. She managed to stay silent despite the terror that threatened to snap her sanity. Hands reached at her from all sides but Razzaq barked again in Arabic and they left her alone.

'Lock her in here,' he said, 'while I think about what to do with her.'

With that she was thrown face down on a bed, hands behind her back and head still in a bag, as she heard the men leave the room.

• • •

'My mission is to destroy the telescopes.'

Conan's eyes widened in amazement.

'The radio telescopes? The Giant Array you mean?'

'Yes. I am to go there early tomorrow morning ... destroy the main control building and as many of the di ... erm ... '

'Dipoles.'

'Yes. The dipoles … as many as possible.'

'But why?' demanded Conan. 'Why on earth would a remote observatory be a target for a terror cell?'

Asif shrugged.

'I am told the scientists perform the ultimate blasphemy … to gaze upon the work of God in the moment of His creation.'

The hair tingled on the back of Conan's neck. He had heard those words before – Jen Khataten quoting Major Lammas.

'Could that be why Lammas was meeting with Razzaq?' he wondered aloud. 'They're in this together?'

'I saw them,' agreed Asif. 'To the world they are enemies but they meet secretly as friends.'

Conan glanced at the time function on his OzBrace, it was an hour since he had left Mel.

'I'd better get back to my friend … but what do you want to do?'

'I want to be out of the Tong … and protection for me and my family.'

There was a genuine earnestness about Asif which put Conan at ease and convinced him the man could be believed.

'You'll have to give us information,' warned Conan. 'Lots of information.'

'I am prepared to do that. It is the only way out.'

'Okay. I'm not authorised to promise anything but I'll put you in touch with someone who is.'

Conan called Loongy and was surprised to hear the man himself pick up almost immediately.

'So … you didn't go home, Tools.'

'No … and I need a covert extraction team right now at … '

'That's okay … I've been talking to Kenny Cook. I can pick you up from your OzBrace signal. Or is it Sergeant Marsh's signal?'

Ten minutes later, Conan and Asif were in the back of a black transit van with dark windows, and Loongy himself was there.

'I owe you an apology, Tools.'

'You do?'

'Someone's been screwing us around for the last few weeks. Someone high up somewhere. I thought you'd been sent to spy on us.'

'Why would you think that?' asked Conan, embarrassed to be

having such a conversation in front of Asif. It seemed Loongy now trusted everyone.

'The timing,' said Loongy. 'The circumstances. It looked bad.'

'No,' insisted Conan. 'I was just sent to look into those two murders … although no one seems to want me to.'

'Something very strange is going on,' agreed Loongy, staring out the window at hundreds of people dancing about in yellow.

'You mean *Illumination*?'

'No … I mean the conflicting orders we keep getting in respect of *Illumination*. We've been preparing for weeks to maintain a big covert presence and just today we were told no more than standard ops. Standard ops to cover a million people!'

'Why?'

'Some bullshit about upsetting the festival goers. Fuck the festival goers! We should do things properly.'

The traffic was moving very slowly and Conan was getting anxious about Mel, who was nowhere to be seen when they drove through the intersection of Kerr and Whitlam.

'Are you able to do another Brace trace?' asked Conan, sipping on some bottled water.

'Who?'

'Her name's Captain Melodie Roberts.'

'Do you know her Medicare number?'

'No.'

'Phone number?'

'No … she doesn't have a phone or I'd call her.'

'No phone?' said Loongy, 'What is she Tools, a fucking caveman?'

Conan smiled weakly, wanting to encourage Loongy's change of attitude towards him.

'Have to wait till we're back at the office to run a trace without numbers. By the way … I had you bashed.'

The water exploded from Conan's mouth and nose, and Loongy laughed.

'I was trying to discourage you … but no hard feelings, eh Tools?'

Conan's fingers touched against his still bruised face.

'No hard feelings! I was put in bloody hospital!'

'You shouldn't have pulled a gun. It made them panic. I've got your watch too ... the one you threw in the dark to lose them. Very clever.'

Conan couldn't help but laugh despite the outrage he should have been feeling. Loongy's matter of fact manner made the admissions somehow funny.

'What about the murdered blokes' property?' asked Conan.

'What about it?'

'Who moved it down the corridor?'

'It was moved?'

'Totally cleared out ... moved holus bolus a few doors down the corridor.'

'Really? Why would anyone do that?'

The van pulled into the basement of the AFP building and Loongy led Conan and Asif to the lift.

'Can I leave you with Asif,' asked Conan. 'I really need to find Mel ... it's been two hours.'

'We can do it all in my office,' said Loongy, 'presuming my office hasn't been taken over by ... whoever is changing the rules.'

Two minutes later the three of them were in Loongy's room – Asif anxious to tell his story but told to wait by the others. Loongy set up a triPod and ran an ID check on Captain Melodie Roberts. He then activated the OzBrace search and a map appeared instantly with a marker in the middle of a building.

'Where's that?' asked Conan.

'Not far.'

He adjusted to real time street view and Conan stared in incomprehension.

'What's that place?' he wondered aloud. 'And what is she doing there?'

'It is the house of Razzaq,' said Asif.

'Oh fuck.'

'Razzaq?' queried Loongy.

'He is a member of my Tong ... a fanatic.'

The three stared at the virtual scene with people coming and going in the narrow lane outside the rundown four storey building.

'Could she be hiding?' wondered Conan, '... trying to get information covertly?'

'If she is inside that building you can be certain she is a prisoner,' said Asif. 'It is a safe house … a fortress. A fly could not pass security there.'

'We have to get her out,' said Conan, getting out of his chair. 'Now.'

'Wait,' said Loongy. 'There is much to consider … you for a start,' he said turning to Asif.

'No,' said Conan. 'He can fucking wait.'

'A self-confessed terrorist conspirator can wait?'

'That's right Loongy … self-confessed. It means we can trust him … isn't that right?' he said, turning to Asif.

'Yes, you can trust me.'

'This is completely fucked up, Tools,' said Loongy, '… and I know someone high up will …'

'She's in danger, Loongy … and busting this house could mean preventing a terror incident.'

Again he turned to Asif for confirmation.

'Almost certainly,' agreed Asif.

Loongy's lips tightened. There was a tap at the door and the smiling Agent Ping said, 'You called sir?'

'Yes … we need the fast response team ready to go, right now.'

'Of course,' said Ping, glancing at Asif, 'Do you need me to take any statements?'

Loongy turned to Asif who said, 'If you don't mind, I need to get home. Can we do it tomorrow?'

Loongy nodded but Ping reminded him that an early statement was always recommended and the proper protocol.

'We don't have time for proper protocol,' said Loongy irritably and waved Agent Ping away to arrange the fast response team.

'Of course,' said Ping, his usual smile fading. 'Of course.'

'Ping!'

Loongy called him back.

'Do you know anything about the Fong and Wing Ho property being moved?'

Ping's smile returned.

'No.'

• • •

Razzaq put his phone down, thinking furiously.

'Lammas swears he did not send the woman.'

'Of course he said that,' sneered Ah Cheng.

'I believe him. He says the woman dishonoured him and that he wants nothing to do with her.'

'Dishonoured? How?'

'She has been seeing another man.'

'Just seeing?'

'Who knows? Who cares?' said Razzaq. 'They are all whores these Australian women ... but the man she has been seeing is an agent of the Federal Police.'

Ah Cheng's eyes widened and he glanced toward the room in which Captain Roberts was held.

'She wears an OzBrace,' said Cheng. 'They could be tracing it right now.'

'Everybody out!' shouted Razzaq, getting up and striding into the next room where half a dozen men were eating a light meal.

'Quickly,' said Cheng. 'Leave everything but the weapons and explosives. At once!'

There was an immediate scramble as the men abandoned their meal and snatched up packs.

'We meet at my house in one hour,' said Cheng. 'Go!'

The men were gone in seconds, instantly obeying orders as they had been trained.

'What about the woman?' asked Razzaq, pulling a long knife from his belt.

Ah Cheng considered.

'She knows nothing about us, except that you met with Lammas.'

'That is too much,' said Razzaq.

'Yes,' agreed Ah Cheng. 'But after tomorrow night ... it will no longer matter.'

'Best to be certain,' said Razzaq and Ah Cheng nodded. The two of them turned towards the door when a loud noise came from outside. They glanced up at the street monitor which showed two black vans parked out the front and men in black scrambling out with armalite rifles.

'Quickly,' said Ah Cheng. 'Move!'

• • •

Conan went in behind the fast response team.

They cleared the ground floor, meeting no resistance, then swarmed up the stairs. The house certainly was a fortress. The front door was reinforced with armour plating and several deadlocks, but had been left ajar as though abandoned.

There was shouting on the next level but no shots and by the time Conan reached the first floor it was already clear there was no one left in the building.

Except Mel.

They found her face down on a bed, trussed and hooded, and crying with relief when Conan released and held her.

'How did you get here?' he asked.

'I just wanted to help,' she sobbed, 'but they caught me … and …'

'Say no more … for now.'

Mel was plainly unhurt, despite a nasty fright, and after a ten second hug Conan let her go. The house would be secured and searched forensically, and the results would be available to Loongy, but just in case there was something obvious he had a quick look around.

'Conan?'

He was glancing through some documents in what appeared to be an office, but they were all in incomprehensible languages and scripts.

'Mmm?'

'They didn't know I speak Arabic and Cantonese.'

'Neither did I.'

'Well, I do … and they said things you might be interested in.'

Conan dropped the papers onto the desk.

'Yeah?'

'I think they intend to let off bombs tomorrow.'

'At the Giant Array?'

'Well, yes … they mentioned that, but other bombs also.'

'Did they say where?'

'They did … and we'll be in a lot of trouble if they succeed.'

'So where? Please don't tell me *Illumination*.'

'No … not *Illumination*.'

Chapter 27

Going Off Like a Madman

It was the party to end all parties at the Dedd Reffo club house.

They had arranged for The Phobes to play – a skinhead metal/punk band who specialised in songs about killing refugees and other patriotic pursuits. Most of the blokes were jumping and thrashing about to the music or getting stuck into the half dozen or so hookers who'd been hired for the night.

Chris was going off like a madman and Robbie was just about able to give himself up to it. The bass and drums hit him in the guts and gonads and the frenzied guitar set his head on fire. He drank like there was no tomorrow but occasionally reflected that, in fact, there was a tomorrow.

But only one.

Five had put their hands up.

Besides Chris and Robbie there were two other blokes (Bruno and Ron) who'd agreed to make the ultimate sacrifice for Australia's salvation.

And, of course, there was Tim.

Robbie was not remotely surprised when he shuffled forward under the proud gaze of Lemon when volunteers were called for that afternoon. Tim didn't make eye contact with Robbie but he did seem to enjoy the applause when he received his blast suit from Jimbo.

Now all five were wearing their thin wetsuit type suits with skullcaps – a bit like the bio-suits the death gamers wore watching drop shots, but instead of flashing colours in time with your pulse they showed the status of an imminent explosion. Jimbo reckoned they were usually used for mining and setting off remote charges mentally. In this case, the charges would not be remote. They would be worn in special pockets on the back – which was a bit of a relief. It was one thing to be a suicide bomber, but you didn't want the bloody thing going off in your face.

The Five, as they were known, were the guests of honour at the party and given first choice of the hookers, if they wanted them. Chris had twisted Robbie's arm, so early in the night he'd picked the one who most reminded him of Kate and gave it to her something fierce. Then he'd hated himself for a half hour or so until Chris told him to snap out of it.

'Is this how you're gonna spend your last night on earth? Moping about with a face like a smacked arse?'

Chris was dead right, Robbie decided, and from that moment he let the alcohol and music sweep him away – determined to wring as much juice as he could from the evening.

'Best give yourself a filthy hangover for tomorrow,' shouted Chris. 'That way it'll be a fuckin' relief when … '

Robbie laughed.

'You always did know the right thing to say, mate.'

The two of them hugged like they'd just won a football match and then started jumping about with the rest as The Phobes launched into their biggest hit – *Give the Cunts Mixo*, about a radical strategy for reducing migrant numbers.

'We got our own radical strategy!' shouted Chris. To Robbie, pissed and screaming with adrenalin, it seemed like the funniest thing he'd ever heard.

• • •

Lemon had promised.

They were going to do it at some point that night.

'When you least expect it,' she'd teased.

Tim was jumping out of his skin. It had been … how long?

His mind sheered away from the embarrassing truth that it had been nearly three months since they'd last done it – on a train in Sydney. She'd been laughing her head off at the time and he hadn't been comfortable on the narrow benches. She'd wanted the CCTV to capture his arse going up and down and he'd been happy enough to oblige, but it wasn't the most romantic shag they'd ever had. And she'd never been in the mood since so Tim was just about busting with repressed need.

Now that he was thinking about sex, he couldn't help but remember that his last two encounters had been with Chris and Robbie. He didn't want to think about Robbie.

So he thought about Chris.

He didn't much like Chris, and knew Chris despised him. But he also knew Chris had never met his eye since the incident in the tent. Tim grinned. It meant he had a sort of power over Chris, if he wanted to use it.

He glanced over at Chris who immediately looked away and Tim burst into laughter.

'What's funny?' demanded Lemon.

'Oh, nothing.'

'Then why are you laughing if nothing's funny?'

It was difficult to have a conversation with the music so loud, so Tim shrugged, smiling, and Lemon's eyes narrowed.

And in that instant, Tim understood that he could have power over Lemon, if he wanted it.

'What?' she demanded.

Tim just continued smiling to himself as Lemon got increasingly paranoid.

'I'm not fucking you until you tell me what you're laughing at.'

'Nothing,' insisted Tim. It was all he could do not to laugh. He noticed Robbie was also laughing and immediately stopped laughing himself.

'That's better,' said Lemon, with her usual look of triumph.

'She thinks she's made me stop laughing,' realised Tim in a moment of small epiphany. 'That's important to her ... to control me.'

Tim was astounded that he had never quite understood that before. He knew she was *difficult* and he'd always had to carefully navigate her moods, but he'd not realised it was calculated – that she actually got a kick out of manipulating him.

So how did she feel tonight?

• • •

'Jeez I'd like to smack that prick.'

'Who?' asked Robbie.

'Fuckin' Tim,' spat Chris. 'Look at the cunt grinning to himself.'

'Why do you hate him so much,' asked Robbie, feeling guilty again at the sight of Tim's black eyes and bruises.

'HT turd,' muttered Chris. 'What is he doing here?'

'Same as us,' shrugged Robbie. 'Just another Anzac hero waiting to jump out of the trench.'

Chris stared at Robbie angrily.

'Like fuck he is! You wanna be put in the same basket as that cocksucker?'

'What do you mean?'

'When it all plays out in the press,' said Chris, getting pretty riled, '... our names will all be listed as the Reffo Five or whatever, and Cocksucker Tim will get the same billing as Chris Majkic and Robbie Bennett!'

'Who cares?'

'*Who cares?*'

Chris put his beer down and the old battle stare came into his eyes.

'Leave him alone, Chris,' said Robbie. 'He's had enough. Look at the poor bastard.'

'He's not real good at making friends, is he?' said Chris. 'I'd shake the hand of the cunt who did that to him.'

Robbie winced with embarrassment and Chris grinned with sudden knowledge.

'You did that?'

Robbie didn't respond and Chris laughed delightedly.

'Way to go, Robbie! Why didn't you say?'

'Because I'm not proud of it man. It was a misunderstanding and I feel like shit about it.'

'Feel like shit? You should feel great. In fact why don't we both go finish the job?'

'Leave him alone, Chris. Let him enjoy his last night.'

Chris allowed himself to be eased back, but sent another warning glare in Tim's direction.

'He better not come near me, that's all. I might not care what I do on my own last night.'

Tim allowed himself to think about Robbie and was surprised to realise that he still liked him, despite what had happened.

Tim couldn't remember anyone being as kind and considerate as Robbie had been – before the misunderstanding. Certainly Lemon had never showed anything like the compassion and friendship that Robbie had shown in just a few days of knowing him. Obviously Robbie was a genuinely decent human being and Tim remembered how he had felt when Robbie said he loved him. Tim had never thought of himself as being attracted to men, despite the things Lemon had occasionally got him to do when they'd been desperate, but his heart had leapt when Robbie had said those words in the dark and all he wanted to do was get close to him and please him.

He stole a furtive glance at Robbie, dancing with Chris, and was shocked to discover he was jealous.

In normal circumstances his mind would have baulked at that line of thinking but the circumstances were far from normal. If tonight was his last night there was no reason not to explore fully any line of thought which occurred to him.

The song ended.

Chris grabbed one of the girls and led her away by the hand, and Tim decided to save Robbie's life.

Chapter 28

The True Enemy

'They have four groups,' said Mel. 'With four targets.'

'And one is the Giant Array?'

'Correct.'

'And the other three?'

'The water treatment plants.'

'Jee-zuss.'

'Conan!'

Conan smiled weakly, then glanced at Loongy.

'So you set up a perimeter to protect the plants, right?'

'You not thinking straight, Tools.'

'Why not?'

'Because there's just about no one I trust right now. I give orders to protect the plants, that sends a message straight away to … to whoever …'

'The Shadow Group we're calling them,' said Mel.

'Okay, to the Shadow Group, that we're onto them. I have to protect the plants but it needs to be a small scale operation. Maybe Ping.'

'Shadow Group?' queried Conan. 'Isn't this an HT operation?'

'Is it? When HT are meeting with the Army of God? And AOG are meeting with Chard and Kwai? Who are also meeting with Ah Li Wu? And Dr Chen you say. They're all in it together, Tools, and there are clearly people in my organisation who are part of it also. I trust you, Mel and even Asif right now more than I trust half of my own people.'

Asif had been sent home. He had been told to continue his preparations as though he intended to go through with the mission, but that he would be arrested as soon as he trespassed on the Giant

Array site. Later he'd be sent into the witness protection program and moved to Sydney, after giving evidence against Ah Cheng and Razzaq.

'Why on earth would Chard want the treatment plants sabotaged?' asked Conan.

'Why would anyone?' asked Mel.

'The only reason to destroy the plants is to make Ord City unviable,' said Conan. 'But OC is Chard's power base. She's not gonna jeopardise that.'

'They don't mean to blow up all the plants,' clarified Mel. 'Just plants Alpha, Beta and Gamma … they're leaving the new plant alone.'

Loongy and Conan stared at each other, then Loongy brought up the public webpage of the new treatment plant Delta. Among its advertised key metrics was its ability to process up to ten gigalitres per day – effectively doubling the city's capacity.

'The city could get by,' said Loongy. 'But it would be a major risk depending on just one treatment plant for two and a half million people.'

'I went past there with Dave Marsh a couple of days ago,' said Conan. 'The place was crawling with suits and spooks it looked to me.'

'So what's so special about treatment plant Delta?' mused Loongy.

'Is it possible,' asked Conan, 'that by causing a water crisis, Chard increases her power in Ord City?'

'How?' demanded Loongy. 'She's already got power. What more can she gain?'

'It might give her an excuse to declare an emergency,' said Mel. 'In which case …'

'She could suspend the First Wave,' anticipated Conan.

They all stared at each other with raised eyebrows.

'It makes sense,' admitted Loongy, grudgingly. 'But why? And why reduce the clean water supply if there are more people depending on it when the First Wavers are prevented from leaving?'

'Jeez,' breathed Conan. 'There'd be a bloody riot if they tried to stop the First Wave.'

'Which would harden opinion in mainstream Australia,' said Mel, '… make it easier to legislate to stop it permanently.'

'Is that what they want?' asked Loongy.

'It's what half of Australia wants,' said Conan. 'There's always been opposition to the seven year visa policy … letting the terrorists loose, and all that.'

'But the government,' insisted Loongy, getting excitable, '… they are the terrorists if they blowing up treatment plants.'

There was a silence as the three of them considered that possibility – appalled at the idea of an Australian government sabotaging its own infrastructure and policy.

'I sincerely doubt it's government policy,' said Conan. 'Even if Chard is involved. But who can we ask? Who can we trust … besides ourselves?'

'No one,' said Loongy. 'I can't tell anyone about this because the risk of alerting the … the Shadow Group is too high. Maybe I tell Ping … he can co-ordinate protection of the treatment plants.'

'Dave Marsh is okay,' said Conan. 'Can we stop him getting on a plane?'

Loongy immediately brought up Dave's number on his triPod and Conan called it.

'Hello?' asked the familiar voice, sounding a little wary.

'Dave, it's erm … me.'

'Hello Me.'

'Very funny. Don't get on the plane. We need you urgently.'

'I knew I shouldn't have answered the phone! I'm in the boarding queue!'

'Well get out of it. We've got a major situation here.'

'Far out! My bag's on the plane!'

'Sorry, mate,' said Conan. 'We'll make it up to you.'

'How?'

'I dunno … we'll send you to Hawaii when it's all over. Put my OzBrace in a security bag and give it to the flight steward, then get your arse to the AFP HQ.

'Oh for fuck's sake!'

• • •

Asif arrived home and Tanya was uncharacteristically anxious.

'That's not fair,' Asif admitted to himself. His own actions had been uncharacteristic so her anxious response made perfect sense.

'Please Tanya … it is nothing,' he assured her. 'Why don't you paint?'

After her initial anger she had withdrawn and turned on the television – something she did rarely.

'I'm not in the mood,' she told him, without taking her eyes from the screen showing preparations for *Illumination* – thousands of people joyously setting up or practicing dance routines. Even the prime minister, Margie Yunupingu, was going to be there, and she and her wife were shown being greeted at Ord City airport by Colonel Chard.

'Would you like me to make you something to eat?'

'Do what you like,' she shrugged.

Asif's heart was breaking at the distance that had come between them, but knew it was his own fault. And if he had to lose her to protect her, then that was the price of his seven year folly.

He went out to the kitchen and started to make kalia. She had always loved his cooking but kalia took a while to prepare. 'That didn't matter', he thought. 'I may not have another chance to make kalia so this must be the best ever.'

The meal was simmering nicely and she had started to thaw a little as the smells wafted through to the living room.

'I am sorry, Asif,' she said, coming into the kitchen. 'I am not used to you going off like that. I shouldn't pry.'

'No … it is my fault,' he insisted. 'There was a small matter I had to deal with but now it is done.'

A smile came onto her face and she put her arms out.

He went to embrace her, his heart filling with joy once again, but at that moment there was a knock at the door.

'Who could that be?' wondered Tanya. 'It must be one of our neighbours as it wasn't the bell from the street door.'

Asif went to answer, hoping Tanya was right about a neighbour, but as he opened it Razzaq pushed past and told him to close the door.

'Razzaq? What are you doing here?'

Razzaq didn't answer, but strode into the living room, staring angrily at the various pictures and half-made sculptures.

'What decadent rubbish is this?' he sneered, standing in front of Tanya's self portrait.

Asif fought down the anger and fear, glancing nervously at the kitchen.

'It is Tanya's work,' said Asif. 'She is quite famous for it.'

'It is pornographic garbage,' said Razzaq, as Tanya entered the room.

'Asif?'

'Darling … this is my friend Razzaq. We go to the football together.'

'Oh. Hello Razzaq … what can we do for you?'

Razzaq pointedly ignored her and said to Asif, 'Cheng sent me.'

The frank admission that Ah Cheng was in charge sent a cool thrill up Asif's spine. It meant something had changed.

'To do what?'

'To ask where you went this afternoon.'

Tanya came and stood by Asif.

'What's this about?'

'It is none of your business,' snapped Razzaq. 'Go to the kitchen, where you belong.'

Tanya flared with anger but Asif took her by the shoulders and looked into her eyes.

'Please, my darling … do as he asks.'

She stared at him, her eyes filling with tears, but she left the room.

'Cover this up before I destroy it,' said Razzaq, jerking his thumb at Tanya's painting. Asif pulled a sheet off the floor to comply.

'Sit,' said Razzaq.

Asif sat and waited, wondering whether he could successfully attack and subdue Razzaq, who was much smaller than him, despite his reputation for fighting.

'Tell me where you went this afternoon.'

'I went nowhere,' said Asif. 'I was home nearly all day.'

'You were seen arriving home at 12.43,' said Razzaq. 'Then you arrived again at nearly five. That means you went out the back way and were gone for anything up to four hours. What time did you leave and where did you go?'

'What does it matter?'

'It doesn't matter why it matters … answer the questions.'

Asif stared at the angry little man, wondering how he had become mixed up with such a maniac. But Asif had been angry himself, he remembered. That was how.

'I often go out the back way,' said Asif. 'There was an ingredient I needed for the kalia so I went to the spice market around four thirty. I was only gone a little while.'

'This can be confirmed by the seller?'

'Perhaps … it was busy.'

Asif sensed that Razzaq was tempted to believe him.

'We can go there now,' said Asif, 'if you don't believe me.'

'No. We will stay here.'

'We?'

'Yes. My house was raided this afternoon by the Federal Police.'

'No!' said Asif, who had been present when the decision to raid Razzaq's house was taken.

'It was Lammas' whore who came to my house after following me through the streets. It was she who triggered the raid … she is connected with the police … but I no longer trust Lammas, and it was he who asked for your mission.'

'It is a good mission,' said Asif, 'to destroy the work of the scientists.'

'Yes and no,' said Razzaq, who seemed to be relaxing slightly. 'If they mean to look upon the work of God then that is truly a great blasphemy and must be punished … but such punishments can backfire.'

'What do you mean?' asked Asif, increasingly anxious about Tanya and how she must be feeling.

'Why do we do what we do?' demanded Razzaq. 'The teaching of the Habal Tong Way and the destruction of the facilities set up by the authorities … how are they linked?'

'We teach the Way to bring enlightenment … and we … at least I … destroy the facilities because I am ordered to do so and I obey the Tong.'

Asif hoped it was a good answer but Razzaq sneered.

'Do not pretend to be simple Asif … it makes me mistrust you. But the real battle of our times is the battle against atheism and apathy.'

Asif glanced toward the kitchen, wondering what Tanya was making of the loud conversation.

'People must choose!' said Razzaq. 'Even Christianity is better than nothing! It is deluded and arrogant … but at least they believe in God. In this, we and Lammas agree … the atheists and the indifferent are the true enemy.'

'So why the science facilities?'

Razzaq was pacing the floor in his agitation and took some moments to answer. Asif glanced again towards the kitchen.

'The atheists take strength from science ... which in their arrogance they believe superior to the teachings of the faiths and The Way. Science must therefore be destroyed.'

Asif just nodded.

'I will stay here this evening,' said Razzaq, '... and in the morning I will accompany you on your mission, to ensure it is done properly.'

Chapter 29

Dirty Little Secrets

It was already dark when Conan, Mel and Dave Marsh cruised past treatment plant Delta on the far side of the river. They could see no one at the plant but the place was lit up like a Christmas tree.

Dave's police boat had been retrieved from the small island where they'd left it when hijacked. It was none the worse for the experience but the mere sight of the boat reminded Conan of the men with guns who'd left them for the crocodiles.

'I don't reckon they really meant us harm,' said Conan. 'Clearly Ming was a part of their operation and it was her job to set us free once they'd gone.'

'But how'd they even know we were coming?' asked Dave. 'It's a bit elaborate. And why Mel?'

'Loongy said he can't trust his own people,' said Conan. 'Obviously someone's letting them know our movements. Although why Ming would go to such lengths, I couldn't tell you. Neither can I answer the Mel question. Maybe just her association with me?'

'I'm not defined by the company I keep,' snapped Mel.

All three were dressed in black with their faces painted in camouflage green like the security people from the plant. Conan hadn't wanted Mel to come but she'd insisted, and it was the best way to keep an eye on her.

'What sort of security are they likely to have?' asked Dave.

'The works,' said Conan. 'Movement and infra-red detection … barbed wire, probably electrified. We'll only have a very short window.'

Loongy had called in a favour from a friend. A very big favour. The friend was an AFP associate who worked at the electricity company and was overfond of gambling. All AFP heads cultivated friends inside the local utilities so Loongy had bailed him out a couple of times, and now he was ready to repay the favour by cutting the power to the local substation. The treatment plant would certainly have its own back up generators but there would be a reset window of anything up to a minute. In that minute they had to cut through the fence and get inside the facility which would be on full alert once the power went down.

Conan checked his new OzBrace for the time.

'Fourteen minutes … let's go.'

They anchored the boat a hundred metres upstream and waded ashore – all of them anxiously aware of crocodiles. Then they crept the hundred metres to where giant pipes from the river led through the fence and waited for 9.55 – the appointed time.

There was no one in sight inside the facility, which blazed with light. There were three huge reservoir towers all interconnected with pipes and walkways with a main building like a giant metal barn in the centre. All doors were closed except for one roller door gaping like a missing tooth.

'How exactly does this place work?' whispered Mel.

Dave shrugged, but Conan said, 'I don't know the exact details, but basically they take water from the river … treat it somehow, to make it fit for consumption … and then send it off to the main reservoir.'

'So how do they treat it?'

'No idea,' said Conan. 'I guess they take out any salt and add chemicals like chlorine to kill giardia and other waterborne bugs. Does it matter?'

'It might. Why is this plant the only one not targeted?'

'It's probably the capacity,' said Conan. 'This is the only one capable of serving the city by itself … so this way the damage would be dangerous without being catastrophic.'

'Does that really make sense?' asked Mel.

'Nothing they do makes sense,' said Conan, getting impatient. 'Now … when we get through the fence, bolt for the open door and regroup inside to the left.'

They'd been able to examine a tri-dee blueprint of the plant in Loongy's office, so knew the offices were off to the right with an open storage area to the left.

'We need to get in then take stock once the lights come back on.'

Conan checked his watch again – three minutes.

At that moment, two men walked out the open door and strolled midway towards the fence. They were both dressed in black and had holsters strapped to their hips. They lit cigarettes.

'Shit,' muttered Conan.

'How long does it take to smoke a cigarette?' whispered Mel, looking at Dave.

'Dunno,' he shrugged, 'I've never timed it … but longer than we've got, I'd reckon.'

'They won't hang about when the lights go out,' said Conan, glancing again at his watch.

'They've got guns,' whispered Mel.

'Stay here then,' said Conan.

'Maybe I should. Maybe someone needs to keep watch and let Edward know if something goes wrong.'

Conan grinned and Mel immediately bridled.

'Screw that,' she said. 'I'm coming with you.'

'Screw that? Your language has become appalling in the last couple of days, Captain Roberts.'

'It's the company she keeps,' said Dave. 'It defines her.'

'Et tu, Dave?' asked Mel, but she was grinning nervously.

Conan looked at his watch again.

'Thirty seconds.'

But at that moment, all the lights went out.

'Fuck! He's early.'

Conan and Dave were armed with tin snips and both attacked the fence, relieved that it wasn't powered by its own generator.

'They've dropped their cigarettes and gone,' said Mel as Conan and Dave clipped frantically and removed a small section of wire in the shape of a gothic arch. Dave went first then Conan pushed Mel through and squeezed in behind. They all ran for the door – a deeper darkness against the looming bulk of the main building and got there just as the lights came back on.

They all went left and managed to get behind a small truck parked in an open space about thirty metres square. Besides the truck there were a number of other vehicles parked. To their right was a large open plan office behind windows, and directly in front were more doors and a staircase leading up to another level with more offices – only one of which had a light on. There was also a strong chemical smell that reminded Conan of his father's back shed.

He led them, doubled over, behind a line of cars to the staircase, glanced about quickly then slipped up the stairs.

'Now what?' whispered Dave, puffing a little.

'This way. You need to give up the fags, mate.'

Conan tiptoed to the office door next to the one with the light on and tried the handle, which was locked. The body language of the other two immediately registered anxiety, but Conan pulled a cigar shaped metal device from his pocket, and Dave grinned.

'What's that?' asked Mel.

'It's a stinger,' said Dave. 'An electronic key and highly illegal.'

'Never leave home without one,' whispered Conan, holding the stinger against the lock until the door seemed to open by itself.

They slipped inside the office which was half lit from outside. Voices could be heard faintly from the office next door and Conan gave Mel the stinger to mind while he produced something like a stethoscope from his backpack. He held it against the wall and gave one ear piece to Mel. Dave glanced about the office, found a glass half full of water which he emptied into a waste paper bin then held the glass against the wall and listened.

'… all secure. Looks like the substation went out briefly but it's back up again.'

'Okay … better check the fences.'

'Don't tell me how to do my job, Greg. Of course we're checking the fences.'

Conan wasn't entirely sure but he thought one of the voices was the bloke who'd led the team that captured him and Dave and left them for the crocs. The other voice he couldn't place but guessed was Greg Ferrier, who was in charge of the plant.

They heard the door open and ducked down as two men walked past outside. One was dressed in black fatigues and the other in a suit. Conan was fairly certain it was Ferrier but he didn't remember him that well from Ronny Kwai's dinner. Footsteps could be heard descending on the metal mesh stairs.

They watched from the dark side of the glass as the two men strode past the truck and out into the glare of the compound.

'Let's go,' said Conan.

They left the office and went to the room next door with Greg Ferrier's name on a plaque. Conan tried the door which, to his surprise, was open and they slipped inside.

'Bloody hell!' whispered Conan.

In the middle of Ferrier's desk was yet another copy of Ming's book, *Asymptotically Approaching Certainty: Chaos As The New Normal*.

'What's so special about this book?'

It was a sparse office with few other books and no paper. There was a triPod sitting on the desk in screen-saver mode – a map of Mars spinning slowly. Conan passed his hand over the red globe but it was locked.

'You got any techies who could open this up?' asked Conan.

'Yeah, maybe,' said Dave. 'It's probably cryp-locked.'

'Good enough.'

Conan hit the hard shut down at the base, scooped up the triPod and dropped it into his pack.

'I reckon this is all we need. Let's go.'

They left the office and went quickly down the stairs without being seen. Then they retraced their steps behind the parked vehicles and got to the open bay door. The compound was hyperlit but there was no one in sight.

'We're dressed almost the same as the security people here,' whispered Conan, 'so when we get outside, don't run. Just walk as though you've every right to be here and we'll go straight for the fence where we got in. And don't touch the fence getting out!'

The other two nodded and, after another peek outside, Conan headed for the fence.

But over to their left there was a bit of a commotion from a small cluster of people near one of the reservoir towers. They were cheering and laughing and Conan paused.

'Keep going,' hissed Mel. 'We're nearly there.'

'You go,' whispered Conan, his confidence rising. 'I'll just have a quick look at this.'

Mel gave him an anxious glance, pausing with Dave while Conan walked towards the small group, who were mostly in black.

They were being addressed by Greg Ferrier, standing on a platform atop a small flight of stairs.

'So after tomorrow,' he said, 'this will be one of ... if not the most ... important facilities in Ord City. There will inevitably be interest in what we do here, which makes you people critical.'

There were nods and murmurs from the black dressed crew where Conan hung on the outer edge.

'Our work is far too important to be interfered with by outsiders ... so we rely on you people to keep everything that happens here secret.'

At that moment, Conan was stunned to recognise Ming standing behind Ferrier. She seemed to be staring straight at him but her eyes moved on and Conan remembered his green war paint.

Ferrier finished his address and the men in black began to disperse. Then he and Ming went inside the reservoir building and, as no one took the slightest notice of him, Conan decided to follow.

Inside the building was a vast water tank, several storeys high. At its base, inside the silo, were metal buttresses and banks of controls with a million winking lights like the interior of a Bond villain's fortress. It smelled like an indoor swimming pool.

Ming and Ferrier were talking to a couple of technicians so Conan took the opportunity to go left, clockwise around the silo. It was all very new – polished concrete floor and gleaming metal. There were numerous plastex tubs full of pale greenish liquid with the formula $Ca(ClO)2$, and other tubs with pinkish liquid and a much longer formula – like nothing Conan had ever seen before. He pulled his phone out and snapped a couple of pictures, including the chemical formulae. Then he emailed the pictures to himself and Loongy and deleted both photos and emails from his phone.

Conan had nearly circumnavigated the silo and could hear Ferrier talking to the technicians about rates of flow and mixture density – whatever they were – and felt suddenly reluctant to push his luck further. With a mounting sense of urgency he retraced his steps around to the far side of the silo and had just made it to the door when the alarms rang out.

'Shit!' thought Conan, 'Please don't be Mel and Dave.'

He ran through the door as the harsh klaxon blared and men in black were shouting in the compound. Some were running for the fence and with a sinking heart, Conan followed towards the place they'd entered. The hole in the fence had been found, but Dave and Mel were nowhere to be seen.

Most of the others in black were shouting instructions and waving guns and Conan felt suddenly conspicuous – not least as he was the only one wearing face paint – but no one seemed to take notice of him.

'Lock down!' shouted the leader. 'No one leaves or enters. Emergency stations all personnel.'

Conan immediately strode away, trying to look as though he was obeying orders and going to a pre-ordained station.

'You!'

Conan turned, to see the head of security striding towards him.

'Where's your station?'

'Erm … front gate.'

'Stay here and guard the hole.'

'Erm … okay.'

Conan could hardly believe his luck, and grinned at the prospect of slipping out as soon as all the backs were turned.

'What's so funny?'

'Nothing sir.'

The man stared hard at Conan and looked like he was formulating further questions, but he turned on his heel and walked away as others scurried about with guns and torches.

Conan stood by the wire for a minute, then dropped to the ground and wormed through the hole, being careful not to touch the sides. No one raised any further alarm so he ran, doubled over, back towards the trees that concealed the riverside path leading to the boat.

He gave a whistle as he waded towards the boat and was disturbed when no one responded. Neither Mel nor Dave were aboard and Conan felt a jolt of adrenalin as he realised they may not have got out.

'Far out!' he muttered angrily. There was no choice other than to go back inside, so he had to do it quickly.

He took off the backpack with Ferrier's triPod and hid it under the dash. Then he waded ashore and ran back to the edge of the trees, and was relieved to see that his absence had not yet been noted. Once again doubled over he ran to the hole and squeezed back through.

'Forget something mate?'

Torches were blazing in his eyes and hands took hold of him. Only half way through the gap, he couldn't struggle without risking electrocution so had no choice but to submit. He was dragged upright by two men and the head of security peered at him closely.

'Fuck me dead!' he laughed. 'It's Tooley!'

• • •

Conan was taken back to Ferrier's office and the green paint was wiped off his face.

'Oh Christ!' said Ferrier when he recognised Conan.

Ming also was present but said nothing.

'What the hell are you doing here?' demanded Ferrier, a small nervous man now that Conan could see him up close.

'Just having a look,' said Conan, with what he hoped was a casual shrug.

'Why are you having a look?' asked the head of security, and for the first time Conan saw a small silver badge on his left breast that said Roger Manderson.

'Because I understand this place is gonna be pretty important after tomorrow.'

Ferrier paled (if it was possible for him to pale further) and said, 'How would he know that?'

'He has been pursuing us,' said Ming, speaking for the first time, '… and more effectively than we realised. Examine his phone.'

Conan blew her a kiss, which she ignored.

'I'd better consult my father.'

'Oh, don't drag him into it,' said Ferrier.

Light suddenly dawned for Conan. 'Your father is Ronny Kwai?' Ming continued to ignore him as Manderson searched his pockets and found his phone.

'No calls or messages in the last hour,' said Manderson.

'He may not have been working alone,' said Ming. 'Sweep the area.'

'It's being done,' said Manderson, and Conan regretted hiding the backpack on the boat. There was a fair chance it would be discovered.

Ming pulled out her own phone and took a photo of Conan. Then she started speaking in what Conan assumed was Cantonese.

'My father,' she said, switching back to English, 'insists you tell us why you became interested in this facility.'

'Major Lammas told me,' said Conan, hoping to spread some confusion by misinformation.

'Lammas?' echoed Ferrier, astonished.

'He's lying,' said Ming. 'Lammas doesn't know about this operation.'

'He was told by Razzaq,' said Conan, making it up as he went. 'But now it's time I went back to headquarters, so if you'll just excuse me …'

He went to stand but was pushed firmly back into his chair by Manderson.

'I'm sorry,' said Ming, 'but this is where the adventure ends. You should have stayed on the island, from where you would have been rescued in another day or so.'

'Isn't he supposed to be back in Sydney?' said Manderson. 'His Brace trace says he's in Sydney.'

Ferrier glared at Manderson.

'Why don't you just tell him everything?' snapped Ferrier.

'It doesn't matter what he knows,' said Ming. She spoke briefly in Chinese to the person on the phone. Then she hung up.

'Agent Tooley must shortly be removed from the game,' continued Ming, '… so what does it matter if he knows we have access to his OzBrace account?'

'Where's my triPod?' Ferrier suddenly wondered.

A silence fell, and Conan grinned.

'Where's my fuckin' triPod?' demanded Ferrier, the panic obvious.

'TriPod?' asked Conan.

'For fuck's sake!' shouted Ferrier. 'It's got everything on it.'

'Be quiet,' said Ming.

Conan laughed. 'It's already on its way to AFP HQ,' he said. 'They'll be unravelling your dirty little secrets as we speak.'

Ferrier paled even further, but Ming waved a hand dismissively.

'He's lying,' she said. 'Why would he still be here if he had taken the main prize? But if it really has gone to AFP headquarters … so much the better.'

Conan stared and Ming gave the ghost of a smile in return.

'There is not much happening at the AFP we don't know about …
or direct ourselves … both here and in Sydney.'

'Eh?'

'That's why you were chosen for this mission,' she continued,
enjoying the surprise on Conan's face. 'We wanted a screw up to be
appointed, and your record suggests you are impetuous … impulsive
… unsystematic … a risk taker.'

'You had me appointed to the Wing Ho, Fong murders?'

Ming laughed and Ferrier said, 'Why are you telling him this?'

'Because he will shortly be gone … and he has worked so hard for
the answers to a very confusing matter. It would be most unkind to
let him die wondering.'

'I also had you invited to Mister Kwai's party at the stadium,' she
said to Conan, '… to get a closer look at you. No doubt you thought
me quite a conquest.'

'You seemed to enjoy it,' said Conan.

Ming shrugged. 'It was adequate. I prefer women … not so messy,
and they don't need constant reassurance about their performance.'

'What about my triPod?' interrupted Ferrier. 'What if he hasn't
sent it to the AFP? What if he's got it somewhere else?'

'I doubt it's gone far,' said Ming. 'I suspect it's still on this base,
or close by … but one thing intrigues me, Agent Tooley. You were
captured coming back in after you had left. What brought you back?'

Conan said nothing and again Ming shrugged.

'It doesn't really matter why … after tomorrow everything will be
different and you will no longer be in a position to annoy us.'

'So what's so important about this treatment plant?' asked Conan.
'Why blow up the other three and leave this one intact?'

'He knows about *that*?' squeaked Ferrier.

'Shut up!' snapped Ming. 'You are a fool … a panicking fool.'

'But who else knows?' pleaded Ferrier. 'This has become too risky
… we should wait until a security audit can be done.'

'No!' insisted Ming. 'It must be before the temporary visas are
confirmed … before *Illumination*.'

'I'm guessing you're trying to bring about a state of emergency,' mused Conan, '… to justify a suspension of the visas. Then there'll be riots … enough to justify a reversal of the seven year rule.'

'Not bad for a screw up,' said Ming, 'but there is more to it than that. Much more.'

'Don't tell him,' said Ferrier.

'Greg,' said Ming, '… from tomorrow there will be three treatment plant directors looking for work. You are expendable. If you tell me what to do, or not to do, one more time … I will not be responsible for what Mr Manderson does to you.'

She raised her eyebrow at Manderson, who grinned nastily at Ferrier.

'So … much more you said,' continued Conan, hoping to keep her talking. 'It must be something to do with the pink chemical in the silos.'

Ferrier shrieked and Manderson slapped him hard.

'Last warning, Greg,' said Ming.

'The chemical goes in the water,' continued Conan, '… it's the only source of fresh water, so people have to drink it … and it does what?'

'That's enough,' said Ming, and at that moment there was a knock on the door.

One of Manderson's black uniformed crew entered with a grin holding Conan's back pack and Ferrier's triPod.

'Thank Christ!' said Ferrier, who seemed immediately to regain his composure.

'It was hidden on a state police boat moored just up river,' said the man, handing the triPod to Ferrier.

'State police?' asked Ming. 'Why not an AFP boat?'

'They wouldn't lend me one,' said Conan, hoping they wouldn't guess that he had help on hand.

'No … they don't like you, do they,' smiled Ming. 'You see how deeply our influence runs?'

'What do you want done with him?' asked Manderson.

'Tie him to the chair. He can go to the Giant Array early in the morning. That will give the authorities something to wonder about.'

Manderson laughed and produced some plastex ties. Conan's arms and ankles were bound tightly to a metal and plastic chair, and then the inevitable black bag went over his head.

'I don't expect to see you again, Conan,' said Ming. 'Better luck next life.'

There was some shuffling, a little more whinging from Ferrier, and then the door closed leaving Conan alone with his thoughts.

Chapter 30

An Acceptable Camouflage

The kalia was served but Asif took no pleasure in it. Tanya was white faced and silent and Asif's heart was breaking. He tried to catch her eye but she stared resolutely at the table and refused to eat.

Razzaq, however, was in a better mood and complimented Asif on the excellence of the kalia.

'You should have worked for me at the restaurant,' said Razzaq. 'This is the best I have tasted.'

'Thank you,' said Asif, flatly.

'You should be proud of your man,' Razzaq said to Tanya. 'He will be a great hero tomorrow.'

'A hero of what?' she asked.

'A hero of Habal Tong,' said Razzaq. 'The time for secrecy is past, Asif. You can tell her.'

Tanya showed no interest in the conversation so Asif was glad enough to say nothing more for the moment.

'If you don't wish to tell her,' said Razzaq, '... I will. Asif is going to destroy the great blasphemy of the scientists.'

'The *what*?' asked Tanya, allowing her asperity to show.

'The Giant Array of telescopes, where they presume to look upon the work of God. It cannot be permitted.'

'What has that to do with the teachings of Habal Tong?' demanded Tanya. 'If all is nothing and nothing is all then surely we are indifferent to the beliefs and actions of others. Their science does not affect us.'

'What do you know of The Way?' sneered Razzaq. 'A white-bread painter of disgusting pictures. I suppose you believe The Way permits and encourages such filth in the same way it permits the blasphemy of science?'

'I know that The Way is personal to all of us and is supposed to be inclusive,' she said, ignoring the insults. 'If you really understood The Way you would embrace rather than destroy.'

Razzaq stared at her in furious disbelief, then turned to Asif.

'I knew it was perilous for you to take up with such a woman, but I did not hinder it for the sake of your mission. She is an acceptable camouflage but her opinions are dangerous.'

Asif nodded numbly and stood to carry dishes to the sink.

'She is like all white Australians who follow Habal Tong,' sneered Razzaq, '... they are tourists ... cultural tourists who dip a toe in The Way for their spiritual amusement but they have no depth ... no real conviction. They take what they want so long as it validates their lust and greed and weakness. When the revolution happens in Ord City they will all be purged ... burned off the face of the earth with the other unbelievers!'

'How dare you,' seethed Tanya. 'How dare you come to this house ... this country ... and presume to lecture on The Way.'

'And how dare you!' fired back Razzaq. 'How dare you question the teachings of Ah Li Wu, who says that ...'

Asif smashed the pot half full of kalia onto Razzaq's head. Then again. Then once again until he stopped moving.

Tanya stared at him aghast, and burst into tears.

'What have you done, Asif?'

'Bought us some time ... I hope.'

He examined the back of Razzaq's head, then checked his pulse.

'He is alive.'

He glanced again at the heavy pot, but knew he could not finish the job.

'We should leave.'

'And go where?' cried Tanya. 'What are you involved in Asif? Are you really a ... a terrorist? Is that why you lived with me ... to cover your tracks?'

'No,' he said fiercely. 'I will explain everything when I can but for now it is too dangerous to stay here. The house will be watched.'

He glanced at the clock in the microwave oven and wondered how to get in touch with Conan Tooley at eleven o'clock at night. Tooley had his phone number but he had not been given Tooley's, or Loong's.

'Just grab a couple of things,' he said, wiping up the worst of the spilled kalia. 'We have to go.'

'But our whole life is here,' she said. 'We can't just leave it.'

'We have no choice my darling … you must trust me.'

She stared at him for a moment, her eyes filling again with tears, but then she went to the bedroom.

When she was gone, Asif opened the fridge and pulled out the packet of haloumi. He then retrieved his small work esky from the freezer and placed the haloumi inside.

He was ready to leave.

• • •

Once again Asif left via the back door into an empty lane, but this time Tanya was with him.

'Where are we going?' she whispered.

'To the federal police,' he replied. 'That's where I went this afternoon, trying to put a stop to all this.'

'To all what?'

'Not now, my darling,' he said, glancing in both directions. 'We must hurry … and be silent.'

He led her quickly through the back lanes, gradually filling with people despite the hour. Many thousands performed shift work in Ord City so there was always a need for food and entertainment, but Asif's eyes swept back and forth, knowing that some would be on the lookout for him. Doubly so once Razzaq recovered and raised the alarm.

But no one seemed to give them a second glance and Asif found himself breathing more easily as they reached the taller buildings towards the city centre. On the corner of Abbott and Gillard Streets, the Australian Federal Police building was unremarkable and unadorned – all tinted glass and steel, with harsh bright lights in the entryway. Asif had never really noticed the building until he'd been inside it that afternoon.

'This way,' he said, with a last glance about. But no one was watching. They went quickly up a ramp and then entered the foyer where a single officer sat at reception. Asif was keenly aware of the various cameras trained on them as they approached the desk.

'Hello … what can I do for you?' asked the officer, a young man of white European extraction.

'We need to see Agent Tooley … urgently.'

'Who?'

'Agent Conan Tooley,' repeated Asif, feeling the merest premonition of danger.

'I don't think we have an Agent Tooley here,' said the young man.

'Yes, you do,' insisted Asif. 'I was with him this afternoon … and Edward Loong also.'

'Edward Loong?' enquired the young officer. 'Are you sure?'

'Yes,' said Asif, sensing the rising panic in Tanya at his side. 'Please call him … this is very urgent.'

'He's not on duty,' said the young man waving his hand over a triPod and scrolling through a number of screens. 'I can call Agent Ping.'

'Please.'

The young man picked up a phone and pushed a couple of buttons, but got no answer so left a message. 'Agent Ping, this is reception. There are a couple of people who need to see you … '

'Urgently,' said Asif.

'Urgently,' added the officer. Then he put the phone down. 'Have a seat. I'm sure he won't be long.'

Asif led Tanya to a large red plastex lounge under hot, bright lights. The harsh lights made them feel uncomfortably exposed and Asif sensed Tanya's anxiety reaching critical levels.

'Please relax, my darling. We are safe here.'

'It doesn't feel safe,' she hissed. 'And safe from what, Asif? Who are we running from? What have you been doing?'

'I got involved with some bad people when I was young and angry,' he said. 'But since I met you I have been healed. My anger is gone and I want no part of their terror.'

'Who are they?'

Asif glanced up at the twin cameras trained on the lounge, then examined the standard lamps at either end.

'Best not say too much now. I promise I will explain it all.'

'This can't be good for the baby,' she moaned. 'Where is this man we're supposed to be seeing?'

'Hello … I'm Agent Ping. What can I do for you?'

They looked up to see a door had opened in the otherwise featureless wall, and a tall Chinese man stood there smiling at them. It was the man who had come to the doorway of Edward Loong's office. Asif felt strangely unwilling to deal with him.

'We need to see Edward Loong,' said Asif, '… or Agent Tooley.'

'Neither are here tonight,' said Agent Ping, his eyes dark and difficult to read. 'Perhaps I can help you?'

He motioned them towards the doorway but Asif was wracked with uncertainty.

'I really do want to see Agent Tooley,' said Asif. 'Can you not contact him?'

'Quite impossible, I'm afraid.'

Asif had expected that and nodded.

'Perhaps we should come back in the morning.'

He stood up and turned to Tanya, but Agent Ping said, 'Are you in danger?'

'Yes,' said Tanya, before Asif could stop her.

'I see … and what kind of danger exactly?'

'It's okay,' interrupted Asif. 'We'll be fine until morning.'

'If you need sanctuary,' said Agent Ping, 'but would rather be somewhere less … official than our HQ, I can give you the address of a safe house.'

Tanya looked pleadingly at Asif who, despite his wariness, agreed.

'The address is 242 Ruddock Lane,' said Agent Ping, lowering his voice. 'It is several blocks east of here, off Abbott Street. It does not look very safe but that is just window dressing to keep unfriendly eyes away. You will be taken care of, I promise.'

Tanya thanked him and stood, one hand clutching at her belly. Asif stared hard at Agent Ping, who smiled evenly back at him.

'Thank you,' said Asif.

• • •

Feeling more exposed than ever, Asif and Tanya left the bright glare of the AFP building and re-merged with the crowds on Abbott

Street. Everyone seemed to be dressed in yellow in preparation for *Illumination* the following night.

'Why didn't you want Agent Ping to help us?' asked Tanya.

'I don't know,' said Asif. 'Edward Loong said this afternoon he no longer knew whom he could trust. And better mistrust undeserved than … '

Suddenly Tanya grabbed Asif's hand and dragged him over to a café where a table had just become available.

'Now … Asif,' she said, 'I want you to tell me everything. The whole truth and nothing but the truth.'

Asif sat, but his eyes were constantly sweeping – watching for any apparent interest in them.

'Asif! Look at me!'

'Sorry … but I must keep an eye out. Razzaq's people may be looking for us.'

'Razzaq's people!' she snorted, making Asif uncomfortable with the loudness of her voice. 'You still haven't told me who they are.'

'They are a radical sect of Habal Tong … dedicated to revealing the racism and avenging the hypocrisy of mainstream Australians.'

'So why did you join them?'

'Because I was angry. I was more than two years in the camps before the law changed and it was horrible … like being in prison with rape and murder happening all the time … and the guards not caring … and the officials always lying to us but refusing to believe our stories.'

'Yes … you told me all that.'

'I did not tell you the half of it,' said Asif, with a touch of his old anger. 'We were treated like animals … worse than animals … and the Australian officials were so smug and arrogant, always lying to us about what they would do to make the camp safer … or lying to us about our refugee applications. Of course we were refugees! Why else would we leave our homes if not in desperation? My home was under water!'

Coffee was brought and they both leaned back to stir sugar and sip. Asif lowered his voice, which had been rising as he remembered his anger. 'I hated the Australians and their always-changing rules … and I hated the other prisoners … crawling over each other like rats in the vicious hell created by the authorities. The only way to survive was to join one of the gangs and I chose Habal Tong.'

'But Habal Tong is peaceful,' objected Tanya. 'Inclusive, empowering and enlightening … that's what attracted me to it.'

'It is all those things for people with money and freedom,' agreed Asif. 'For people who do not have those things, the idea that nothing is all is very attractive. It means if I have nothing then all shall have nothing. I will destroy myself and take them all with me.'

Tanya stared at him, her mouth open in shock.

'And so I planned to do,' he said. 'I met Razzaq … and Ah Cheng … people who shared my anger and contempt for the Australians and it seemed like the most natural thing in the world to join them. We would meet regularly and talk about how we would get revenge on Australia one day and before I knew it I was part of their plan … they were my friends.'

'But not anymore?'

'No. That's when the best thing ever to happen to me came along.'

He reached across the table and took her hand.

'Tanya my darling … I cannot begin to tell you how much I love you … admire you … worship you. From the day we met I began to heal in heart and spirit and I learned many things … not least that true happiness between a man and woman can only be achieved when both are equal. Neither you nor I own or rule the other, so we play an equal part in all things and both of us are happy.'

'Equals don't hide the truth from each other,' said Tanya. 'How can you say we were equals when you were part of this gang planning … planning what exactly? The destruction of telescopes?'

'Razzaq said it was a great blasphemy … the work they do there.'

'Is that what you think?'

'I do not know,' said Asif, 'but the one thing I have now realised is this … leaders call upon the led to do things in the name of The Way, but the true reason for the action may be to serve an entirely different purpose. I realised I was being used.'

'And that is why you wanted to be out of the Tong?'

'No.'

Asif glanced over both shoulders, his sense of danger growing ever stronger.

'I wanted to be out because, as I said, I was healed … by you. My anger was gone and I just wanted our life together to continue. The only way to achieve that was to leave the Tong … but that is not an easy thing to do. The federal police have promised to send me to Sydney with a new identity … a new life.'

He glanced round again and froze. Razzaq and Ah Cheng were striding through the crowd with what seemed to be a group of other men, but they had not yet been seen.

'Inside! Quickly!'

He took her hand and drew her deeper into the crowded café. Moments later, Razzaq and Ah Cheng swept past followed by half a dozen others. Razzaq was still covered with red brown stains from the kalia sauce and his head was wrapped in a gauze bandage. His face was set in a furious rage and Ah Cheng also looked very different from the cheerful Chinese Asif had always known.

'We should go to the safe house,' said Tanya, when they had passed.

'Perhaps,' said Asif. He picked up the plastex bill but Tanya took it and held it against her OzBrace until it buzzed. Once again, Asif's eyes filled with tears as he perceived the significance of her gesture, but he stood and said:

'Let us take the back door … and consider again outside. I would like to find Agent Tooley.'

Chapter 31

Scorned and Hated
by all Decent Folk

Conan didn't know how long he'd been in the dark but had quickly given up struggling. He knew very well that the more you struggled against plastex ties the harder they gripped. People had lost limbs or even died from struggling so he did his best to stay still in the slightly rickety chair.

He wondered about Mel and Dave. Had they escaped? Hopefully they'd had the sense to get out when the commotion of his capture was happening. Even now they might be leading Loongy and his agents to the scene to release Conan and prevent a major terrorist incident.

By whom exactly?

Conan was still not entirely sure who was behind it all. Neither was he certain he knew the full details of what the Shadow Group intended, but he had to prevent them blowing up the other treatment plants and he was fairly sure the pinky-red chemical ought not be getting into the water supply.

The bag over his head was stuffy and sweaty. He would have tried to shake it off except that every movement seemed to jerk and tighten the plastex ties. He concentrated on breathing and tried to make a plan for what he would do when they came for him. They meant to take him to the Giant Array, they had said, which Conan knew was supposed to be Asif's target. That meant the Shadow Group knew what Habal Tong had planned and, of course, Conan had seen Ah Li Wu at dinner with the Shadow Group. They were in league, he now perceived, to some terrible end and Conan was to be a victim of their effort – destroyed in an explosion at the Giant Array? That would confuse the authorities, when his DNA was discovered there, especially if the Shadow Group were to concoct a story about a rogue AFP agent bent on some terrorist action himself.

Conan realised, under his hood, that he wasn't particularly scared of death. But he was horrified at the prospect of being blamed for something terrible. He seemed to see in his mind's eye the millions of media reports naming him as responsible for the destruction of the Giant Array – one of the most important scientific installations in the world. He would be hated! Scorned and hated by all decent folk and the name Tooley would be forever listed with names like McVeigh, Monis and Milat.

Please get out, thought Conan of Mel and Dave. Please get out and bring the authorities. Don't do anything stupid.

He heard a click come from the direction of the door and his body went rigid with anticipation.

He heard the handle turn and the door opened.

Then it closed.

'Conan?'

Conan felt a wash of relief immediately followed by a surge of frustration.

'What the fuck are you doing?' he shout/whispered.

'We can leave if you like,' said Mel, angry and astonished by his stupid question.

'Sorry,' said Conan. 'I hoped you'd already gotten out and were bringing help, but never mind. Sorry.'

They pulled the bag off his head and Dave produced a blade to cut the ties. In a matter of moments Conan was up and rubbing his wrists and ankles, getting the blood flowing again.

'We used the stinger,' said Mel, proudly. 'It's very clever.'

'Thanks,' said Conan, taking it back. 'I'm very glad I got you to hold it, but where have you been?'

He snatched up his phone which had been left on the desk, noting the time was one thirty.

'No signal,' he muttered.

'Yeah,' said Dave. 'We've been hiding in the truck downstairs, and straight after you were captured we lost the signal. They must have a local scrambler.'

'So we'll have to sneak out,' sighed Conan, 'but we'll take this.'

He picked up Ferrier's triPod which was still on the desk, and dropped it back into his backpack.

'Okay ... let's go. Really quietly now.'

'Quietly?' grinned Dave. 'I've got a much better idea.'

• • •

The three of them paused in the open doorway but there was no one in sight. They slipped down the stairs and dashed behind the truck where Dave and Mel had spent the last hour.

'Can you drive a truck?' whispered Dave. 'Because the keys are inside.'

'I don't know,' said Conan. '... but are you crazy? They'll spot us straight away.'

'They'll spot us anyway,' said Dave. 'The security cunts are ...'

'David!'

'Sorry Mel ... the security gentlemen are on high alert after you were caught. They're all patrolling the perimeters right now and the fence is electrified. This way we can just smash the front gate down. Trouble is ... the truck's manual and I've only ever driven autos.'

Conan considered Dave, grinning like a crescent moon and clearly failing to appreciate the seriousness of the danger.

'There's even the hope,' said Dave, 'that no one will respond to the truck starting up as everyone will just assume it's one of their own doing it for some legitimate reason.'

'They might,' agreed Conan. 'Or they might think what the fuck's that? and come running with guns.'

They opened the passenger door on the darker side of the truck and Conan climbed aboard, followed by Mel and then Dave. The keys were sitting in a well behind the two gearsticks and Conan examined the controls with a sinking heart.

'I have driven a manual,' he said, 'but that was yonks ago and far less complicated than this lot.'

'Oh, for heaven's sake,' said Mel. 'It's not that hard. I'll do it if you like.'

'You've driven a manual truck?' asked Conan in surprise.

'No, but the bus used by the mission where I work is manual. I've driven it many times.'

'No way, Mel,' said Conan.

'How disappointing. I didn't realise you were sexist, Conan.'

'I'm not … at least I don't think so, but these people have guns, Mel, and the driver is very likely to be shot at.'

'Oh.'

'That's why I'm not doin' it,' grinned Dave.

'So … you don't mind if I have a go?' asked Conan.

'Um … no. That's fine. Sorry.'

Conan checked out the gears again, which fortunately were written on the stick. With the engine switched off he used the clutch to feel his way around the gear box, then took a deep breath.

'Okay … maybe you guys better lie on the floor.'

He pressed the starter button and the truck roared into life, sounding like a Hercules bomber in the previously silent chamber. Someone walked towards the window in the open plan office on the bottom level.

Conan forced the gear stick into reverse and the clutch ground squealing. The truck lurched backwards and then stalled.

'Fuck!'

Conan pressed the starter again but nothing happened. The person in the window could be seen beckoning someone else.

'Put it in neutral,' hissed Mel.

'Christ!'

'Conan!'

'Shit, sorry. Fuck!'

He got the gear stick back into neutral and the truck growled into life again. He'd already made a bit of space backwards so threw it into first this time and swung hard to his right. The truck stalled again.

'Jeezus fuck!'

'Conan! Say that again and I'm getting out.'

'You can't get out you mad cow!'

'I *beg* your pardon?'

He got the truck back into neutral and pressed the starter again and once more the engine rumbled. People were rushing to the window inside the office and Conan knew time was running out. Easing his foot more gently off the clutch this time the truck moved forward but there wasn't enough room for a right hand turn.

'Fuck it!' shouted Conan and crashed into the office window where several people were showered with glass smashed into a million shards. Conan threw the truck back into reverse and, getting the hang of the clutch a bit better, slammed the truck backwards into a couple of cars, forcing one of them into yet another car.

People were running towards them but now there was room for a proper right turn and Conan swung hard on the wheel.

'Down!' he shouted as one of the black-kitted security men ran into the entrance and aimed a gun as Conan accelerated straight at him. The windscreen exploded in hard confetti but none of them were hit (except by flying glass). And then they were outside.

'Where the fuck's the gate?'

'To the left!' shouted Dave. 'Between the silos!'

More men were running at them but Conan just ignored them, concentrating on finding the road. More shots rang out and bullets were hitting the truck but the shooters were diving out of the way and their aim was off.

The truck gathered speed and leaned over as Conan careered hard round a bend and through a carpark where he bounced off several more cars.

'To your right!'

'Fuck!'

Conan missed the road to the right and screeched to a halt, but remembered to keep his foot on the clutch. He could hear gun shots but couldn't see who was firing as he slammed the truck into reverse and beeped his way back the thirty odd metres by which he'd missed the turn.

'The gate's straight ahead,' shouted Dave as more people came running through the carpark. Conan suddenly flinched as though a bee had stung him on the forehead, but he threw the truck forward, gathering speed again.

'There it is!'

There were people at the boom gate aiming guns at the truck and Conan shouted, 'Get down!'

Then, having pointed the truck at the gate, he ducked down himself, keeping his foot flat to the floor. Guns banged about his ears and a metallic shriek sounded as they tore through the gate and bounced violently as the truck hit the kerb. Conan was up again but couldn't see properly. He fumbled at the stalks on the side of the wheel and was hit in the face by the windscreen wiper reaching through the non-existent windscreen.

'Fuck!'

'Conan!'

He got the lights on just as he smashed into another parked car and bounced back into the middle of the road.

'I can't fuckin' see!' he shouted, and that's when he realised he was bleeding.

'Conan,' said Mel, 'let me drive.'

Conan wiped his eyes but they kept filling with blood.

'Anyone behind us?'

'Not yet,' said Dave, looking back through the rear window, which was also gone.

Conan hit the brakes, stopped in the middle of the road and climbed over Mel, letting her slide underneath him.

'Conan ... you're all bloody.'

'Sorry Mel ... very rude of me and I apologise.'

'Are you okay?'

'Well, I've been shot in the head ... but I think I'll manage.'

'Here they come,' said Dave.

Mel put her seatbelt on and then carefully placed the truck in first gear.

'Put your seatbelt on Conan.'

'Please just drive Mel.'

'I'm not going anywhere until you put your belt on.'

'You'd rather they shoot me again?'

Mel stared daggers at him, but moved slowly forward along an empty road servicing the industrial area on the eastern bank south of the city, which loomed ahead like a vast pile of jewels pulsing with light.

'They're coming,' warned Dave.

'Where are we going?' asked Mel, as the truck gathered speed in third gear.

'Back to my shop,' said Dave.

'We'll never get through the traffic,' said Conan, still wiping blood from his eyes.

'Turn here,' said Dave, and Mel expertly slowed, putting the truck into second for the left turn. 'And right ... better get a move on, they're coming.'

'I'm still waiting for your apology, Conan.'

'Sorry?'

Conan was twisted in his seat with a hand over his eyes to keep the blood out, trying to watch through the rear window.

'You called me a mad cow and I'm absolutely furious with you right now.'

'Put your foot down, Mel!' shouted Dave, as a car rounded the corner in pursuit.

'Oh, for heaven's sake.'

The truck increased in speed but was getting closer to the city where traffic and pedestrians would make evasive driving difficult, even at two in the morning.

'We'll never make it to K-town,' said Conan. 'We'll have to find a place where we can ditch the truck and get away on foot.'

'No worries,' said Dave. 'Get onto the ring road coming up and we can dive out under the flyover towards the bridge. There's a real warren of streets there and if we can just get a head start we should be able to lose 'em.'

Conan pulled his shirt off as Mel concentrated on the road and Dave kept up a commentary on the pursuit behind and the options ahead. He wrapped the shirt like a bandanna round his head and tied the sleeves behind. His vision cleared but his head was throbbing with pain.

They flew up a ramp onto the ring road and Mel, her confidence increasing, pushed the truck ever faster as the car followed some 100 metres behind and the city loomed above – a mass of light and colour, and warm cooking smells rushing through the broken windscreen.

'They're trying to shoot the tyres out,' said Dave, as sparks flashed off the road. 'Down there!'

Mel flung the truck onto an exit ramp – tyres squealing – and they seemed to descend into darkness under huge buildings.

'Fifty metres!' warned Dave. 'There's a service bay. Pull in there, then we all get out my side and run.'

The truck levelled out and they could all see a blue layby sign just ahead on the left. Mel slammed the truck into the narrow space, colliding with a concrete barrier.

'Out!'

Dave was out and Conan was dragging Mel across the seats as the following car squealed to a stop next to the truck in the middle of the road.

'Run!' shouted Dave, and took off through a dim lit alleyway toward a blaze of lights. He twisted right, then left, then right, then left, then left, before pausing to look back. There were people around them now. One or two stared at Conan's head gear and the blood on his face and chest, but most just flowed past.

'Okay, said Dave, 'I don't reckon we're home just yet, but it's looking alright. This way.'

He led them at a brisk walk through another maze of streets full of intoxicating smells and vendors crying their wares like any mediaeval town. At two in the morning!

After ten minutes or so of pushing through throngs of people they had completely lost any sense of pursuit, so slowed to a walk and then stopped.

'So,' said Dave, '… I reckon we get back to my station and hand that Pod over to our techies, yeah.'

'You certain you can trust them?'

'Reasonably certain, but … '

'But what?'

'Something like that Pod … it's probably got a positional locator on it. We're probably drawing the next lot of hunters after us right now. And it might have other features like reverse screening.'

'Right.'

'They could be watching us the second we turn it on and taking over any local network.'

Conan considered, lips set in a thin line of frustration.

'In fact,' he mused, 'chances are they've got access to the Quantum … which means the instant we turn this on it'll network itself and obey some preset commands … including a sensitive data and history wipe.'

'What you're saying is,' remarked Mel, 'we can't use it, but it can help them find us.'

'I suppose so.'

'Well?'

There was an overflowing garbage skip nearby so Conan lifted a plastic bag full of shredded paper and pushed the backpack underneath.

'Remember this place, just in case we want to retrieve it,' he said.

Dave led them on, relieved that they were no longer drawing the Shadow Group heavies after them.

'The Pod would have been nice, but we don't really need it,' said Dave. 'Once we're back at the station we'll be able to start alerting a whole bunch of authorities as to what's going on … even the army maybe. Too many for the Shadow Group to have infiltrated all of them.'

He continued to lead them through mazes of streets and laneways – twisting and turning so that no pursuer could possibly have found them unless by the most outrageous happenstance.

'Not far now,' said Dave. 'I'd kill for a coffee … and a ciggy. Left 'em on the boat.'

'I'd kill for a bed,' muttered Mel, and Conan nodded to himself. He was crushingly tired now the adrenalin was wearing off, and his head was hurting.

'And you need a hospital,' said Mel.

'I'll be right,' said Conan, feeling a little braver now they were just about home.

They rounded a corner onto Whitlam Street and stopped. There were several black transit vans parked out the front of Dave's state police station and a lot of people going in and out with files and computers.

'Oh shit,' said Dave, his cheerful mood vanished.

Conan stepped back behind the corner and watched as Agent Ping stood out the front, talking into a phone and clearly in charge.

'This isn't good,' said Conan, aware that Ping had also been given the job of co-ordinating protection of the water treatment plants.

'Now what?' said Mel, sounding tired and defeated.

'Back to your place,' said Conan.

'I beg your pardon? No way.'

'Okay, we'll go to the one place they won't expect.'

. . .

Conan was a little surprised that the key still worked at Ming's apartment, which was not far from Dave's cop shop. He did a quick sweep from room to room but it was empty, untouched in fact since they'd last been there. Dave put on the coffee machine and Conan headed for the shower.

He was pleasantly surprised when Mel followed him in. She hadn't been exactly friendly in the last little while, but they'd all been under a lot of stress.

'Let me look at your head.'

He went to strip the shirt off but it was stuck to the dried blood on his forehead.

'I'll have to get under the shower first.'

Conan kicked his shoes off then started pulling his trousers down, all but falling over in his tiredness. By the time he turned the shower on and had stepped out of his underpants he realised Mel was already naked herself – looking very odd with her green face.

'That's right … we're a couple,' said Conan. 'I'd almost forgotten in all the excitement.'

'Almost forgotten … how romantic.'

But she stepped into the shower with him and, after rubbing the camouflage paint off her face, they just clung together under the warm water, eyes closed and enjoying the brief moment of sanctuary. Then, as she felt him stir against her thigh, Mel stepped back and said, 'Right, let's have a look at that head of yours.'

The wet shirt was pealed away with only minor disruption to the scabbing process, and Mel looked relieved.

'You're very lucky. A couple of millimetres closer and it might have killed you.'

'Lucky? A couple of millimetres the other way and it misses me entirely!'

'Why didn't you shoot back at them?'

Conan did have his own weapon but he hadn't fired back, had never, in fact, fired his gun in the line of duty.

'I'm a lover, not a fighter,' he said, examining his wound in the mirror.

'Really? Well there won't be either tonight … at least, not with me. I'm too tired.'

They got dressed and went out to the kitchen where Dave had made coffee and was sitting at the table where the contents of Ming's medical cabinet were displayed.

'Gauze bandage there,' said Dave, 'but no dressing so it'll stick.'

'It was only a scratch,' said Conan, sipping coffee. 'I'm better off without a bandage … although I could do with a clean shirt.'

He repeated the gist of what he'd learned regarding Ming and the Shadow Group's plans. The three other treatment plants were planned for destruction that night, as was the Giant Array. Also, the Shadow Group seemed to be directing operations at the AFP.

'They even had me appointed to the Fong, Wing Ho murders.'

'Why you?' asked Mel.

'Because I'm a screw up,' said Conan, ignoring Dave snorting with laughter. 'They wanted a screw up so there'd be no risk of progress in the case.'

'So, speaking of progress,' said Mel, 'what do you propose we do to stop the explosions and expose the Shadow Group?'

'I haven't told you everything,' said Conan. 'They pretty much admitted this was all about causing an emergency to justify a moratorium on the seven year visas … but there's something else. Inside one of the silos at Delta there were vats of some red chemical. They're putting it in the water but didn't say what it's for.'

The three of them sat in silent contemplation for a few moments.

'The problem is,' said Conan, '… who can we trust?'

'You trust Loongy, don't you?' said Dave.

'I did … but why are the AFP going through your station like a dose of salts?'

'Why not just put it out there on social media?' asked Mel. 'That might alert too many people to enable them to go through with it.'

'And might also start a riot,' said Conan. 'There's no way we can just put this out there. It has to be contained or there'll be anarchy.'

'Well, whatever we do,' said Mel, 'it's nearly four o'clock and I desperately need a few hours sleep first.'

She stood up and looked at Conan.

'You coming?'

Conan couldn't help but feel that the proper cause of action was to remain vigilant and undertake some heroic action, but Mel looked absolutely gorgeous and he was so tired.

'I'm desperate for a few winks myself,' said Conan, pulling out his phone. 'But I'd better just make one call before I do.'

Chapter 32

Remade Clean and Perfect

Asif and Tanya decided to go to the safe house. Agent Ping had said they wouldn't like the look of it, and he was right.

The house at 242 Ruddock Lane was burnt out and with the remnants of blue police tape still across the entrance.

'Maybe it's the tape that makes it safe?' mused Asif. But neither of them took any further step towards the derelict house.

'I don't like it,' said Tanya, 'but where else can we go?'

When they entered the laneway behind the large apartment buildings they were aware of how still it was – as though they had entered a sound-proof bubble. They could make out traffic din in the distance but here the lane was quiet, and smelled of cooking oil, cabbage and cat piss.

'There's no one here,' said Asif, his nose wrinkling at the stench. 'How can a deserted house be safe?'

'Maybe there is a better room inside,' said Tanya. 'It's just presented like this to keep people away?'

She took a step towards the blackened house, then froze as a sound came from the end of the alley to their right – a plastic bottle had been kicked along the ground, but no one could be seen.

'A dog or cat?' suggested Asif, a note of panic in his voice.

Then their heads snapped around as the same noise came from the left, and an empty drink bottle lay in a pool of light under a streetlamp, slowly spinning to a halt.

'Quickly … inside!' said Asif. At that moment his phone rang. The number was withheld but he answered, hoping it might be Agent Tooley.

'Hello?'

'Asif?'

'Yes?'

'Conan Tooley. Did I wake you?'

'No,' said Asif, dragging Tanya down the short path and through the dark doorway of the burnt out house, '… but we are in trouble.'

'Where are you?'

'Inside an AFP safe house, but there are bad men coming and we are frightened.'

There was silence and Asif checked his phone to ensure it was still working, as Tanya drew him by the hand deeper into the house which smelled of charred wood and urine.

'Agent Tooley?'

'Yeah … hang on. Where are you?'

Asif could hear people in the front yard.

'The address is 242 Ruddock Lane.'

'What?'

'242 …'

'I heard. Who sent you there?'

'Agent Ping.'

There were noises coming from the front of the house.

'Get out!'

'What?'

'Get out! Whatever you do, get out!'

• • •

Conan put his phone away and swore in frustration.

'Have you got a firearm?'

'I left it in the boat,' said Dave. 'What's up?'

'We've got to get to Ruddock Lane … *really* quickly.'

He went into the bedroom where Mel had already got into bed.

'I've got about ten minutes in me if you want to fool around,' she said, with a look that could've defrocked a bishop.

'Sorry Mel, no rest for the wicked. I need to make a mercy dash.'

He snatched up his gun (which was still in the en suite) and strapped it into place. Then he threw on his jacket.

'I can't stay here without you!' protested Mel.

'Why not?'

Mel moaned and started getting out of bed, causing Conan to groan with frustrated desire when he saw she was naked. He pushed her gently back down.

'I haven't got time to wait, Mel. Stay here and I'll be back ASAP. Have a rest.'

'What about Dave?'

'He's coming with me. See you soon.'

He kissed her on the forehead and strode back into the living room where Dave was waiting by the front door throwing down the last of his coffee.

'Where are we going?'

'Ruddock Lane ... the house where the Fong, Wing Ho murders happened.'

• • •

'What are you doing Asif?'

'Looking for another way out,' he said, and rejoined her from where he had been poking among the debris on the far side of the room.

'Stay close. I don't like it here.'

There were more noises from the front of the house. The moon was shining in through holes in the roof so the various beams of light were like ghostly columns in the blackness. There was movement.

'Asif?'

The voice was Agent Ping's and Asif felt his blood run cold.

'Asif ... I am here to help. Where are you?'

They were suddenly dazzled by a flashlight and heard more voices laughing.

Hated voices.

Razzaq and Ah Cheng stepped into the light, grinning like wolves.

'As I said, this is a safe house,' smiled Agent Ping, '... a place where secrets are made safe for ever.'

Tanya screamed and Asif grabbed her by the shoulders, then pulled her towards him.

'Will we leave the Dedd Reffo marks this time?' asked Ah Cheng. 'Or the Habal Tong?'

'Why not both?' said Razzaq. 'Did you bring your knives?'

'What is going on?' demanded Asif.

'What does it look like?' snapped Razzaq. 'You have betrayed the Tong! There is only one penalty for that.'

'The Tong betrayed me,' insisted Asif. 'In any case, you must let Tanya go. She has done nothing to you and she is carrying a child.'

'Then there shall be three deaths today,' said Ah Cheng, opening a bag from which he produced a long thin blade.

'Down,' said Agent Ping, producing a gun and waving it towards two filthy looking mattresses in the corner.

'Asif!' wailed Tanya, clutching at her belly. 'Asif!'

But he did not answer, as Razzaq and Ah Cheng came forward and pulled Tanya, shrieking, from his arms.

'If you don't shut up,' said Agent Ping, 'the pain will be worse … much worse, I promise.'

Tanya stopped screaming but sobbed in devastated distress – staring at Asif and waiting for him to do something, but he seemed to have accepted his fate.

'All is nothing and nothing is all,' murmured Asif, like a prayer, or a meditation.

'Nothing will be all very soon,' agreed Ah Cheng. 'But there are some formalities first. We will need to carve your foreheads before death or the blood will not flow. Those who discover your bodies must know you died in terrible pain.'

'What about the eyes and tongues?' asked Razzaq.

'They are more easily done postmortem,' said Ah Cheng, 'but is there anything else that needs to be chopped off in this case? It is a serious betrayal.'

All three of them laughed at Asif, who seemed almost to be unaware of them.

'All is nothing and nothing is all … All is nothing and nothing is all … '

'Asif! Please!' wailed Tanya, but he ignored her.

'Enough!' said Agent Ping. 'Get down on the mattresses.'

Tanya was forced down but Asif got down onto the mattress

himself and lay on his back.

'All is nothing and nothing is all ... All is nothing and nothing is all ... '

'I have to say,' said Ah Cheng, 'I admire your stoicism Asif. What a shame that same calmness in the face of death could not have been applied to our cause. Still ... your death will serve an important purpose.'

He examined his blade, then stepped towards Asif with a terrible grin.

• • •

'This way, quickly!'

Conan and Dave raced through the streets just south of the main CBD, which were incredibly full of people at four in the morning. Most of the people were revellers in the yellow of Habal Tong, but there were also packs of aggressive youths looking oddly out of place. The city had filled in the last 24 hours, and not everyone was celebrating.

'Is this the right way?' panted Conan, unsure of his whereabouts.

'Absolutely,' replied Dave, who suddenly stopped with his hands on his knees, gasping for air.

'Fuckin'... fags ... '

'Down here?' shouted Conan, pointing along Abbot Street.

'Yeah ... it'll be the second or third on the right ... I mean left.'

'Left?'

'Um ... yeah. Definitely left. You go ... I'll catch up.'

Conan took off again, running. Abbott Street was less crowded than the last warren of lanes and alleyways they'd just negotiated, and ran fairly straight. He went past Hanson Alley and Bob Brown Lane and there was Ruddock Lane – on both sides of the street.

'Fuck!' shouted Conan, and ducked into the left turning, hunting numbers. Typically for Ord City there were few buildings with numbers displayed and Conan had gone some way before he found one – 373. And the street didn't look at all familiar.

'Fuck it!' he shouted.

'Tools!'

Conan spun round and Dave was summoning him back.

'You went the wrong way!'

'You said left!'

'I meant right,' he shouted, pointing. 'It's that way.'

Two cars and a motorbike screeched to a halt as they ran back across Abbott Street and plunged into the deeper dark of Ruddock which began to twist and turn. The tall buildings became lower blocks of flats and the road seemed filled with overflowing skips and abandoned cars. A block with a number in faded paint said 282-284 and the alley twisted again.

'Not far,' wheezed Dave.

Conan had only seen the lane in daylight but this stretch of it was beginning to look familiar. And there seemed to be a glimmer of grey light in the east. It was pushing dawn.

'Asif!' shouted Conan. 'Where are you.'

The lane turned yet again and Conan knew the house was close.

'Asif!'

The house was on the right side of the street looking dark, unwanted and utterly evil in the thin grey glow of the pre-dawn.

Conan drew his gun, and took a deep breath.

And then the house lit up red and yellow as a fireball ripped through it.

Conan and Dave dropped as the noise hit them. Tiles and bits of broken wood were falling all around and a fire was roaring in the right half of the house.

Conan staggered up, appalled at the heat.

Then he heard the scream.

'Fuck, no!' muttered Conan, but he only paused a moment to pull his jacket off and wrap it around his head, which had started bleeding again.

'Come on.'

They ran through the doorway into the house which was well ablaze. If anyone was in the right half of the house they were beyond help as searing heat and flame blazed at the would-be rescuers.

The main room of the house, where Fong and Wing Ho had been found, was brightly lit, hot as a furnace, and like a scene from a nightmare.

Conan could see bodies and bits of bodies and the whole wall and floor was painted wetly red. Then one of the bodies moved.

Conan ran to where the mattresses were, utterly soaked in blood, and realised at least one person was alive but in a dreadful state.

'Quickly!'

He took the burned and blood drenched person who was lying face down by the shoulders and as he lifted saw there was another person underneath – a woman – who looked in better shape because she screamed again.

'Asif!'

'Come on, Dave!'

He lifted the man off the woman and Dave pulled the woman to her feet. Then they dragged what was left of Asif past the encroaching flames and out into the coolness of the street where two men were watching, with faces like cardboard.

Conan didn't have time to worry about whether they were wrong 'uns. He lay Asif down in the roadway and ran to find a hose.

The woman seemed dazed but not badly hurt. She collapsed next to Asif, wailing and crying as she kissed his face, which was also covered in blood and Conan could see that a crude D had been carved in his forehead.

Dave was on his phone calling for emergency services but they could already hear sirens. Sirens everywhere. It seemed like the whole city had woken in panic.

It felt like the end of the world.

• • •

Melodie Roberts was drifting through a golden cloud with occasional glimpses of idyllic woods and streams and sometimes of beautiful crystal cities, like the vision of a far future when the world had been remade clean and perfect.

She was being held also – safe, warm, enfolded in her lover's arms. She could feel him beside her – sharing her journey – and she felt herself surrendering, willingly, to his gentle caress.

Mel had so rarely had sex dreams in the past, and if she had she had always roused herself to prevent the shocking liaison from developing.

But not this time. She welcomed his attention and remained asleep when she might easily have woken.

His hand reached from behind and stroked her breasts – now gently, now firmly – then slid along her hip, her thigh, pulling her leg back over his and opening her up to further exploration.

She heard herself moaning, then realised the moan was her lover's – a deep, profound longing that only she could answer. It was a liberating, enlivening feeling – to understand that only she could fulfil such need and she felt herself like a clear vessel filling with love as the hand increased its urgency.

The moaning seemed to get louder and increase in pitch, to the point that it became an irritation.

'No,' she murmured, distracting and confusing herself with her own waking voice.

The moaning was not a human sound. She woke further to realise it came from outside – a scream, or a siren. Lots of sirens, and the hand cupping her vulva was suddenly unwelcome.

'No,' she repeated and tried to twist away.

'Yes,' whispered a voice in her ear.

For a second she relaxed, but then she was bolt upright in the bed and staring in shock at the Chinese woman who was also naked.

'What are you doing in my bed?' demanded Mel.

'I was about to ask you the same thing,' said Ming.

PART FOUR

Chapter 33

Psycho-blast

On the morning of Friday the 25th of January – the day before Australia Day – the people of Ord City awoke to chaos.

Three of the precious water treatment plants had been destroyed in the hour before dawn, leaving the city vulnerable to both lack of water and to outbreaks of waterborne diseases such as giardia, dysentery or even cholera. There was an immediate call (from the right wing media) for the suspension of the *Illumination* festival and also for a suspension of all visas to prevent the First Wave from becoming full citizens at midnight.

But the Ord City administrator, Colonel Joan Chard, made a stirring, Churchillian speech to defy the terrorists and reassure the many tens of thousands that both *Illumination* and the First Wave would go ahead.

'We do not bow down to terror!' she said.

'The terrorists want us to suspend *Illumination* … that much is evident from their timing. They want to set us against each other … Australian against new Australian … and if we do suspend *Illumination* and the First Wave … the terrorists win! They get the conflict they need to drive a wedge between us who ought to be partners in Australia's glorious future.

'Well, it won't happen! Not while I'm in charge. There will be additional security around our last functioning water plant which, thanks to our foresight, has the capacity to provide for the entire city. There will also be additional security at *Illumination* tonight so enjoy your celebration. And tomorrow I, and the Prime Minister, will welcome forty-two thousand new Australians and invite you either to stay in Ord City or go anywhere in the country you like.

'So, for tomorrow ... happy Australia Day ... to each and all of us!'

• • •

Conan needed sleep.

He was desperately tired but there was no rest just yet. Asif was remarkably unhurt. He had a rough D cut into his forehead and his buttocks and back had been scorched in the blast, but the blood in which he'd been covered was not his own. Mostly.

In the moments before Agent Ping and the others had entered the house, Asif had stuck a remote detonator into the nine strips of mangalite in his esky and concealed it in the debris on the far side of the room from the mattresses. Then he had concentrated on triggering the detonators via the psycho-blast suit he had donned earlier and had endured even the carving of his forehead while counting the final sixty seconds.

Ah Cheng and Razzaq had been so lulled by his quiet acceptance they had not restrained him and were surprised when he leapt up from the mattress and covered Tanya with his body. Two seconds later the manga exploded, smashing anyone standing to smithereens, while mainly passing over those prone.

Agent Ping, Ah Cheng and Razzaq would not have felt a thing as they were instantly vaporised but Asif and Tanya would surely have died in the fire if Conan and Dave had not shown up at the very last second.

Asif and Tanya were on their way to hospital, but Conan and Dave were once again in the back of a black transit van, with the two cardboard men who had flashed ID cards from the ONA. The Office of National Assessments was the most senior and secretive of the Australian intelligence agencies, answering directly to the Prime Minister's department.

'We've been watching you for some days, Agent Tooley,' said the one whose ID suggested he was Agent Green. The other was Agent Smith. If Conan was not looking at either he found it impossible to remember their faces, which were featureless and without expression.

Like cardboard.

'Why have you been watching me?'

'Because we're very interested in Ord City and you were chosen for a mission up here which didn't match your profile.'

'I protested at the time,' said Conan, 'but it was forced on me. Anyway … Dr Ming Li Chen says her organisation arranged it.'

'Because he's a screw up,' explained Dave.

'We know about Dr Chen,' said Agent Smith, ignoring Dave. 'Do you know who she works for?'

'For whom she works? Some of them. We had to make sure you weren't working with her before we approached you. We think we can now cross you off the list.'

'So who *does* she work for?' asked Conan, ignoring both the grammar correction and the implication he'd been under suspicion. 'We've been calling them the Shadow Group … for want of a better name.'

'They don't have a name,' said Agent Green, '… as far as we know, but their contacts go to the very top of government, business and the intelligence community.'

'Except ONA,' said Agent Smith.

'Except ONA,' agreed Agent Green, as the transit van pulled into a tunnel leading to a ramp that went deep under a building. Everything went black except for the dim green glow from the dashboard.

They emerged into a hyperlit space, closed off in front, and a metal door slid shut behind them. The driver, who hadn't spoken, pushed a card into a slot by his window and another door slid open.

'How can you be certain that ONA hasn't been infiltrated,' asked Conan, feeling tired and stupid. 'How can anyone really know anything about anyone?'

'We have our ways,' said Agent Green as the van was parked in a bay. 'This way please.'

They were led along a grey corridor with numerous grey doors only visible due to the touch plates that gave entry. At the end of the corridor, Agent Green palmed a door open and they entered a dark room with a large triScreen glowing sky blue with clouds floating past in screen saver mode. It was like standing on a cliff staring into blue infinity.

'This is our operations room,' said Agent Smith, passing his hand over an authority node causing the blue sky to be replaced by the holograms of several people Conan knew and a few he didn't. They seemed real, standing in space, eyes blinking and seeming to follow the viewer.

'Holy fuck!' said Dave, unused to such resources, but Conan was familiar with the technology.

'Here they are,' said Agent Smith. 'We've slowly been working out the connections but ... maybe you can help with that.'

Razzaq and Ah Cheng were standing on the far left, with a number of other Asian men of various ethnicities, including Asif. Then closer to the centre were the Majors Lammas and Maddox, then Ronnie Kwai, Greg Ferrier, Joan Chard and an elderly Chinese who looked like Ah Li Wu. Behind them was yet another elderly man in wire spectacles who looked like an extra from a Nazi film. Further to the right was Conan himself with Edward Loong and Agent Ping, and on the extreme right were Ming, Richie Farr and Jen Khataten. Alongside each person was a holo-plaque shimmering in the air with name, job title and a few other notes about their connections and activities. Conan knew it was possible to change dates and times for the whole scenario and watch the various groupings blend and separate as they had been observed in reality.

'Yep, they're all here,' said Conan. 'Who's the old bloke at the back?'

'Hermann Van Der Kock,' replied Agent Green, and Conan finally recognised him.

'Oh, right ... he's aged.'

Van Der Kock had been a government minister back in the twenty twenties. In fact he'd been Immigration and Home Affairs Minister at the time Ord City was promulgated but had retired a few years back.

'What's he got to do with it?' asked Conan.

'Maybe nothing,' said Agent Smith, 'but he's Dr Chen's father.'

'He is? I thought that was Ronny Kwai.'

'No. Dr Van Der Kock lives in Ord City for part of the year but spends most of the time on his estate near Brisbane with his Chinese wife. We are uncertain whether he is involved in ... the Shadow Group as you call them.'

'Jeez,' said Dave, '... he must have been pretty ancient when Ming was born. He's more like her grandfather.'

'He was a specialist obstetrician and researcher before going into politics,' said Agent Green, with a slight shrug. 'Dr Chen seems to have followed in his footsteps ... but she has other interests.'

'But what are they doing?' asked Conan. 'What's it all about?'

'They have destroyed three water treatment plants in the early hours this morning,' said Agent Green, indicating the group on the left.'

'That was the sirens?' asked Dave.

'Apparently,' replied Agent Smith, indicating the men around Razzaq and Ah Cheng. 'Now all of these men are dead ... the price of their missions.'

'Not him,' said Conan, pointing out Asif. 'His job was to blow up the Giant Array, but he backed out ... didn't want to be part of it. Now he's in hospital.'

'He is still a conspirator,' said Agent Smith, '... but the Giant Array ... another connection.'

He manipulated a Pod and most of the Asian men turned blue, but the holo of Asif walked over to stand near Jen and Richie.

'I think,' said Conan, 'that the reason the plants were destroyed was simply to make the entire city dependent on water from Plant Delta.'

'A feasible deduction,' agreed Agent Smith. 'But why?'

'They're putting some pinky red chemical into the water there ... and Ming was there last night with Ferrier and Roger Manderson ... their head of security. He's the bloke who kidnapped us and left us on an island surrounded by crocodiles.'

Agents Green and Smith stared at Conan for a few moments.

'A red chemical?' asked Agent Green.

'Yeah. I mean, maybe it's perfectly legit ... I don't know what normally goes into water, but it could be a drug ... or a poison. I took a snap of the formula.'

He pulled out his phone and downloaded his messages – including one with a couple of photos taken from inside the Delta plant silo, one of which was of a long, weird looking chemical formula on a label attached to a large plastic drum.

Agent Smith asked him to forward the photos to a special number and within seconds the photos were blown up and in 3D before them.

'That's just calcium hypochlorite,' said Agent Green when the pale greenish tub came up, '... pool chlorine, which also goes into drinking water ... in much smaller quantities'

'Thought so,' said Conan. 'But what about this one?'

The photo with the pinky red tub came up and they all stared at the formula, half consisting of the periodic table notations with which Conan was familiar, and half a strange looking script with non-whole numbers. $C2.42$ and $H1.79$ both featured among the first few characters.

'It's part of the customised isotopic spectrum,' said Agent Green.

'The what?'

'Elements normally have a reactive valency based on their natural states, and those valencies are whole numbers, but researchers using the Quantum computer can build stable isotopes and allotropes beyond and between the natural valencies and blend them with other such isotopes to make a vast new range of compounds with properties entirely unknown.'

'They can even,' said Agent Smith, 'start from the basis of a certain desirable outcome ... and reverse engineer their way to a chemical, or set of chemicals, which achieves exactly that condition. This is very advanced stuff.'

'And highly classified,' added Agent Green. 'Access to the Quantum to build this chemical must have been granted at a very high security level. Let's just do a search ... '

He trailed off and took a screen shot of the formula, then fed it into a browser.

'This is a quantum browser so it should know something about the chemical's history.'

'You have access to the Quantum?' asked Conan.

Agents Green and Smith glanced at each other, then Agent Smith said, 'That's the chief purpose of ONA these days. We use the Empyrean.'

Dave and Conan stared blankly.

'The Empyrean is the highest order function of the Quantum,' said Agent Green. 'Not all the capacity of the Quantum computer is available for government agencies. We keep the Empyrean separate so it can be used for self monitoring and security.

'To answer your earlier question ... what are they doing? The Quantum can monitor its own metadata, if you like, and certain commands and functions were identified as anomalous. Members of what you call the Shadow Group had been ... aah ... here we go.'

The blue sky had returned during the search but vanished as a number of hits were listed on a shimmer field.

'There must have been some serious security and decryption required for the Quantum to take that long,' said Agent Smith, '... but that seems to be par for the course with these people.'

'Holy shit!' said Conan.

After searching the webs for reference to the formula on the plastic tubs, the top hit referred them to a chapter from a book by Dr Ming Li Chen - *Asymptotically Approaching Certainty: Chaos As The New Normal.*

'Bloody hell,' said Conan. 'That book's been turning up everywhere.'

The chapter was entitled *Plasmas and Peoples: Predicting Populations and the Chaos of Crowds.*

'Perhaps we'd better read it,' said Agent Green.

'Knock yourselves out,' said Conan. 'But not me. I am absolutely rooted with tiredness so I'll have to grab a few hours sleep.'

Agents Green and Smith said nothing for a moment, then Agent Green said, 'We can provide stimulants to keep you awake ... there is no time for sleep just yet.'

'Sorry, this is obviously your jurisdiction now. It's out of my hands and I have to get back to Mel.'

'Impossible,' snapped Agent Smith, the first time he'd shown anything other than total robotic calm. 'This is a matter of the highest national security and you are needed.'

'For what?'

'A complete debrief for a start,' said Agent Green. 'There is clearly information you have that we do not. We need to know every possible detail from the moment you became involved in this matter.'

'Oh no ... '

'Then we need to liaise with the local and national authorities, get updates on all potential terror activities and determine whether any preventive action is needed for the festival tonight.'

'Oh fuck,' said Conan, his brain filling with apathy and toxins.

'Why don't you just arrest the Shadow Group and get to the bottom of it all?'

'On what charge?' demanded Agent Green.

'Well ... erm ... blowing up the treatment plants?'

'That was done by the Habal Tong extremists led by these men,' said Agent Smith, waving at Ah Cheng and Razzaq. 'They are now dead and their accomplices are all dead also.'

'But there's a connection between them,' said Conan, pointing at Lammas, Razzaq and Agent Ping.

'We can't prove the connection,' said Agent Green. 'And even if we could we would need a smoking gun. The whole point of getting others to do your dirty work after all is so you can't be blamed for it.'

'Arrest Lammas then. Asif told me he gave Razzaq and Ah Cheng their instructions. We know he met with the honchos in the Shadow Group.'

'I agree Lammas must be our focus,' said Agent Smith, 'but all you have is hearsay. There is no real evidence against him. You should watch him today.'

'Sorry. I already told you ... tools down.' He let out a massive yawn and could have fallen asleep on the spot if there was a chair handy. 'How do I get out of here?'

Agents Smith and Green stared at each other with thin lips, then Smith nodded as though a psychic exchange had taken place.

Agent Green said to Conan, 'As a member of the AFP you will be aware of the seniority of ONA among Australia's security agencies.'

'Yes, but so what? I'm not in your chain of command so you can't compel me.'

'We can, actually,' said Agent Smith. 'Conan Daniel Tooley ... I hereby implement the authority given to me under rule 21E of the Office of National Assessments Administrative Order of 2027. By virtue of the clear and present danger to national security, the ONA's authority to enlist special agents is activated. You are now a Special Agent of the Office of National Assessments ... for the next seven days.'

'You can't do that. I don't consent.'

'The Administrative Order says nothing about consent,' said Agent Smith. 'It is not necessary.'

'What about him?' said Agent Green, indicating Dave.

Agent Smith, who seemed to be the more senior of the two, rubbed his lips, considering.

'We don't know a lot about him ... but he'd help our diversity figures.'

'Eh?' said Dave, 'Are you calling me a fuckin' token?'

'The casual salary rate is approximately four times that of a Western Australian police sergeant,' said Agent Green. Conan burst into laughter at the look on Dave's face as he tried to maintain his righteous anger while processing the thought of his new salary.

'Special Agent Token Marsh reporting for duty,' said Dave, grinning.

Chapter 34

In Flesh as Well as Fantasy

Major Tom Lammas was up early on the day he had long dreaded.

Illumination.

He sneered as he strode along the footpath which was unusually clear at that time of the morning. Fridays were usually the busiest day of the week for the street traders and the city was fuller than ever with the hordes of deluded participants and onlookers who'd come for the festival and the celebrations which would follow the First Wave.

Mind you, it hadn't started well. Lammas had smiled to himself when he'd been woken in the night by so many sirens, then he'd gone back to sleep and dreamed his favourite dream about a world entirely arrayed in the livery of the Army of God, with him as Grand Marshall exhorting the masses to greater and greater displays of adoration.

Arrayed.

The few people who were up and about were talking anxiously among themselves and gesturing at their various news media. Something big had clearly occurred.

He sat in his favourite café and disciplined himself to wait until his coffee was served before opening his triPod and bringing up the *Ord City Times*.

He managed to look stern and disapproving, but inwardly he was laughing in triumph at the reports of destruction. Three water treatment facilities had been blown up, leaving only one to provide for the entire city, but Major Lammas found himself scanning ahead looking for any mention of the Giant Array.

Nothing.

He abandoned the lead article and hunted through the other top stories which were mainly about *Illumination* and how the focus of the world was on Australia and the fruition of an enlightened refugee policy. The only other explosion reported was a derelict house in Ruddock Lane, believed to have been started by a leaking gas canister.

Lammas slammed his cup down in disgust.

He had known Razzaq and his people were unreliable. The removal of inconvenient nobodies was within their capability, but the sabotage of a poorly defended remote facility was utterly beyond them.

He couldn't even call Razzaq to find out what had happened as Razzaq was notoriously hostile to the idea of giving out his phone number. 'There must be no metadata between us!' he had always insisted. Lammas had seen the sense of that, but it was a source of frustration in an emergency.

It was possible, he knew, that Razzaq was simply delayed and that there would be more breaking news about the destruction of the Giant Array, but something about the clear light of day said the opportunity had been lost. The magic uncertainty of night made all things possible and Lammas found himself furious at Razzaq's incompetence. Or duplicity. The Giant Array – the Great Blasphemy – needed to be destroyed on the same day as the *Illumination* Festival. Before the *Illumination* Festival for its best impact. Where on earth was Razzaq?

Lammas drummed his fingers on the table.

There was a possibility, if he dared. As part of their arrangement, he had allowed Razzaq to store some of his explosives at the K-Town chapter house. It was kept in an out-of-date tofu packet in the bottom of the large freezer in the kitchen and was simple enough to use. Razzaq had told him that all you needed to do was stick the detonator – a small round metal ball with a spike on one end and a light at the other – into the explosive, which was like plasticine. Set the timer and off you go. He'd also said it was best to somehow contain the blast or it was mostly wasted upwards. 'Put it underneath what you want to destroy,' Razzaq had said, and Lammas found himself making the journey mentally out to the Giant Array.

There was no security there. That had always been one of the tempting aspects of the target, and all available security people now would be onsite at the water treatment plants or at the Festival. It was possible the site would be completely abandoned for the day as he had heard the bitch Khataten enthusing about *Illumination* and how she was looking forward to attending.

He drummed his fingers again.

It was a major risk for a man in his position – a man soon to become a Colonel.

Michael would help.

• • •

Robbie Bennett fought the urge to wake.

Back into the sanctuary of sleep is where his spirit fled, but in so striving he was aware of his condition, which pushed him closer to waking.

There would be consequences.

Clinging to the evanescent shards of a dream, he could already feel the poison in his system waiting to remind him of his folly.

There was also something else, but for the moment he didn't have to think about it.

Kate had been in the dream and while he knew he'd be depressed upon waking (as he always was after dreaming of her) he couldn't help but welcome the bliss of any time with her at all. It wasn't a sex dream. Just an ordinary dream of simple domesticity, which in its way was better than a sex dream because most of a couple's life is spent away from the extremes of passion. It's important to be comfortable together and he was so happy with Kate, in his dreams.

She was walking towards him, reaching for him …

The first dull thud struck between his ears as the grandaddy of all hangovers announced its arrival. Kate's face faded in a blur of tears as Robbie squeezed his eyes shut against the searing blast of pain and a surge of nausea.

He was going to be sick.

Not yet. There were still precious seconds of semi-sleep between the incoming waves of agony. It became a rhythm – pain, relief, pain relief, pain.

His foot touched against another, and for half a second his heart erupted with joy. Kate was with him, in flesh as well as fantasy.

But no, it wasn't Kate. And there was the other thing and it was necessary to think about it.

Not yet.

A sudden surge of toxins and his mouth filled with saliva. There were only seconds so he jack-knifed off the bed and fled into the bathroom, just managing to get his head over the toilet before his guts exploded. Heave after heave he poured dead beer and ex-food into the bowl as the sweat sprang up on his forehead and pain speared his brain.

His body felt old. Filthy. Disgusting.

'Are you alright?'

He ignored the voice, and swayed on his feet, still doubled over and spitting strings of bile into the toilet.

'Robbie?'

He gave an inarticulate grunt that might have meant: I'm fine; but might equally have meant: fuck off and die.

Die.

That was the other thing.

That's what had to be done today.

That's what had made last night possible.

• • •

Lieutenant Michael Rice was proud.

Since Captain Roberts had gone on compassionate leave (as Major Lammas had explained it), Rice had been acting officer in charge of the K-Town chapter house and enjoyed the authority.

Enjoyed it so much, in fact, that he was already lamenting the fact that Captain Roberts would inevitably return and resume her duties, relegating Rice to reading bible stories or making tea at the Great Debate. With Roberts away he was running his own show and had already instituted changes to improve the efficiency and effectiveness of the mission.

'I'm working on a way to measure belief,' he told Major Lammas.

'Measure belief?'

'I have faith it can be done,' enthused Lieutenant Rice. 'There must be an algorithm … it's just a matter of agreeing on the variables.'

Major Lammas was Lieutenant Rice's hero and it wasn't often that

Lammas had paid him much attention in the past. But Captain Roberts' absence meant they now spent time together discussing the accounts, planned events and any need for Major Lammas' participation – like at tonight's vigil in opposition to the *Illumination* Festival.

'Why would we want to measure belief?' asked Lammas.

'Why? Well ... any number of reasons,' said Rice, 'but mostly to show how we've made a difference. If we could report to our superiors that belief at our mission was up, say ... 3% in the month ... that'd be fantastic.'

Lieutenant Rice's heart sank as Lammas laughed but then, to his surprise, Lammas said, 'You know what Michael ... it's a fine idea.'

'You think so?'

Major Lammas had never called him Michael before. It was a sign of his confidence and a deepening intimacy.

'Yes. Obviously it needs to be thought out properly ... all the variables, as you say, taken into account. But I see no reason why you shouldn't do a paper on the matter for the next synod.'

'Wow! I'd love to do that.'

They were drinking coffee in the chapter house kitchen and managing to ignore the local brethren holding a Bible study in the main hall. They had a full day's activities planned culminating in the vigil at eight pm to counter the pantheist heresy of *Illumination*, but depressingly few had shown up so far. Even the believers were infected by the city's excitement.

'Well, I've always believed in encouraging talent,' said Lammas, with a friendly pat on the shoulder. 'You know, Michael,there is a chance Captain Roberts won't return.'

'That's a shame,' said Lieutenant Rice, barely able to contain his excitement.

'A terrible shame,' agreed Lammas. 'She has problems ... personal problems about which I can't say too much. But there is a likelihood ... almost a certainty that she won't return and I'll have to find a replacement.'

'I see.'

'Now ... you are a fine young officer with many admirable qualities,' said Lammas, watching Rice closely.

'Thank you, Major.'

'However … you are a lieutenant … a fairly new lieutenant … and the role requires a captaincy. You'd normally have to spend three years as a lieutenant before being eligible for promotion. How long since you graduated from the academy?'

'Nine months,' admitted Rice, his heart sinking as soon as it had soared.

'Nine months,' repeated Lammas. 'It's not long … but neither is it a total impediment to you being promoted.'

Rice looked up at Lammas, quizzical.

'There does exist within the regulations,' said Lammas, 'provision for advancement in special cases … where some outstanding duty has been done.'

'Like my paper you mean?'

'Your what?'

'My paper. The one you said I should write for the synod.'

'Oh! Absolutely! Brilliant idea … but I have something else in mind.'

Major Lammas lowered his deeply hypnotic voice.

'Something that would require action … boldness … and complete discretion.'

'I'm your man,' said Lieutenant Rice, excitedly. 'What needs to be done?'

'Something that will seem on the face of it to be wrong … but it must be done for the glory and future of our mission. And for this service … which must remain utterly secret … I will guarantee your captaincy. I will have that authority when I am made colonel.'

'Why will it seem wrong?' asked Rice.

'It is not wrong,' said Lammas, his voice basso profundo with passion. 'Not if you believe utterly in the rightness of our mission.'

'Oh, I do,' insisted Rice, mortified that Major Lammas could doubt him.

'The church has often done things … over the centuries … that might have looked wrong from the perspective of historians. But those things were only ever done for the glory of God and the primacy of His church. Such ends justify any means and sometimes, in being the instruments of His mysterious ways, we are called to do things that we might deplore … or even be called to martyrdom. In His cause, can there be any higher honour?'

'No,' breathed Lieutenant Rice.

'It's like the *Epistola Clementis*,' said Major Lammas, lowering his voice even further.

'The what?' asked Rice, the hair rising on the back of his neck with the Major venturing into such dangerous territory.

'The *Epistola*,' repeated Major Lammas. 'We do not talk openly about it for it is one of the church's greatest secrets ... but it was clearly a forgery that came to light by happy convenience at a critical time. The church could well have perished without it. But whoever was responsible for the forgery ... that forgotten scribe ... is without doubt one of the greatest heroes of the church and sits at the right hand of Christ in Heaven among all the saints, none of whom have any higher honour.'

'Wow.'

'Wow indeed,' smiled Major Lammas. 'I am not suggesting our mission is as critical to the church as was the *Epistola Clementis*, but it is critical nonetheless. Will you help me Michael?'

'Of course,' said Lieutenant Rice, his voice heavy with emotion. 'I mean, you haven't told me what the mission is ... but of course.'

'Thank you, Captain Rice,' said Major Lammas.

• • •

Five people – two men and three women – sit before a huge picture window looking over a vast city, with an ocean to the north under a pink sky waxing gold and blue. A servant pours tea and departs silently. None of them speak until all have savoured the tea and replaced their cups.

'A strong beginning,' says the larger man.

'But not an unqualified success,' says the youngest woman. 'Not everything went entirely to plan ... and we have lost important pieces.'

'Important pieces, yes,' agrees the smaller man, to whom they all defer. 'But no piece is irreplaceable. Not even you my dear ... in the wider game.'

The young woman bows her agreement as the eldest woman says, 'The part that went wrong was the side operation arranged by our colleague. I knew it was a distraction but at least it was not crucial to our own plan.'

'It will be interesting to see how he responds,' says the large woman. 'Two disappointments in one day … '

'He will not respond,' says the larger man. 'The one we need to worry about is Agent Tooley. He has proven surprisingly able and resilient.'

They all turn to the youngest woman, who sips her tea thoughtfully.

'His profile suggested otherwise,' she shrugs. 'But it doesn't really matter. He cannot hinder our main purpose.'

'Nevertheless,' says the smaller man, his voice unusually harsh, '… we have planned this day too long to countenance failure, and Agent Tooley is the greatest risk to our success. You will not underestimate him again!'

The younger woman stares, then lowers her eyes in acceptance of the rebuke as the smaller man continues.

'The elimination of Agent Tooley from the game is now a main priority.'

The others all nod their agreement and sip their tea.

The Great Day, which will be forever remembered in the secret history, has begun well.

Chapter 35

Liberation and Power

'I really ought to check on Mel,' said Conan, glancing at his watch.

'Let her sleep,' said Dave, who was absolutely wired after the pills that Agents Green and Smith had given them to stay awake.

'What are they?' Conan had asked at the time, but Agent Green had given an evasive answer.

'They will keep you alert for a good twelve hours,' said Agent Smith. 'That is all you need to know.'

That had been an hour prior and now, at nearly ten o'clock, they were once more in the coffee shop across the road from the Army of God chapter house.

Both were disguised.

That is, both had had their appearance altered in a small way to deflect the scrutiny of anyone who might be looking for them. Conan had a high quality fake moustache that looked very real, along with a baseball cap and shades. It was simple but his mother would have passed him in the street. And no sooner had he thought of his mother when his phone rang.

'Oh shit.'

'What's up man?'

'It's my ma,' said Conan. Before he knew what had happened, Dave had snatched the phone out of his hand and answered it.

'Hey Conan's ma? How ya goin'?'

Conan shook his head in disbelief as Dave, clearly affected by the pills they'd taken, giggled into the phone.

'Yeah, sure … I'll put him on.'

'Thanks a fuckin' lot,' mouthed Conan as he took the phone.

'Hi Ma … this is a really bad time.'

'Your friend sounds nice,' said his mother.

'Implying that I don't?'

'I didn't say that.'

'No … that's the thing about implication … '

She laughed, and Conan sighed. She never laughed at his jokes, unless she wanted something.

'So how's the retirement village?'

'Same as it was last week when you didn't visit me.'

'Sorry, Ma … it's just … I'm on a really important job.'

'It's to do with *Illumination* isn't it.'

'I can't say.'

'Of course it is … there's no other reason for you to be in Ord City. I hear our slut of a prime minister will be there.'

'That's not very nice.'

'Neither is she. I can't believe what's happened to this stupid country.'

'It's called democracy, Ma. Gotta go.'

'Your girlfriend came to see me.'

'Who?'

But Conan knew. Who else but Lucia would seek out his mother, presumably to send him a message that couldn't be traced to her own phone or a public phone.

'She's *your* girlfriend, Conan … didn't you tell me some westie bogan name. A bit rough I would have said, but that's the fashion these days … all tattoos and piercings … and weird haircuts. The girls look rougher than the boys.'

Yes, definitely Lucia, thought Conan, his heart sinking in guilt.

'Did she leave a message, Ma?'

'Your guess is as good as mine.'

'Why?'

Dave nudged him and pointed with his chin. Lammas was walking down the steps of the chapter house, in company with Lieutenant Rice.

'She said you needed to go back to the thing you were supposed to protect in the first place.'

'Eh? What does that mean?'

'Sorry, Conan, I'm not a mind reader … but it seemed urgent. She was all edgy and watching out the window ... like she was scared or something.'

Conan's heart sank even deeper, guessing the danger Lucia must be in and the risks she must have taken.

For him.

'Okay ... the thing I was supposed to protect in the first place,' mused Conan. 'Are you sure she didn't say anything else?'

Lammas and Rice were disappearing down a side street and Dave was paying the bill.

'Oh yes, she did say one other thing.'

'Yeah?'

'She said she was looking forward to seeing you again, and ready to do what you've always talked about.'

• • •

Tanya stared at Asif, lying on his front, his head bandaged and his back and buttocks burned from the explosion. Those burns would have been on her face if he had not protected her with his body.

She had been checked over when they'd arrived in the ambulance but, apart from the hideous memories, was unhurt. Now she sat in a chair in his room watching over him as he slept sedated with some special ointment on his burns.

Tears crept into her eyes again, but they were mainly tears of relief. The horrible men had been destroyed and whatever it was Asif had been mixed up in was over. It would take time to heal but heal they would, because if Tanya was certain of one thing, it was that Asif loved her deeply enough to throw his own life away to protect hers. That was worth a lot and she would always remember it.

The pain he must have suffered when they cut his forehead! The pain he was suffering now, or would when he woke.

At least they were safe in the hospital. A policeman was standing outside the door and she might have been terrified of policemen if not for the reassurance of Agent Tooley straight after the explosion. It was Agent Tooley and his friend who had pulled them out of the fire, and Asif seemed to know them. Agent Ping, who had seemed the worst of the bad men, was a one off bad guy according to Agent

Tooley, so now they were safe. Protected by the federal police in the Army of God hospital.

'How's the patient?'

Tanya looked up to see a fat, middle aged woman in a black uniform with gold crosses on her collar.

'He's sleeping,' said Tanya.

'You should be sleeping also,' said the woman. 'Would you like to go back to your room?'

'No thanks.'

The woman picked up a tablet at the end of Asif's bed and scrolled through a number of charts. Then she checked his drip.

'He seems comfortable enough,' she said. 'I'm Major Maddox, by the way.'

'Hello … I'm Tanya Cahill.'

'The painter?'

'Yes.'

Tanya smiled despite her instinctive dislike of the woman, who seemed bossy and officious.

'I went to an exhibition of yours, about a year ago,' said Major Maddox. 'It's not really to my taste, I'm afraid, but I could tell you're very talented.'

'I get that a lot,' said Tanya.

Major Maddox placed the tablet back in its plastex sheath.

'I understand that Asif was injured in an explosion.'

'Yes. He was hurt protecting me from some very evil men … me and my child.'

'You're pregnant?'

'Yes.'

'So he's a double hero?'

'He's always been my hero,' said Tanya, feeling guilty for her initial dislike of the woman.

'And people were killed in the explosion?'

Tanya opened her mouth to answer, then remembered the warning from Agent Tooley.

'I think so … but I'm not supposed to talk about it.'

'That's alright dear,' said Major Maddox. 'The policemen have their rules, I suppose, but I'm just here to help you recover and talking helps sometimes. Have we given you some breakfast?'

'Erm … no,' said Tanya, suddenly feeling hungry.

'Why don't I get us a nice cup of tea … and some toast perhaps?'

'That would be lovely,' said Tanya, warming even more to the considerate woman who left the room with a reassuring smile.

Five minutes later she was back with two pots of tea and a plate of toast with butter, jam and honey.

'Still sleeping?' asked Major Maddox, with a glance at Asif as she placed the tray on a side table and poured the tea. 'Milk and sugar?'

'Just milk, thanks,' said Tanya. The smell of tea and toast was heavenly and emphasised, somehow, a return to normality. She spread toast with butter then applied the jam very liberally. 'I'm quite ravenous, thank you.'

'I'm amazed you're still awake after your ordeal,' said Major Maddox. 'Usually people crash after expending all that adrenalin in a stressful situation.'

'I expect I will later,' said Tanya, sipping her tea and relaxing a little more.

'You're obviously Australian,' said Major Maddox, '… and Asif's from where?'

'Bangladesh. He gets his citizenship tomorrow … or tonight at midnight I suppose.'

'Ooh … a First Waver. How did you meet?'

Tanya felt herself relaxing completely and was happy to chat to the nice woman about how she and Asif had met at a Habal Tong gathering shortly after she had moved up from Sydney. Asif had been very shy but she had been drawn to him from the moment she laid eyes on him – tall, slim and silent with an air of mystery about him.

'He seemed full of secret promise,' remembered Tanya, then flushed as she realised how correct that assessment had been.

'And what drew you to Habal Tong in the first place?' asked Major Maddox.

'Curiosity,' said Tanya. 'I grew up in a Catholic house, then later found Buddhism, then I found Habal Tong which seemed so much more liberating and empowering than other religions … or philosophical pursuits. Habal Tong is not a religion … it's a tool for life.'

'You didn't find liberation and power in Christianity?' asked Major Maddox.

Tanya snorted milky tea through her nose. 'Oh ... sorry,' she laughed, embarrassed. 'But no, in all honesty I found the opposite in Christianity.'

'What a shame. But the Catholics, of course, are a bit more heavy with the rules than some.'

'Perhaps,' admitted Tanya, '... but all religions, to my mind, are about asserting power over believers. That's why I liked Buddhism ... which teaches you to find the divine within yourself. And Habal Tong was even better because it required no sublimation of the self to any authority, human or divine ... and its various axioms were powerful tools of meditation to help you reflect upon the cosmos and your place within it. I'm never so alive and free as when I'm meditating on The Way with a brush in my hand. When the muse comes over me I can work for hours without even knowing what I'm doing and I seem to snap out of a trance and there in front of me is a finished painting in which the muse has been captured on any number of levels. I've never known such magic ... it's intoxicating and deeply fulfilling.'

Suddenly Tanya yawned, her brain reeling with tiredness.

'You are very passionate about it,' said Major Maddox. 'I'm almost tempted to look into it myself.'

'You should,' yawned Tanya, fighting to keep her eyes open.

'Drink this, dear,' said Major Maddox, holding a glass of red liquid up to Tanya's lips.

'I think I need a rest.'

'You have a sleep darling ... but first drink this medicine. It's like raspberry juice.'

'Okay.'

• • •

'The thing I went to protect in the first place,' muttered Conan for the fourteenth time as he and Dave followed Lammas and Rice through the half-filled streets.

Dave lit up a cigarette and sighed with pleasure, 'Must be fuckin' hours since I've had a fag.'

'That's great,' said Conan, waving away smoke. It was mid-morning and the streets were strung with posters with Habal Tong axioms in English and a dozen other languages, and filling again with revellers getting ready for the biggest Australian party since the Sydney Olympics. The sun was high enough to be blazing down into the concrete canyons of the CBD and Conan felt sweaty and vaguely toxic, certain that lack of sleep and the mysterious stimulant were bad for his health.

'The thing I went to protect … I didn't come to protect anything,' protested Conan. 'I came to look into a double murder.'

'Fair chance you've solved that too,' said Dave. 'The blokes killed in the explosion … going through the same modus operandi with Asif.'

'Yeah, maybe,' agreed Conan.

Lammas and Rice had paused outside a lockup garage and were in close discussion. Rice was carrying a plastex box that may have been a small esky. Conan pulled Dave behind a stand filled with faded, curling postcards and watched the crowds streaming past as the garage door opened.

'What does it mean though,' asked Conan, 'if Razzaq and Ping were working together? It partly explains the total lack of interest in the case by the AFP, but does that mean Loongy's involved also?'

'Go ask him.'

Conan was aware that he hadn't reported Agent Ping's death to Loongy, although the forensic crew were all over that particular scene so his ID had doubtless been discovered by now. In all likelihood the AFP were looking for Conan and Dave also, but they wouldn't be able to trace them. They now wore ONA replacement OzBraces and their previous accounts had been deleted from all records. Their location could now only be traced by the Empyrean computer used by the ONA.

Of course the AFP wouldn't be the only people looking for Conan. The Shadow Group wouldn't have given up, but hopefully their minimalist disguises would defy the facial recognition software employed by CCTV and micro-drones all over the city.

'If Ping's linked with Razzaq then he was also linked with the Shadow Group via Lammas,' decided Conan. 'The pieces are falling together.'

'The pieces are leaving,' said Dave, as a small maroon car nosed out of the garage.'

'Shit,' said Conan. 'We need a vehicle.'

'Cab?' suggested Dave. 'Follow that car and all that?'

The maroon car pulled into a break in the traffic and Conan looked desperately for a cab. There were usually millions of the bastards.

'Fuck me dead!' he shouted, furious, as the maroon car sped away down the weirdly empty street which miraculously filled again in seconds with empty cabs all honking and going nowhere.

A garish sign above them in green, red and gold said, *When you ask a question, you take one step from the answer. The Way.*

Conan glanced at his watch – 10.27.

'Not a good start to our ONA careers,' said Dave, tossing his cigarette into a puddle caused by the seemingly random plumbing work going on everywhere.

'They should've given us a car,' said Conan, thinking desperately. 'Lammas wouldn't get in a car unless he was leaving town, would he?'

'Maybe.'

'So if he is leaving town … where's he most likely to go?'

'Delta water plant?' asked Dave.

'Possibly. We know he's got a link with the Shadow Group … maybe they're having a top brass meeting there?'

'Wouldn't be easy for us to sneak back in,' said Dave. 'Although there *is* a big new hole at the front gate.'

'Whatever we do, we need a car,' said Conan, as they started heading back to the ONA office, '… but I don't think it's the water plant we need to visit.'

'No?'

'No … I'd never heard of it when I came here, and Lucia's message was to look into what I first wanted to protect.'

'Our orders are to watch Lammas.'

'And we don't know where he's gone. So the logical thing to do is go to the place most in jeopardy because that's where he might turn up if he's linked with the Shadow Group.'

Dave's face twisted oddly as he worked through Conan's reasoning.

'Okay, that makes sense … I guess … but what place is most in jeopardy.'

'The National Broadband Node. That's what I was trying to protect when I first got involved with Ord City. That's where we need to go.'

Chapter 36

Science Came Too Late

It was good to get out of the city again. The place was so crowded in preparation for the big night it felt hard to breathe with everyone in such close proximity, fighting for the same oxygen. And of course everyone was out on the streets shouting about the destruction of the water plants.

'Why can't they panic in private?' wondered Conan, switching off the radio. There was nothing on except the Festival and the treatment plants, and the visit of the prime minister, Margie Yunupingu.

Conan and Dave had requisitioned a car from the ONA pool and were heading south on the Argyle Highway. The car was a powerful German model with driverless function, but Conan enjoyed handling the controls himself as he'd never driven such a beautiful (and hugely expensive) vehicle.

'Soon catch that maroon shitbox in this,' laughed Dave as the mulga flashed past.

The road to Halls Creek loomed up and Conan said, 'Right … we have to measure fifteen ks from here. Then there's a turnoff.'

He reset the trip meter and put his foot down a little harder.

'Just as likely to be highway patrol out here,' warned Dave. 'State coppers don't like Ord City so they tend to assert themselves on the edge of their jurisdiction.'

'Duly noted,' laughed Conan and put his foot down even harder. Almost too quickly they reached the turnoff – an unmarked asphalt track – slightly west of the highway heading back towards the river. About half a klick from the turnoff they saw a large yellow sign with the coat of arms and black letters: *Commonwealth of Australia: Authorised Personnel Only Past this Point.*

'Should have a look at the Giant Array, too,' said Conan. 'That was supposed to be Asif's target until he jumped ship.'

'You're the driver,' said Dave as they approached a low ridge.

'Speaking of driving,' said Conan, slowing down, '... it occurs to me that once we top that ridge we'll be exposed to whoever might be watching on the other side.'

'So?'

'So the NBN facility is not far from here. If there's something dodgy going on I'd rather not announce ourselves.'

There were a number of indentations in the rock face so Conan pulled off the road and hid the car. The low cliff looked an easy climb so instead of going back to the road they scrambled up the escarpment which was like a giant staircase with hard, wiry vegetation thrusting out of every crack.

'Fuck!' shouted Dave, as he happened upon a large brown snake sunning itself on a wide shelf.

'It's only a snake,' laughed Conan. 'Didn't your lot used to eat them?'

'Not my lot,' said Dave, edging away from the snake that was quickly moving in the opposite direction. 'We're the coffee tribe ... coffee and Marlboro.'

They moved more slowly towards the top of the escarpment and then crept on hands and knees to look over the edge to the west. The ground fell away towards the river glittering about two kilometres away. In the middle foreground was a facility like an old-style electrical substation, surrounded by two lines of razor wire fence. The sun was behind them so Conan brought out his mini-binox and looked long at the NBN facility.

'No maroon shitbox,' he said, 'but a few other cars, including a couple of black transit vans. There's also a couple of blokes in suits at the gate.'

'It's probably always like that.'

'No. When we were chatting at the football Richie said he was usually by himself and it got pretty lonely. Jen Khataten is mostly by herself too at the Giant Array ... she certainly was that time I turned up there ... although ... '

'Although what?'

'Well … I told you Jen was completely starkers when I ran into her at the GA … '

'Yeah, but tell me again.'

'She wasn't wearing anything at all, but when she was going back out … after taking me back to her office to use the landline … she picked up a big sunhat and some water and forgot her technical gear. I thought it odd at the time because … why didn't she have a hat and water in the first place?'

'It was still early?' shrugged Dave. 'She didn't need them until the sun was higher?'

'Maybe. Or maybe she was trying to distract me.'

'From what?'

'I wasn't just trying to get to a phone, remember. I was also following Ming's footprints … or suspected I was. What if Ming and Jen *are* in cahoots? Jen had a copy of Ming's book … and the ONA had her and Richie among their various connections.'

'Getting her kit off is going to pretty extreme lengths to distract you … and how did they know you were coming?'

'Successful tactic, though, if that's what it was … I didn't give Ming another thought. But as for how did they know I was coming? They can tell if a gnat farts on Alpha Cen-fucking-tauri at that place. Besides, Ming would've guessed I might follow.'

Dave stared hard at the NBN facility, then shrugged.

'And what if they are in cahoots? For what purpose? Aaah fuck!'

He jumped up and slapped at his legs. And at that moment Conan realised there were ants everywhere. He slid back from the edge and brushed at himself as Dave jumped about swearing.

'Get off the ridgetop Dave … they'll see you.'

'Fucking ants!' yelped Dave. 'Shit!'

'Too many spooks here,' decided Conan, calmly turning back to the car. 'Let's go have a look at the Giant Array.'

'Fuck!'

• • •

Dave's legs were dotted with red lumps from where the ants had feasted and he still gave the occasional yelp as another emerged from the inner folds of his clothing to bite where he was most vulnerable.

Conan managed to ignore his whingeing and considered the problem in front of them. It was another twenty ks to the Giant Array but half a kilometre after the NBN facility the road was unsealed. Conan pulled over at the edge of the sealed road and stared into the distance – a flat red plane dotted with low scrub and a handful of stunted trees.

'Nowhere to hide out there,' he said. 'Our dust cloud will be visible for a long way.'

'You're not suggesting we walk, I hope.'

'Not the whole way … but maybe the last two ks?'

'Jee-zuss!'

Conan headed slowly onto the flat red track but, despite his care, a small dust cloud rose behind him.

'Keep an eye out for any dust clouds in front, in case someone's coming the other way.'

Conan was also watching out for any concentration of trees or mulga that might shield the car if they had to get off the road. And twelve klicks past the end of the sealed surface he noted three large termite mounds clustered together and standing up out of some thick mulga. They might hide the car, but they also attracted the eye – better than nothing.

'Dust cloud ahead,' said Dave. Conan immediately slowed to a halt, turned round and drove back to the termite mounds. They were about fifty metres on the river side of the road and easy enough to get to but they would have to raise dust and leave tracks. He parked at the best angle he could to maximise concealment, switched the engine off, and waited, watching through a gap between the mounds.

About a minute later, the dust cloud coming from the Giant Array was observable beyond the mounds and a flash of dirty red went past to their left, heading back the way they'd come.

'Maroon shitbox,' confirmed Dave. 'You want to follow?'

Conan sucked his teeth and weighed his options.

'Maybe we'd better have a look at the GA office. I'd like to know what they were up to out there.'

● ● ●

With the maroon car headed back towards the city, Conan decided that speed was more important than caution so flew along the dirt track heedless of the red cloud billowing out behind like a Martian dust storm.

Suddenly they were driving through vast fields of the white metallic spiders – dipoles they were called – which received radio signals from the edge of the universe.

'Why isn't there some sort of security for this place?' wondered Dave.

'They can't have anything electronic or electrified,' said Conan. 'The super-faint signals they collect would be smashed by an electric field. Just its remoteness is all the security they need … usually. And it's not as though it presents any sort of threat to anyone … except those scared of science.'

'Where's the office?' asked Dave.

'God knows. Somewhere along this road, I'd imagine.'

They proceeded up a long low slope like a military cemetery with its thousands of identical white dipoles. As they reached the crest they saw the demountable office building, like an old school room, about half a kilometre ahead. Conan slowed down and looked around, looking for signs of movement or recent activity.

'What do you reckon they were up to?'

'I don't know for certain,' said Conan, 'but given Asif was supposed to blow this place up … the great blasphemy and all that … I reckon Lammas might've come out to finish the job.'

'You mean … Lammas has just set this place to explode?'

'There's a fair chance of it.'

'Then what the fuck are we doing here?' demanded Dave.

'Our civic duty,' said Conan. Rolling up to the demountable, he switched off the engine and took a moment to check out the building. There was nothing to see or hear so they got out of the car.

'But … a bomb could go off any second?'

'Good chance,' said Conan. 'Come on.'

He walked quickly around the building but could see no sign of anything wrong. It simply looked abandoned.

As he stepped onto the stairs Conan had to fight off the idea that his presence might be triggering something. That idea gave him a paranoid sense of urgency and he opened the door without bothering to scrutinise it for booby traps. And inside was the first shock – a light was flashing yellow on a ball set on top of a small esky, sitting on Jen's desk.

'What the fuck's that?' asked Dave.

'I'd say it's a bomb,' said Conan, emboldened by Dave's nervousness. 'For God's sake don't touch it, but if it turns orange let me know.'

'Why?'

'Because it looks like a standard mining safety detonator ... they flash green, yellow, orange, red for the same interval and then kaboom.'

No sooner had he said the words than the flashing light changed to orange.

'Shit! Get out,' said Dave, but Conan grabbed him by the arm.

'Stand here and time it,' he said, while I have a quick look round. Let me know when it turns red.'

Dave backed away to the doorway, his face grey, but he nodded and looked at his watch.

And at that moment there was a huge explosion from outside.

'Fuck!' yelped Dave and would have bolted but Conan grabbed him by the collar.

'Clearly they've set other bombs among the dipoles,' said Conan, as the massive blast finished reverberating in their skulls and bits of debris hit the roof. 'The only bomb we have to worry about is this one ... and it's still orange.'

'Oh man,' said Dave clutching his stomach, '... I think I need a shit.'

'Just be glad you haven't already had one,' said Conan and strode off to look around the rest of the office-cum-lodgings.

It was more or less unchanged since he'd last seen it. The bed was unmade and there was a vague smell of perfume that he recognised from the time before. Another thunderous blast went off outside and more debris rattled the house.

'Conan! It's gone red!'

'What was the interval?'

'Erm ... about ninety seconds, I think.'

'Okay ... coming.'

He took one last glance around the bedroom, then realised he hadn't looked in the en suite. Almost against his better judgment, he stifled his rising sense of panic, and forced himself to look in the bathroom.

At first it looked completely empty, but through the translucent shower screen he could see something dark.

'Conan! Quickly!'

'Still got a minute,' shouted Conan as he struggled with the screen door, which wouldn't budge. 'Shit! Dave … get in here!'

'No way man, I'm leaving!'

'There's someone in the shower!' shouted Conan. 'Come and help me for fuck's sake!'

Fired by adrenalin, Conan wrenched at the door which still refused to budge so he backed away and then threw his full weight at it and managed to crack it open. The door still wouldn't move but he managed to kick a few big plastex shards away and could see inside. Richie Farr was fast asleep, wedged into the floor of the shower with his mouth gagged and his hands tied.

'Oh fuck!' whined Dave from the doorway, then gave the shower another few boots until Conan was able to reach in and grab Richie under the shoulders.

'Twenty seconds,' shouted Dave.

Conan heaved in desperation and fell to the floor, but he'd got Richie half out of the shower. Dave took over as Conan scrambled to his feet and together they took a shoulder each and pulled him clear.

'Grab his legs!'

They had to go back past the bomb which was flashing an angry red and much faster than before.

'Five seconds!' cried Dave. 'Get out now!'

With a last superhuman heave they crashed through the door and collapsed off the steps with Richie on top as a giant force seemed to wash over them and a vast roaring filled the entire world. Conan thumped into the ground and seemed to see darkness and fire all around him. Bits of the building were crashing into the ground dozens of metres away and a small bar fridge smashed the back window of their car.

Bit by bit the fireball and dust diminished and Conan staggered to his feet. The house was just about razed to the ground and burning fiercely, but they'd missed most of the blast by getting below floor level in the moment it went off.

'Come on, Dave!'

Dave was writhing in pain on the ground and Richie was still snoring, oblivious to the fact his life had been saved by the tiniest margin. Conan dragged him away from the fire and behind the car, from where he could see, not far away, the results of two other explosions where dipoles were scorched and flattened. Those would have done little damage to the installation but the office, and any evidence it held, were completely destroyed.

• • •

Lieutenant Michael Rice was in two minds.

On the one hand, his natural conservative nature abhorred what they had done. On the other hand, and he glanced at Major Lammas sitting grim-faced in the passenger seat of Rice's old Toyota, he now shared a dreadful truth with his hero. They were joined together forever with a massive secret.

'We must never talk of this,' said Lammas. 'Not to anyone … not even to each other.'

Rice nodded, relieved but also a little disappointed.

'Can we at least talk about what the explosions mean?' asked Rice. 'After all, if it had been someone else who set them off we would certainly talk about the impact.'

Lammas was silent for a moment as they passed the NBN facility on their left.

'Yes, we can talk about the impact. What does it mean to you, Michael?'

'It wouldn't have meant much at all until you explained what they were doing.'

'I detest the way the scientists pretend to have the answers,' said Lammas. 'They subtly rule the world because their work underpins the apparatus of modern life. Science builds cars and planes and modern medicine. People trust their lives with these things in a visceral way they never quite do with the church. That means that they believe more in science than they do in God … and that cannot be tolerated.'

'No,' agreed Rice. He could see smoke beyond the horizon in the rear view mirror.

'That Agent Tooley,' said Lammas, his voice quavering with hate, 'told me he didn't believe I believed ... didn't believe that anyone had ever *truly* believed in God.'

'Really?'

'Do you have any concept of how profoundly offensive that is?' demanded Lammas. 'Or how dangerous?'

'It's certainly offensive,' agreed Rice, '... but why dangerous? No one cares what Tooley thinks.'

'It's dangerous because he's put his finger on the biggest problem facing the church ... the biggest problem the church has ever faced ... and that comes back to the war between faith and science for the hearts and minds of all people. We could leave them to their cars and planes and medicine ... we could let them have just about everything but there is one thing we could never let them control.'

'And what is that?' asked Rice, slowing to take the turn left onto the Argyle Highway, and back towards Ord City.

'The beginning,' said Lammas. 'In the beginning was the Word ... and the Word was God. If science can go back to the very beginning ... look upon the work of God as it unfolded ... they will submit it to their usual profanities ... measuring, calculating, proving and disproving.'

'Disproving,' echoed Rice,

'Disproving,' repeated Lammas. 'Everything we've done ... two thousand years of effort and toil in the name of God. It will all evaporate like a puddle in midsummer if the glaring light of science is shone upon the deepest mysteries of our faith.'

'My God!' said Rice, deeply moved.

'That's why our actions are completely justified,' said Lammas. 'But, like the heroic scribe who created the *Epistola Clementis*, our work must remain hidden. You must never speak of it ... you must learn to forget it even happened.'

Rice felt just a twinge of worry as he recalled the silver car mostly concealed behind some termite mounds that he had spotted on their way back from the Giant Array. He hadn't mentioned it. It was highly unlikely the car's occupants – presuming there were occupants – would be able to identify his car and link them with the explosions, but he knew Major Lammas would regard it as a security concern and want to do something about it.

Best not to worry about it.

The sign on the left said 25 kilometres to Ord City. In the distance the first lights and sirens sped towards them, then flashed past seconds later as science came too late to the rescue of the Giant Array.

Chapter 37

Let the Brunt Bearers Dance

'I really should check on Mel,' said Conan, as they flew north along the red dirt track towards the NBN and the Argyle Highway.

'We also need to get this bloke to a hospital,' reminded Dave.

Richie didn't seem to be hurt but he was out like a light, clearly drugged as they had not been able to wake him with shouts and slaps. They had at least removed the plastex bindings around his wrists and now he was stretched out across the commodious back seat, snoring.

'Whatever we do,' said Conan, 'we can't be identified. There're too many people hunting for us and I've no idea who we can trust. The AFP ... or at least that part of the AFP working with Ping and the Shadow Group ... will have tentacles everywhere, including the Fireys and the hospitals. Even the ONA blokes didn't know exactly who was kosher and who wasn't.'

They went past the cluster of termite mounds and then minutes later the NBN facility loomed up on the left. The entrance was a couple of hundred metres off the road but they could see a group of people clustered at the fence looking to the south where black smoke twisted into the sky. There were a couple of flashes which Conan knew would be the sun glinting off binoculars swinging from the smoke towards their car.

'We still don't know why Lucia wanted us to check out the NBN either,' muttered Conan, and then put his foot down harder. The last thing they needed was another road chase from people at the NBN taking an interest in them.

'I reckon we'll learn something when Richie wakes up,' said Dave. 'Mind if I smoke?'

'Yes, I do.'

Conan glanced at his watch. It was after twelve and Mel would surely be awake and wondering where he was.

'Maybe we'd better take Richie to the ONA office. They can call a doctor to check him out and then we can ask him who tied him up and left him for dead.'

'Well, we know who did that,' said Dave. 'Lammas and Rice.'

'I doubt it. They wouldn't have had time. In fact, I reckon there's a fair chance they didn't even know he was there.'

'So who put him in the shower?'

'Whoever's in charge at the NBN right now ... Richie's supposed to be in charge of it after all. And they probably did it early this morning expecting Asif to turn up and blow the Array. That's what they intended for me too, back at Delta.'

'Nasty.'

At that moment a fire engine roared over the crest and careered past them, lights flashing and siren shrieking.

Then another, and another, as Conan pulled over to the left to let them past.

Last in the line was an unmarked black car with dark windows which, rather than hurtling after the fire engines, rolled to a stop in the middle of the one lane track.

'Oh shit,' said Dave. 'Who the fuck is this?'

Conan eyed the gaps in the mulga to their left and prepared to shoot off the road to get around the black car – which then rolled slowly forward and stopped alongside them. The window began to slide down and Conan reached for the pistol strapped under his left arm.

But it was Agent Green behind the wheel of the black car, and he motioned for Conan to lower his own window.

'Well, you seem to turn up everywhere,' said Agent Green. 'Weren't you following Lammas?'

'It was Lammas who blew the Array,' said Conan. 'He's ahead of us in a maroon Toyota, but that's not the main game.'

Conan explained about the people at the NBN and the attempted murder of Richie Farr, the NBN director.

'Have to get a warrant to invade the NBN,' mused Agent Green, '... and enough men to enforce it.'

'Call in the army?' suggested Conan.

'It may come to that,' said Agent Smith, also in the other car. 'But any sort of armed forces manoeuvre today ... of all days ... is going to involve a lot of people and inevitably warn the ... the Shadow Group I suppose we're calling them. We need to involve as few people as possible and strike at exactly the right moment.'

'That sounds fine in theory,' said Conan, 'but what exactly are they planning? You can bet something will happen tonight.'

'Yes,' agreed Agent Smith. 'How are the pills helping?'

'I'm alright,' sighed Conan. 'Dave's giggling like a schoolgirl but ... he generally does.'

'Pills aren't bad,' agreed Dave. 'I wouldn't mind a few more.'

'You only took one, didn't you?' asked Agent Green.

'No, I took all of 'em,' said Dave.

Agents Green and Smith stared, then Green said, 'Well, it's Friday today ... make a note in your calendar for next Wednesday. You might be ready to sleep by then. In the meantime, Agent Tooley, you'd better get Mr Farr to hospital, and then I suppose you'd better arrest Lammas, if you can find him again.'

· · ·

Back in the city amid hordes of yellow-dressed revellers, Major Lammas began to relax.

Of course, he had little to worry about once he was out of Michael's car. Lammas had instructed Michael on how and where to set the bombs, but he had stayed in the car himself, wearing sunglasses, on the off chance there were security cameras sending images to the cloud. If there were, then only Michael would be in the line of questioning, and Lammas was confident that he was inspired enough by the forgotten scribe of the *Epistola Clementis* to keep silent about Lammas' involvement.

Stuck in heavy traffic towards the centre of town, Lammas started feeling nervous again.

'I might get out here, Michael.'

'Are you sure? It's only another kilometre or so.'

'I need to see someone,' said Lammas, opening the door in the middle of Keating Road, which was like a car park with its hundreds of stationary vehicles and streams of pedestrians flowing past and through them.

'Okay,' said the putative Captain Rice, disappointed the shared adventure was over. 'I suppose I'd better get back to the chapter house. See you later, perhaps?'

'In all likelihood,' said Lammas, checking his watch. 'I do have other chapter houses in my sector ... and the cathedral of course ... but I may turn up for your vigil.'

He shut the door and, without a wave, merged with the crowd – relieved to be out of the incriminating car, but aware that the streets of Ord City were teeming with filament cameras and micro-drones. If anyone had taken an interest in Michael's car, it's journey could be monitored, including the part where he got out of the car in the middle of the road.

His mouth set in a thin line, Major Lammas strode through the ridiculous Habal Tong devotees, many of them singing and dancing, and already making their way towards Rinehart Stadium and its precinct – the main site for the *Illumination* festivities.

There are those who make history, he thought with satisfaction, and those who bear its brunt. Let the brunt bearers dance while they could. Later they would be forgotten – remembered only as statistics.

The building to which he was headed rose up on his left and he noted with annoyance a strong security cordon and clearance area. So much for a discreet entry. He gave a thin smile to the security personnel and submitted to their screen and search before entering the foyer of the Town Hall. There was a queue at the information and reception kiosk but Lammas forced himself to be patient rather than attempt to pull rank. After nearly ten minutes he was finally at the head of the queue.

'Major Lammas,' said the girl with a bright smile. 'Do you have an appointment?'

'No ... but I need to see Joan ... erm ... Colonel Chard, ASAP.'

The girl gave him another smile as she picked up a telephone and spoke briefly with a colleague.

'That's fine, Major,' she said handing him a security pass on a lanyard. 'The Colonel will see you shortly. Just go straight up.'

Lammas thanked the girl and headed to the lift which needed the security pass to access the top floor. He waved the pass over the sensor and was aware of the numerous cameras recording his presence, as they always did these days.

There were only a few people milling about on the executive level but all were absorbed in their work. No one even glanced up as he strode across the old parquetry floor to Colonel Chard's personal assistant.

'Hello, Megan,' said Lammas in his most mellifluous baritone.

'Hello, Major Lammas,' said the PA. 'Would you mind taking a seat?'

'My need is fairly urgent ... '

'I'm sure ... but the Colonel has other visitors and she knows you're here. She won't be long.'

Major Lammas was not accustomed to being kept waiting but he kept the annoyance off his face.

'I see you are wearing yellow,' said Lammas.

'Everyone's wearing yellow today,' replied Megan.

Lammas glanced around and noted she was correct. 'I had no idea that the teachings of Habal Tong had reached as far as the Chief Administrator's office.'

'They haven't really,' said Megan, with a small shrug. 'But we've been told to show solidarity with the populace ... especially because of ... '

'Because of what?'

Megan glanced about then lowered her voice: 'Because of the threat of ...'

'Welcome, Major,' said Colonel Chard standing in the suddenly open doorway to her office. 'What can I do for you?'

Lammas was intrigued to continue his discussion with Megan but that could wait. He smiled at Chard and walked towards her with his hand out.

'Thanks for seeing me at short notice, Joan. I need to consult you on an urgent matter.'

'Very well,' she said, standing back to let him through but Lammas stopped in the doorway when he saw Major Marjory Maddox sitting at the round meeting table.

With Dr Chen.

'Am I interrupting?' asked Lammas, eyeing Maddox coolly.

'Not at all,' said Major Maddox, looking suspiciously pleased with herself. 'Good to see you, Thomas.'

'And Dr Chen also,' said Lammas, taking a seat. 'What an interesting trio.'

'Well … you're welcome to join us Major,' said Colonel Chard. 'We were just congratulating Dr Chen.'

'You were?'

'She's been appointed head of the new maternity hospital,' said Major Maddox.

Lammas was stunned at the revelation – even outraged – but he fought to keep his reaction measured.

'Really? What happened to Dr Coutts Hempel?'

'He's decided to take early retirement … and Dr Chen is the best possible replacement.'

Major Lammas felt a cool thrill of fear that he was losing control which he did his best to ignore.

'Congratulations, Dr Chen,' he said. 'I presume you went through an exhaustive selection process.'

'It would have been a waste of time,' said Chard. 'No one is better qualified in all of Australia.'

'Do you believe in God, Dr Chen?' asked Lammas.

'I believe in power,' said Ming, with a smile. 'Don't you?'

'I believe in authority,' said Major Lammas, '… the moral authority of the Army of God.'

Colonel Chard smiled to reassure Major Lammas.

'Doctor Chen's medical qualifications are first rate and she is one of the most published researchers in antenatal science … in the world. I think we're lucky to have her.'

'No doubt,' responded Lammas, finding it harder to keep the irritation out of his voice. 'But it's not your decision who leads an Army of God hospital.'

'No, it's mine,' said Major Maddox. 'And I agree that Dr Chen is an outstanding appointee. She's been brevetted a captain in the AOG.'

'A captain … even though you wanted her removed from a junior position in the main hospital just a week ago?'

'She was overqualified for that role,' said Maddox, smoothly brushing his objection aside. Lammas forced himself to accept the new reality, knowing he would be isolated if he resisted a decision which had already been taken.

But it got worse.

'Of course,' said Major Maddox, '… brevet captain is just temporary rank until she is confirmed by the synod. She will be Major Chen from that time.'

Lammas paled.

'She'll be a major? But there are only two majorities within our division.'

'Correct,' said Maddox, with a nasty smile. 'I've just been made a colonel.'

Major Lammas was utterly floored by the news that Marjory was now his superior. He opened and closed his mouth like a baffled guppy but made no articulate sound.

'So, Thomas,' asked Colonel Chard pleasantly, '… what brings you here all a-fluster on this pleasant afternoon?'

Lammas was still reeling and had no desire to reveal his problem in front of his AOG colleagues.

'Sorry Joan, it's … erm … a private matter that needn't delay our friends.'

'I don't mind being delayed,' said Maddox, smiling sweetly at him.

'No secrets in this room,' said Colonel Chard. 'What do you want Thomas?'

Lammas thought furiously, weighing up his conflicting but urgent needs.

'I need a favour from your most trusted technician in the Roads IT department.'

'Hah!' laughed Ming. 'He wants the tapes wiped to hide something … the exercise of his moral authority, no doubt.'

'Is that true Thomas,' asked Chard.

'Yes, but it's a very small matter.'

'Wiping the tapes is a very large matter,' said Chard. 'You wouldn't ask me to do it for a very small matter.'

'I would prefer not to be seen getting out of a particular car on Keating Road at about 12.33 pm,' said Lammas lamely. 'That is all.'

'But if it's only a small thing,' said Maddox, '... no one will ever search the tapes anyway. No one will ever care what you were doing at 12.33 on Keating Road.'

'But they might care what he was doing before that,' said Ming. 'And the authorities ... whoever they be ... might have an interest in a particular car in a different time and place. A lot of bad things have happened today.'

'And still the night to come,' sighed Chard. 'I'll see what I can do Major Lammas.'

'Oh ... well, thank you.'

There was a very pregnant silence and Lammas realised, to his embarrassment, that they were waiting for him to leave.

'I think we had better talk later,' he said to Major ... Colonel Maddox, trying to reassert some authority.

'I doubt I'll have time later,' she said airily. 'We have an extremely busy afternoon and then ... '

They all knew it would be a hectic evening.

'Right ... '

Major Lammas rose heavily and nodded, and left the room in a cold, humiliated fury. He was back on the street by the time he realised he hadn't finished speaking with Megan about a 'threat' that evening.

There was no way he could go back in.

Chapter 38

The Colour of the Hated

Conan and Dave dropped Richie, still sleeping, at Kununurra Private – a non-denominational hospital – and arranged for a guard.

Conan was getting anxious about Mel. She still – as far as he knew – was yet to get a phone, so he couldn't contact her, but she could have contacted him. It was well into the afternoon and surely she was awake by now.

'So … we're hunting Lammas again?' asked Dave.

'I guess,' said Conan. 'But I'd better check on Mel first.'

The traffic was a bloody nightmare. The roads were closed around the stadium and adjacent square, leaving a huge precinct that was already filling with revellers for the evening's festivities. Besides the thousands dressed in yellow there were many in darker colours. As they sat motionless in traffic on Keating Road, Conan could see a few knots of aggressive looking young men in red and black – the official colours of Dedd Reffo. And some were waving the Eureka flag – their unofficial symbol.

'Gonna be trouble tonight,' said Dave.

'Yep,' sighed Conan. 'I wonder why Dedd Reffo wear black and red?'

'Black skin, red blood,' said Dave and Conan raised his eyebrows.

'Aren't they anti-refugee? Refugees are mostly Asian rather than black.'

'Black has always been the colour of the hated,' said Dave, somehow cheerful despite his words.

There were other groups also wearing bio-suits that pulsed in time with music or with the wearer's heartbeat. Some of these were walking blindfold through the barely moving traffic in a show of pointless bravado. The suits were still dim in the afternoon light but would be a riot of colour once night fell.

'This is fuckin' hopeless,' said Conan, glancing at his watch – 2.42 pm. 'I'll just pull over here and we can leg it.'

'We're going on foot?'

'We'll take for ever otherwise.'

Conan managed to get the car up onto a footpath.

'You can't leave it here,' said Dave, but then he shrugged. Parking violations were the least of their problems.

They pushed through the throng into a laneway that led to Abbott, up Bob Brown, through a warren of other half-full lanes and emerged not far from Ming's apartment block. It looked the same as ever – fairly quiet in contrast with the frenzied activity going on elsewhere. They went in through the open street door and trotted up the stairs to the first floor. Conan produced his key. It didn't fit the lock.

'Oh shit.'

'Wrong key?'

It was the only key Conan had. He tried it again, but could only get it halfway in.

'Fuckin' hell!'

Dave went to knock but Conan grabbed his arm.

'The lock's been changed.'

Conan considered his best course of action and decided there was only one.

He pulled out his stinger and held the shiny metal tube against the lock until it clicked, but the door wouldn't budge.

'They've put in a bolt,' muttered Conan. 'It can only be opened from the other side. Fuck!'

He put the stinger away and took his gun out. Then he knocked.

The knock seemed overly loud in the small stairwell and they listened for footsteps on the other side of the door. But nothing.

'What do you want to do?' asked Dave, also holding a gun. 'Break in?'

'We really need a warrant for that … but if we ask for a warrant …'

For a start it would take time, and secondly, it would certainly alert the Shadow Group.

'They already know we know about the place,' said Dave, guessing Conan's thoughts.

Conan tested the door with his shoulder.

'Feels pretty solid. I don't think we're getting in there without shooting the locks off.'

'Mel might be tied up inside.'

'I doubt it. They would've taken her somewhere else, surely … but we don't know she's been captured.'

'So what do you want to do?'

Conan aimed his gun at the lock.

'Stand back.'

But at that moment the door opened and a small Chinese man stared round eyed at the gun aimed at his chest.

'Who are you?' he shouted. 'What's this about?'

'Sorry,' said Conan, putting the gun back in its holster. 'We're police. We're looking for Melodie Roberts.'

'No Melodie Roberts here! Only my family!'

'But we left her here only a few hours ago.'

'Not here,' insisted the man. 'Somewhere else … this my house.'

Conan pushed past the protesting man and walked into the same apartment he had left that morning – the same but different. It was extensively furnished with many Asian style paintings on the walls, and the fridge was covered with bills in the name of Jingyi Wan.

A woman shouted in Chinese at Conan and then at the man who shouted back in the same language, gesticulating angrily. Conan ignored them and went into the bedroom, where he was certain he could still catch a hint of Mel's natural scent.

The Chinese man ran up to Conan and aimed a phone at him.

'There, I have your picture and make complaint!' he shouted.

'You won't be making any complaint,' snarled Conan. 'I know who put you here and they won't want any trouble.'

'I make complaint,' repeated the man.

'Let's go,' said Conan, glancing at his watch.

It was 3.33 pm.

• • •

Melodie Roberts was tied to a bed, and once again had her head in a bag – the third time since she'd befriended Conan Tooley.

Not that she was getting used to it.

The bed at least was comfortable but her nose itched and it was impossible to scratch with her hands tied above her head. There was also an unpleasant smell of disinfectant so she guessed she was in a public building, like a school or a hospital.

She had been mortified upon waking to find herself in bed naked with Dr Chen, who had also been naked. She was even more mortified by the frisson of curiosity that situation had aroused in her but she banished that thought from her mind and focussed on her anger.

And her terror

Dr Chen had been accompanied by armed men who had stared openly at her body as though she was no more than a pornographic image. She was humiliated – the exact opposite of the feeling of arousal and empowerment she had enjoyed when inviting Conan to stare at her. In fact the idea of being seen naked by any man now seemed like the worst thing in the world.

Second worst. They had taped her mouth shut and removed her OzBrace. Then they wrapped a short dressing gown around her, put the bag over her head and hurried her out of the apartment and into a car. Sometime later she was taken out of the car and held tightly by two men as they marched her along echoing corridors with that smell of disinfectant and floor polish, and into a room where she had been tied down on the bed. They had at least left her feet free and peeled the tape away so she could breathe through her mouth, but warned her she was far from help so there was no one to hear her scream.

'Why are you doing this?' she had cried, acutely conscious of the fact that the dressing gown didn't quite cover her nakedness.

'You should not have stuck your nose into our business,' said Dr Chen.

'But I didn't,' insisted Mel. 'I've just been caught up in matters I don't understand. I don't have the slightest clue who you people are or what you're doing.'

'You know who I am,' said Dr Chen, 'and I'm afraid that knowledge is dangerous. Very dangerous.'

And to her shame, Mel started to cry.

'Please don't hurt me. I just want to forget all this and go home to Melbourne. I'm so sick of it up here.'

'What does your boyfriend know about us?'

'Not much ... he's completely confused by everything and unable to put the pieces of the puzzle together.'

'And yet he constantly turns up where he is most unwanted.'

'Well ... I don't know why that is,' sobbed Mel. At that moment she heard a moan – someone was in pain, or emerging from sleep.

'Who else is here?' she asked.

'You have a couple of friends,' said Dr Chen, '... but don't worry about them. They're both asleep and unlikely to wake.'

'Unlikely to wake?' queried Mel.

Dr Chen just laughed and moments later the door was closed.

Mel called out a few times but her voice just seemed to die in the confined space.

She had never felt so alone.

• • •

Conan and Dave had no choice other than return to the ONA office, which fortunately was not too far on foot.

The crowds were getting thicker on the streets and traffic was at a standstill with hundreds of drivers shouting and gesticulating angrily. Only the motorbikes were making any sort of headway but even they had to thread slowly around the gridlocked cars and pedestrians.

'Just imagine if a bomb went off among this lot,' said the ever-positive Dave. Conan nodded grimly. There had, of course, been bomb threats reported in the papers from Dedd Reffo and there were plenty of Reffs on the streets, but there were also huge numbers in bio-suits who would be trying to find the likely places for bombs and cluster there, flaunting their nerve with slowly pulsing lights.

Back in the office, neither Agents Green nor Smith were in but Conan and Dave had access to the operations room and Conan ran a trace on Mel's OzBrace.

'Not far away,' said Conan, bringing up the street view. The signal was coming from a crowded filthy lane and he stared for a few moments until he recognised the skip where they'd hidden Ferrier's triPod.

'Oh shit!' said Dave.

'Looks like they've got the Pod back and left Mel's OzBrace there,' said Conan. 'Or Mel herself. It'd almost be funny if it wasn't such a worry.'

'It's their way of saying they're smarter than us,' agreed Dave.

'Well … we may as well go check it out,' said Conan. But that moment he realised someone else was with them in the operations room standing motionless among the holos of the Shadow Group.

'Hello, Agent Tooley.'

Conan stared at absolutely the last person he expected to see in the Ord City office of the ONA.

'Lucia?'

'Agent Baresi to you.'

He continued to stare at the unsmiling Lucia.

'My god, Lucia … I thought you'd been arrested.'

'No … extracted. I've long been a member of the ONA within the AFP. It's not uncommon.'

'But … erm … '

'But what?'

'But you, erm … '

Conan didn't know where to start. He'd been about to make an ignorant comment about her comparatively junior status within the AFP and realised immediately that a role within the communications department was perfect for an other service infiltration. She had access to everything and everyone.

He also felt as though he should embrace her but something about her aloof stance made that impossible.

'Why were you extracted?'

'Why, indeed?' replied Lucia. 'Partly your fault, Agent Tooley. Your constant unauthorised requests were destroying my credibility. No one could go on complying with such requests without drawing attention to themselves.'

'Oh.'

'Oh,' echoed Lucia. 'Very articulate. No one else could put such an infinity of meaning into one syllable.'

'Yes … erm … I got your message about the NBN. I think Smith and Green are looking into that.'

'I know,' said Lucia. 'I've spoken with them … and you're supposed to be arresting Major Lammas.'

'Yes.'

'So why are you still here?'

Conan shrugged helplessly and glanced at Dave.

'Hi Lucia … Agent Baresi,' said Dave, sensing Conan's discomfit and trying to come to his rescue. 'Conan speaks very highly of you.'

'If he's mentioned my name to anyone outside the AFP that's a breach of the Act and his service agreement,' replied Lucia without taking her eyes off Conan.

'Oh.'

'Okay,' said Conan, clapping his hands together, '… we'd better find Lammas, and go check that OzBrace trace.'

'Off to save the damsel in distress?' asked Lucia.

'If we can,' said Conan. 'Bit of an emergency … but I guess we'd better have a talk when I get back.'

'Perhaps,' said Lucia. 'By the way … the cryp number you asked me to look into belongs to Dr Ming Li Chen.'

'Right,' said Conan, still feeling as though the earth had shifted dramatically under his feet. 'I thought it might.'

He turned to Dave and, with some relief, said, 'Let's go.'

• • •

It did occur to Conan that Mel's OzBrace could have been bait for a sniper, but there were quite a few people milling about the lane with the overflowing skip and Dave kept a look out as Conan pulled away the bag full of shredded paper. Mel's OzBrace was exactly where they had left Ferrier's triPod (which was gone) with a green post-it note stuck to it which said: *If you want to see your girlfriend alive, go to the stadium and wait outside Gate C for further instructions. Take no further part in any investigation. You are being watched.*

Conan scooped the OzBrace and note into a forensic bag and dropped it into his pocket.

'Now what?' asked Dave, glancing about at the scores of people within view, any of whom could be watchers, or snipers.

'I think we have to ignore the note,' said Conan, trying to keep the worry out of his voice.

'So we go after Lammas?'

'No other choice, really.'

The Army of God chapter house was about a ten block walk, but was at least in the same general direction as the stadium, in case they were being watched.

'You sure get mixed up with some interesting women,' said Dave. 'Ming, Mel, Lucia … '

'You should have met my wife,' said Conan. 'Lisa would have eaten those three alive.'

'Yeah? My wife is pretty good.'

Conan turned to Dave in surprise. 'That's the first time you've mentioned her. I didn't even know you were married.'

'Yep … thirteen years,' said Dave with a lopsided grin.

'Really … what's her name?'

'Cathy. She was born the night Cathy Freeman won the Olympics.'

'So she's only thirty? Bit young for you, isn't she?'

'Yeah. Good, eh? She was just legal when we got married. I used to arrest her all the time.'

'What?'

'Only way to keep her out of trouble. Her old man was grateful.'

'So, where is she?'

'Buggered if I know. She goes bush a bit with her mum and the old sheilas.'

Conan was incredulous but careful to say nothing that might seem ignorant.

'Best way to keep the marital fires burning,' said Dave. 'Next time you get married you oughta send her off walkabout every six months. She'll be all over you like ants on a dead snake when she gets home, I guarantee it.'

'I'll bear it in mind,' said Conan.

They were nearing the chapter house and the crowds were unbelievable getting this close to the stadium. It was pushing five o'clock and the program was kicking off at six, but nearly a million people were pouring into the precinct and it was already bedlam.

Most were in various shades of yellow but there were tight knots of black and red and flocks of young death gamers in flashing bio-suits brightening up as the light faded in the chasms between the buildings.

For all that, there was an empty space out front of the chapter house. Conan stood across the road and watched for a couple of minutes but no one seemed to be entering or leaving. There was a sign out the front advertising a vigil from seven o'clock and Conan found himself grinning.

'The focus of the entire planet is gonna be on *Illumination* tonight. The whole world will be watching … and Major Lammas will be fighting his irrelevant fight in total obscurity.'

'He must be used to that,' said Dave, as they crossed the road.

'I don't know that he is,' mused Conan. 'I reckon he likes being in the spotlight among the movers and shakers, so I can't see him hanging about all night in an empty hall.'

They walked up the stairs and paused in the double doorway. There was no one to greet them and inside the main hall it was dim and all but silent. The little Chinese man in the blue shorts and white singlet was present, talking earnestly with Lieutenant Michael Rice. Conan could tell from twenty metres away that Rice was intensely bored, until he glanced up and saw them, and his face turned white.

'Good evening, Lieutenant Rice.'

'Oh … erm … hello Agent Tooley.'

'Any idea why we might be here?'

Rice swallowed and licked his lips, and glanced towards the kitchen. Then he shook his head.

'Not much of a mob here this evening,' said Dave.

'No … but it's only five o'clock,' said Rice, glancing at the old digital clock on the wall. 'I know they'll be rolling in before seven.'

'Including Major Lammas?' asked Conan.

'I hope so,' said Rice. 'He said he would try, but he does have other responsibilities. He's a very important man.'

The little Chinese man was looking curiously from one to the other as the conversation proceeded. Lieutenant Rice blinked first.

'Lee … would you mind giving us some privacy? These men wish to talk with me.'

'He's fine,' said Dave. 'We don't have any secrets, do we Agent Tooley?'

'We don't,' agreed Conan. 'But Lieutenant Rice might.'

'Actually, it's Captain Rice.'

'Captain,' echoed Conan. 'A sudden promotion?'

'It's only provisional,' amended Rice. 'With ... erm ... with Captain Roberts' departure the leadership of this chapter requires a captaincy.'

'Aah, Captain Roberts,' said Conan. 'Any idea where she might be?'

'I'm sure you'd know better than I,' said Rice, attempting to assert himself but sounding small and peevish.

'We think she's been kidnapped,' said Conan, glancing about the empty hall. 'Or worse. You seem to have done well out of her disappearance.'

Rice blushed pink and glanced again at the small Chinese man who suddenly got the hint and backed away with a small bow.

'I swear I know nothing about Captain Roberts,' said Rice. 'I liked her.'

'Liked? You're using the past tense?'

'Like her,' amended Rice, miserably. 'I do hope she's okay.'

Conan sat in one of the chairs arranged before the low stage and considered things while Dave stood behind Rice with his arms folded.

'Where did you go this afternoon?' asked Conan.

'Nowhere.'

'You were here all afternoon?'

'Erm ... mostly,' replied Rice.

'Mostly? So where else did you go?'

'Nowhere important,' said Rice, trying to sound defiant. 'Why do you ask?'

'Just putting all the blocks together,' said Conan.

'Well, I don't see why you should regard me as one of your blocks.'

'No? What about Lammas?'

'What about him?'

'Is he more ... blockworthy than you?'

Rice frowned, trying to gather his thoughts.

'I don't really know what you mean, Agent Tooley ... but I know Major Lammas is innocent.'

'Of what?'

'Of ... erm ... of anything. He's a good and decent man.'

'Good and decent men have often been guilty in the past,' said

Dave. 'The whole history of your Christian church is full of good and decent men doing evil in the name of God.'

'Which is why the Army of God was formed,' said Rice, on more confident ground, '... to establish an organisation that is just about God and has nothing to do with the sexual abuse and worldly ambition of the traditional churches.'

'You're not ambitious ... Captain?' asked Conan.

'Only so far as it helps me to do God's work,' insisted Rice.

'So, you were doing God's work this afternoon when you went for a drive in your maroon Toyota?'

Rice had been getting more relaxed but his face went white again and he didn't answer for a moment.

'I hope I'm always doing God's work,' he said, finally.

'Does God's work include murder?'

'What?'

'Did you know there was a person tied up in the shower when you set the bombs at the Giant Array this afternoon?'

'No! I mean ... no, I didn't set any bombs.'

'So Lammas did it?'

'No!'

Conan eyed the panicking Rice and felt the old satisfaction, the certain knowledge that a subject was about to break.

'You are aware, I presume,' said Conan, 'that the roads between here and the Giant Array would have literally millions of filament cameras. Your entire journey there and back has been recorded. There are also some thousands of cameras at the Giant Array sending recordings into the cloud. I could probably bring them up for you right now on my Pod.'

Rice said nothing but looked absolutely stricken.

'Here's your choice,' said Conan, '... you get charged with all the same crimes as Lammas and serve the same sentence – which is gonna be long, I guarantee it – or you come over to our side and tell us everything. You still might see the inside of a gaol, but it won't be anything like what Lammas has got coming.'

And to Conan's surprise, Rice started sobbing.

'I didn't know there was anyone in the shower ... I swear it.'

'Did you look?'

'No.'

'Well, the court will call that murder by recklessness. At the very least it's manslaughter … which carries the same potential sentence as murder.'

'So … someone was killed?' asked Rice, his voice squeaking with emotion.

'Why should you care now when you didn't before?'

'I do care,' insisted Rice, tears rolling down his face. 'I would never have done it had I known.'

Rice covered his face with his hands and started howling. Conan knew he was being duplicitous letting Rice think someone had died in the explosion, but at the same time he had nothing but contempt for the man who had let off a bomb in a house without checking anyone was home. He deserved to be first man eaten in a movie, and Conan enjoyed being the monster.

'Sit down,' said Conan, offering him a chair into which provisional Captain Rice all but collapsed.

'So, why did you do it?'

'Major Lammas said it was God's work … to prevent scientists looking upon the moment of creation.'

'The ultimate blasphemy,' said Conan.

'Exactly,' agreed Rice. 'But I'd never have done it if … if … '

'No one was killed,' said Conan.

'We nearly were,' objected Dave.

'Well, yes … we were nearly killed but we got out in the nick of time and brought Dr Richie Farr out also. But he would've been killed, which makes the charge attempted murder.'

'Thank God he's alright,' said Rice, bursting into tears again.

'God had nothing to do with it,' said Dave, with some feeling. 'It was all our work … moving in mysterious ways.'

Rice suddenly looked defiant again and opened his mouth to speak, but Conan interrupted him. 'Regardless of who saved Richie … us or God … there's still gonna be hell to pay, Captain Rice … unless you help us bring down Major Lammas who, just quietly, is guilty of a whole bunch of other bad shit.'

'Alright,' said Rice, '… what do you want me to do?'

Chapter 39

The Highest Form of Existence is Non-Existence

Robbie was starting to feel okay again.

Better than okay. The hair of the dog was stirring the ashes of last night's debauch and his hangover had started to ease. The party had resumed in the Dedd Reffo house with everyone getting stuck into the piss and a few of the hookers were back also – working pro bono to support the cause.

Robbie wasn't interested in the hookers. The one that looked a little like Kate was back, wearing a pink sleeveless top really similar to one Kate sometimes wore. He winced every time she caught his eye – he'd never done it with a prostitute until the previous night and was embarrassed that he'd somehow cheapened his unrequited love. He was also embarrassed as he knew he'd been boorish and graceless in his treatment of the girl – it had felt like a violent rape despite the fact she'd been paid for her consent.

'Have this.'

Robbie looked up as Chris offered him a small red vial.

'What is it?'

'Crimson … there's fuckin' shitloads. It's free.'

Robbie had never had Crimson, or any other illicit substance apart from the occasional toke on a joint to be sociable. He was more of a drinking man.

'No, thanks.'

'Why not?' asked Chris, 'What have you got to lose?'

Chris tipped the vial down his throat, then held a couple more out to Robbie.

'Come on man, I've already had three … you need to catch up. Last night on earth remember … don't die wondering!'

In spite of himself, Robbie laughed and took the two vials and drank them. They tasted like raspberry.

'Is that Crimson?'

The hooker who looked like Kate had appeared at Chris's side, and spoke with an exotic accent.

'Sure,' said Chris, 'I got a few more somewhere.'

He patted his pockets and produced four more vials. He gave two to the girl and put the others away for later.

The girl thanked him and drank, then eyed them both.

'I hear you're part of the special group tonight.'

Robbie opened his mouth but Chris put a hand over it to stop him speaking.

'Sorry, love,' said Chris, suddenly much less friendly, '… don't know what you're talking about.'

'Oh.'

Chris gave Robbie a meaningful stare, and then stalked away.

'I didn't mean to upset your friend,' said the girl.

'That's okay,' said Robbie. 'He never stays upset for long.'

There was a bit of a weird silence (despite all the noise around them), then Robbie said, 'Look, I … want to apologise for last night.'

'Why?'

'Because … I don't think I treated you very well.'

'Seriously?'

'Yeah. Sorry.'

The girl laughed, heart achingly like Kate, and Robbie felt himself blushing.

'What's your name?' she asked.

'Robbie.'

'I'm Siobhan.'

'Are you Irish?'

'Aye.'

'On a working holiday?' asked Robbie, then winced as he realised what that meant.

'No … I'm a refugee.'

'You're kidding!'

'Absolutely not. Europe's a total basket case these days. Australia's got its problems but at least there's still some space and a bit of spunk here.'

Again Robbie felt himself blush as he resisted the urge to make the obvious joke.

'I didn't know folks from Ireland had to wait in the TCZ to get citizenship,' he said.

'Course we do. Same rules for everyone ... which is another thing I like about Australia.'

'Don't the rules apply the same to everyone over there?'

'On the surface perhaps. The feudal system lives on in subtle ways.'

She had Kate's strawberry blond hair and pink-brown skin with a dusting of freckles across her nose, but she had a fresh, open, intelligence and suddenly seemed really attractive to Robbie.

'How does the feudal system work in 2030?' he asked, wishing he knew more about history.

'Try getting a job in England or Ireland if your family doesn't own the business,' she said. 'Robots do everything else ... they'll do my job soon.'

Yet again Robbie blushed.

'If you don't mind me asking ... how did you get into this sort of work?'

'Why?' she demanded, her smile fading.

'Just wondering.'

'The question implies a judgment.'

'Sorry ... I ...'

'Men are always so sad about women working the streets ... not that it stops them using the service mind.'

'It's just that ... ' Robbie paused, desperately not wanting to insult her, '... I mean, you're obviously very smart.'

'And why shouldn't working girls be smart?' she asked. 'It's an easy way to make money ... surely the eejits are the ones who give it away free.'

Robbie laughed and suddenly felt a profound certainty that everything he thought he knew about the world was completely wrong. What's more, he was starting to feel an incredible sense of well-being and clarity – a kind of breathless joy which he suspected was the onset of the Crimson.

'God, I love Crimson!' said Siobhan. 'So … are we going to fuck, or what?'

But before Robbie could respond, his shoulder was grabbed and he turned to see Jimbo looking flushed and sweaty.

'You're wanted in the planning room,' said Jimbo. 'Now.'

The whole point of the evening, forgotten for the few minutes he was talking to Siobhan, came crashing back to the front of Robbie's mind.

'Seeya,' said Siobhan with a cute little wave.

Robbie opened his mouth to say something about later.

But there wasn't going to be a later.

• • •

The atmosphere was very different in the planning room.

The Five, as they were now known, sat in the seats of honour wearing their blast suits – all of which pulsed with a pleasant pastel green.

Robbie, Chris, Bruno, Ron and Tim.

Robbie knew the Crimson was now strong in his system although he didn't feel drugged in the alcohol or pot manner. It was more like a sense of supreme clarity combined with a feeling of exhilarated power. He felt like he could do anything, overcome any obstacle, and somehow the idea of being an Anzac warrior and jumping out of a trench to charge the machine guns sounded a lot of fun.

For all that, he was avoiding Tim's eye and wishing he would stop looking at him with that lost puppy dog look. Lemon was clearly suspicious that something was up, but kept her thoughts to herself in the (mostly) solemn silence.

'Okay,' said Mungo, '… time to prepare.'

He opened an esky and started pulling out strips of something like plasticine, or blue tack. They were about twenty centimetres long and slipped perfectly into the four pockets sewn onto the back of the suits. Mungo and Jimbo went around the Five and fiddled with their pockets and Robbie felt Jimbo pat him on the shoulders when it was done.

'You'd normally need detonators for manga,' said Jimbo, 'but these safety suits have got inbuilt receivers which can spark the charge.'

'Safety?' asked Ron, and so funny did it seem that all of them burst into loud laughter.

Except Lemon. 'It's no laughing matter,' she said hotly

That seemed even funnier to Robbie.

'Righto … this is it,' said Mungo. The laughter ceased and the serious mood was back. 'The Dedd Reffo Five will tonight make the ultimate sacrifice to try and keep Australia free for Australians.'

There were murmurs of assent.

'You've each got four strips of manga which is one hell of a blast. You won't feel a thing yourselves, but the idea is to do maximum damage to Habal fuckin' Tong. Try and get close to their leadership but that won't be easy with the security. If you can't get near the leaders at least try and get where the yellow cunts are most heavily concentrated. The gates of the stadium are good places … especially when the first bomb goes off and everyone's in a panic to get out.'

Bruno and Ron grinned at the prospect of maximum damage, but Chris, Robbie and Tim were quiet as the reality of what was happening sank in. It seemed to Robbie that the imminence of death made him focus in a way that he had never previously done. In fact, death didn't seem scary at all on Crimson – it was more a kind of adventure, or even a philosophical riddle that suggested the highest form of existence is non-existence.

'Now, tomorrow,' said Jimbo, 'the papers 'll want to know something about youse. Anyone got anything they want us to say.'

'Fuck Asians,' said Ron, and most of the room laughed.

'Isn't it refugees generally we're against? Not just Asians?' Robbie found himself saying.

'They're mostly Asians,' said Jimbo, dismissively.

'Yeah … but I was just talking to an Irish refugee and I feel a bit weird about a white Irish woman being welcome and us being more focussed on the blacks and Asians. I don't mind being anti-refugee but I don't want to be thought of as racist.'

'What the fuck are you talking about?' demanded Pauly, and Chris swore with disgust.

'It's a legitimate question,' said Tim, standing annoyingly close to

Robbie. 'I don't want to be thought of as racist either.'

'Robbie,' said Chris, his voice straining with repressed fury, '…
are you with us or against us? Because I can't take this piss weak shit
another second.'

Robbie couldn't help but feel a pang of guilt, as though he was
somehow betraying his oldest friend, and nodded numbly as the
Crimson surged again in his brain.

'We good?' asked Mungo, sensing it was time for gentleness rather
than bombast.

Robbie and Tim nodded.

'Because we can certainly emphasise to the media that Robbie and
Tim weren't racists,' said Mungo, and everyone laughed again.

'Now for the good news,' said Mungo. 'These safety suits usually
need a mental signal from the wearer to set off the charge but you lot
won't have to worry about that. Tonight we'll be sending out a series
of override signals to the suits which trigger the explosions separately.
So youse blokes don't need to make any conscious decisions. You just
need to be in the right place at the right time.'

'Cool,' said Bruno, and everyone laughed again.

'What about the bad news?' reminded Lemon.

'Oh right,' said Mungo. 'It's not really bad news … not for those
who are truly resolved to make the ultimate gesture and go down in
history as the Dedd Reffo Five.'

'What is it?' asked Robbie.

'We erm … we just thought it might be best to help you all with
the resolve. The blast suits are made of bio-plastex which is super
tough … you'd need a laser to cut it. The manga pockets are all sealed
shut, but the suit itself has extra ties that can go under your legs and
through some loops at your waist.'

He demonstrated with Ron's suit as he went.

'Now we just attach a combination lock … and voila!'

Ron was now completely incapable of removing the blast suit – in
case that might occur to him later.

'How do you send the signal?' asked Robbie.

'Don't you worry about that,' said Jimbo. 'You just focus on getting
close to Ah Li fuckin' Wu.'

'Shit, yeah,' said Mungo, 'that's the main target. Anyone takes out

Ah Li Wu your place in history is guaranteed, like Lee Harvey Oswald. You'll be on Trivial Pursuit cards for a thousand years!'

Everyone laughed again. Jimbo nudged Tim aside and took hold of the ties on Robbie's blast suit, fed them under his crotch and pulled them through a couple of loops at his side. Then he pulled them tight at the back and Robbie heard a click.

The lock was in place.

'Your turn, Timbo,' said Jimbo, to Tim who, was, as ever, hovering at Robbie's side.

Tim and Chris were trussed like the others, then even more Crimson was passed around.

Robbie's skull seemed to open up to embrace the cosmos. He felt utterly immortal.

Chapter 40

Strong Tang

Major Lammas glanced at his phone and was annoyed to see Michael Rice was calling him.

'What is it, Captain Rice?'

'Major ... we need to talk ... urgently.'

'What about?'

Lammas was brusquely dismissive. He had an idea Rice's car would be identified going to and from the Giant Array and he wanted to minimise any association with a man who was likely to be charged with those crimes.

'I shouldn't say over the phone ... but it's urgent.'

Major Lammas was supposed to be at the Army of God Cathedral, according to his schedule, and no doubt people would be wondering about him. Instead, he was standing among the teeming crowds near Rinehart Stadium and staring at a new building on the edge of the square – the recently opened Army of God Maternity Hospital, so new the scaffolding was still up on two sides.

'It can't wait until tomorrow?'

'No, Major, it's urgent ... of the highest urgency I should think.'

Lammas' lips pursed and he had a bad feeling about meeting Rice, but didn't see how he could reasonably refuse.

'I'm down at the Maternity Hospital ... you know where that is?'

'Of course.'

'Meet me out front as quickly as you can.'

'Yes. Thank you, Major.'

Lammas hung up and continued to stare at the building which had only been open a couple of months and was not yet fully operational. There was a strong security cordon – far stronger than Lammas would have thought necessary considering the revellers would have no interest in it. Maybe it was being used as a potential emergency station – the papers were full of imminent terror threats after all.

'I really ought to know more about the hospitals,' thought Lammas, still furious that Marjory Maddox had won the precious colonelcy which Lammas had assumed would be his. What strings had she pulled? And why was she suddenly in cahoots with Dr Ming Chen?

Captain Chen and soon to be Major!

Lammas knew that somehow he had taken his eye off the ball and was no longer at the centre of all things as he thought he had been. Something big was going on – even bigger than the things he knew about – and it had something to do with the hospital.

Should I just walk in? he wondered. He had no doubt the security people would let a major into an Army of God facility, but it would alert Marjory and if he did enter he would prefer to do it anonymously.

He decided to do a circumnavigation, pushing through the crowds at the front and into the less populous lane at the side. It was a box shaped building about four storeys high – no architectural triumph but functional, no doubt. Fewer windows were lit up at the side and construction fences continued the security cordon all the way around.

The lane at the back was almost deserted and there was a place where the construction fence was partly obscured by one of the overflowing skips ubiquitous to the city.

With a glance in both directions, Major Lammas found a toehold and swung himself onto the top of the seven-foot barrier. Then he dropped onto the inner side and was mostly hidden from the street by plastex hoardings. The first two doors he tried were locked, but then he came to a large open entry bay which looked like an ambulance station. With the onset of dusk, everything was in near darkness but there were two plastex saloon style doors which he pushed through and found himself in a dimly lit corridor.

The building felt empty, somehow, although he knew there would be people at the front and on the higher levels. He opened one of the many doors off the corridor and discovered it to be a room with two beds in it – a birthing suite he guessed, with a second bed for family members.

He tried a second door, but it was locked, as was a third. There was a familiar smell which he couldn't quite identify – a chemical he knew from a different context – but as he continued along the corridor it was replaced by the antiseptic odour characteristic of hospitals.

He was almost at the end when he heard something. He paused, then retraced his steps and stood outside another door, listening.

Someone was inside, and crying from the sound of it.

· · ·

Captain Melodie Roberts had almost cried herself dry.

No one could hear her.

No one would find her.

She couldn't even be sure that Conan would know she was missing just yet. He was tremendously busy and for all he knew she was safe and waiting for him.

She had given up straining at the manacles, knowing they would only tighten if she did that, and had tried to twist her body so that the flimsy dressing gown might cover more of her. That of course only resulted in the dressing gown falling away and leaving her shamefully exposed.

She had called out a few times but her companions must have been asleep. She could hear deep breathing and occasional creaks from the next bed, but that was it.

There was a click at the door and she heard it swing open. She was mortified by the knowledge that she was fully exposed to whomever was present.

There was silence.

Melodie couldn't tell whether anyone had entered.

'Hello?' she said.

But there was no response.

· · ·

He knew it was her, even before she spoke.

He'd never seen her naked – not properly – despite the fact they had enjoyed sexual congress on two occasions. But somehow he had immediately recognised the beautiful female body lying manacled to the bed with her face covered. A wave of anger came over him, blended with contempt and a surging arousal.

It did occur to him to wonder how she had ended up in this predicament. No doubt it was a consequence of her shameful liaison with Agent Tooley, and fully deserved.

'Is someone there?' she asked, her voice slightly muffled by the black bag over her head.

Major Lammas glanced out the door. There was neither sight nor sound of anyone else in the building.

She was so vulnerable, her legs drawn up to hide her nakedness. He realised this was a priceless opportunity to redress his grievances against her, not least the fact that she had always hidden herself from him, even during sexual intercourse. Now, in the dim light from the corridor, he would feast his eyes.

• • •

Melodie felt a strong hand seize her ankle and drag it straight onto the bed.

'No, please!' she cried. 'Cover me up and let me be.'

She couldn't fight against the hand and felt another of the plastex manacles being wrapped around her ankle. She kicked out with her other leg and heard a male grunt of pain. Then she shrieked as a vicious slap caught her on the thigh. Her right leg was yanked tight again and before she knew it she could not move it. Then her left ankle was caught and she no longer even tried to resist but just sobbed as she was left spreadeagled and immobile.

• • •

'Fucking bitch,' thought Major Lammas as he rubbed the blood off his lip. He hadn't seen the kick coming in the dim light and it caught him hard. She would pay for that.

Having completed tethering her, he was able to admire his handiwork. She was indeed a prize specimen – exquisitely formed – and he felt some regret that he was not to spend his life with a woman of such physical perfection. His erection raged painfully against his trousers and almost before he realised what he was doing, he had unzipped it and stood over her, holding his penis and gazing down at the woman who had betrayed him.

She was writhing against her bonds and the movement of her hips was profoundly inviting, as though she was making love to him, from a distance.

• • •

Melodie had no idea what was happening.

There had been no further sound from the door and she had heard no footsteps. She presumed he, whoever he was, was still in the room and staring at her body. She forced herself to stop struggling and tried to squeeze her knees together, but they were drawn too far apart and then she was crying again.

• • •

It was the tears that did it.

He'd wanted to make it last but the tears were such a turn on he couldn't hold back. Semen spilled between his fingers and onto her thigh. He spasmed several times, then wiped his hand on her breast and zipped himself awkwardly, ignoring her protestations of disgust.

He did feel a moment's regret that he hadn't mounted her, but that regret was then replaced with a kind of dignified pride. He had behaved with restraint when most men would certainly have raped her.

Most men were animals.

Major Lammas glanced at his watch and was aware that Michael Rice was probably waiting out the front for him, but he hadn't yet had a proper look at the building.

Something very big was clearly happening and Major Lammas was determined to get to the bottom of it. He closed the door on the weeping Captain Roberts and continued towards the end of the corridor where an elevator and stairway were located.

It was at that moment that Lammas realised from where he knew the strange chemical smell.

He went back along the corridor to the two doors which had been locked, and again encountered that strong tang, which he now remembered from earlier in the day.

The first door was securely locked but there was a glass panel fixed in place. He pressed his face against the glass and after a few moments made out a green light winking in the darkness.

The door opposite was also locked and a peek through the similar glass panel gave a similar result.

Both rooms contained mangalite explosive and were rigged to detonators in the safety mode.

Chapter 41

Chemical Consensus

Provisional Captain Rice had not been very helpful.

Under interrogation it quickly occurred to Conan that either he was an exceptionally good liar, or he had simply not been included in most of Lammas' affairs. The latter was more likely, so Conan decided to let him temporarily off the hook after instructing him not to tell Major Lammas that he was under investigation.

Conan and Dave had then left the chapter house and waited across the road in the café Conan had visited a couple of times before.

Less than ten minutes later, Rice had emerged wearing a baseball cap and dark glasses – a pointless disguise, given he still wore his Army of God uniform. He glanced about furtively then strode off in the direction of the stadium.

'Reckon he's going to Lammas?' asked Dave.

'I told him not to,' said Conan, draining the last of his coffee with the second of the endurance pills Agent Green had given him. 'Just in case it didn't occur to him.'

They got up and followed, one on either side of the road, and managed to keep him in view despite the tens of thousands filling the streets as they approached the stadium precinct.

There was loud music everywhere and, amid all the yellow, the pulsing bio-suits were getting really bright as the last of the light faded. People with bullhorns were shouting Habal Tong slogans and reciting the glosses of Ah Li Wu to throngs of devotees. In all the chaos they had to get closer and closer to Captain Rice who, clearly lost in both the crowd and his anxieties, ignored all of it and no longer snatched glances over his shoulder.

When they reached the great square in front of Rinehart Stadium it was getting a lot harder to push through the crowd. Fortunately, Rice skirted the main crowd so they made steady-ish progress. There were still many thousands in cluster parties around the edges and anything that looked remotely like a target for terrorists – even rubbish bins – was where they gathered to show their bravery in tight, brightly pulsing throngs.

'Crimson,' said Dave.

Conan nodded. The streets were awash with the drug. Vials had been offered to them on several occasions and Conan even accepted a couple from one particularly aggressive thug who was shouting about the importance of chemical consensus. Better just to agree with such idiots than get stuck in an argument.

Then Rice was glancing about again, but Conan managed to step behind a couple of yellow clad young women who were kissing passionately and utterly lost in the moment.

Tai Chi style music was blaring from the many tannoys around the square, with occasional interjections from the teachings of Ah Li Wu and Conan started to feel a bit drugged through lack of sleep and his sense of occasion. Rice had stopped moving and was now standing out the front of the new maternity hospital which was surrounded by scaffolding and a security barrier.

Conan and Dave found a corner of the barrier that was more or less unoccupied and sat on the ground to watch Captain Rice as he glanced anxiously from side to side. He was obviously waiting for someone and Conan would bet a year's salary that someone was Major Lammas.

• • •

Major Lammas had made a decision.

The existence of the explosives, plus the plight of Captain Roberts meant he now held a couple of aces, which he would use to extract information from Marjory Maddox. He refused to think of her as Colonel Maddox and held out some hope that that ridiculous decision could still be reversed.

Instead of using the stairs he summoned the lift to the basement. It required a security pass to access the upper levels but his OzBrace was sufficient to turn the sensor green and he pressed the button for the top floor.

As he rose, he felt himself hardening, ready to take back the initiative and never surrender it again. He realised he had been complacent – mistaking Marjory's diffidence for tacit acceptance of his innate authority. He had therefore treated her, more or less, as an equal and she had abused that favour by politicking behind his back for the role that was rightly his. That could never be forgiven.

His phone rang and he saw that Michael was calling. Michael could wait.

The lift reached the fourth floor and the doors rolled apart to reveal a softly lit open plan space very different from the antiseptic glare of the operational levels below. Only one person was in view, a receptionist sitting at a desk outside an office with a closed door. She looked up as Lammas approached and he saw her face set hard in anticipation of an argument.

'Is Major Maddox within?' asked Lammas.

'Colonel Maddox is in a meeting,' said the girl, picking up a phone. 'Would you please wait here, Major Lammas?'

Without further word, Lammas strode past her, seized the handle and thrust the door open.

• • •

Conan was getting impatient.

Whoever Rice was waiting for was taking their time and Conan sensed he needed to get onto the front foot.

'Dave ... you stay here and watch who comes and goes, but I'm gonna have a look at this hospital.'

Dave nodded and Conan got up and glanced at his watch.

'If I'm not back in half an hour, send me a text. If I don't respond within a minute it means I'm in trouble and you'd better come looking for me.'

'You're always in some sort of trouble,' laughed Dave, and Conan felt uneasy that he was trusting his backup to someone totally wired on industrial strength No Doze.

With an eye on Captain Rice, Conan considered the security

cordon at the front and decided to get in the back way if possible. He started walking down a side alley but, glancing up at the building, saw a ladder at one end of the scaffolding. The scaffolding, of course, was on the wrong side of the security fence but it was a handy way in or, at least, up.

Further down the alley the people were fewer so he started looking for means of getting over the fence. There were the usual number of skips – mostly full of building debris – and in a flash he was over the fence. There was no scaffolding on that side of the building (it was all at the front and the far side) so he continued around the back and found himself in a dark open space that looked like an ambulance bay. There were big plastex double doors that looked like a way in, but Conan decided to have a look from the scaffold first. He would come back to the ambulance bay if necessary.

At the back corner of the rectangular building the scaffolding resumed and Conan was about to go up a ladder when he saw two men approaching with torches. Immediately he ran back to the ambulance bay, up some stairs, and hid behind a pallet of building materials. Perhaps a minute later the men with torches shone them briefly about the ambulance bay and passed on.

There was something about the double plastex doors that Conan found inviting but he resisted the temptation to take that route and resolved to go by his original plan.

Back to the scaffolding he went and up the ladder onto the layer of metal planks that constituted the first level. He knew the next ladder was at the front of the building and that was where he was most likely to be seen, so he walked quickly and carefully the sixty metres or so to where lights shone out of some windows and a blaze of light came from the stadium and numerous holoscreens set up around the square.

Conan knew the best way to remain concealed in full view was to act as though he had every right to be where he was, so he climbed as casually as he could to the second level. At that height he had an excellent view of the vast numbers in the square. Captain Rice was still standing out front of the hospital and fiddling with his phone, but Dave was hidden by a crowd at the far corner.

At the front of the building and two levels up, Conan could see into a large entry foyer with a lot of security people and virtually no one else. A little further towards the back of the building there was darkness but Conan could see lights on in rooms on the top floor.

He had to go all the way to the back to reach the third ladder, and then had to come all the way forward to reach the last ladder to the top floor. The men with the torches made another pass beneath him and Conan paused until they were gone. The view from the top level was stunning and Conan found himself mesmerised for a few moments watching the hordes like slowly eddying currents in a seething cauldron. All about the square were lamp posts, holoscreens and tannoy speakers which seemed to be the most popular nodes where vast numbers clustered – here in shades of yellow, there in Dedd Reffo's red and black, and everywhere the pulsing bio-suits like fairy lights in a deep forest of humanity.

He lifted his eyes to the stadium itself, looming over the scene like Uluru. They were supposed (according to the note in the skip) to wait by Gate C for further instructions. He would do that if unable to find Lammas, but it would not be easy to get through.

Wrenching his attention away from the crowd was like coming out of a trance but Conan forced himself to engage with the problem at hand. He had been most interested in the lights at the top of the maternity hospital and those lights were close by now, coming from a large room with a series of French windows. The scaffold was illuminated by the wash from the room so he knew he could be observed from inside. He just needed to get a little closer to see whether anyone was there.

He got down on hands and knees and edged forward until he could see the back of a woman in a black AOG uniform – probably Major Maddox. She was sitting in a chair next to another woman – probably Joan Chard by the stylish grey/blonde hair. Chard looked angry and Conan pulled out his phone, now equipped with the cheap listening app Mel had shown him.

• • •

Lammas stared at the women who stared back at him – Chard angry, Maddox embarrassed and Dr Chen behind a large desk, inscrutably amused.

'Double, double, toil and trouble,' said Lammas, '... the same three meet again.'

'What are you doing, Thomas?' demanded Maddox, trying to assert her authority.

Lammas remained calm and closed the door quietly.

'Exercising my prerogative as a member of the War Council,' he said, dragging a chair from the conference table and placing it next to Chard in front of Dr Chen's desk.

'This meeting has nothing to do with the War Council,' said Maddox.

'How did you get in?' asked Dr Chen. 'I gave instructions that no one was to be admitted to this floor without my permission.'

'Are you suggesting that I ... a major in the Army of God ... could be prevented from accessing one of our facilities within my own jurisdiction?'

'The hospitals have always been my jurisdiction,' said Maddox. 'It would have been at the very least polite of you to knock rather than barge in as though hoping to catch us out at something.'

'Well, perhaps I have caught you out,' said Lammas as he sat in his chair and crossed his legs.

'I beg your pardon?' demanded Chard.

'Yes, explain yourself Thomas,' said Maddox. 'And might I remind you I am now your superior.'

'You'll never be my superior, Marjory. Neither you nor anyone else in your little gynocracy.'

Dr Chen laughed. 'Gynocracy! Excellent!'

'So,' said Lammas, 'I think it's about time you explained what you've been doing behind my back.'

'You are being offensive, Major,' warned Colonel Chard.

'Yes,' agreed Dr Chen. 'He cannot help his male manners ... but none of us like being left out of the secrets.'

Maddox and Chard were clearly surprised by Dr Chen's conciliatory tone, and in that moment Major Lammas perceived that both Chard and Maddox deferred to her. What on earth was going on?

'You seem to be calling the shots,' he said to Dr Chen. 'So perhaps you can explain to me why there are rooms downstairs full of explosive and my ex-fiancée is tied naked to a bed?'

Maddox exclaimed with anger, but Ming Chen just laughed.

'She is still tied down? You didn't release her?'

Lammas did not respond and Ming said, 'You see? He did not release his former fiancée … even though she had to be in dire peril. That can only mean Major Lammas is already on our side.'

'He has not been through any of …' began Maddox, but Ming interrupted.

'Everything comes to a head tonight, and we already know that Major Lammas has been very bad today … out at the Giant Array.'

Lammas said nothing.

'Therefore,' continued Ming, 'he knows he cannot betray us without betraying himself.'

'Betray what about you … precisely?' asked Major Lammas.

'You would work it out in the morning,' said Ming.

'After the new hospital is destroyed and certain people killed in the blast,' mused Lammas. 'I would know that you had blown up the hospital … but why?'

'Why, indeed?' replied Ming, smiling.

'I'm uncomfortable with this,' said Chard, to Ming. 'Major Lammas is too bent on his own agenda. We could never trust him.'

'We could if we brought him fully into our circle and promised him advancement as one of us rather than relying solely on his own merits.'

'What are you talking about?' demanded Lammas, annoyed at being patronised.

The three women glanced at each other as though a wordless conversation continued for a few moments. Then Ming said, 'Our networks and ambitions are greater than you imagine, Major Lammas. Considerably so, I should think.'

'Which means what?'

'Which means there are patterns and movements happening beneath the superficial reports that people hear about in the media or read in history books. We drive those patterns, Major. Mostly in the shadowy background, but sometimes there must be substantial adjustments requiring more direct action. Tonight will be one of those occasions, but we have prepared for it a long time. Longer than you might think.'

• • •

Conan was in an agony of indecision.

He was fascinated by the conversation, but horrified to have learned that Mel was tied up somewhere in the building, which was set to explode. In normal circumstances he would have pulled the plug by now and called in the Fast Response Group to take over the building, but there was no way he could call in anyone to help as he had the impression from Ming (and from his own experience) that the Shadow Group had so completely infiltrated the AFP and other agencies that any attempt to alert the authorities would also alert the Shadow Group. He would trust Lucia, Dave, and Agents Smith and Green, and maybe Loongy, but only if he could talk to them in the flesh. Any electronic message was bound to be intercepted.

The second problem was that he didn't know where in the building Mel would be, so searching would take time. He needed Dave's assistance, but even texting Dave would be risky.

Those problems were bad enough but far worse was the cold metal that was suddenly forced against the back of his neck, and his earplugs were torn away.

'Get up ... slowly.'

Conan felt a flood of adrenalin hit his guts – firing his flight response – but there was nothing for it. He had already recognised the voice of Roger Manderson, the security chief from the water treatment plant, and knew him to be a dangerous man.

With Conan still on hands and knees, he felt himself being quickly and expertly frisked and his own gun was removed from its inner holster. His phone also was taken.

'On your feet.'

Conan stood and saw there were two men in black uniforms, both with guns trained on him.

'That way,' said Manderson, pointing further along the top level. Conan walked, wondering whether he dared to run and trust his luck, but he had no idea where the scaffolding led in the darkness towards the back of the hospital.

About halfway to the back there was a turn to the right where the scaffold accessed a balcony. Manderson's accomplice held Conan's collar with a gun pressed into his spine as Manderson produced a key and opened a door into a darkened office.

Manderson pulled out a phone and after a few seconds said, 'You were right … he turned up but I've got him safe.'

He listened for a few moments, then said, 'Are you sure?'

Immediately he apologised, then rang off.

'Bring him,' he said to his accomplice and Conan was propelled through a door along a dim lit corridor towards the front of the building. For a moment, Conan thought he was being taken to the room where Ming and Lammas were, but instead he was taken to a lift, and Manderson hit the down button.

'What …' began Conan, but the gun was immediately pressed against his forehead, and he closed his mouth.

In the lift, Conan's face was pressed into the corner so he could not see his captors. They did not speak and Conan perceived what experienced professionals they were, calmly performing their duties despite the enormity of the potential consequences. They were almost certainly ex-military, with the implacable air of seasoned mercenaries.

The lift continued its descent, then halted. Conan could not see which floor they were on but found himself in another dim corridor which continued into darkness.

Once again he was marched by the collar with the gun thrust into his back. Conan guessed they were on an operational floor due to the strong smell of antiseptic. There was some other smell also he couldn't place, a faint chemical reek under the cleaning materials.

They stopped in front of a door he could barely make out in the dim light and Manderson opened it.

Inside, Conan could just make out, in the semi darkness, a woman lying trussed and naked on a bed, and a couple more bodies lying on another bed.

'Mel?'

'Conan?'

'Quiet!' snapped Manderson.

One problem solved, thought Conan. It would have taken forever to find her in this building. Now he just needed Dave to work out he was in trouble and come to the rescue.

But Ming came instead, with Major Lammas.

'Well, Agent Tooley,' said Ming, gazing appreciatively at Mel's naked body. 'It was interesting crossing swords, but this is truly the end.'

'Have you searched him?' she asked, turning to her security chief.

'Taken his gun, and phone,' said Manderson.

'They sometimes have other useful items,' said Ming. 'Search him again.'

The accomplice pressed his gun hard against Conan's temple as Manderson went through his pockets, and found the vials of Crimson he had accepted from the aggressive thug and hadn't had a chance to discard.

'Crimson,' said Ming. 'How appropriate.'

'Why is it appropriate?'

'Because I invented Crimson, Conan. Can't you perceive the ironic perfection in that? The cosmos has a way of playing tricks on us with coincidence and synchronicity. Almost makes me believe in God, as most people will by the end of the night.'

'Believe in God?'

'Yes … and I will make it happen.'

At that point the man on the other bed stirred and moaned and Conan realised Asif was with them.

'Asif?' he asked.

There was no response but Ming was delighted.

'You see what I said about synchronicity? You know these people? This is wonderful.'

'Conan?' asked Mel. 'What is happening? And please cover me up.'

'Don't touch her,' snapped Ming as Conan moved to comply. 'In fact, take off your own trousers.'

'I beg your pardon?'

'Remove your trousers,' repeated Ming, smiling again.

Manderson's accomplice placed the gun back against Conan's head.

'Okay,' said Conan, bewildered as well as angry, and scared. He fumbled with his belt then stepped out of his trousers which were taken by Manderson and tossed into the corner.

'Underpants also,' said Ming.

Conan complied and, at that moment, heard his phone chime. Manderson looked at the phone and laughed softly, 'Your mate Dave Marsh wants to know whether you're okay. I'll put his mind at ease.'

Manderson then dictated as he replied to Dave's text, 'All good. See you soon.' He turned off Conan's phone and tossed it into the corner.

Ming told Conan to place his left hand where Mel's right hand was tied to the bed. Manderson attached a plastex manacle, then Conan was forced to kneel between Mel's legs and his right hand was stretched over to where her left hand was tied. With that hand tied also he was forced to lie on top of Mel who started sobbing with anger and humiliation.

'She needs something to relax. Give her the Crimson,' said Ming. Manderson pulled off Mel's hood, unstoppered one the vials and forced it into her mouth.

'Conan may as well have the other one,' laughed Ming. 'It was clearly brought to this room by God for this very purpose.'

'I don't want it,' said Conan.

'Of course you do,' said Ming. 'You have about half an hour to live so why not have a new experience while lying between the legs of your lover? You see how good I am to you?'

At that moment, Mel recognised Lammas, and screamed her fury at him.

'You filthy piece of shit!' she snarled. 'I knew it was you!'

As she screamed, Manderson was attempting to force the Crimson into Conan's mouth and Conan suddenly sucked it all in, vial and all. A flood of raspberry filled his mouth and he tried not to swallow, but before he knew it the Crimson was gone, leaving an aftertaste that reminded him of children's cough medicine.

'I don't know what you're talking about, Captain Roberts,' said Lammas, 'but you always were a little confused, not least about your loyalties.'

'How dare you!' snarled Mel. 'You disgusting, pathetic wanker! I would kill you if I could!'

'Well, you can't,' said Lammas, feeling aroused again by his ex-fiancée's helpless fury.

'Why are you doing this?' asked Conan.

'Because you have been too persistent, Agent Tooley,' said Ming. 'If you'd left us alone you wouldn't be in this predicament.'

'But why are you blowing up a brand new hospital?'

'How does he know that?' Ming demanded.

Manderson shrugged.

'It doesn't matter what he knows,' said Lammas, 'as very soon he will know nothing.'

'True,' said Ming. 'But we are not blowing up the hospital, Agent Tooley … that is being done by Habal Tong extremists. That is what the reports will say tomorrow.'

'So why are the Habal Tong extremists blowing up the hospital?' asked Conan, trying to be sarcastic but oddly amused as a wave of euphoria hit his brain. His desperate situation suddenly seemed funny and he knew it was the drug, probably blending with the lack of sleep and the pills Agent Green had given him.

'Two reasons,' said Ming. 'There is the obvious political aspect … which doubtless even you could guess.'

'And the other reason?' asked Conan, trying not to laugh, or be distracted by the feel of Mel's naked body against his.

'The other reason is to destroy the lack of evidence.'

'The what?'

'Don't you think this has gone far enough, Dr Chen?' said Lammas, glancing at his watch.

'What can they do?' replied Ming. 'And I so rarely get a chance to explain my handiwork … not that most people could ever understand it.'

'I know you've been using chaos theory to dabble in trans-plasmatic chemistry,' said Conan. 'No doubt Crimson is a product of that … but you won't make a lot of money giving it away.'

'I'm impressed you've worked out that much,' said Ming. 'But if you think I created the drug to make money then you are still a long way from perceiving my design.'

The drug was fantastic.

Conan had never felt so alive.

The weirdness of his situation didn't trouble him at all and neither did the prospect of imminent death. It almost seemed like a tantalising riddle that could somehow be worked out and transcended. Mel also, he noted, was no longer distressed but was lying beneath him with her eyes closed and a strange little smile on her lips.

Lips that looked so beautiful and kissable, but Conan wrenched his mind away from the drug's seductive hedonism and pursued the argument with Ming.

'Your design,' he mused, '... to destroy the lack of evidence? And we're in a hospital, so it's a lack of medical evidence?'

'Dr Chen,' warned Lammas.

'Correct,' she smiled, ignoring Lammas. 'And what sort of hospital are we?'

'A maternity hospital,' said Conan. It felt like his brain was able to encompass the entire hospital, seeing it like a three dee image and able to penetrate virtually its many rooms and corridors. He sent his consciousness to find the records room that he knew must exist, even though he had never seen it in reality. Then immediately stopped, realising he was surrendering to some fantasy vision inspired by the drug.

'A maternity hospital,' echoed Ming, '... but there is no evidence of babies here.'

'Because you're also putting Crimson in the drinking water,' said Conan, '... and it affects fertility?'

'Bullseye!' laughed Ming, as Lammas exclaimed with anger. 'You are far cleverer than I realised, Agent Tooley. What a shame it has to end like this.'

Conan laughed himself, knowing it was the drug that made him amused, even though he should have been horrified by what he had discovered.

'So you are blowing up the hospital to obscure the fact it has become obsolete,' said Conan, '... there are no babies being born. And at the same time you are causing a political and security storm which will justify the suspension of the First Wave visas.'

'Oh, that's awful,' laughed Mel, and Conan sniggered himself.

'What that means is ... you'll effectively turn Ord City into a massive concentration camp. People are allowed in but they will never leave and few children will be born.'

'Very good, Agent Tooley. You've worked it out ... or most of it. But Crimson does have one other important effect. I'll leave you to think about that.'

With that she left the room, followed by Manderson and his crony. Lammas lingered for a moment, bent over Mel and said, 'Well, well ... parting is such sweet sorrow and all that.'

'You are a disgrace to the church,' said Mel, furious despite a bit of a giggle.

'Perhaps,' said Lammas in a rich baritone that seemed to drip like honey through Conan's crumpet brain. 'But tomorrow I will be one of its greatest heroes. Unfortunately you won't be around to see it.'

Mel and Conan erupted in laughter and Lammas left the room, closing the door and leaving them in total darkness.

Chapter 42

An Interesting
Philosophical Puzzle

Just after seven o'clock the Dedd Reffo Five, with a few of the others, left the club house and headed down towards the main square where *Illumination* was happening.

Borne up by yet another vial of Crimson (and with more in his pocket) Robbie felt an amazing peace descend. It was a peace derived from clarity. His perception was so pure and strong, it was like his mind encompassed the entire world and all its people.

Some of whom Robbie was about to destroy.

They were Habal Tong after all, so that made it easier. Or would have done but for a few things Tim had said over the past few days.

Robbie glanced at Tim who was walking with Lemon but happened to be looking at him with a smile. Robbie felt a flush of embarrassment, which suddenly passed and he didn't care if Tim wanted to show his affection so openly.

What did it matter after all?

At that moment, Chris threw an arm round Robbie's shoulders and shook him.

'Up for it, mate?'

'Absolutely,' replied Robbie.

It was weird how the drug made him so eager to test himself against an explosion. It was almost like he could see it all in advance like a sort of video game. The rapidly expanding plasmas and particles of the blast could – if he was quick and clever enough – somehow be negotiated, leaving him not just alive but stronger than ever. The people around him were unlikely to manage it but …

'I'm gonna get as close as I can to Ah Li Wu,' laughed Chris. 'That'll teach the prick!'

'Teach him what?'

'Teach him not to come here to spout his bullshit … and steal all the fuckin' jobs,' shouted Chris, sneering at the thousands of people around them, mainly dressed in yellow and dancing to a hundred different tunes.

The sights and smells and massive sense of occasion were almost as intoxicating as the Crimson. Robbie was aware that what he was doing was wrong and would see him remembered for appalling reasons – but somehow he didn't care. It was not just the Crimson (although that helped) because he had made the decision to do it unaffected by anything but alcohol and the hopelessness of unrequited love.

Fucking Kate.

He had determined not to think about her tonight, but thinking about Kate only made him think about Tim.

Again he glanced at Tim who was still smiling at him, and Robbie smiled back. Lemon stared at Robbie, then stared at Tim. Then her mouth, set in a thin line of suspicion, was so funny Robbie burst into laughter.

'What's up, man?' asked Tim.

'I was just thinking what a beautiful night it is,' said Robbie, and Tim grinned. Then he stepped towards Robbie and before Robbie knew what was happening they were embracing in the middle of the street. Clinging tight and laughing, uncaring, as Chris, Lemon, Jimbo, Pauly, Mungo and all the rest stared at them in silence.

Then they broke apart, still laughing – staring into each other's eyes and laughing.

'What the fuck's this about?' demanded Chris, angry despite a burst of sniggering.

'They've become bum chums,' said Lemon, and Robbie and Tim roared with laughter, still staring joyously into each other's eyes.

'What the fuck?' demanded Jimbo.

'I wondered where Timmy got to last night,' said Lemon, the only one not laughing with the impact of Crimson. 'Now we know.'

'Is that true, man?' asked Chris, his heart cracking with betrayal.

'Does it matter?' asked Robbie.

'Yes, it fucking matters,' said Chris striding forward and taking a swing at Tim.

Robbie saw him coming and blocked the punch. 'Run!' he shouted.

Tim blinked in confusion and then ran, with Robbie haring after him as they dodged and twisted through the crowds, laughing their fool heads off.

Chris ran a few paces after them, utterly furious but laughing because of the drug, until he found himself standing in the middle of the road, surrounded by yellow clad dancers and weeping – so consumed with hatred he could gladly have set the blast suit off at once to clear those fuckin' Habal Tongers out of his path.

'We'll get 'em,' said Lemon, with a hand on Chris's shoulder.

'Fuckin' oath,' said Jimbo. 'Mind you, they can't get the suits off. When the signals go out they're toast.'

'Who sends the signal out?' asked Chris.

'That's secret, sorry,' said Mungo. 'No one's allowed to know for security reasons.'

'What if they find the police and dob us in?' asked Lemon. 'The police could cut their suits off if they don't go off before.'

'Can you send a message to anyone, Mung?' asked Jimbo, 'To get the signal brought forward?'

'Nope,' said Mungo. 'We get our orders ... that's it.'

'We better find 'em then,' said Lemon. 'Find 'em before they fuck up everything.'

'They're fuckin' dead,' snarled Chris, pounding a fist into his hand and then started laughing again.

Laughing and crying at the same time.

• • •

Tim and Robbie ran for the best part of ten minutes – dodging and weaving through the crowds – until they finally stopped and looked back the way they'd come. There was no sign of pursuit.

'Robbie?'

'Yeah?'

'I think we lost 'em.'

They stood, chests heaving with exertion and watching the crowds nearby anxiously, but there was no commotion. The crowd, like a vast liquid, had resettled into its resting state after the agitation of their own passage.

Tim turned to Robbie and said, 'What happens now?'

'I don't know. I guess these bomb suits are gonna go off sooner or later ... '

They both laughed.

It was really hard to take death seriously on Crimson – your own death at any rate. Causing the death of random others was just a tad more sobering, but even that seemed more like an interesting philosophical puzzle than the moral outrage it truly was.

'Even though we're about to be totally vaporised,' said Tim, '... finding your friendship in the last few days is the greatest thing that ever happened to me.'

Robbie found himself melting and laughing at the same time. They embraced – just holding each other – and Robbie felt the weirdest, most powerful emotion he had ever known. He could almost see Tim's entire history like a flash movie and the injustice suffered due to his gentle spirit being constantly abused. Robbie felt that if he could somehow hug the pain away he would at least have made some sort of positive contribution to someone else's life before his own miserable time on earth ended.

Tim broke the embrace.

'Robbie?'

'Yes, man?'

'When they were putting the lock on your blast suit ... I stood behind Jimbo and saw the combination.'

'Eh?'

'If you want me to ... I can get your suit off.'

Robbie stared at Tim and was amazed at the response that welled up from the very depths of his soul.

'No way, man. If your suit stays on, then so does mine.'

Tim's face broke into the sweetest smile Robbie had ever seen and said, 'Well okay ... if you're sure ... but the option's there.'

'Fuck the option,' said Robbie. 'Let's go have a look at *Illumination*.'

He held out his hand and Tim took it with a look of pure adoration.

Then, hand in hand, they walked into the crowd.

· · ·

It was pitch black but there must have been some tiny diffuse light coming from somewhere – under the door perhaps – as Conan could just make out a dim glitter from Mel's eyes.

Despite the terrible danger, he was also profoundly aware of her body against his and had a raging erection. He didn't know whether it was just the Crimson making him so turned on and insouciant of death. He had heard that people threatened with death get super horny as though it were some sort of race memory reflex – a last chance to pass one's genes when confronted with destruction.

Mel, also, was clearly in the mood. She was moving against him, manoeuvring into a position where the deed might somehow be done despite their strictures. Conan was so turned on he felt his brain would snap if he couldn't get it in, but there was something more important to do.

'Mel?'

'Mmh?'

'We erm … we don't have time.'

'Time?' replied Mel in a dreamy voice. 'That's all we've got, Conan, and I think we'd better make the most of it.'

She was grinding harder against him and it was all he could do to resist. The urge to let it happen was so powerful, but there was definitely something more important.

'Mel … I've got a vial in my mouth … one of the vials the Crimson was in.'

'So?'

'So, if I can bite down and break it, and spit the shards into my hand, I can cut your manacle.'

'Don't you dare spit, Conan. It's disgusting.'

Despite himself he started laughing, and of course the Crimson made him laugh even harder, and then Mel was laughing also.

'Stop it,' he cried, tears of mirth rolling down his cheeks in the dark. 'This is serious.'

That set them off even worse and it was at least a minute before he could speak again.

'Listen, Mel … hold your hand next to mine so we can make, like, a catcher's mitt.'

'You want to spit into my hand?'

'It's not spit … it's glass. Broken glass to save our lives perhaps.'

'Is it really worth living in this stupid country in this stupid world?' asked Mel. 'I suddenly don't care.'

'That's just the Crimson,' said Conan. 'It takes away fear … you definitely want to live.'

'I really don't know that I do,' said Mel. 'I think Crimson makes you see more clearly and now I see I'll never be happy in this world. There's too much evil.'

'Evil people have always been in charge,' said Conan, 'that's the nature of politics. But two people can still make a happy life together, no matter how hard the leaders want to fuck it up for them.'

'You really believe that?'

'Yes I do, Mel.'

'And you think we could be happy together?'

Conan, once again, was confronted by his vague promises to Lucia but there was an excitement and a connection with Mel he couldn't deny.

'I think we already are happy.'

'Oh Conan … '

She kissed him, then said, 'Very well, you may spit in my hand.'

There was another thirty seconds or so of laughter and then they arranged their hands together – his right and her left.

Conan bit down gently on the vial and felt it break into several small pieces. If they could just catch one …

He manoeuvred the shards to the front of his mouth, then aimed at their hands – about two feet away in the darkness.

He spat.

Chapter 43

Behind, Beyond and Beneath

The square was filling with people. Thousands and thousands were flowing in and milling about the stadium which seemed to draw them in like the vortex at the centre of a whirlpool.

Dave Marsh got up to stretch his legs and wondered for the twentieth time whether he ought to go into the hospital. Conan had left a message suggesting everything was OK, but that was a while ago.

It was now quite dark but the many people wearing bio-suits were like Christmas lights, clustered or strung out amid the churning dark mass of humanity. Huge holoscreens around the stadium walls or placed about the square showed colourful images that danced in time with the music which was still Tai Chi in nature but getting a little more urgent. Pulsing rhythms started to wind through the music, giving the crowd a small taste of the excitement to come.

It was quite mesmerising to Dave who was beginning to regret taking all the pills. He was feeling more than a little wired and a tad toxic, and it seemed as though the dancing images on the screen were sometimes a little too real for his comfort. He glanced at his watch again – 7.22. Conan had been gone for a while.

Another text couldn't hurt. He pulled out his phone and sent the same message as before: Everything OK?

A minute passed.

A large group of HT women dressed in yellow and openly swilling vials of Crimson pushed into his place by the wall and Dave allowed himself to be moved aside. He was getting concerned.

Another minute passed without response.

The building was brightly lit at the front but faded quickly into darkness, like an iceberg. The dangerous part is always out of sight thought Dave, wondering how he was going to get in.

He was just about to make his way down the same lane Conan had gone to find access, when he saw people being pushed back from the security barrier at the entrance. Dave hurried over, as best he could, through the ever-thickening swarm and saw Lammas walk out, accompanied by Ming and Colonel Chard. They were escorted by a small troop of security people in the same black uniforms Dave had seen at the treatment plant, and those security people now forced a passage through the crowd.

They were headed for the stadium.

Dave was confronted with a dilemma: should he look for Conan, who had still not responded, or should he follow these members of the Shadow Group?

The crowd were starting to flow back into place where the Shadow Group had gone and Dave took off to run after them, timing his movements to fill the gaps just before someone else did and staying some five or so metres behind. He was still dressed in the black fatigues they'd worn to infiltrate the water plant so, in the dark press, he could almost pass for one of them.

• • •

Major Lammas' head was whirling.

He had learned a lot in the last half hour, but still wasn't entirely sure how he felt about Dr Ming Li Chen being the main power behind, beyond and beneath all that was happening. It was infuriating to perceive how he had been used, an unwitting pawn on the edge of their network, but exciting suddenly to be part of it, even though it meant accepting his place in the hierarchy – a place beneath Dr Chen and even Marjory.

Still, and he glanced left and right at the people filling the square in front of the stadium, it was thrilling to know the real reason they were here and to be a part of the future – as it had been explained to him.

Most of the people wore yellow, he noted and although the main part of the festival had not yet commenced, most were already transported by religious ecstasy brought on by drug-fuelled visions.

Major Lammas had his doubts about the means but was very sure about the end.

Everyone needed to believe.

• • •

Conan spat, and felt something hit his hand.

'Yuck!' said Mel.

Conan instinctively closed his hand over hers. 'Don't move,' he said. 'I think it's trapped between us.'

With infinite caution, Conan moved his hand and, yes, there was at least one shard of glass caught between their palms.

'Whatever you do, don't move,' repeated Conan. 'This is the tricky bit.'

The angle of her hand meant that if he took his away, the glass would fall onto the bed or the floor and they would be unable to reach it.

Weirdly enough, the Crimson helped. Conan, somehow, could visualise – almost as though the lights were turned on – the delicate piece of glass that might effect their freedom but was defying his efforts to retrieve.

'Ow!' complained Mel as he pressed the shard a little harder into her flesh.

'Sorry … I'm just trying to get it to stick to your hand so I can pick it up.'

'You're hurting,' she complained, but she continued to hold her hand hard against his.

Slowly, ever so slowly, he slid his hand over hers until he could transfix the shard with a finger. Then he got his thumb in place and held the piece of vial. It was a good piece, with a part of the slightly thicker glass of the base and a bit more than a centimetre in length.

'Okay … hold very still as I try to cut your manacle.'

His hand shifted in the dark – three fingers feeling for the plastex tie as index finger and thumb held onto the precious glass blade. It was more than a little awkward but he found a place at the side of her wrist that he could reach.

'Ouch!'

'Sorry.'

'You're cutting me!'

'Sorry, Mel … can you try and pull your hand to the left?'

He felt an infinitesimal shift away but that was enough to feel more plastic than flesh beneath his fingers and he tried again.

'You're really hurting.'

'Sorry, Mel, it's cutting me also but I am getting the plastex as well. Be brave.'

Mel gritted her teeth as Conan bent his wrist uncomfortably to get purchase. He felt the shard bite deeply but Mel flinched and the glass broke leaving him with only half.

'Shit … don't move.'

'Ow! Conan … I can feel blood on my arm.'

'Sorry, darling … I'm nearly there.'

Conan, with profound care, used his middle finger to feel where most damage had been done to pick the best point of attack. It was amazing how Crimson somehow converted the sensory information to vision – it was as though the lights had been turned on – and with some precision Conan picked the deepest gouge in the plastex and sliced down hard.

'Ow!' shrieked Mel and the shard was knocked from his fingers.

'Fuck! I've lost it.' But another feel of her manacle revealed the plastex was hanging on by a thread.

'Give it a pull, Mel. It's nearly cut through.'

Mel was audibly in a bit of pain, but she braced herself for a massive tug and was surprised when her hand broke free with enough force to clout Conan in the face.

'Fuck! What are you doing?'

'It's payback for slashing my wrists,' she said, not at all unhappy about hitting him.

'Okay,' said Conan, recovering. 'See if you can find another bit of glass on the bed.'

Mel groped about as best she could with her left hand.

'Here's one. It's very small.'

She did at least have a lot more freedom of movement than Conan and it didn't take her as long to cut through his right manacle. Then Conan found quite a good sized piece and quickly freed his left hand and Mel's right.

It was a difficult manoeuvre to free their ankles. Conan, with splayed legs was able to twist partly aside while Mel tugged at the sheets beneath her.

'What are you doing?' he asked.

'Wiping my chest.'

'Why?'

'You don't want to know.'

She managed to lean forward and cut through his ankle ties, and then her own. They were free.

'Don't turn the light on just yet,' whispered Conan. 'We don't want to alert anyone.'

Asif and Tanya were still sleeping on the next bed but after a couple of shakes, Asif woke.

'What ... what is happening?'

'Asif, it's Conan ... Agent Conan Tooley.'

'Agent Tooley? Why is it dark? Where am I?'

'No time to explain, but we have to get out of here.'

Asif and Tanya both had only one hand manacled to the bed so Conan freed them quickly. Then he groped his way to the corner and found his phone, gun, trousers and underpants.

'Do you want to put my undies on?' he asked Mel and she giggled, still strongly affected by Crimson.

'They're a bit big,' she said, 'but better than nothing I suppose.'

While Mel arranged herself as best she could with the silk dressing gown wrapped tight around her, Conan turned his phone back on.

'Hmmm ... Dave texted me about ten minutes ago. I didn't respond so he's probably trying to find us.'

Conan sent another message to Dave, warning him to stay clear of the hospital and that they would meet outside.

He then inched the door open and peered up and down the dim corridor.

'Okay, can you walk Asif?'

Asif was still badly injured from the burns on his back and wearing only a surgical gown.

'Yes, I think so, but Tanya will not wake up.'

There was a lot more light in the room with the door open so

Conan went over to the bed and picked up Tanya. Then he led them out of the room and away from the front of the building, deeper into darkness where he hoped to find the double plastex doors to the ambulance bay he'd seen from outside.

'Where are we?' asked Asif in a stage whisper.

'We're in the new maternity hospital … but we have to get out,' said Conan, grunting with the effort. Tanya was heavier than she looked.

'Hang on … I need a rest.'

He lowered her to the floor and leaned against a wall. He could just make out the plastex doors about twenty metres away. They were going to make it.

He went to pick up Tanya again but something flickered in the corner of his eye. He turned back and saw a green flash through a window set in a door.

He took a closer look and saw a green blinking light inside a room. The door was locked and Conan swore.

The light turned to yellow.

• • •

Dave felt his phone buzz and glanced at the message – Conan was telling him to stay outside the hospital and meet up there.

That was fair enough, but Conan didn't know he was on the trail of the Shadow Group. Dave put his phone away and concentrated on staying close.

It was getting harder as they approached the stadium. The gap forced by the security guards was tighter and refilled more quickly, meaning Dave had to stay hot on their heels to keep up. If they turned now they would stand a good chance of recognising him. Certainly Ming would know him – she had worn his shirt for a while on the island and Dave grinned at the memory. Clearly she was up to her neck in something very dodgy, but he couldn't help but like her. She was brave, utterly gorgeous and probably the smartest person he had ever met. That stuff she wrote about – trans-plasmatic chemistry and the morphological rationale of populations – weird shit, and how the fuck did they fit together? You'd need a brain the size of a pumpkin to sort that out.

Closer to the stadium doors there were huge clusters of bean bag chairs scattered about and people were swarming over them – dressed and undressed. The music was still vaguely Tai Chi in style but getting more modern. The drums and sequencers cutting through it all were forcing the crowd to move in massive unison. Even the people bonking in the bean bags were in sync with the beat and Dave found himself strangely wired by the pills he'd taken. When he turned his head, it was like anything he'd been looking at retained the ghost of an image on his retina, like staring at sparklers dancing in the dark.

They were just about at the main gates now and though thrown wide open the press to get in was like a mediaeval shield wall. Thousands of people were pushing and shoving and even the security people were struggling to make progress – but progress they made and Dave forced himself along in their wake. He could have touched Lammas if he wanted to – in fact, he could have touched all three, so tight were they packed. It was a pickpocket's paradise.

Or a frotteur's. Legions of young men and women looked like they were doing anything with anyone as the lights and music pulsed and huge holos flickered into life above their heads. It was still mainly lights and abstract images but now and then they seemed to coalesce into figures and faces. The excitement in the crowd was like nothing Dave had ever known and it was all he could do to maintain his concentration.

Suddenly he fell forward into a less populous zone just inside the gates. Lammas, Ming and the others were being shepherded through a security check point and before he'd properly realised what was happening, Dave was through as well. They passed through a doorway into the bowels of the stands and one of the security guards held the door open for him.

Dave passed through the door into a long corridor and hurried after the Shadow Group, trying to keep the fool grin off his face.

• • •

Acting Captain Michael Rice was in a torment of indecision.

He had been desperate to meet Major Lammas, and had been

shocked to see him leave the hospital in company with Colonel Chard and Dr Chen. Something very large was happening, on the biggest night since the promulgation of Ord City. Rice was keenly aware he was supposed to be leading the vigil back at the chapter house and that his absence could do irreparable damage to the fragile devotions of his brethren, but Major Lammas needed to understand that the authorities were hunting him.

Now even more so, as when Rice had started after Lammas in the crowd he had seen Agent Marsh following closely behind him.

Rice had done his best to keep up but the tightness of the crowd had seen him slowly pushed aside until he was lost in the swirling maelstrom in front of the gates. The sensation was like drowning – like being lost overboard and watching the lights of the ship pass over the horizon – but Rice would still do his duty despite the fact he had been warned against it.

He got his phone out and managed to send a short message to Lammas: You are being watched by the Federal Police. They know about the bombs at the GA. Please meet me at the stadium Gate C!!! Please!!!

• • •

Conan pushed through the plastex doors carrying Tanya and climbed carefully down the stairs. He wouldn't put her down until they were beyond the likely blast zone. God knew how much explosive was in the room.

She was heavy, or Conan was tired, and he felt her slipping, but with Mel's help managed to get her outside and away from the ambulance bay entrance. They made it to the corner of the building, still inside the security barrier and obscured from the street by plastex hoardings. Conan wanted to use his phone but the noise even a block away from the square was deafening.

He tried the number Agent Green had given him for emergencies and was surprised when it answered – even more surprised that he could actually hear the conversation.

'Tooley?'

'Yes.'

'Where are you?"

Conan had a sudden paranoid thought that he might be talking to one of the Shadow Group, but thrust that down given his urgent message.

'Is that Green?'

'You're ringing the number I gave you, aren't you?'

'Yes but … never mind that. There's a bomb at the maternity hospital. You need to get everyone out.'

'Another bomb? Wonderful.'

'You can deal with that? I've also got some hurt people who need looking after.'

'We can hardly get a car in there,' mused Green, 'it's bedlam. I have some other news by the way.'

'Yeah?'

'Edward Loong has been arrested … and so has Kenneth Cook.'

'Fuck!'

'Quite.'

'Arrested by whom?'

'Their own people. We don't have all the details, which is a worry in itself … but what it means is this: the Shadow Group are moving to take over all security services on the night they're needed most. I even have concerns about the integrity of this supposedly secure line.'

'I thought you guys were in charge of the Empyrean,' protested Conan, '… the highest Quantum function ruling all communications.'

'So did we,' said Green, 'but something's happened out at the NBN node. They've obviously patched in a bypass that gives them control … at least of their own operations. I must say they've arranged and timed it all extremely well. First class job.'

Conan could hardly believe his ears.

'You sound awfully calm about it.'

'No point panicking, Agent Tooley. I suggest you try to find Dr Chen … she seems to be pulling all the strings right now.'

'Any idea where she is?'

'Not with the patch in place … but if the stadium is the focus of the night's festivities, you can probably assume she won't be far away.'

Conan thought furiously, enjoying the way the Crimson seemed to kick in like a turbo when he needed to concentrate. It was like he could see the problem as a series of abstract numbers that just needed resolution and the answer would present itself.

'Is there anything we can do to disrupt the patch?' he asked.

'Not without taking out the NBN for the entire city,' said Green. 'A bit drastic ... but we may have no other option.'

'Is there a local substation that serves the stadium.'

'Yes, probably.'

There was silence for a few moments, then Agent Green was back.

'There is a substation in Bob Brown Lane ... like a big green meta-plastex box ... but I don't see what can be done at this late stage. You'd need an army tank to hurt it ... or about fifty strips of mangalite.'

'Mangalite?' repeated Conan. 'Okay ... gotta go.'

He hung up and looked at Asif.

'How are you feeling?'

'Better, but Tanya is still sleeping. I am very worried about—'

'Don't worry about that now. I've got a job for you.'

Chapter 44

The Proximity of Death

Chris and Lemon led the others like a pack of wolves hunting their prey – rabbits hiding among other rabbits.

Chris was devastated by Robbie's actions, his anger refuelled by Lemon's non-stop narrative regarding Tim and Robbie's betrayal.

'Nice pair of fuckin' ratbags they are,' she said. 'After all I've done for Tim … this is how he repays me?'

She was spitting chips about it, but if she was angry about Tim it was nothing compared with the white hot fury that consumed Chris.

'I thought we were mates!' he kept saying, bitter tears alternating with wild laughter as the Crimson affected his moods.

Lemon was the only one who didn't seem too affected by the drugs. She remained very focussed and kept pestering Jimbo and Mungo about the blast suits.

'You must know when they're timed to go off,' she kept saying. Eventually Mungo snapped. 'Aah for fuck's sake! Sometime after Ah Li Wu starts his fuckin' speech, okay? That's all I fuckin' know. Time you blokes got in place.'

The crowd was already impossible but Ron and Bruno took off into the thick of it, vowing to find Ah Li Wu and boasting about how many yellow shitcunts they were gonna take with them.

Chris shared their hatred of all yellows and their HT fuckin' bullshit but he now had a more urgent priority.

'I'm gonna find fuckin' Tim,' he snarled. '*And* Robbie!'

'Well, get a fuckin' move on,' said Jimbo. 'Ah Li Wu is due to hit the stage just after eight and it's not far off.'

Chris nodded grimly then shoved his way into the crowd, followed by a grinning Lemon

$$\bullet \quad \bullet \quad \bullet$$

The *Illumination* festival was amazing.

Robbie and Tim no longer needed to push through the crowd. Somehow, probably via the Crimson – and despite the bombs strapped to their bodies - they just seemed to flow through its eddies and streams, exulting in the bond they felt for all people. The Tai Chi music was getting a lot rockier and seemed almost visible as they moved into the centre of the square in front of the stadium. There were bean bags everywhere, and dozens of people were handing out vials of Crimson which Tim and Robbie accepted eagerly.

'It's a bit like the early stages of alcohol,' said Tim. 'It makes you uninhibited, happy and full of energy.'

'It's a lot better than that,' said Robbie, gazing about in awestruck wonder. 'There's a sense of freedom and indestructability. I feel like there's nothing that can't be achieved. All you have to do is want something and it's gonna happen.'

Clad and unclad women (and some men) kissed them on the lips as they merged deeper into the throng. The sense of profound connection with all around them became more intense. Huge groups were clustering in massive hugs with every sex act imaginable going on.

'That explains the bean bags,' laughed Robbie. 'The organisers had that sussed.'

They hadn't properly realised, until that moment, that they were walking hand in hand, and Robbie was amazed to understand that he wasn't remotely concerned about it. He felt so connected with Tim that it would have seemed wrong *not* to be holding hands.

They moved out of a section of yellow-clad dancers into a vast group in bio-suits like a living, breathing forest of light. Like the yellows, the bio-suits were clustering, anonymous, polymorphous. Robbie's brain seemed to be filling with a white noise of ecstasy and two naked girls embraced him. Another two embraced Tim, kissing him and pulling at his clothing which they couldn't remove.

'My suit can't come off,' laughed Tim. 'But Robbie's can.'

With that, he took hold of the lock at the back of Robbie's blast suit and, seconds later, flung the opened lock into the random crowd.

'What are you doing?' cried Robbie.

'You don't need to wear it, man,' he said, grinning like stars, as the girls tore at Robbie's suit.

'Why can't yours come off,' demanded one of the girls. 'We all need to be naked ... that's the way we were made and how we should always be.'

'It's locked on,' said Tim, 'so I can't escape my secret mission.'

'What's your mission?' asked the girl.

'To kill Ah Li Wu.'

'Really?'

The girl laughed and swallowed another vial of Crimson. Her friends now had Robbie naked and were kissing him all over, but Robbie had eyes only for Tim.

'Um, would you two prefer to be together?' asked one of the girls.

'We're *all* together,' cried Tim, snatching up Robbie's discarded blast suit, '... now and forever. The only way we could get closer is if our component molecules were to come apart somehow and fuse back together into one all-knowing, omnipotent being.'

'We need a bomb!' yelled one of the girls. The bio-suit wearers were ever searching for means of testing their bravery and all night they'd been gathering in places where terrorist bombs were most likely to be placed, to prove their courage with slow pulses in the proximity of death.

'I *am* a bomb!' shouted Tim.

All of the girls eagerly embraced Tim, leaving Robbie naked and laughing, but he reached past two of the girls and threw his arms round Tim's neck.

The music had morphed into a blend of Tai Chi techno-trance with occasional splashes of rock guitar and drums like a bickering argument that slowly soothed into loud agreement. Now and again the music would fade and a succession of speakers would introduce one of the Habal Tong axioms and expand upon it.

'Love is money and money is love ... the more we have the richer we are. Anything can be purchased with the currency of love, if you have enough.'

The voices themselves, mainly female, were pure music, and the words like deeply profound poetry opened doors in Robbie's mind he'd never known were there. He tried to get closer to Tim but the girls clung like mistletoe, and yet others were forcing themselves closer to Tim as the news spread that a bomb was at hand.

'Call Kate!' shouted Tim.

'What?'

Robbie could barely see Tim with all the bodies forced between them.

'Call Kate!' shouted Tim. 'Tell her you love her!'

'But I don't,' yelled Robbie. 'I love you!'

• • •

The light was still flashing yellow.

Conan, to his disbelief, was back inside the hospital and holding his pistol against a door. For the first time in his career he fired his weapon and the door blew open to reveal two large eskies filled with mangalite strips and wired to a single detonator.

The light changed to orange.

'Just gone orange,' said Conan, '... which is a good sign. It means the intervals between status changes are fairly long.'

'I work with explosives all the time,' reminded Asif.

'Of course you do,' apologised Conan. 'So ... what happens if we just pull the detonator out?'

'The charge will go off immediately.'

'Are you certain?'

'I earnestly request a two minute head start if you wish to try it.'

Conan considered the two eskies.

'Are they safe to carry?'

'As long as it is still cool. And we must be careful not to detach the wire coupling.'

They lifted the eskies in unison after Conan hid the blinking light under a sheet pulled from a bed. Then, with Asif leading, they carried the eskies out of the room and started moving towards the ambulance bay.

'Wait!'

Conan paused to look into the room opposite and saw, to his dismay, another blinking light – also orange.

'Jee-zuss! There's another bomb.'

Asif stared blankly and Conan shrugged.

'We'll deal with it if we have time. For now we need to get this lot to where it might do some good.'

They made their way down the corridor and lowered the eskies onto the edge of the ambulance bay. Then they ran down the stairs, collected the eskies and resumed their careful conveyance.

It was almost completely dark at the back of the hospital and the protective barrier was a major problem. They carried the eskies to the corner of the building where Mel's white face loomed anxiously out of the shadows. Tanya was still comatose on the ground.

'Okay,' said Conan, 'I'll get over the fence, then you two need to lift the eskies. I'll balance them on top until Asif gets over and we can lift them down together.'

'What's in them?' asked Mel.

'Erm ... '

'Very powerful and extremely unstable explosive,' said Asif.

'What?'

'It's fine, Mel,' said Conan, '... and we haven't got time to debate it.'

'What do you mean by unstable?'

'It is a warm night,' said Asif, '... as the explosive heats up it is less predictable.'

'Which means we don't have time to debate it,' repeated Conan, climbing the fence.

'Quickly,' said Asif to Mel, '... it will only take a moment.'

Mel thrust down the feelings of panic, and anger, and took a deep breath. Then she took hold of the esky, as Asif did, and lifted on his count.

'It's heavy.'

'Good girl!' encouraged Conan, taking hold of both eskies as Asif leapt on top of the fence and helped Conan lower the eskies to the ground. Then he was quickly back over, lifted Tanya over his burned shoulder, and ignoring the pain, climbed awkwardly back across, helped by Mel.

There were any number of people in the laneway but no one took the slightest notice of what they were doing.

'I am *not* a good girl, Conan.'

'Eh?'

'I said I'm not a good girl.'

'Fair enough ... I prefer bad girls anyway.'

Conan hadn't been able to resist the retort but from the look on her face knew it would require some serious back-pedalling – not that they had time for that.

'I must stay with Tanya,' said Asif, '... get her somewhere safe.'

Conan knew they had a journey of about 600 metres to get the eskies to the NBN substation on Bob Brown Lane and Mel was looking mutinous.

'I'd like your advice when we get to the substation,' said Conan. 'Maybe if Mel carries one esky and you carry Tanya ... we could all go together?'

'Are you insane?' demanded Mel.

'Of course. If that is alright with Melodie,' said Asif.

There was an awkward silence, then Mel groaned, 'Very well, but I'm not happy, Conan ... not happy with any of this.'

'None of us are,' agreed Conan. 'But thank you darling ... I really need your help. The whole city needs your help.'

Without another word, Melodie lifted one of the eskies as Conan lifted the other. Then, with Asif carrying Tanya over his shoulder and leading the way, they headed back towards the square.

Just as the blinking light turned red.

Chapter 45

The Fight Against Ignorance

Six people – three men and three women – sit before a huge picture window looking over a vast city, with an ocean to the north under a purple sky fading to black. A servant pours champagne and departs silently. None of them speak until all have savoured the sparkling wine.

Major Lammas was absolutely delighted to be back in Ronny Kwai's private suite at the top of Rinehart Stadium. It was just as lavish as before but those present were fewer in number, and far more important for the future.

Most he knew – Kwai, Chard, Chen and Maddox – but he had to be introduced to the smallish, elderly man in a khaki safari suit with white shoes who peered at him through round rimless spectacles.

'Major Lammas,' said Ronny Kwai, 'allow me to introduce the greatest visionary in Australian history ... Doctor Hermann Van Der Kock.'

Lammas was nonplussed for a couple of seconds, but then he remembered. 'Ah ... you were the Minister for Immigration when Ord City was established.'

'Immigration and Border Protection,' said Van Der Kock, 'and I maintain yet an affectionate interest in Ord City's affairs.'

'You have some affection left for me, I hope.'

Dr Ming Chen slipped an arm through Van Der Kock's and gazed at him adoringly.

'Of course, my little dove,' he replied. 'Are you content with the arrangements?'

'Yes,' said Ming, '... one or two complications but ... they've been dealt with.'

'Complications?'

'No longer relevant,' she pouted, holding up her phone. 'And the bypass is stable … the fireworks can begin as soon as you give the word.'

'Very well. We shall proceed, Duyfken.'

Some of the guests drifted off to examine the buffet, but Lammas found himself staring at Dr Van Der Kock – transfixed by his presence.

'I understand,' said Van Der Kock, 'that you have been accepted within the inner sanctum.'

'Yes. It is a great privilege,' responded Lammas. 'Thank you.'

'You have, of course, been on the edge of our network for some years,' said Van Der Kock, sipping champagne. 'You were a conduit between us and the Habal Tong but you didn't know that did you?'

'I knew I was working with people dedicated to the fight against ignorance,' said Lammas.

'And so you were, but ignorance takes many forms. The cabinet of which I was a member for example, they refused even to consider … well … that is in the past.'

Major Lammas felt his head whirling with all he had learned, but knew there was more to come.

'I feel like the world I know has come apart at the seams,' he admitted.

'A fair observation for a man in your position,' replied Van Der Kock. 'Do you know why we have embraced you fully within our fold?'

'No.'

'Full membership of the leadership group is not something we take lightly. Come.'

Van Der Kock led Lammas outside to where the stadium seating overlooked the main arena – heaving with people but especially concentrated around a stage erected at the northern end.

'Our prime minister … Mrs Yunupingu is down there with the official party,' said Van Der Kock. 'She thinks … as she always does … that she is presiding over the main event, which will culminate with an address by Ah Li Wu.'

'I met him,' said Lammas, 'at a local restaurant.'

'Did you?'

'Yes. An interesting fellow … if rather misguided.'

'That interesting fellow,' said Van Der Kock, 'is an actor.'

Lammas stared, once again feeling stupid among the staggering revelations.

'An actor?'

'Yes, employed by us.'

Lammas felt his mouth open and close, but wisely remained silent.

'In case you haven't worked it out yet,' said Van Der Kock, waving an arm to take in the stadium and everyone in it, 'I created Habal Tong.'

'You did?'

'Of course. And obviously, I also created Dedd Reffo. There must always be a balance.'

If Lammas had been thrown before by what he was learning, he was now completely stunned.

'You both fought and assisted that balance with your Army of God organisation … which is why you were useful to us … but it was your willingness to take bold action out at the Giant Array that alerted us to the fact that you are not constrained … like most … to inconvenient temporal laws. You were willing to take major risks to achieve what you perceived to be the rightness of your cause.'

'Well, of course.'

'That makes you worthy of joining us,' said Van Der Kock. 'Our organisation has always dared great risks in the name of our mission, and so it will continue.'

'Your mission?' asked Lammas.

'Our mission is the same it has always been … for two thousand years.'

'Which is what?'

'Control, Major Lammas. That is all … control.'

They were joined by Dr Chen.

'Have you briefed him, Daddy?'

Yet again Lammas was amazed.

'Doctor Chen is your daughter?'

Van Der Kock laughed.

'My little Duyfken, yes … she is over fifty years younger … but entirely my creation.'

'Although I like to think I have improved on your work, Daddy darling.'

'Of course you have. Your work in chaos based neuro-chemistry would be worth a dozen Nobel prizes if we were ever to allow its full publication. But we have our own needs, do we not?'

'I understood from the conversation with Tooley,' said Lammas, 'that the chemical released into the water reduces fertility.'

'Conversation with Tooley?' snapped Van Der Kock.

'Don't worry, Daddy. Tooley is the irrelevant complication. He is tied to a bed in the hospital and the blast sequence has already been initiated. He will be gone very shortly.'

It was Van Der Kock's turn to stare uncertainly.

'You spoke with a federal agent about the water supply? The fellow captured at Delta whom I told you to destroy?'

'He is being destroyed, Daddy. He is bound hand and foot and drugged … and way beyond help.'

'Even still, I suspect your need to reveal your triumph over adversaries has again affected your judgment.'

Dr Chen looked chastened and bowed her head.

'You are right, and I apologise. I must learn to enjoy my victories discreetly.'

Van Der Kock smiled at her.

'The best victories are those the enemy does not perceive. If we do our work properly then no one blames their misfortune on us. They blame it on God … or the devil.'

'Well … let us toast the many victories to come,' said Dr Chen. 'After tonight our work will be easier for a time.'

Daughter and father raised their glasses and Lammas drank politely.

'You said, sir, that your organisation has been around for two thousand years?'

'Yes,' said Van Der Kock. 'Two thousand years. Probably longer but that is when we first understood the power of belief and turned it to our purpose.'

'Belief?' echoed Lammas, trying to keep the disapproval out of his voice as he adjusted yet again to his new reality.

'Yes belief … and passion … they go ever hand in hand. Our organisation has been in the vanguard of nearly every faith and philosophy … every *ism* if you will, since the conversion of Constantine.'

'No ... '

'Of course we have. Whatever the prevailing social, political, economic paradigm, our people have always been there to help guide the appropriate credos and systems into existence to keep the masses in their place.'

'We are philosophical midwives,' said Dr Chen.

'An excellent analogy,' laughed Van Der Kock, '... especially given the current circumstances.'

Lammas felt his phone go off again, but ignored it as his head continued to whirl.

'The *Epistola Clementis*?' he asked.

Van Der Kock smiled. 'Yes, one of our better results. Christianity might have withered on the vine without it.'

'But ... does this mean there is truly no God?'

Van Der Kock's good humour was immediately replaced by anger.

'You of all people should know the answer to that Major. Of course God exists!'

'But ... '

'We are not an atheist or agnostic movement,' said Dr Chen. 'We have always helped the people to see God.'

'And tonight,' said Van Der Kock, 'they will see Him like never before. I think it is time for the formal part of the evening. Come my little Duyfken.'

● ● ●

Dave Marsh was standing just inside the door to Ronny Kwai's suite, staring about in amazement. He was with a small detachment of black uniformed guards and no one had really paid him any attention, such was the excitement in the room. None of the guards, except Manderson, were permitted to go beyond the outer chamber but they were allowed to drink light beer in honour of the occasion. Most were watching screens showing the crowd in the main arena but Dave was watching Lammas talking to Ming Chen and an old bloke he recognised from the holo-figures in the ONA operations room – Van Der Kunt, or whatever his name was.

He pulled his phone out to contact Conan.

Dr Van Der Kock excused himself and moved off to speak with Ronny Kwai, followed by his daughter.

Major Lammas shook his head for the hundredth time, then pulled out his phone. There were several messages from Michael Rice – each more hysterical than the last, and all implying that Lammas had been involved in the explosions at the Giant Array.

Lammas' teeth gritted in anger at Rice's stupidity. There was no evidence against Lammas except for the messages on Rice's phone and his own potential testimony.

Rice himself was the only danger, the only fly in Lammas' glorious new unguent, won through his willingness to dare great risks.

Major Lammas' jaw set grimly, as he realised what had to be done.

He pulled out his phone and sent Rice a message: Meet me by Stadium Gate C in fifteen minutes.

Chapter 46

All is Nothing
and Nothing is All

Robbie was naked in a crowd of semi-naked men and women. Many still wore bio-suit tee-shirts, but were unconstrained from the waist down, and clustering together in a wild, orgiastic passion.

He could no longer even see Tim at the centre of the knot, but his heart was filled with a weird love for him.

Call Kate?

That's what Tim wanted him to do, but his phone was gone, lost with the blast suit which was now buried under many writhing bodies.

He realised there was still a vial of Crimson in his hand and, despite having already had at least four, pulled the stopper and downed the raspberry flavoured juice as the music changed again. A series of guitar power chords announced another change of feel and a massive bass sequencer kicked in. Immediately the crowd adjusted, timing its movements to the beat.

'Time and space are the fourth dimensions, we are told,' spoke the mellifluous female voice, 'but Habal Tong is also a movement. Which means we are required to move in time … in our own space.'

Robbie was tempted to lie in a bean bag chair which had suddenly become available, but the music was too compelling. He found himself moving, at first just vaguely, but ever more emphatically as the words danced in his brain and the music possessed him.

There were holo-screens and speakers all around the square and laser light shows were pulsing madly, but there was somehow a coherence to it all. No matter how frenzied the lights and movement,

Robbie could perceive an order in the chaos.

'Order is chaos and chaos is order,' said the voice and Robbie laughed. It was as though the voice was speaking to him alone, like a psychic dialogue. He could almost see the voice, lines of colour in the air around him coalescing into cognate shapes.

'Tonight is a special night … the pinnacle of our movement,' announced a different voice – a musical male voice – and a massive roar erupted as the hundreds of thousands in the square and stadium realised that Ah Li Wu was before them.

In the flesh.

It was almost like waking from a trance as the multitude focussed their attention on the many holo-screens where Ah Li Wu – the reclusive legend and creator of Habal Tong – gazed upon his people.

'A special night, indeed. I can see and feel the commune … the engagement … the connection between all peoples here tonight … and those who can't be here but are with us in spirit. Are we connected?'

There was a roar of agreement and acclamation and Robbie found himself swept up by the ecstasy – the power of connection. All around him people were joining hands and Robbie also was held by intimate strangers.

'All is nothing and nothing is all,' said Ah Li Wu. 'This is how we bring the purity of our purpose to the rest of the world … to lose the self and become part of something greater … like a leaf on a tree, like a tree in a forest.

'All is nothing and nothing is all,' cried the crowd, Robbie with them, as they all began to dance again in slow unison.

'This is the path to immortality' said Ah Li Wu. 'Only through losing the self can you become part of something greater … something that can live forever.'

'Live forever!' responded the crowd, speaking with one voice.

'All is nothing and nothing is all!'

'Live forever!' screamed the crowd, as the first of the explosions went off.

• • •

Conan heard the explosion but knew it wasn't the hospital. It had come from the direction of the stadium to their right. The hospital was behind them.

They were moving as quickly as they could, skirting the edge of the square and heading for Bob Brown Lane, carefully carrying the eskies.

'What was that?' demanded Mel.

'Nothing.'

'It sounded like an explosion.'

'Well no one's panicking,' said Conan. 'It can't have been.'

That much was true. If anything the crowd had started to move towards the explosion, and the voice of Ah Li Wu continued, soothing and caressing with its lilting message.

'He makes a lot of sense,' said Mel. 'I like listening to him.'

'That's because you're strung out on Crimson,' said Conan. 'If you were sober you'd think it was meaningless drivel.'

'I disagree,' said Mel. 'There's something to it … all is nothing and nothing is all.'

Conan kept an eye on the light flashing red, which he'd partly covered to keep Mel from worrying. He reckoned they had about seven minutes to get the manga to the NBN substation and then clear the street. The journey was about 400 metres. It would have been simple in normal circumstances, but with so many thousands packing the square and surrounding streets, progress was slow.

'No need to be polite Asif,' shouted Conan to his point man, who kept apologising to those he pushed past.

Conan felt his phone go off but didn't have time to check.

'How long do we have?' asked Mel.

'About nine minutes.'

'Are you sure?'

Conan glanced at his OzBrace for the time and knew it was really only six. Six and a half tops.

• • •

'Who was that?' asked Lemon.

'Not me,' said Chris.

They'd heard the explosion about a hundred metres away and knew it was one of the Dedd Reffo Five being translated to glory. There was a fifty-fifty chance it had been Tim or Robbie, but Chris was determined to keep searching.

He'd do the fuckin' job himself if he got the chance.

• • •

'Live forever!' chanted the crowd in time with the music and it morphed into a song – everyone singing the words without needing to learn them.

'At this point we are standing at the gates to The Land Where Everything Is True,' said the voice, and it seemed to Robbie that the holo-screen view of Ah Li Wu had moved inside his head, so strong and real was the image. No, not inside his head, it was a figure standing before him – before everyone – as real as anyone else.

'This is the place where communication is so perfect … so profound … we understand instantly, as though we are, each of us, neurons within a vast communal brain.'

'Yes!' shouted the crowd in simultaneous epiphany.

'Once you tap into the thought of the communal brain you have reached the ultimate … the highest point. You are privy to the thought of God Himself. Behold!'

And it seemed to Robbie that a flash of purest insight gave him a glimpse – the briefest glimpse – of an androgynous face filled with wisdom, sadness and impossible joy.

'It is enough to know that God exists,' continued Ah Li Wu and Robbie's heart and soul filled with love for all humanity. 'Now it is time to dance. Dance for God.'

Another explosion went off in the distance. Robbie was aware that it was likely one of his colleagues but somehow it didn't seem to matter. Only dancing mattered.

Without being taught the steps, the crowd moved in perfect unison. Even those who actively tried to do something different found they were still mirroring exactly the moves of all others, as though both group and individual impulses had become streamlined into one. Every soul was filled with ecstasy but the realisation that they were truly part of something bigger was the biggest revelation and wonder.

'Dance for God!'

• • •

Provisional Captain Michael Rice was probably the only person in the crowd who had not taken Crimson.

Nevertheless, he had learned to flow with the crowd rather than fight it, and so made better progress in the direction of the stadium gates.

The behaviour of the crowd was incredibly disturbing. He could hear Ah Li Wu spouting his gibberish, but rather than laugh and reject him, the massive crowd was moving and singing in disturbing unity. Rice knew he could never get his congregation to display such devotion and, despite his certain knowledge that his Redeemer liveth, felt more than a tad jealous of Habal Tong's impact on believers – deluded heretics though they were.

He was also keenly aware that a couple of explosions had gone off in the last few minutes but, rather than flee, the crowd seemed ever more excited and – to Rice's shock – many seemed to have removed their clothes and were writhing about in group orgies. No, his congregation would never behave like this.

A couple of girls grabbed him by the arms and tried to pull him onto a bean bag. For half a second he let them, but then tore himself away with a furious cry, aghast that he could have been tempted by such obvious harpies of hell.

It was critical he find Major Lammas to warn of the danger.

• • •

It was easier to move once they made it out of the square, but there was still a long way to go. At least two hundred metres Conan knew, and only three minutes max before the manga went off.

'Can we put the eskies down a moment?' asked Mel.

'No. Keep moving.'

'But they're heavy! My arms are tired and I think I'm going to drop mine.'

'Oh for fuck's sake. Five seconds rest … that's all.'

They stopped and lowered the eskies carefully, then Mel flung her arms around Conan's neck and said, 'I'm so tired … can't we just leave the eskies here and tell everyone to get clear?'

'No … and that's enough rest. Come on.'

For an instant he thought she would refuse, but with a white-faced resolve she lifted as he did and continued towards Bob Brown Lane. Conan wasn't sure but he thought the red light was flashing slightly faster. Surely they had at least two minutes.

'Can we move a bit faster?'

Asif responded by upping the pace and Conan urged Mel to keep up.

'Nearly there … just another hundred metres.'

'Then what?'

'You'll see.'

'Don't patronise me, Conan.'

'Okay … we're going to blow up the NBN substation.'

'What?'

'Sorry … I thought that was clear.'

'We are doing no such thing!'

There was no time for niceties.

'Asif,' shouted Conan. 'Leave Tanya here with Mel, and take Mel's esky.'

Before Mel could properly understand what was happening she had been relieved of her esky and Tanya had been laid at her feet. Conan hurried away with Asif, knowing they had about a minute. She opened her mouth to complain but – on reflection – perceived that carrying large amounts of unstable explosive set to go off at any moment was not something she was that passionate about. Mind you, Conan's manner had been infuriatingly high-handed and there *would* be repercussions!

Conan could feel the sweat pouring off his brow and beading under his clothes. His hands felt slippery on the plastex esky but he still moved as quickly as he dared, trying not to jolt the mangalite into a precipitate reaction. There were still a lot of people about, even this far from the square, and he realised he would have to clear the street as soon as the manga was laid.

Where was the fucking substation?

Bob Brown Lane was not well lit and there were the usual numbers of overflowing skips about. He wouldn't see the substation until he was right on top of it.

'There it is,' said Asif, and Conan realised he'd been about to walk past it – obscured by a temporary campsite erected by a middle-aged couple in HT yellow.

'Get out of the way!' shouted Conan, carefully placing his esky against the substation.

'Go and get fucked!' snarled the woman, pushing sixty with grey dreadlocks.

Without a word, Conan grabbed her by the arm and dragged her to her feet. Then, ignoring her screams and her raking claws, he pulled her down the street, shouting for everyone to get clear. Most were staring, immobile, those that paid any attention at all.

'Get clear! Quickly! There is a bomb!' shouted Asif.

And to Conan's bewilderment, half the people in the street – those in madly pulsing bio-suits – started running towards it.

It was too late for further warning. Conan released the screeching woman's arm and ran for his life, remembering he hadn't had time to remove the eskies from the other room in the hospital.

• • •

Dr Ming Chen was incandescent in her glory.

The fulfilment of her life's work was playing out beneath her – in the stadium, in the square, in the city at large. All people did exactly as she required them to do, saw as she required them to see.

She wielded power far greater than any pope or emperor, greater even than a pharaoh because all of that required belief. Her power, wrought by signals sent to a brain rewired by Crimson, made them perceive reality – her reality, controlled from her phone, and no belief required.

'All of us together, component parts of the communal brain,' she said, her phone on speaker, 'constitute the ultimate genius.'

She switched the phone off speaker so they wouldn't hear her laugh. She was talking about her own genius of course, and that of her father whose pioneering work she had continued. Even now he watched her proudly as she strolled about the small Olympus above the stadium, making her pronouncements and binding all to her vision and will.

'We will make this country a perfect place … an example to the world … and all peoples will know Habal Tong … the only true and certain path to God.'

There was a massive roar from inside and outside the stadium and then a huge explosion, which she knew must be the hospital as all other portable bombs, carried by the Dedd Reffo fools, were controlled from her phone.

She felt a moment's regret that Conan Tooley was now reduced to his component atoms – there was something there she might have enjoyed moulding into an acceptable partner, for when she felt like a man. But she banished that regret and chose another of the Dedd Reffo bombs – only three left.

'All is nothing and nothing is all,' she said, as she pressed her finger against the icon on her phone.

• • •

Robbie Bennett was filled with joy and wonder as he beheld the countenance of God.

'All is nothing and nothing is all,' said the glorious figure, hyper-real before him.

'Yes, I understand that now,' said Robbie, his eyes filling with tears of adoration. 'But what do you want of me?'

'I want …'

The face seemed to flicker for a moment, like bad TV reception, then came back sharply into focus – indescribably beautiful but filled with sadness and wisdom.

'Please,' implored Robbie, '… please tell me what you want of me.'

'There's been a mistake,' said God.

'A what?'

But God never spoke again. S/he just seemed to shrug and then disappeared.

Robbie found himself shaking his head – weirdly disoriented, as though he'd just been woken from an unexpected nap. Others around him were also shaking their heads, staring about in vague bewilderment. Tim was nowhere to be seen.

The music had ceased and all the holo-screens were blue spheres of static. The only sound was confused whimpering, which got louder as thousands of people began to complain and hunt for their clothes. Robbie found a pair of football shorts which covered the key parts of his nakedness and started wandering, staring about at the mass confusion. People were streaming away from the stadium but Robbie was confounded as to what had happened. Even now it was getting hard to remember the visions which had been so sparkling and real just moments before.

He saw a sign saying Gate C and pushed against the flow of bodies.

There might be answers inside the stadium.

• • •

Lieutenant Rice was confused utterly.

The whole world was going mad, but at least the naked masses had stopped their fornication and were putting clothes back on.

'What are you staring at?' snapped one of the girls who a minute before had tried to entice him onto a beanbag.

'Nothing,' he mumbled, averting his eyes and pushing into the crowd flowing in the opposite direction.

He had to warn Major Lammas, and then get back to his chapter house where the vigil had been held without him. Gate C was about fifty metres away and he forced his way through, desperately avoiding contact with the mostly naked flesh.

It was inconceivable what had happened. For a while, Rice had felt as though he was in a painting of hell by Hieronymus Bosch. Then it was like the lights came on and everyone woke from a weird mass hypnosis.

At least it was – in some way – a return to reality. Or towards reality. But as things felt increasingly normal, Rice got ever more anxious. Major Lammas had to know the authorities were hunting him.

My God, thought Rice. What if Lammas was arrested? It would certainly be the end of his captaincy, and possibly worse. It could even mean gaol and complete humiliation for Rice himself – Rice who had only ever wanted to serve God and had somehow found himself mixed up in matters way over his head.

Tears pricked at his eyes as he realised his peril.

Only Major Lammas could save him.

. . .

'There he is!' cried Lemon.

She was the only person who had stayed focussed after everyone else seemed to lose their minds. She pulled Chris by the hand past the thousands of whining, complaining semi-naked fuckwits who wandered about like Brown's cows after the holo-screens died.

Now, through a gap in the slowly dissipating crowd, she'd caught a glimpse of Robbie Bennett and dragged Chris towards him. 'There's your so-called best mate!' she shouted.

Robbie stood blinking at the threshold of Gate C, and Chris's eyes narrowed.

'Right!' said Chris, his fingers curling into fists.

. . .

'What is happening?' demanded Dr Hermann Van Der Kock.

'I'm not sure,' said Ming. 'I … I think the bypass has gone.'

'Meaning what … precisely?'

'We no longer have control.'

Van Der Kock's mouth tightened and for a second Ming thought her father was going into one of his epic screaming fits, but he managed to control himself.

'Out!' he shouted to Manderson. 'Executive group only … down to the car park at once.'

. . .

Dave Marsh was thoroughly amused by the sudden panic among the Shadow Group honchos, even if he had no clue as to what had gone wrong. He'd heard Van Der Kock mention the car park, so slipped out of the door and ran for the lift, determined to get there first.

He pulled out his phone and was relieved when Conan finally answered.

. . .

'Thank God!' cried Michael Rice as he saw Major Lammas standing under the Gate C sign.

'Hello Michael.'

Major Lammas looked pale and tired, as though all the cares of the world had descended on his shoulders. It wasn't fair, reflected Rice, that so much trouble should come looking for such a good and decent man. He would do what he could to help the Major – and himself.

'Major … the AFP agents …'

'What about them?'

'They seem to know a great deal about our activities this afternoon.'

The Major's face flushed with anger.

'How could they possibly know? What did you tell them?'

'Nothing! But … I think they followed us. They saw my car and said they had footage.'

Major Lammas glanced about at the dazed hordes still pouring from the stadium, then dragged Rice by the collar away from the light blazing around the gate.

'Show me your phone!'

Lieutenant Rice was shocked at being manhandled but surrendered his phone.

'What is the password?'

'Oh … erm … it's L, A, M … erm … I mean 526627.'

Lammas gave Rice a withering look then deleted his last few texts.

'Do you have any concept of your own stupidity?' enquired Lammas. 'Of course you don't or you wouldn't have committed such an imbecilic act.'

'I'm so sorry, Major,' sobbed Rice, on the brink of tears. 'Just tell me what you want me to do and I'll try to fix it.'

'It's too late for that,' said Lammas dragging Lieutenant Rice deeper into a pool of shadow. Lammas' hands on his collar were rough – outrageously rough – and, as Rice started to protest the mistreatment, his words were choked off by thumbs pressing viciously into his throat. He clawed at the hands but Lammas was bigger and much, much stronger, and after a moment of purest agony a gentle peace began to descend over Lieutenant Michael Rice.

• • •

Robbie never saw it coming.

One moment he was staring in bewilderment at the people flowing out of Gate C, and the next he was on the ground in dazed agony after Chris's king hit took him totally by surprise.

'Treacherous fuckin' cunt!' shouted Chris, kicking Robbie in the face as Lemon shrieked with excitement.

'Kill him, Chris!' she screamed. 'Kill your best mate!'

Robbie curled into a foetal ball as kicks and punches rained over him – one kick to the temple felt like his brain had snapped in half. Then it stopped. Through kaleidoscopic tears and blood, Robbie looked up and saw Tim dragging Chris away, clutching at him, pinning his arms to his side as Chris butted him again and again. Lemon also was raking her nails into Tim and trying to tear him off.

Robbie knew he needed to come to Timmy's defence but his body refused to obey him. He couldn't move and he couldn't speak and for some reason Timmy's blast suit was flashing red.

Then the whole world turned into thunder and fire.

And blackness.

Chapter 47

Australia Day

On Saturday morning, Australia Day 2030, the prime minister, Margie Yunupingu, nodded at the producer, watched his fingers count down to zero and the camera light flash on.

She settled her spectacles and stared solemnly into the cameras, sending her three dimensional image into every living room in Australia.

'My dear Australians ... by which I mean all Australians, oldest to newest. Last night, the terrorist group Dedd Reffo set off a number of bombs at the *Illumination* Festival in Ord City ... including at the new maternity hospital. Why anyone would want to bomb a children's hospital is utterly beyond me, but ... at least no one was hurt in that particular blast.

'The same cannot be said for the rest of the festival. It saddens me deeply to advise that four other explosions, including three suicide bombers, accounted for over forty killed ... including Major Tom Lammas, a senior officer of the Army of God and a true Australian hero ... and nearly two hundred injured. These come hard on the heels of the terrorist bombs which destroyed three water treatment plants and part of the Giant Array telescope.

'The secret service ... whose outstanding work prevented many more deaths ... advise me that the purpose of the Dedd Reffo group was to force a moratorium on the First Wave of new Australians given full citizenship after the expiry of their seven year visas. I am proud to announce that their plan has failed. The First Wave are now at liberty to go anywhere in Australia they wish ... as will the Second Wave,

Third, Fourth and Fifth. Australia … on this very special Australia Day … welcomes all peoples displaced by the world's problems and my government will continue to find solutions for all that … '

• • •

Five people – four men and a woman – sit before a huge picture window looking over a vast city, with an ocean to the north under a pink sky turning gold and blue. The woman switches off a holo-screen as one of the men stifles a laugh.

'What's so funny, Agent Tooley?' asked Lucia – Agent Baresi as Conan supposed she should be called.

They were drinking coffee in Lucia's large office at the top of the ONA building, early Saturday morning after less than three hours sleep.

'I was just laughing at the spin our prime minister has put on the situation.'

Lucia sipped coffee and shrugged, looking weirdly poised and corporate. Her change in demeanour (not to mention status) was just about the strangest thing Conan had had to cope with in the last two weeks.

'She's just doing what politicians always do,' said Lucia. 'Now that the Dedd Reffo group has been blamed for all explosions, the snap polls are suddenly very pro-refugee. She'd be mad not to exploit that.'

'And,' said Agent Green, '… she has substantially less than half the details as to what truly transpired.'

'Isn't it our job to fill her in?' suggested Conan.

Lucia shrugged again.

'You will eventually learn, Agent Tooley, that the message must always be managed.'

'Precisely,' agreed Agent Smith. 'If we give the elected officials an unfiltered and unrefined report they'll cause a panic. Can't have that.'

It had been a busy night, although not entirely successful. The city was back in the hands of the proper authorities, led by the Australian Federal Police, bolstered for the moment by army units and a large detachment of the Western Australia state police. The Crimson had been removed from Water Treatment Plant Delta and would disappear from the streets once the glut was fully consumed.

'There can't be much of it left,' said Dave Marsh. 'It was bloody well everywhere last night.'

'So where is Doctor Chen?' demanded Lucia.

That was the loosest of the loose ends after *Illumination*. Conan and Dave Marsh had arrested the Shadow Group as they tried to leave Rinehart Stadium in a black transit van, but Ming had not been in the van.

'I couldn't watch all of them at once,' defended Dave. 'A lot of the CCTV had to be rebooted after the NBN went out, and even Van Der Kock might've gotten away if not for that explosion at the gate.'

The last explosion of the night had occurred at Gate C – the very gate where Conan had been told to wait by the Shadow Group. It might've been his body torn apart by the suicide bomber rather than Major Lammas's. His colleague Lieutenant Rice had survived but with horrific injuries.

'How did that last blast suit go off?' wondered Agent Green. 'The others were set off remotely by Doctor Chen, but she'd lost control of her phone by then.'

'Asif reckons the suit must have been deliberately set off by the wearer,' said Conan. 'Sure made a mess of him … and the people who apparently tried to stop him.'

Witnesses claimed that just before the Gate C bomb had gone off, a man wearing a flashing suit was seen fighting with another man and a woman. There was almost nothing left of them, and the explosion had also killed Major Lammas who'd been only a few metres away. Fortunately, the blast had caused hundreds of idiots in bio-suits to come running towards the incident, hoping for more of the same, and it was that congestion which prevented the Shadow Group from getting away. Conan and Dave had arrived with their weapons drawn and all in the car – Van Der Kock, Ronny Kwai, Colonels Maddox and Chard and Roger Manderson – were now refusing to talk in grey rooms in the bowels of ONA headquarters.

'Why did Chard make that speech about not letting the terrorists win when that's exactly what they wanted?' wondered Dave Marsh.

'Have to show willing,' said Lucia. 'She had to make it look as though a moratorium against the First Wave was a reluctant but reasoned response to a crisis ... and that's what they would have done this morning if their plan hadn't gone awry.'

They now understood that Van Der Kock, as the minister for immigration and border protection when Ord City was established, had devised a plan to create a giant concentration camp from which no refugees would ever be released. An antenatal scientist himself, he had started research on a drug – perfected by his daughter – which could be added to the water supply to control fertility and enhance belief. Refugees would come to Ord City, but the political situation would always be managed so none would be permitted to leave, or even want to leave given the power of Habal Tong. And few children would ever be born.

'So, all this time,' said Dave, 'the world was holding the Australian government up as a shining light of how to provide for refugees, and in reality we had no intention of ever letting them into the country.'

'That's not entirely true,' said Agent Smith. 'It was Van Der Kock's plan, aided and abetted by the Shadow Group and Colonel Chard, but there's no evidence it was ever government policy.'

All five glanced at each other with thinned lips.

'No evidence,' agreed Agent Green, '... and the government has changed twice since Van Der Kock's party were in power so ... I think we'd best leave it there.'

'We still have to find Doctor Chen,' insisted Lucia. 'That is a first order priority ... not least as she could set up another Crimson manufacturing operation somewhere.'

Besides its anti-fertility function Crimson, taken as a concentrate, had certain other properties – not least was its propensity to rewire the brain in the presence of certain electromagnetic signals causing the perception of reality to be profoundly changed and remotely controllable.

'The invention of Crimson is, in fact, a work of genius,' said Agent Smith. 'There is a whole new spectrum of pharmacological possibilities opened up by trans-plasmatic chemistry. Crimson ought to be studied but it cannot be permitted to be manufactured illicitly.'

They all turned to Conan, who had managed to turn the tide at the climax of *Illumination*, even while under the influence of Crimson himself.

'There's been a mistake?' asked Lucia, with a slow smile.

'It was the best I could think of … top of my head,' said Conan. 'I've never played God before.'

When the two eskies full of manga went off in Bob Brown Lane, the blast took out the NBN substation, disrupting the local patch the Shadow Group had created from the NBN Node out near the Giant Array. That meant the ONA was back in charge of the Quantum computer and all communications. Conan was able to advise them of Ming's phone number, written in the copy of her book found among Fong and Wing Ho's effects, and Lucia was able to give him control of her phone just as God was talking personally to all Crimson users.

'What you said was very good, really,' said Agent Smith. 'Vague and uncertain … as religion ought to be. You could hardly have said anything better to restore the status quo when nearly a million people were wallowing in an orgy of religious certainty.'

The masses had emptied the square, scratching their heads and blinking in the dim light, wondering what had happened and already finding it hard to remember any particular detail.

'You know they want to have *Illumination* again next year,' said Agent Green. 'For the Second Wave.'

'I'm sure it won't be a problem next year,' said Lucia. 'And without Van Der Kock writing new verses for the Habal Tong Way, it'll start to run out of steam … most new religions do.'

'Unless Ming takes over,' said Conan.

'As I said,' said Lucia, '… she's a first order priority. Your priority Agent Tooley … and can I please ask the others to allow us a private word?'

Conan's heart sank as Agents Smith, Green and Marsh rose from their chairs and left the room. He'd been dreading the inevitable private interview.

Lucia – Agent Baresi – waited until the door was closed and said, 'Congratulations, Conan, not just for your work last night, but also on resolving the Fong, Wing Ho murders … just brilliant.'

'Well,' said Conan, tiredness swamping his modesty, 'we'll never be entirely certain that's what happened … but it's as good an explanation as anything else.'

Once Conan understood how Crimson worked in the presence of a certain electromagnetic signal, he had immediately remembered the Fong, Wing Ho toxicology and asked Agent Green to run the Quantum Empyrean over a new search on the *Epistola Clementis*. That search, now that the Shadow Group's patch had been destroyed, quickly brought up the webpage with the crossed keys which Conan had seen frozen on Bruce Fong's laptop.

'You remember I had you look up the *Epistola*?' said Conan, and Lucia visibly shuddered at the memory.

'As you said,' agreed Lucia, 'the absence of any information on the web … of something so interesting … was itself interesting, but once we regained control of the Quantum, it was possible to find what the Shadow Group had hidden.'

Bruce Fong and Michael Wing Ho had been alerted to the existence of the *Epistola*, by Major Lammas himself at the Great Debate. They had then done a search while on Crimson and when they downloaded the page it sent a signal to their laptops which gave them a powerful vision, similar to the vision unleashed at *Illumination* to the Crimson-soaked masses where God himself seemed to appear.

The vision, replayable for anyone on Crimson, promised them membership of God's own secret society and included a phone number – Ronny Kwai's number – which they had rung, only to receive directions to the site of their own murder by Agent Ping and Asif's former colleagues – Razzaq and Ah Cheng. It was the Shadow Group's way of establishing that the signal actually worked in the presence of Crimson, but then preventing anyone talking about it before the main event.

'And Ming's book with her phone number that we found in the apartment just down from Bruce and Michael's … where all their stuff had been moved,' said Conan, '… it was Agent Ping's copy. He'd been seeing Ming … she was using him for information on AFP movements … but that was the link between Lammas, Razzaq and the Shadow Group with Ming as the puppet master, fooling them all, even when some thought they were following their own agendas.'

'Including you,' said Lucia.

Conan didn't answer, just reddened in embarrassment for all the things said and unsaid over the years he'd known Lucia – or thought he had.

Loongy and Kenny Cook had been restored. The resumption of control meant ONA had been able to trace Agent Ping's communications with Ming and more senior members of the AFP – all of whom were now under arrest and being questioned in similar buildings around the country.

'What about Jen Khataten?' asked Lucia.

Jen Khataten was also in one of the grey rooms downstairs, but not refusing to talk.

'She'd also been seeing Ming, although I think she regrets it now. She says Ming had been using the Giant Array dipoles as quasi-neurons to perfect her brain modelling … to match it against Crimson.'

Lucia stared at him for a moment.

'That is completely astounding,' she said. 'The mind control possibilities of Doctor Chen's drugs are … well, terrifying.'

'For all we know we're being controlled right now,' laughed Conan, as Lucia eyed him coldly.

'So what now?' she asked him.

'What do you mean?' he replied, knowing exactly what she meant.

'Shall we throw it all in and go travelling together? As you always promised?'

It was the abruptest of about turns and Conan didn't know what to say or where to look.

'I suppose I have misled you over the years,' admitted Lucia, with a sigh. 'But I could hardly disclose my true status.'

'Are you saying you really want to go travelling? After all this?'

'I am human, Conan,' sighed Lucia. 'And I feel as though I've reached a stationary point. It wouldn't be a bad time to just stop and be a wife … and a mother.'

Conan reddened further. Lucia gave him a look of profound sadness and said, 'But I suppose it's too late for all that … I suppose you have other plans?'

'Well … I have made certain promises to … erm …'

'That's fine,' said Lucia, instantly switching back to her corporate persona. 'We can continue to have a professional relationship. I want you to stay on as a field agent, Agent Tooley.'

'I'd like that, but ... erm ... first ...'

'You want to go travelling with Captain Roberts?'

'It's just Melodie Roberts ... she's quit the AOG.'

Lucia gave him one last aching glance and turned back to her computer.

'Leave is approved for one month, Agent Tooley. Report to me in Sydney.'

Realising he'd been dismissed, Conan rose with relief and started walking to the door, as his phone rang.

He winced as he recognised his mother's number.

'Hi, Ma.'

'Conan ... you're alive?'

'Yes, Ma.'

'What on earth is going on up there in Ord City ... it's all over the news.'

'It's over now.'

'It got me thinking Conan ... if anything were to happen to you ...'

'Yes?'

'Well, you *have* mentioned me in your will, I hope ... it's just that Virtual Youth is so expensive and ...'

Conan laughed as he ended the call.

He kissed Mel who was waiting outside the building. 'What now?' she asked.

'London,' said Conan. 'Let's go to London.'

• • •

Asif was warm, lying in his own bed with Tanya's arms around him.

So much had happened, but – almost inconceivably – he was now a full Australian citizen and able to travel anywhere in the country. What's more, Razzaq and Cheng had been destroyed and many more in their network. The likelihood was that no one in the radical network – if any were left alive – knew about him.

He was free.

Tanya had finally woken from the long-acting drug and blessedly knew little of their ordeal. He was happy to keep it that way.

'Asif?'

'Mmmm?'

'Have I told you today how much I love you?'

'Only four times … I am happy to hear it again.'

'Okay … I …'

Tanya paused.

'What is it?'

'Oh, Asif … '

She took his hand and held it against her belly.

'I think I felt a kick.'

Asif's eyes filled with tears and he hugged her fiercely.

They were free. All of them.

• • •

Robbie Bennett was cold.

He'd been fighting the urge to wake which seemed to come in waves, adding memories like debris on a beach, which he slowly put together as his consciousness returned like a torchlight probing a fog of drugs and pain.

Still, he kept his eyes shut for now, keeping out the worst.

Chris was dead.

He knew this and felt deeply sorry despite the fact that Chris had beaten him so badly … might even have killed him if not for the bravery and sacrifice of Tim.

It was the loss of Tim that really saddened Robbie. They had become close friends so quickly it was outrageous. Robbie had never understood that a friendship that intimate was possible with another male.

Robbie knew it wasn't a lovers' relationship. There had been one or two ambiguous moments but it was just a really deep friendship which somehow went beyond trivialities like sexual orientation. Robbie felt devastated for its loss, but also much older and wiser, as though knowing Tim had taken him to a whole new level of understanding of the strange lives of men and women.

As for women …

Robbie heard a chair scrape and knew it was time to open his eyes.

There was a young woman sitting next to his bed, smiling anxiously. It took him a few moments to recognise her with the new hairstyle, and it was a really long time since he'd seen her smile.

'Kate?'

If you enjoyed

Welcome to Ord City

please take a moment
to give it a rating on

www.goodreads.com
or
www.amazon.com.au

Also by Adrian Deans

The Fighting Man

In the year 1060, young Brand Holgarsson's family are wiped out in a Viking raid arranged by his treacherous uncle Malgard. Malgard is named thegn of the town of Stybbor in East Anglia while Brand is outlawed and hunted by Malgard's men, determined to extinguish the last possible claim to Malgard's thegnship.

Aided by a strange young woman, Valla, who claims to be 242 years old, Brand escapes and is befriended by Harold Godwinson, Earl of Wessex and the choice of the Saxon nobles as successor to the childless King Edward (the Confessor). Brand nurses his dream of vengeance over Malgard while sharing Harold's perils and waiting for Valla who will only return from The Place of Dreams if Brand has remained true to his promise to lie with no other woman.

All stories come together at the Battle of Hastings, where Harold's great banner, The Fighting Man, flew above the field at Senlac Ridge in opposition to the papal cross carried by William the Bastard.

A tale of love and revenge set against history's bloody backdrop.

'The Fighting Man is a rollicking read, a non-stop action-packed adventure full of romance, battle and humour. I read it on the train, walking down the street, well after my usual bed time and when I was supposed to be working. Even though I knew exactly where the story was headed, I was compelled to know what happened next.'
— Jane Rawson, *From the Wreck*

'Historical novels that feel truly authentic are one of life's great joys. Not since reading Sharpe have I felt such a sense of being in the story. Outstanding.'
— Stuart Quin, Full Circle Films

www.adriandeans.com

Also by Adrian Deans

Mr Cleansheets

Eric Judd is 39 and his girlfriend wants him to give up playing football. Eric (aka Mr Cleansheets) is a goalkeeping legend at his amateur Sydney club because in his youth he received a letter inviting him to trial with Manchester United. The letter said to 'come when you're ready' — and six days before his 40th birthday, Eric is finally ready.

Inspired by the dying wish of his Uncle Jimmy, Eric travels to England, but does not quite receive the welcome he had hoped for. Instead, he encounters all manner of villains: murderous football hooligans, Irish mafia, dodgy agents, beautiful pop stars, international terrorists and a range of supporting players with any number of overt and hidden agendas.

But he does get to play football.

The ultimate holiday read — a non-stop rollicking yarn that keeps the pages turning, and if you're anything like me, you'll be starting to panic as the pages disappear in your right hand.
Lawrie McKinna, Central Coast Mariners

If you put Lock, Stock & Two Smoking Barrels, the News of the World and Four Four Two into a blender, the result might well be Mr Cleansheets.
Simon Hill, Fox Sports

Adrian Deans is at his best when writing about football.
Dan Silkstone, The Age

www.adriandeans.com

Also by Adrian Deans

Straight Jacket

Morgen Tanjenz is a lawyer with an overactive sense of justice. His mission in life is to reward the virtuous, punish the ignorant and avenge those who won't avenge themselves. He dispenses justice via his favourite pastime ('life sculpture'), in which he takes an anonymous interest in strangers – pulling strings in the background to change their lives as he thinks they deserve.

But Morgen isn't the only one changing lives in the city. There is a serial killer on the prowl who taunts police in letters to the local rag but, as the body count rises, Detective Sergeant Blacksnake Fowler can hardly focus on the job with so many distractions. His boss hates him, his deputy is trying to undermine him, and the woman he loves is having an affair.

Straight Jacket is not only a well-thought-out and exciting crime thriller, but also hilarious entertainment.
Newtown Review of Books

Deans has a great feel for the relaxed narcissism that oozes from Sydney's professional classes, and the middleclass banality of Sydney's northern suburbs provides a surprisingly good setting for a book about psychopaths and serial killers.
Law Society Journal

The first person narrator is unconventional, hard to sympathise with, and generally unlikeable for most of the book. However, there is something about Deans' writing that makes you want to read more. The novel doesn't let up, going deeper and deeper into the psyche of the narrator, and into the origins of his warped sense of justice.
Crime Fiction Lover

www.adriandeans.com

Also by Adrian Deans

THEM

Rob Lasseter is the great grandson of a legendary explorer. His prized possession is an old parchment, which is thought to be a map showing the location of the fabulous reef of gold. Unfortunately, there are no points of external reference on the map. The only words are 'You are here', next to an X, but Lasseter doesn't know where X is – he doesn't know where to start looking.

Inspired by the strange disappearance of the White Haired girl, and the receipt of a letter addressed in his own handwriting from a place he had never been, Lasseter (with his friend Miles, who claims to be dead) embarks upon an odyssey into the centre of Australia and has some very strange adventures. Lasseter thinks he is looking for gold, but instead he finds something far more interesting.

The ultimate solipsist journey - an Australian story of pan-cosmic enormity.

www.reallybluebooks.com   www.adriandeans.com

Also by Adrian Deans

Political Football:
Lawrie Mckinna's Dangerous Truth

Growing up in darkest Scotland as the son of the local poacher and then rampaging across Europe with a pack of Rangers hooligans is not the best preparation for high office in Australia.

Father at 18, professional footballer at 20, Lawrie McKinna was living the dream until he uprooted for Australia at 25 to play in the NSL. Then he became a successful coach (NSL, A-League and China) and ultimately was elected to political office as an independent after being courted by both mainstream parties due to his massive popularity. These pages chronicle his journey, telling his dangerous truth with fearless candour, infectious enthusiasm and a wicked sense of humour.

Very readable, but not for the PC at heart.
Andy Harper

I read it in five hours flat and could not put it down.
Roy Hay

Compelling and mesmerising.
Con Stamocostas

An amazing journey.
Ashley Morrison

www.adriandeans.com

www.ingramcontent.com/pod-product-compliance
Lightning Source LLC
Chambersburg PA
CBHW030544020726
47494CB00005B/1480